The Hawaiian narrative is one of both profound triumph and, sadly, deep injustice. It is the story of Native Hawaiians oppressed by crippling disease, aborted treaties, and the eventual conquest of their sovereign kingdom. These grim milestones remind us of an unjust time in our history.

Barack Obama
King Kamehameha Day 2010

The last lava flow occurred here so long ago that there are none now living who witnessed it. . . . There were doubtless plenty of Kanaka sentinels on guard hereabouts at that time, but they did not leave casts of their figures in the lava as the Roman sentinels at Herculaneum and Pompeii did. . . . They probably went away. They went away early, perhaps. However, they had their merits; the Romans exhibited the higher pluck, but the Kanakas showed the sounder judgment.

Mark Twain
On a visit to Hawai'i Island in 1866

Daughters of Fire

Tom Peek

Published by Koa Books, PO Box 988, Hana, Hawai'i 96713
www.koabooks.com

Printed in the United States of America. Distributed in North America by SCB Distributors. Distributed in Hawai'i by Native Books and The Islander Group

Publishers Cataloguing-in-Publication Data
Peek, Thomas R.
Daughters of fire / Tom Peek. — Kihei, Hawai'i : Koa Books, ©2012.

p. : ill. ; cm.

ISBN: 978-0-9821656-2-1
Includes pronunciation guide, glossary, and suggested further readings.
Summary: An adventure of cross-cultural romance, political intrigue, goddesses, myth, and murder set amid the cultural tensions of contemporary Hawai'i.—Publisher.

1. Hawaii—Fiction. 2. Cultural fusion—Hawaii—Fiction. 3. Hawaii—Politics and government—21st century. 4. Murder—Hawaii—Fiction. 5. Volcanic eruptions—Hawaii—Fiction. 6. Mystery fiction. 7. Romantic suspense fiction. I. Title.

PS3616.E326 D38 2012

813.6--dc23 1210

CONTENTS

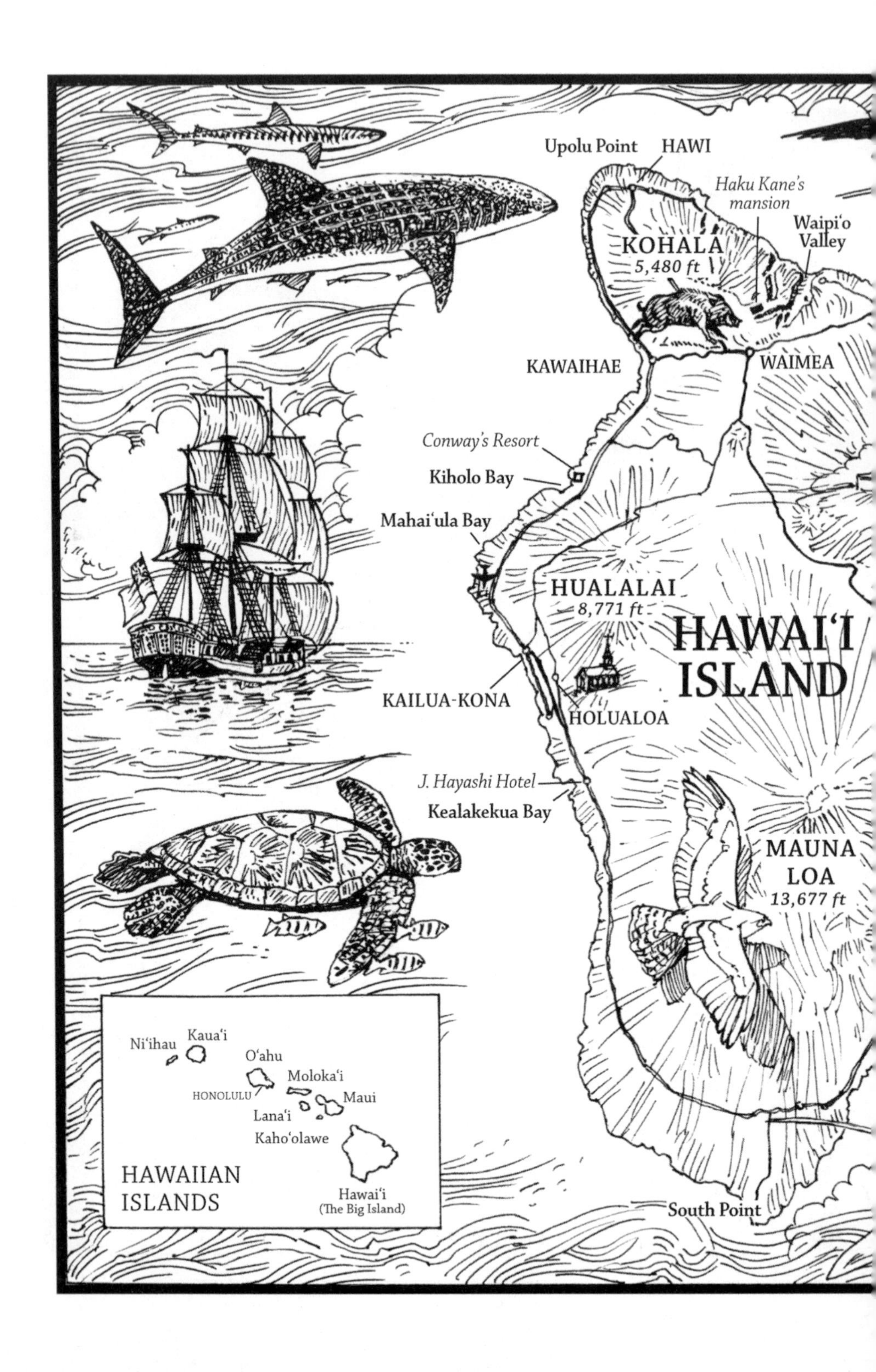
Upolu Point
HAWI
Haku Kane's mansion
Waipi'o Valley
KOHALA
5,480 ft
KAWAIHAE
WAIMEA
Conway's Resort
Kiholo Bay
Mahai'ula Bay
HUALALAI
8,771 ft
HAWAI'I ISLAND
KAILUA-KONA
HOLUALOA
J. Hayashi Hotel
Kealakekua Bay
MAUNA LOA
13,677 ft
South Point
Ni'ihau
Kaua'i
O'ahu
Moloka'i
HONOLULU
Maui
Lana'i
Kaho'olawe
HAWAIIAN ISLANDS
Hawai'i
(The Big Island)

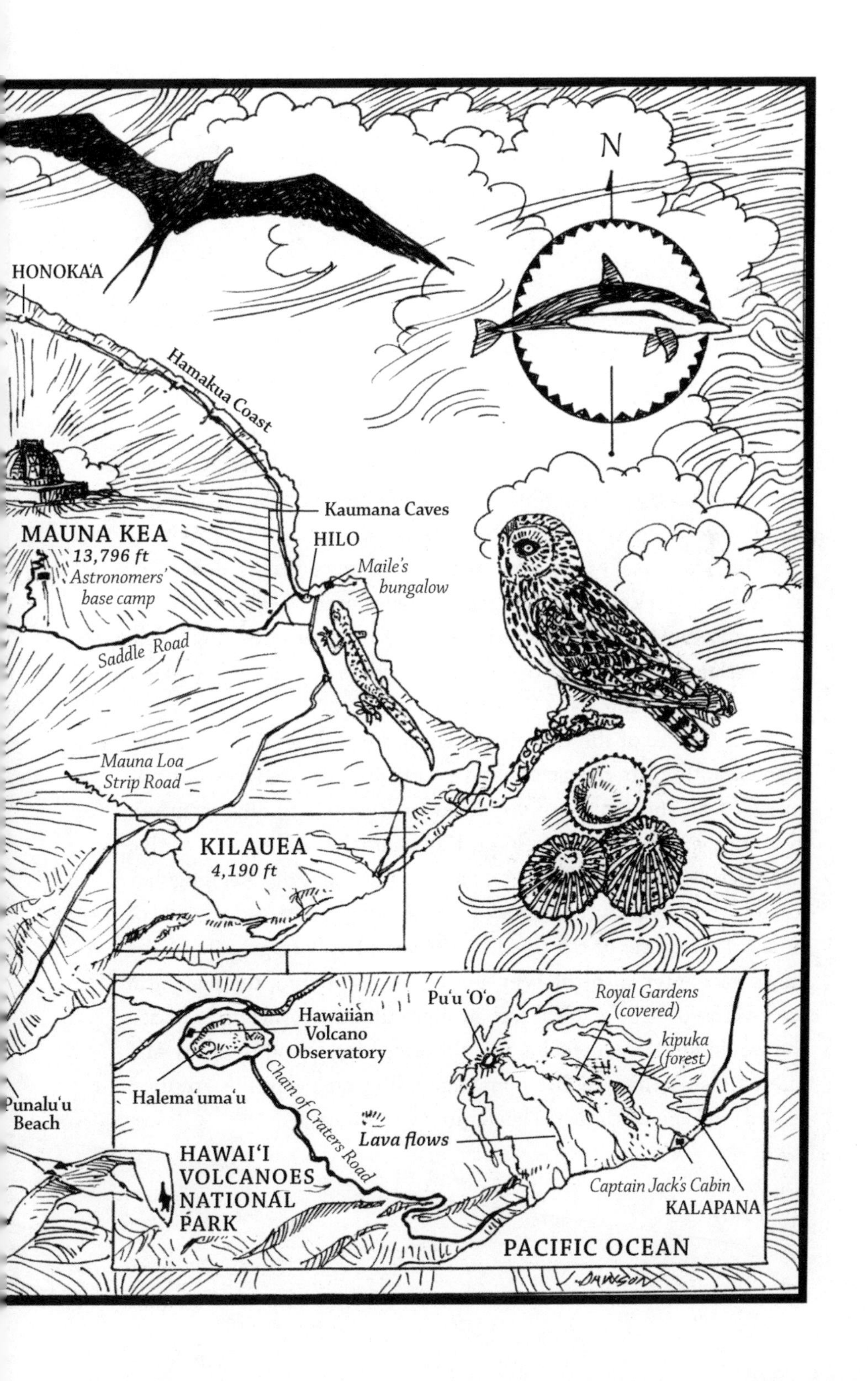

N
HONOKA'A
Hamakua Coast
Kaumana Caves
MAUNA KEA
13,796 ft
Astronomers' base camp
HILO
Maile's bungalow
Saddle Road
Mauna Loa Strip Road
KILAUEA
4,190 ft
Hawaiian Volcano Observatory
Pu'u 'O'o
Royal Gardens (covered)
kipuka (forest)
Halema'uma'u
Chain of Craters Road
Punalu'u Beach
Lava flows
HAWAI'I VOLCANOES NATIONAL PARK
Captain Jack's Cabin
KALAPANA
PACIFIC OCEAN

Author's Note

THE ISLAND OF HAWAI'I lies 200 miles southeast of Honolulu—far removed from the tourist glitz most people think of as Hawai'i. The island's volcanoes still erupt with gusto, and mountain blizzards bury its 14,000-foot peaks in snow. Native Hawaiian culture is alive here, and twenty-first-century logic must coexist with ancient customs, not the least of which is a reverence for deities that have long dwelt on the island. Sightings of the volcano goddess Pele are still written up in local newspapers.

Most stories of the Hawaiian Islands are mythic, and this novel is no exception. Its characters and events are pure fiction—but not untrue. One incident, memorialized in legend, actually occurred. In 1801 the great Hawaiian king, Kamehameha, acting on a native oracle's warning, made a personal sacrifice to Pele, begging her to stop the devastating rivers of lava flowing from the craters of Hualalai. Accounts of the incident preserved only fragments of the king's encounter with the seer, but on several points the historical record is clear—the goddess was so angry that the royal family feared she would kill Kamehameha, but the wise king found humility and offered his sacrifice to the female god. The next day the eruption ceased, and the volcano has been quiet ever since.

Mahalo nui loa

to the Polynesians of Hawai'i and the South Seas
whose guileless, open hearts restored my
shaken faith in human nature.

Prologue ∫ Pele and the King

THE ISLAND OF HAWAI'I'S KONA COAST—1801

King Kamehameha towered over the crew of his double-hulled canoe as it sailed into the ravaged village of Kiholo. None of the panicked reports he'd received from messengers prepared him for the destruction he now saw with his own eyes. Most of the village was gone, buried by lava from Hualalai, and the stench of smoldering animal carcasses—dogs, chickens, and pigs burned alive—scented the smoky air. The charred canoes at the shoreline stunned Kamehameha, for lava had streamed down the volcano so quickly villagers couldn't even launch their precious craft out of Pele's way.

A crowd gathered on the beach, led by the village *ali'i*—members of Hawai'i's royal class—their robes of red and gold feathers vivid against the steaming black lava. Kamehameha, barely waiting for their welcoming chant to finish, leaped off his canoe into the rising surf lashing Kiholo Bay, followed by his bodyguards and other attendants. Agitated waves clung to the hem of his feather cloak as blustery winds shook the lofty arch of his feather helmet and nearly toppled the two men bearing his royal standards of golden plumes. The legendary warrior strode onto the beach, its coral sands speckled with pumice and the glassy gold threads of Pele's hair. A tingle crawled up the back of his neck.

None of the panicked reports he'd received prepared Kamehameha for the destruction he now saw with his own eyes.

High up the volcano, his grove of breadfruit trees smoldered, and down at the shore, a pillar of steam billowed from the sea where lava had overrun one of his royal fishponds. Village women frantically emptied huts still endangered by flows, while a procession led by a native priest hauled yet another squealing pig up the lava-scarred slope. The *kahuna* chanted toward Hualalai as the men heaved the shrieking beast into a torrent of lava, its blazing hulk conveyed seaward atop the molten flow. Villagers followed with bundles of red *tapa* cloth, red *'ohelo* berries, red fish, and more pigs—offerings to appease the goddess.

The king and his bodyguards strode into the courtyard of the main village temple, with its thatched hut, sanctified tower, and wooden images of the gods. This *heiau* was dedicated to Kamehameha's war god, Ku, but the king's mission that day concerned Pele and the oracle he'd summoned from Kilauea who knew how to communicate with her.

"The goddess has rejected all our offerings!" a village priest cried out as Kamehameha pushed past him. The king signaled his guards to remain, and he alone stepped into the hut.

"*Aloha*, Kamakaokeakua," said the king to the oracle, whose very name meant "the eye of the god."

The old kahuna rose slowly from his woven mat, the braids in his grizzled beard dangling. A robe of white tapa draped his wiry body, bark fabric handed down through generations of men and women possessing the *mana*, the divine spirit, of seers. From his neck hung a garland of red *lehua*—blossoms of the *'ohi'a* tree, symbol of the volcano goddess, Pele. Knots on the ends of his bone-white hair kept it clear of his enormous black eyes. "Aloha, Kamehameha," the kahuna replied, peering into the great warrior's face and detecting fear in his eyes.

They sat down on the mat across from each other.

"The volcano has been quiet many generations," the king said. "Why does it rage upon us now?"

"Pele is angry." The priest studied the king's face. Kamehameha's royal blood ran all the way back to thirteenth-century conquerors from Tahiti, and few dared cross him, but the priest held on to the truth. "She is angry with *you*."

The king's back stiffened. "With *me!*"

"Why else would she erupt in the middle of your royal breadfruit grove, then send her flows straight to your prized fishpond? She watches you, sees what you are doing with this kingdom you've built on her island. She wonders if you've become so powerful that you now see yourself as more important than the gods."

"I have always respected the gods!"

"And Pele has always been your ally. Without her, your kingdom would not have been possible. Your cousin's armies would certainly have overwhelmed you had she not annihilated them on Kilauea with her suffocating cloud of ash." Yet as he spoke, the kahuna wondered whether Pele had simply grown weary of the cousin's warring too.

"But," the oracle continued, "history shows that Pele can change allegiance. All of this—the buried village, your scorched breadfruit trees, the entombed fishpond of Kiholo—all just warnings!"

"Why would she abandon me now?"

The priest pointed his bony finger at the king. "Look around you, Kamehameha. You have taken more than your share of fish from the pond, leaving for Pele smaller and smaller offerings with each passing year, and you have forbidden even Pele to receive breadfruit from your royal grove. This has not gone unnoticed by our goddess. Nor has she failed to see how you cooperate with the white-skinned *haole*, sharing with them the fruits of our springs, reefs, and forests in exchange for guns to expand your domain to the other islands."

Anger flashed in the king's eyes. "I will not hear this!"

The earth trembled again, as it had on and off for days, and the kahuna felt power surge into his old bones, as if the goddess herself had joined him in the hut.

"You see, Kamehameha! Look how your triumphs have gone to your head—successes impossible without the help of our gods!"

Kamehameha leaned forward menacingly.

A glint of red flickered inside the kahuna's cavernous eyes. "You *will* listen, because you must. I have heard her voice, a voice of anger and dismay. Watch her bury your kingdom, and you with it!"

The king's face contorted, but he restrained his anger.

"Beware, Kamehameha. The haole have given you the guns you need to take control of these islands, but Pele is the ruler of *this* island!"

Kamehameha rose to pace the hut, his nearly seven-foot frame looming above the kahuna. His hand rested on his *pahoa*, a long dagger—of British iron—but still the priest's eyes defied him.

A commotion arose outside and Kamehameha stepped to the door. "Another fishpond has been taken, sir!" declared his guard.

"*Auwe!*" the king muttered, spotting yet another fiery steam plume at the coast. He turned and exchanged stares with the priest. "What must be done to stop this rampage!"

"Sit down, my ruling chief, and I will tell you."

Kamehameha obeyed.

"Pele demands a sacrifice."

"What! Our war god Ku may accept a human sacrifice, but Pele—a female—cannot!"

"Even so, something must be given to her as a *personal* sacrifice, something from your own body, something containing your mana—and *you* must take it to her altar, the craters of Hualalai."

Kamehameha sat a long time staring at the white-haired priest and his garland of red flowers. "I am afraid of Pele," he said at last, beseeching the priest with his eyes.

"You will not die, Kamehameha. This I know." The oracle leaned forward, close to the king. "But you must be watchful in your dealings with the haole, for one day they will challenge your allegiance to Pele and bring changes that will threaten all you have built. You may hope that uniting the islands into one nation will protect us from these outsiders, but in time, through their influence, all the temples will be destroyed, our people made ill, and the land taken away. These friends of yours bring an ill wind that even your armies cannot quell."

When the king stepped outside into the wind and fumes, his face pale and eyes tentative, his bodyguards glanced at one another. Could the great Kamehameha be afraid?

A few days later, his royal canoe set sail again from his compound at the foot of Kohala volcano, this time bound for the village of Mahai'ula, ten miles south of Kiholo, where Pele now ravaged the king's land. Many high chiefs and chiefesses made the journey, including two of Kamehameha's wives, who feared Pele would kill the king. To help assuage the goddess, they brought along Princess Ululani, who had once in great ceremony offered her dead son's body to Pele, making the child a guardian spirit in Pele's clan. The royal family hoped this spirit would recognize his mother and help protect the king.

The blustery winds that accosted Kamehameha at Kiholo Bay had transformed into a fierce Kona storm, and his double-hulled canoe labored against windswept waves. The entourage huddled on deck, enduring the heavy seas with a sense of destiny and duty, for they could see red rivers streaming down the face of Hualalai and more steam plumes at the shore. Even Kamehameha's most hardened warriors wept at the sight of the village surrounded by seething lava.

As the royal entourage disembarked onto the sand, a wave of expectation hushed the anxious crowd, for if any humans could appease Pele, it would be these rulers, who for generations had acted as intermediaries between the people and their gods. Few failed to notice the great *ti*-leaf-wrapped bundle carried by the king, adorned with buds and leaves gathered with his own hands.

The king's procession ascended the volcano's smoky slopes along the edge of the eruption's main flow, their vivid garments visible against the blackened mountainside. As the storm heightened, gale-force winds tumbled trees to the ground, and heavy rains instantly evaporated on the fresh lava, sending up shrouds of steam. When they finally reached the great bubbling cone, the main lava river separated into several streams, each fronted by an undulating yellow flame. Everyone stopped, recognizing in the fires the vaporous figures of Pele and her clan dancing a hula. Among them, to the family's great relief, was Princess Ululani's son, the brilliant flame gyrating close to her as she offered a chant of love: *"O ka maka o kuʻu keiki ka lamaku . . ."*

The king stepped away from the others and announced, "The kahuna and I shall proceed alone." The pair disappeared into the fumes swirling about the erupting cone, and in the hellish heat chanted prayers the priest had prepared. Below them, veiled by the curtain of fumes, the royal entourage threw in their own offerings, including baskets of the king's breadfruit and fish.

The kahuna studied Kamehameha's face in the orange light, noting that the prayers had properly humbled the king. "It is time," he told the monarch.

Kamehameha set his leaf-wrapped bundle on the bank of the lava river, then carefully removed his great feather helmet and handed it to the priest. He reached up to grasp the tresses of his graying hair and, unsheathing his *pahoa*, sliced off a generous lock for the goddess. Those tresses held his personal mana—divine essence inherited from generations of royal ancestors and strengthened by his bold life of conquest and rule. In the fiery light, Kamehameha spread apart the ti leaves of his bundle and added his sacrifice to the offerings inside.

He cradled the bundle in his hands and moved so close to the molten river that the feathers of his robe curled in the heat. "O mighty goddess," he said in a low voice so only Pele would hear him, "my mana is yours, and I apologize for my transgressions." Bowing well below the green bundle, he tossed it into the fissure. Flames surrounded the offering, but it did not burn.

"Pele!" Kamehameha cried, this time booming so everyone at the erupting cone could hear his plea. "I am your subject! I beg you to once again ally yourself with me!"

His offering burst into flames with a blast of heat that scorched the king's cheek.

"It is done," the priest stated with shimmering eyes.

The dancing flames ebbed, and the lava streams formed again into a single mighty river. As the royal family descended the steamy slopes, the storm abated, and the next day the eruption ceased.

Kamehameha's sacrifice may have satisfied the deity, but other powerful forces would eventually change the world he knew and threaten the nation he formed. Within twenty years he was dead, his bones secreted away to a cave on the Kona coast. His laws were overturned, his wives and children embraced new gods, and the ways of the haole were seeded throughout the archipelago, along with their devastating diseases.

Almost all Hawaiians perished in those early plagues of cholera, measles, and smallpox, but those who survived struggled to keep their ancient culture alive, and they sometimes wondered what Pele and the other gods would think of all the changes. Their reverence for the volcano goddess never died, even as the kahuna went underground, quietly handing down their stories and wisdom to each new generation, waiting for a time when they would be needed again.

The island of Hawaiʻi continued to grow with regular eruptions from Kilauea and Mauna Loa on the other side of the island. But Hualalai remained silent, its volcanic peaks shrouded by clouds.

1 ∫ The Scientist's Inquiry

TWO CENTURIES LATER . . .

One particular volcano intrigued Dr. Gavin McCall, Australian National University astronomer—a gigantic peak on a distant moon that could spew a fiery plume big enough to cover all eight Hawaiian islands. He watched for that cataclysm from the cold windswept summit of Mauna Kea, tallest of five volcanoes on the island of Hawaiʻi and home to some of the world's largest telescopes. In gaspingly thin air 14,000 feet above the Pacific, he held his vigils, waiting for the great cone to blow—a volcano named Pele on a moon called Io, spinning madly around the giant planet Jupiter.

His observations would culminate a yearlong research sabbatical that had given the astronomer some time away from his teaching responsibilities—and another chance to adapt to life without his wife, Annie. Still grieving, McCall had used his first four months to wander alone through Australia's outback, instead of perfecting the infrared camera he had designed to peer at Io's Pele. His withdrawal into the wild abruptly ended with word that his project had been granted observatory time on NASA's InfraRed Telescope in Hawaiʻi that next summer. He could not know that this prized opportunity would pull him into a series of events much wilder and life changing than anything he might experience in the outback.

During a late-night observing run on Mauna Kea, an island-born telescope operator mentioned the *real* Pele, the Hawaiian goddess after whom scientists had named the extraterrestrial volcano. McCall, always intrigued by the fascinating or unusual, thought he would mention this colorful bit of lore in a paper he was writing for an astronomy conference back in Canberra. But the operator, reticent to discuss the volcano deity, gave the scientist the name of the island's leading expert on Hawaiian myths and legends, anthropologist Maile Pili'uhane Chow.

One afternoon, when icy fog cloaked the mountaintop, McCall left the isolated base camp, 5,000 feet below the summit, and headed for the town of Hilo down the winding Saddle Road that crosses the island between Mauna Kea and its sister volcano, Mauna Loa. He found Dr. Chow's office above a restaurant on the main street of the former plantation town, sharing a dimly lit corridor with Sam Wong's Fine Tailoring and Joey's Polynesian Tattoo Palace. *M.P. Chow, PhD* was painted in red on the frosted window of the door, which was ajar.

"Knock, knock," McCall said, peeking into the cramped room.

"Come in," replied a hearty voice.

Maile Chow looked up from an old wooden desk covered with reports, letters, and legal pads scribbled with notes. Chow was a Chinese name, so McCall had not expected her bold Hawaiian features. She was broad-shouldered with skin the color of mahogany and a black cascade of hair that reached below her waist. Gold bangles adorned her wrists above large attractive hands, and a gold chain rested just above her breast. Polynesian features also dominated her face—broad nose, angular jaw, and full lips, whorled at the corners. Only her eyes revealed her father's Chinese gene, the lids more oval than round. But their color was Native Hawaiian—as dark as deepest night, and luminescent. The Australian found it difficult not to stare at them and for a moment was flustered.

"You must be Dr. McCall," she said, reaching to shake his hand. "Aloha."

"Righto, Dr. Chow. I appreciate your willingness to meet with me."

"Please sit down." She motioned toward the rattan chair opposite her desk, next to a tall bookcase. McCall eased his lean six-foot frame into the chair, quickly scanning her collection on Pacific island history and lore. Next to the books stood a large shark-skin drum, worn smooth from generations of thumping palms.

The anthropologist leaned back in her chair and eyed the astronomer. Self-assurance lined his rugged face, a look she had seen all too often on haoles. "You work on Mauna Kea."

"Yeah, we're studying a volcano on one of Jupiter's moons, a monstrous cone named after your goddess Pele."

"And you want some background."

"Yeah." He sank deep into the chair, pulling out his notebook and pen.

"History or legend?"

"Both, I guess." He smiled warmly, his green eyes twinkling.

Maile proceeded to tell the astronomer the story of the goddess. She shared the simple version, good enough for a haole scientist, skipping over the deepest meanings of the tale. But she told it vividly, with resonant voice, flashing eyes, and the storytelling skills inherited from her mother. Gavin could see it all: Pele leaving the mysterious ancestral land Kahiki, guided over the ocean by her shark brother Kamohoali'i; her embattled search for a home in the volcanic archipelago, eventually reaching the island of Hawai'i; her fierce romances with obsessive lovers and battles with jealous rivals; Pele lovingly building mountains, or angrily burning villages when she felt betrayed—stories revealing the islanders' love and reverence for a deity that can create and destroy.

Each episode intrigued McCall, but he grew just as interested in watching Maile's expressive face, and soon ceased taking notes. Staring at her bold features, he could visualize the fiery beauty and formidable will of the volcano goddess.

"And these stories," she said, wrapping up, "only hint at the depth of her power, this woman god so commanding that she once even humbled Hawai'i's mightiest king. But that's another story." Maile relaxed back in her chair.

"Marvelous tale! And first rate in the telling!" he said, his accent exaggerated by enthusiasm.

Maile smiled. "Today you will find people whose devotion to Pele has never flagged, even as the islands themselves have changed beyond belief."

"Are you saying some islanders *still* believe in this goddess?"

"More than believe." Maile leaned forward. "Many worship her."

"*Worship*?" The scientist's eyes glowed against his deeply tanned face.

"They pay homage to her with song, dance, prayer, and ceremony. And they give *ho'okupu*—gifts. Flowers, food, and in modern times, gin."

"Gawon," he said, cocking his head sideways. "Gin?"

"*Bloody* right," she replied, mocking his heavy accent, "though she'll accept other spirits too, as long as they're potent enough!"

He laughed, dimples flanking his smile. "Well, I'll be," he said, leaning forward toward her desk, "and what do you anthropologists make of all that, anyway?"

She planted her elbows atop the spray of reports and propped her chin on her hands. "I suppose that depends on whether the anthropologist is Hawaiian."

He stared quizzically into her gleaming eyes. She peered back, and there was a sudden, not disagreeable, tension between them. Just then the sun dropped into the window, bathing them with golden afternoon light.

"Many things in nature we do not fully understand," she replied, sitting up straight.

"Yes," he nodded, his eyes traveling over her face. "Powerful forces."

There was an odd little silence. McCall fell back into the chair and gazed at the anthropologist. "But Dr. Chow, this is the space age."

"So?"

"Well, surely *you* don't believe in that nonsense about Pele?" He regretted the comment as soon as he made it.

Nonsense? The word thudded inside her chest.

Maile rose behind the desk, revealing her true stature, almost six feet and full bodied. She turned to the window to gaze at the sea. Her raven hair, backlit, glistened with auburn highlights. She looked regal even in her sleeveless blouse and khaki skirt. "Is that how you astronomers view the early observers of the sky? Was Galileo a fool because he couldn't grasp the full dimensions of the universe he was trying to understand? You know, a lot of people *still* think astronomy is made up of far-fetched theories more fanciful than real." She turned back to look him straight in the eye. "You ask much of people to believe your stories—suns created out of gas, planets formed from stardust, all the matter of the universe beginning as a dance on the head of a pin? Really, Dr. McCall."

He leaped to his feet, struck with the realization that he had offended. "Terribly sorry! Bloody tactless of me—"

"Don't worry about that. Just remember that all cultures create revered deities and epic stories to portray powerful things that defy simple explanation—like this volcanic island."

McCall sat back down, looking up at her like a chastised student.

"People here live in the shadows of five volcanoes. Three have erupted in historic times—Mauna Loa, Kilauea, and Hualalai. Is it so odd that they would honor the power of these volcanoes through the adventures of a deity? To islanders, scientific theories of tectonic plates and a convecting hot spot are remote, abstract, and dry. So they paint their picture of Pele with deeper hues."

Maile's speech suddenly lapsed into that special cadence with which islanders almost sing their sentences. It was as if her native dialect, repressed by a professional haole world, was fighting its way back through the passion of her words. She flung her magnificent hair out of the way and sat back down in the chair. "At least Hawaiians have one thing straight. Unlike Westerners, they don't pretend they can *control* these things. They know that humans, although precious in the web of life, are too small for that."

"I'll admit that point," McCall replied, fearing that Maile was about to close the conversation. "Dr. Chow, I really didn't mean to come off so badly. I was just teasing a bit. It's an Aussie habit."

She smiled weakly. "I understand, but the elders have told us the old lore, and we still respect them and the traditions they try to keep alive. Besides, we know the volcanoes." She began straightening her papers. "So Dr. McCall, it's better that you learn now—and from me—that islanders take these things seriously."

"Quite so," he replied, again pushing himself forward in the chair.

"Keep in mind our heritage. Hawai'i was absorbed into the United States a century ago, but it's been part of Polynesia for two millennia. So many Hawaiians, like your Aborigines, still live with one foot in the ancient world—especially on *this* island.

"In fact," she said in a lighter tone, and looking up, "if you visiting astronomers would spend a little more time down here with the community, you might appreciate our island customs, for they are not so unrelated to the mysteries *you're* looking at up there in the heavens."

"To be perfectly honest, Dr. Chow, I didn't realize that Hawaiian culture was still a going thing. I mean, well, Waikiki and Honolulu—so much about these islands seems quite altered. I assumed the deeper traditions were gone."

"Hidden, maybe, but not gone."

The sun dropped halfway into a cloud, but several shafts of gold played across McCall's face, filling his probing eyes with light. "I'm sorry I was so insensitive," he said, extending his hand across the desk. "Will you accept my apology?"

A gleam of surprise swept into Maile's eyes. She wasn't used to apologies from haoles. "Don't worry about it, Dr. McCall." She took his hand and shook it with a firm grasp.

"I can see that I'll need to handle my treatment of Pele with more respect in my article. Dr. Chow, you've opened up a new world of ideas for me. Fact is, your island and your goddess fascinate me. I'd like to know more if you're willing to share it."

Maile paused, scrutinizing the Australian. There was something about him, something about his having come to see her in the first place, that compelled her to say yes. "Well, we can't have you sitting up there in your observatory, studying your moon's volcano without understanding the goddess for whom it's named, can we?"

He smiled brightly. "That just wouldn't do, eh?"

Maile got up and walked to the bookcase. She scanned the tropic-mildewed spines and pulled out a slim red volume. "Like any good scientist, I assume you'll want references." She handed McCall the book.

"This contains the Pele legend," she said, smiling. "Do your homework."

He smiled back. "I will."

Maile glanced at the clock behind her desk. "I'm afraid I have to go."

Gavin frowned. A silent question hung in the air.

She stood looking at him, hands on her hips. "There's a *luau* tonight for some friends moving to the mainland. Would you like to come along?"

He was surprised at the invitation, but pleased, and his face brightened.

"We can finish talking story there," she added.

"Sounds lovely. But I wouldn't want to intrude."

"How would you intrude?" Maile looked at him as if he were from another planet. "Remember, you're in Hawai'i. The custom is aloha"—she paused—"Gavin."

She smiled broadly, and he grinned back.

"Thanks—Maile."

2 ∫ The Luau

Gavin followed Maile's Jeep to an old beachfront community beyond Hilo's industrial quarter and harbor. Her hair danced inside the Jeep as it sped along a narrow lane of bungalows, coconut palms, and flowering trees. The sun hovered low over Mauna Kea, its summit cones shrouded in a frothy cap of clouds. Cars had parked along the roadsides, and a large crowd mingled near three ramshackle pavilions tucked into the coastal jungle. Several gleeful friends hailed Maile before she could even pull over.

"Aloha, Maile!" they hollered, flashing the islands' casual salute—the *shaka*—a hand waved with the middle three fingers folded into the palm, pinkie and thumb outstretched. Women sprinted across the road to hug her through the Jeep's window. Gavin parked his NASA Blazer under a thicket of trees between a battered pickup and a rusty Corolla missing its bumpers and got out to wait for Maile. The muggy jungle smelled of damp vegetation. Hilo's urban bustle seemed much farther than five miles away.

Gavin watched people milling about the little park. Some lounged at picnic tables inside the pavilions, while others hung around a homemade grill where two beefy men lorded over sizzling fish and chicken. In the central pavilion women set out tray after tray of food, a potluck feast for the departing family. A half-dozen elders held court in folding chairs near a lava rock seawall. A younger group sat on the wall, each face shining in the day's last light. Two men, throw nets draped over their shoulders, stalked the shoals for schools of fish. Children played tag under the coconut trees and frolicked in freshwater ponds along the shore, their brown backs glistening in the sun.

Laughter and conversation flowed freely under the jungle canopy, blending with the splash of waves against the rocks. A young man sang traditional melodies in Hawaiian, accompanied by two men on guitars and an old woman on an *'ukulele*. Several little girls with fern garlands on their wrists and ankles practiced their hula under a coco palm while a cluster of women looked on.

Each face seemed to reflect a different ethnic mix—combinations of Polynesian, Chinese, Portuguese, Caucasian, Korean, Filipino, and Japanese blood. A few were pure Hawaiian. Only a handful of haoles had come (mostly the spouses of Hawaiians), and Gavin felt self-conscious. He wished Maile would finish conversing and rescue him.

A shirtless Hawaiian with thick round shoulders stepped out of the battered pickup in front of Gavin's SUV. Each arm bore a tattoo—one an elaborate turtle design, the other simply the word *Saigon*. His dark eyes shimmered, like Maile's.

"Aloha, bruddah," he said, muscling a huge cooler out of the truck bed.

"Cheers," Gavin replied.

"You comin' to da party?"

"Yeah, just waiting for my friend over there." He pointed at the Jeep.

"You wit' Maile?"

The man acknowledged Gavin's affirmative answer island-style—with raised eyebrows and an upward nod.

"My name's Liko."

"Gavin."

Liko rested the cooler atop the tailgate and offered the island handshake—a firm grasp and double shake anchored off the thumbs. It seemed convoluted to Gavin, yet he felt the camaraderie in it.

The Hawaiian grabbed a beer from his cooler and handed it to Gavin. "See ya ova' dere," he said, lugging his burden across the road.

"Good on yer, mate!" said Gavin, awkwardly flashing him the shaka.

"Wha'? Already got da local style?" Maile, walking over, joked in pidgin.

"Huh?" Gavin was startled to hear the PhD anthropologist speak the local lingo.

"We're trilingual, Gavin," she said, shifting back to regular English. "Some of us can still speak Hawaiian, but among our diverse local friends, we'll use the community language, pidgin. It combines all our ancestral tongues. You'll hear plenty of it tonight, especially among younger people. Older Hawaiians who weren't allowed to use pidgin in school or church still speak the King's English. They refused to work on the sugar plantations and never picked it up from the Asian work crews. Locals will slip into pidgin with you too, Gavin, once we get to know you—or when we get emotional about something."

"I'll do me best to keep up."

Maile guided Gavin into the heart of the party, introducing him to friends and family (without the *Dr.* or the surname). All greeted him with the same warmth and openness he'd experienced from Liko at the road. A few spoke such heavy pidgin that Gavin could do little more than nod and smile. Hearing Gavin's accent, some asked if he was from Australia or New Zealand. A few asked him what he was doing "up on the mountain," and all wanted to know how he felt about Hawai'i.

Everyone made him feel welcome, except two young men who, having heard he was a visiting astronomer, got up and left as Gavin was being introduced.

Liko shrugged. "Auwe. Dey no more talk wit' haole guys. Say you guys mess up dees islands bad enough, so no more aloha for dem."

Maile turned to Gavin. "There's growing resentment here . . . but that's a long story."

"I'd like to hear it."

Liko rested his hand on Gavin's shoulder. "Dees days, we got some pretty radical sovereignty guys—dey want their islands back. Dose kids angry, but not really at you." The Hawaiian smiled broadly. "Enjoy da party, bruddah."

Just then two Hawaiian men strolled up to Maile. One, handsome with twinkling eyes, wrapped a muscled arm around her waist.

"What's dis?" He shouted. "Maile Chow? We t'aut maybe you no more come to luau wit d'jour old gang." He turned to his companion. "She got one busy haole-kind PROFESSIONAL job, you know. No more go out with *kanaka maoli* men." Native Hawaiian men.

"Knock it off, George!" She broke free of his grasp and clenched a fist. "I not so *PROFESSIONAL* dat I 'fraid fo' bust you up!"

"Neh!"

Everyone laughed, except Maile.

"George like go out wit' her," Liko whispered into Gavin's ear. "Good guy, but no more her type."

Gavin flashed a curious look.

"She stay stuck between two cultures." He twisted the cap off another beer and handed it to Gavin. "Maile still trying figure out where she belong."

When some women moved in between Maile and the two Hawaiians and started teasing the men with off-color remarks, she took Gavin by the arm and stepped out of the fray, then walked him over to the departing family for whom the luau was held. The young Hawaiian, his haole wife, and their little girl were heading for Seattle, where he'd landed a sales job with United Airlines. His wife seemed almost relieved, telling Gavin that buying an affordable house was impossible in Hawai'i and that she didn't want to raise a family in a rental owned by local Japanese or haole landlords.

This was their last night in Hawai'i, and the young man's eyes gleamed with tears as he talked to Maile. "I'm the first of my family to leave," he said. "We don't know when we'll be back. Grandpa used to say that 'a tree uprooted can't be transplanted without dying.'"

Later, Gavin commented on the young man's remark. "He sounds like many of the Aborigines in the cities back home. Separated from their homeland, they wither . . . spiritually, I guess you'd say. The ones who do adjust become culturally separated from their clans."

Maile sighed. "We know how that is."

A lively group noticed Maile and swept her toward some friends near one of the ponds, so Gavin strolled over to the seawall and struck up a conversation with several elders. When Maile reemerged from her friends, she noticed Gavin listening intently to an elder's story, his handsome profile silhouetted against the shimmering sea. Suddenly he leaned back—mouth open, teeth glistening—and laughed so joyously that its echo gave her a rush of delight. She wondered if Gavin's natural rapport with the islanders was because, even as a white Australian, he, too, was a child of the Pacific. Perhaps he'd even befriended some of its aboriginal residents.

When she drifted back to a pavilion to chat with a friend, Gavin looked up and saw her—Maile's hair ablaze in the last minute of daylight, her regal figure and face profiled in gold.

Feeling his glance, she looked over and smiled.

Torches were lit, pulsating light on the people, pavilions, and jungle. Gavin and Maile joined the long line of friends progressing around the food table. The food was as eclectic as the mingled ancestries gathered there—pork steamed in ti leaves, grilled fish from the reef, and *kalua* pig cooked in a traditional underground firepit. Oriental ginger chicken was heaped on plates alongside Chinese noodles, Japanese rice, American macaroni salad, and Hawaiian *lomilomi* salad. Someone had baked Portuguese sweet bread, served with guava jam and *poha* jelly. And, of course, everyone relished the tubs of *poi*—the always-present taro mash.

Maile interpreted the buffet for Gavin, and his interest delighted the cooks. They heaped his plate with everything and would later tease Maile about her "haole-boy" friend who could "grind" (eat) Hawaiian *kau kau* (food) like one good kanaka maoli.

Afterward, Gavin followed Maile back to the seawall. Crickets chirped in the jungle and geckos chattered as if talking story with the clan attending the luau. The sun had set behind the mountain—now a purple hulk against the fading sky—and Venus beamed in the west. To the east, over the ocean, rose a nearly half moon. Far in the distance, up the Hamakua coast, the yellow lights of former sugar towns twinkled in the purple dusk.

The young singer resumed his performance atop the seawall. His youthful body swayed in the firelight, and his voice shifted into a heavenly falsetto. People joined in the song, tapping their rubber flip-flops against the dirt. Couples gravitated back to each other, children snuggled with grandparents, and those who wanted to get rowdy disappeared into the shadows to smoke pot or drink more beer.

"This is great," Gavin said. "It's like a throwback, something you read about in books written decades ago."

"Ya know, Maile, this place could get under a bloke's skin."

Maile flashed him a puzzled look. "Why do you say that?"

"Look." He lifted his arms as if to embrace the whole scene. "The moon, the stars, mountains, ocean . . ." His voice fell to a whisper as if fearing he might startle the picture out from under his eyes. ". . . food, family, laughter, song—love."

"Gavin, this is what Hawai'i has *always* been for us—what I hope it always will be."

He nodded, his eyes drifting to the ocean, an undulating tapestry of moon and starlight. "Ya know, Maile, this place could get under a bloke's skin. A few nights like this and a man might never go home."

"It's happened before."

At the end of the song, a large woman rose from among the elders, commanding everyone's attention. Although she wore Western clothes—casual slacks and a blouse—she had the same luminescent eyes Gavin had noticed among many of the Hawaiians at the luau.

"Tonight," she said in a loving but formidable voice, "we say good-bye to part of our family, Lohelani and his wife, Betty, and their little one, Lehuanani. Let us pray for their health and good fortune." With that, everyone, even the oldest of the elders, stood.

"*O na akua, O na ʻaumakua,*" she began, addressing the gods and the ancestors. Her deep tremolo echoed through the jungle, and Gavin felt a vibrant tingle, as if electricity ran up his back. A spontaneous moment of silence followed the prayer, and then, without cue, the young singer began "Hawaiʻi Aloha," a traditional anthem sung at the close of gatherings: "*E Hawaiʻi, e kuʻu one hanau e . . .*" (O Hawaiʻi, O sands of my birth . . .) The departing family moved into the firelight, and everyone joined hands and sang. Tears ran freely. When the song finished, everyone held up their clasped hands and then hugged. Even the men kissed each other on their cheeks.

"Thanks, Maile," Gavin said as the group began to disband. "This was really fine. I enjoyed it so much I forgot to ask you those last few questions about Pele."

Maile laughed. "Good. You lost your focus. We analytical types need to remember to do that."

Gavin nodded. They fell silent, absorbing the music and talk and the lap of waves against the shore—keenly aware of each other.

"Say, Maile," Gavin said, eventually breaking his own reverie. "Thanks for lending me the Pele book. How should I get it back to you?"

"When we go to Kilauea. If you really want to understand Pele, you have to visit her home. And I think I should show it to you."

"Too good! When?"

Maile peered into the Australian's shining face. "Tomorrow?"

"Righto."

Gavin hadn't felt this contented in a long time, certainly not in the four years since Annie's death. Driving back to the astronomers' base camp, he found himself smiling all the way up the mountain.

Maile, too, felt happy, and she floated on blue ocean dreams all night. By morning, though, her mind surged with questions, not the least of which was one so many Hawaiians ask themselves after the fact: Was I sharing too much with the haole?

3 ∫ Pele's Fiery Home

FRIDAY AFTERNOON, JUNE 2 . . .

Gavin pulled up to Maile's building in his rusty NASA Blazer, its white paint dusted with red Mauna Kea ash. Maile sat at the foot of the stairs reading a newspaper. She had donned her anthropologist's field clothes—jeans, flannel shirt, and boots scarred from walks on lava rock—and wore her hair in a great heap atop her head, pinned with a chopstick. Two gold bangles adorned each wrist.

Gavin leaned across the seat and flung open the passenger door. "G'day, Maile!" he shouted, his eyes sparkling. "I'm ready to meet your goddess."

She got up from the stoop, smiling. "You think so?"

He plucked the book of legends off the seat. "Spent half the night doing my homework."

"Good for you," she said as she slid into the Blazer.

Gavin didn't notice the hint of sarcasm in her voice. "Say, Maile, thanks again for last night. That was super!"

"I enjoyed having you with me," she admitted, "although I had to set two aunties straight about the professional nature of our relationship."

He laughed so delightedly that Maile had to chuckle. She fastened her frayed seat belt and asked, "This junker belongs to NASA?"

"Yup. The IRTF—InfraRed Telescope Facility."

"Infrared? So your telescope looks for *heat* then?"

"Exactly," he replied, pulling out along the ocean on King Kamehameha Avenue. "We point at Io and if the mirror picks up lots of photons—well beyond the normal heat for a moon—we reckon she's blowing her top. Then we study what she's spitting out."

"How often do you monitor Io's volcanoes?"

"I'll be on the Big Island for the next three weeks. Right now I'm waiting for a couple of hours of clear sky to recalibrate my camera before starting the full-blown observing run. But the weather's not cooperating."

"Clouds?"

"Yeah, I understand that's a rare thing for Mauna Kea, especially in summer. Fact is, the summit's been socked in for two days, with freezing fog and wind. One of the blokes in the kitchen says it's 'cause some astronomer pinched a lava rock for his collection. Apparently there's this superstition about taking lava off the island." He smiled irreverently.

"We're not going to get into a fight again, are we?" she asked, smiling in spite of herself.

"Not a chance. I only brought it up so you could explain it."

"Sure you did. Did you really look at the book I gave you?"

"Read the whole thing last night—after giving up on the bloody sky. But hey, if it weren't for the foul weather, I wouldn't be here with you, eh? I'd be up there, freezing me duff off. And I wouldn't have a chance to see *your* volcano."

"I'm glad there's some consolation."

During the hour-long drive up the volcano, Maile pointed out scenery, but Gavin kept returning to the luau, his infectious enthusiasm lightening her mood—and lowering her guard. Halfway up, they stopped at a family-run store to top off gas and buy *bentos*—Japanese box lunches. Maile strode out of the little tin building and noticed Gavin staring across the rainforest. Five miles away, towering above the trees and ferns, stood a fuming cinder cone.

"That's Pu'u 'O'o," she said, "named for the sacred 'o'o bird—now extinct."

"So the volcano's broken out on this flank?"

"Yes. For decades, lava's been flowing from that cone down to the sea."

"Amazing to see it just over there, only a stone's toss from the petrol station," Gavin said, squeegeeing the dusty windshield. "Ya know, I've always been curious about volcanoes, but didn't really get into them till *Voyager* spotted one erupting on Io during the '79 Jupiter flyby. The US-Australian team I've joined has done a lot of follow-up observations from Mauna Kea. Two of my mates on this run are geophysicists, and I'm the team's infrared man. I helped design the camera."

"You'd think a man studying a volcanic moon millions of miles away wouldn't miss the chance to see an eruption only a few hours from where he's working."

"Terrible, yeah? But time's precious on these big scopes, and I've been working nonstop since I got here. Not that I'd mind taking a few days off, but my colleagues back home already have raised eyebrows, what with me spending summer in Hawai'i at university expense."

"So if the weather hadn't been bad, you wouldn't have visited Kilauea? Or come to see me about Pele?"

"'Fraid so." He cringed, pulling the pump nozzle out of the SUV.

"Talk about having your head in the clouds! Did it ever occur to you hot-shot haole astronomers that you ought to know something about the island that hosts you?" She shook her head. "I'll have to give you a crash course."

"I'd like that . . ." She slid onto the seat and Gavin closed the door, leaning into the open window. "I'd like that very much."

They continued up the volcano's flank, high into the rainforest. Now 4,000 feet above Hilo, clouds skimmed over the treetops and a light mist smeared the windshield. At the national park entrance, the Hawaiian ranger recognized Maile and waved the vehicle through. Some distance beyond park headquarters, Maile directed Gavin to a pullout at a clearing in the trees, the whole area rent with steaming fissures.

"This way," she said, getting out of the vehicle. She pulled the chopstick from her hair, freeing it to dance in the cool wind. As they walked the path toward the cliffs above the summit caldera, long grass lashed their legs and swirls of fume jigged alongside.

"Hawaiians call this area *Wahine Kapu*, the bluffs of the sacred woman," Maile said reverently. "The spirit of Pele's brother, Kamohoali'i, also resides here, so she never blows smoke over these cliffs, no matter how wild the volcano gets."

Gavin looked at her blankly.

"But since you read my little book, you already know that much."

They stepped through the mist, and the three-mile-wide caldera came into view. Long wisps of fume rose from the deep depression.

"Good God, she's a boomer!" Gavin gasped, scanning the vast floor of steel-gray lava flows. "Looks like an asteroid impact crater!"

"The summit's quiet now, but just six months ago she was still spewing fume and ash from a series of explosions that put everyone on edge. For a long time she even reappeared as a churning lava lake. Sometimes the air got so bad that Civil Defense evacuated people downwind from their homes, and the national park closed. Fumes drifted over the whole state and real estate values plummeted. The summit crater glowed red at night for the first time in decades, even as Kilauea continued to erupt downrift at Puʻu ʻOʻo. Geologists think the magma welling up inside the island is growing. Pele eventually moved back downrift, but the scientists, and some of the elders, are still concerned. Explosive eruptions are rare here and can be extremely dangerous."

"What do the elders say?"

Maile stayed quiet a moment. That was not to share, at least not yet. An indirect answer would suffice. "Pele can show herself in dazzling molten displays—lava lakes, fire fountains, wild rivers—but to explode, Gavin, that's something else. In 1790 she did it and destroyed a would-be king's ambitions, annihilating the warriors of Kamehameha's chief rival. The destruction wrought by that outburst is legend."

The astronomer stepped closer to the rim. Inside the caldera's far end was another, deeper crater marked by yellow sulfur and great curls of fume.

"That's where she exploded," said Maile, pointing.

Gavin jammed his hands into his pockets. "Otherworldly," he muttered, his sandy-blond hair tossing wildly about his head.

After giving him a minute to absorb the scene, Maile said, "Now I want to show you where the goddess lives."

They returned to the Blazer and continued along the road, eventually descending right into the caldera to a parking lot near the deeper crater. The area was deserted, the afternoon tour buses having come and gone. As they got out, swirling fumes engulfed them in the tang of sulfur. "Pele's breath," Maile whispered.

They followed the park's rough trail to the crater's rim, its sheer cliffs dropping another 400 feet below the caldera. Around them lay chunks of shattered rock blasted out of the crater and dusted with pink ash. They gazed down at the great steaming hole on the crater's floor that only months earlier had warned of the tempest that seethed beneath it. Maile noticed that the resident tropic birds had vacated their usual domain for the lone white hawk that had soared in above the crater.

"This is Halemaʻumaʻu, sacred home of Pele."

Gavin crept closer to the edge, peering into the pit. He surveyed the frozen features of its once-molten lake and its new fuming hole. And just at that moment, an elderly Hawaiian woman emerged from the vapors swirling about the path, her gray-streaked hair trailing behind her. Of wide girth and solid build, she wore a traditional yellow shawl atop her dress, its corners knotted over one shoulder. Her black eyes glowed in a nut-brown face as she clumped down the trail, a green bundle tucked under her arm.

They watched as she crossed the Park Service rope lining the path, marched to the crater's edge, and leaned so far over the precipice that Gavin instinctively stepped in her direction.

"Gavin, don't!" Maile whispered loudly. "She knows what she's doing."

The old woman placed the bundle on a rock jutting over the recently active pit and chanted in her native tongue. Maile cocked her ears, but the wind caught the words, keeping them a private matter between the elder and the volcano.

The old Hawaiian returned to the trail. As she passed, she noticed Gavin, her dark eyes severe.

"G'day," he said, smiling. She looked away and a moment later vanished into a veil of steam.

Gavin walked over to the green bundle at the cliff's edge. Nearby lay remnants of other gifts—dried flower stems and blossoms, 'ohelo branches bearing clusters of red berries, withered *leis* and rotting cane stalks, and fresh offerings wrapped in the thick, waxy leaves of the ti plant. A flask of gin stood propped against a clump of lava. Curious, Gavin stooped to examine the woman's bundle. A piercing cry resounded directly above him.

He leaped back from the precipice, his eyes flashing upward, then hastily returned to the path, snagging his foot on the rope as he climbed over it.

"Bloody bird startled me!" he hollered to Maile.

"You mustn't disturb a gift for the goddess," she said.

"Guess so." He glanced back at the cliff of offerings, then walked over to Maile. "My curiosity just got hold of me."

"I know, but you should be careful. And more respectful."

"Why do islanders bring these gifts?" he asked, still shaken.

"They're here to praise Pele, or to appease her. Some say a bundle of fish or taro has spared their home from the volcano's wrath or brought their families good fortune."

"So I was about to meddle with someone's future over there," he said, laughing.

A gust of volcanic steam blew across the pair, and Gavin started coughing.

Maile grasped his arm and escorted him out of the acrid air.

"This place is even stranger than up on Mauna Kea," he said when he could breathe again.

Just then a shadow passed over the Australian. "There it is again!"

"*'Io*," Maile said calmly.

"Huh?"

"The island hawk. His name's spelled like your moon, but pronounced 'EE-oh,' and Hawaiians believe he's a powerful spirit, too."

Maile didn't mention it, but she was certain the hawk's arrival was no coincidence. It had come with the old woman—or was there for her.

4 ∫ Metaphors

Despite the crater incident—or perhaps because of it—Maile decided to take Gavin closer to the volcano's deity. They drove out of the caldera onto a road that descended Kilauea's southern flank. After traveling through stretches of devastated forest and along a line of old craters and cones, the road hugged the edge of the volcano's 2,000-foot shoulder, a precipice Hawaiians call a *pali*. Hardened lava spread out in all directions—glassy, black *pahoehoe* broken here and there by stretches of red *'a'a* clinkers that resembled heaps of iron slag. On the brink of the pali stood a spacious wooden deck with picnic tables overlooking the Pacific.

"One of my favorite places on the island," Maile said. They strolled down the path to the deck, buffeted by blustery winds. "Up here you can see over fifty miles, from the fishing village of Kalapana to the island's southern tip."

Gavin gazed out at the vast sweep of volcanic cliffs and coastline.

"You're looking at the district of Ka'u, the most volcanic part of the island—and the place I grew up. See that rugged coast down there? It's dotted with the remnants of abandoned fishing villages, and in the uplands are defunct sugar plantations and cattle ranches. In between is a vast lava desert of ancient ruins and some two-century-old footprints baked into the ash of that 1790 eruption I mentioned, reminders of men, women, and children who died in a war between rival chiefs."

Gavin scanned the landscape, taking it all in, while Maile leaned against the deck's railing, watching him. He clutched the rail like a sailor manning the bow, his pant legs flapping.

"Marvelous!" he exclaimed.

She smiled. "How about supper?"

"Bloody good idea! I'll go get the stuff."

Maile continued to ponder the man as he went to the Blazer, striding up and down the path with a graceful gait. They sat down beside each other facing the steep overlook, now awash in early evening light. Gavin pulled the bentos out of the bag and handed one to Maile.

"How did you get interested in astronomy?" she asked, gathering up her windblown hair and tucking it inside her jacket.

"I was one of those kids who spent all night in the back garden looking at stars and planets through a telescope built by my dad and me. He was a crew boss at the mines, and we lived in the outback, where the sky is unimaginably clear. It was an odd contraption of a scope, but it brought the whole universe into my isolated world. I learned the science of it—the physics—much later. Just the opposite of most astronomers nowadays, who start out gazing at formulas and only later apply it to the sky."

"What was the attraction?" she asked, nibbling a piece of chicken.

"Oh, I mean, you just look up there and your jaw drops! Celestial objects epitomize nature's grandest forces and the possibility that somewhere out there—near a star on a planet too dim for us to see—is life!"

"Then it's not just what you observe, but the *possibilities* it represents?"

He nodded. "Frankly, for me the science is a bit tedious, but the results are fascinating. They reveal the magic all the more."

"But if it's 'magic' that thrills you, why were you so surprised when I told you island people still revere Pele?"

A faint smile broke at the edges of his lips. "Let me turn that into a question for you, Maile. Are you saying Pele is a symbol to the islanders, that those gifts they bring to the crater are actually their way of honoring nature's power?"

She nodded as she poured them cups of coffee from her thermos.

"And the legends are handed down over generations so people won't forget that power?"

"Yes. That's part of it too."

"But yesterday you spoke of her as if she were a real person."

"She's all those things, Gavin—the revered symbol of the volcano, a central character in the epic stories that are the history of Hawai'i's people, and, well . . ." Maile leaned forward over the picnic table. "She's a powerful spirit that people feel and sometimes even see."

Gavin's green eyes twinkled in the sharp evening light.

"Over the centuries—right up to today—sightings occur. Some accounts are full of fear. Others show great affection. But all are testimonies of awe. Some have seen Pele in a dancing flame atop a molten flow or in a swirl of fume leaping from a fissure. More than once, her image has been photographed rising from a lava lake. She can be seen *anywhere*, and in many forms, from rocks to human flesh. Sometimes she's like a voluptuous young woman with flaming eyes and flowing hair, a goddess so beautiful that even great chiefs cannot resist her seductions. Sometimes she's an old woman with weary red eyes who tests her people's generosity by requesting help or food. In that case, you better give her what she wants!"

Maile's eyes seemed to darken despite the bright light bathing the pali.

"Pele can be volatile or tempestuous—and she commands respect. She is, after all, a powerful creative force that, for the benefit of her people, builds or destroys."

Although Gavin loved Maile's storytelling, his face betrayed his skepticism. "And who gets this privilege to see her?"

"An amazing variety of people," Maile replied with a knowing smile. "Not just superstitious fishermen and farmers, but bank presidents, US Army commanders—even scientists."

"Gawon!" Gavin said. "They can barely *imagine* such things."

Maile pointed defiantly into the deep blue sky. "You just said there was magic *up there*."

"Look, saying there's wonder in the cosmos is far different than believing spirits walk the earth. When I say there are things we don't fully understand about the universe, I'm talking about things we *could* understand if we had the science to do it."

"And what makes you believe there's life out there, Gavin?"

"Because conditions exist for planetary formation around many stars we observe. Astronomers agree, there are probably *trillions* of planets, *many* with life!"

"But you *always* believed there was life out there, didn't you? Back when you were looking through your homemade telescope—long before you knew what science would show you. What made you believe?"

"Good question," he said. "I suppose it was the imponderables. I just assumed that in such a gigantic system we couldn't be alone."

"So you *knew* it had to be—before you had the science to 'prove' it?"

"Too right! I get your point. But we *understand* the volcano because we've done the science. So to believe that eruptions are caused by the whim of some goddess is, well, it's—"

"Crazy? Look, Gavin. This volcano is the very thing you're talking about—nature's mysterious power. Pele stories exist because something wondrous or unexplainable happened to someone. All I'm saying is, don't dismiss what you don't understand just because you can't explain it entirely with science—*especially in Polynesia*."

The scientist nodded slowly. "I'll give you that."

"You remember from the book I gave you, Pele's mythic island-hopping down the archipelago, chased by her sea-goddess sister? You can read that as a Hawaiian account of the islands' geologic evolution, starting with Kaua'i and ending with the last born, this island, Hawai'i. What the ancients knew about natural forces they passed on as metaphorical descriptions—*stories*. Is that so different from science?"

"But surely islanders today realize science can explain all these phenomena." Impatience was seeping into Gavin's voice. "Especially with all the knowledge gained during the past fifty years, much of it from scientists right here in Hawai'i."

"Yet during that same period the belief in Pele and our other deities has resurfaced. The old religion, repressed since American missionaries came here, is experiencing a renaissance, along with many other cultural practices. Hawaiians again add their metaphors—their stories—to the scientific ones."

"Somehow I think of scientific discoveries as more than just metaphorical descriptions. They're renderings of the truth."

Maile smiled over the brim of her coffee cup. "Renderings? Isn't that what a story is?"

Gavin looked back quizzically. "You're serious, aren't you?"

"Absolutely."

"It's getting chilly out here," he said, zipping up his jacket. He rose and walked to the railing, staring out across the stark landscape, trying to absorb what he'd heard.

Gavin turned back and leaned against the rail. "Did you get interested in the legends because of your family?"

"That was part of it. My mother was Hawaiian, born here in Ka'u, and I learned some of the old ways from her. But my father was Chinese, originally from Honolulu. He worked hard in his Pahala store so he could afford to send me to college. He hoped I would choose a profession, not just raise a family. I had a knack for science, yet I sensed even as a child that my mother represented something Polynesian that was important . . . and disappearing. So I took up anthropology as a way to stay in touch with my vanishing past and give me a useful profession. Now I lecture part time at the university's Hilo campus and do private consulting."

"Who are your clients?"

"That's the ironic part." She winced. "Most of my contracts are with developers who by law have to conduct archaeological surveys before they build. With the boom in housing and resorts, especially over on Kona side, I've had plenty of work. But these are the very people who destroy the things about the island I value most—the reasons I became an anthropologist. It's the only way I can make a living with my degree unless I teach full time in Honolulu or on the mainland."

"And you want to stay on this island?"

"This is my *'aina*—the land I come from, my roots. For a Hawaiian, to be without one's 'aina is to be disconnected, to live without ancestral continuity."

"I understand," Gavin sighed, setting his empty cup on the table. "But what you've put together here isn't bad. At least you help protect what should be preserved."

"That's what I thought, at first, but only rarely is a project canceled to save a cultural site. Most of the time I go in with a team of archaeologists to identify what's significant, and the most important artifacts are shipped off to the basement of the Bishop Museum in Honolulu. Then the bulldozers come, followed by construction crews. I tell myself it's better to have someone like me saving those little bits of culture than some haole who couldn't care less, but I worry about taking the developers' money to do it."

Maile looked away, her moist eyes distant. "And now they're building that monstrous resort in Kona, transforming one of our richest cultural sites into another Disneyland."

The gusty winds moaned through the timbers of the exposed deck.

"We've all got a living to make, Maile," Gavin said softly.

She nodded and fell silent, watching the shadows lengthen as the sun dipped close to the sea. Gavin finished packing up the picnic remnants, then stepped to the rail to take in another view across the volcano's broad shoulder.

"It's *beautiful*, Maile. Strange as it is, this is one of the loveliest places I've ever seen."

"I thought you'd like it," she replied, a bit more lilt in her voice.

He turned back, peering into her melancholy eyes. "I'm beginning to understand your feelings about the volcano. It's more than just a crater at the top of the hill. I mean, *all* this"— he waved his arm through the crisp, windy air—"and the history that goes with it, is part of Kilauea."

"That's right. And if you make the effort, you'll discover that the *whole* island is like that. Then you might appreciate why many Hawaiians, like that woman back at the summit, still worship the ancient gods."

"You'll have to give me a little more time on that one . . . Say, Maile, do you take all your visitors to this place?"

"No."

They exchanged a long look. Gavin took Maile's hand and helped her up from the picnic table, and they strolled in silence up the path to the Blazer. The last light of the day transformed the pali into a pastel wonderland, and the hawk that had followed them to the overlook soared back to the crater.

5 ∫ Ominous Phantoms

Gavin sped down the steep road that switched back across the pali. The picnic overlook was just a speck on the ridge above them, atop a frozen cascade of lava gleaming in the dying light. Far below on the coast, steam plumes billowed as lava flowed into the sea.

"Fantastic!" Gavin hollered, popping his head out the window for better views. "How close can we get?"

"Right next to it, if you'd like. But I know another place, upslope, where we can look down into a molten river at close range. Let's go there first, while we still have some light."

"Too good!"

They followed the coast for several miles, then turned onto a cinder road leading back up the pali. A sun-bleached wooden sign stood beside the road:

KAPU!
NO TRESPASSING!
VIOLATORS WILL BE PROSECUTED!

"Never mind the sign," Maile said. "That's just to keep tourists out."

"What does *kapu* mean?"

"Traditionally it means 'sacred.' In this case it's saying 'off limits.'"

"Looks pretty adamant to me."

"Don't worry about it."

"Whatever you say." Gavin shifted the Blazer into four-wheel drive and bounced it up the deeply pitted road. They drove through a forest of giant ferns and ʻohiʻa trees, over a cinder berm meant to discourage passage, and onto an overgrown asphalt road leading further uphill, passing several houses with boarded windows, their yards tangled jungle.

"Civil Defense evacuated this area some years ago," Maile said, "after flows cut the subdivision in half and then turned on the village of Kalapana."

"Darn shame," he said. "They look like fairly new homes."

"This was once part of the volcano's vast sacred forest, unspoiled until the 1960s, when speculators subdivided the land. Mostly mainlanders bought the lots, often sight unseen—vacation and retirement properties advertised in travel magazines." Bitterness crept into her voice. "The real estate agents didn't mention that Royal Gardens Estates was built on Kilauea's rift zone."

"And the authorities let them get away with that?"

Maile's face hardened. "Of course they did. There was money to be made, and in these islands, the developers own the politicians. Often they *are* the politicians. It's only gotten worse since statehood."

The pavement disappeared under a ten-foot heap of black rock. "Bloody hell!" Gavin exclaimed, braking the Blazer.

They got out and scrambled to the top of the flow. Strewn about the decimated forest were half-buried remnants of charred houses, vehicles, swimming pools, children's toys—reminders of a community burned and then buried under tons of molten rock. The flow had the texture of a frozen sea—waves of hardened rock, bubbled domes, and whirlpools spun in stone. Here and there a blackened palm or ruined car protruded like flotsam. A disembodied tin roof rattled in the wind, the peak of an ark sinking into the depths. Looming above it all, beyond the dark ridge, was the massive volcanic cone, Puʻu ʻOʻo, belching out amber fumes from its gaping mouth.

The couple leaned against the scorched hood of an incinerated pickup and watched the sun slip into the sea. Darkness encroached quickly, and the distant steam plumes glowed red. Volcanic haze hung over the once-populated slope.

"This place gives me the creeps," Gavin said.

Maile stepped away from the burned hulk. "Follow me."

They stepped over jagged crevices and around deep holes as they trekked across the lava. The utterly black terrain made hiking difficult, and Gavin stumbled on the charred remnant of a fence post. But Maile knew a half moon would soon rise, giving sufficient light to guide them back. They followed a strip of forest not yet destroyed by Pu'u 'O'o's torrents. The vegetation eventually gave way to a recent flow, still hot under their feet, and much of the lava's crust was eggshell thin, cracking under their weight. When they stepped into the open, Maile pointed to an orange glow shining up from a breach in the hillside. They approached the gassy chasm slowly. Leaning over its crusty rim, they peeked into the glowing hole, their faces blasted with heat. So bright was its luminescence that their pupils instantly contracted to pinpricks.

Mouths agape in wonder, they watched in silence as the molten river swept beneath them, iridescent orange sloshing against the cavern's white-hot walls.

"Scientists call this a skylight," Maile whispered. "It's definitely some kind of window."

Gavin grasped Maile's arm and leaned out over the chasm, sweat dribbling orange off his face. "It's like looking into . . ."

"Pele's world?"

Gavin nodded, mesmerized by the dizzying mass of molten stone rushing by.

Suddenly he tightened his grip and yanked Maile away from the hole. "Watch out!"

"What are you doing!" she hissed, pulling her arm free.

"Didn't you hear the edge crumbling?"

This time she heard the cracking. She grasped *his* arm, and they gingerly stepped away from the hole.

Again, the crumbling sound, but even closer.

"Wait!" she whispered, "that's not the skylight." She pointed downslope. "There's someone over there—walking on the fragile lava!"

Two hundred feet below the glowing chasm, in the first rays of moonlight, a line of seven shadowed figures shuffled down the volcano.

"What are *they* doing here?" Maile whispered.

"Security for the subdivision?" Gavin asked.

"There's been no security here since the place was abandoned years ago."

"Tourists, then?"

"Up here?" She shook her head. "I didn't notice any vehicles when we drove in. They must have come a different route."

"Odd," Gavin said, "they're not using flashlights."

The procession stopped, and two men began climbing up toward the skylight. The Hawaiian man in front towered over a shorter Filipino companion.

"Get down," Maile said, grabbing Gavin's shoulders, and they crouched close to the ground, the glassy pahoehoe lava crunching under their feet.

The Hawaiian halted to cock an ear, his eyes gleaming in the gassy iridescence. After a long minute, he led the other man forward.

Gavin put his arm around Maile and nudged her closer. "They haven't seen us," he whispered, his lips touching her ear. "Could they be here to make an offering?"

"It's possible," Maile replied, "but my gut tells me something else."

The two men stepped into the skylight's glow, scarcely twenty feet from the couple hiding in the dark. They peered into the hot, fuming hole, their bodies undulating like scarlet phantoms. The immense Hawaiian had a thick, dark mustache, his aloha shirt half-open in the heat. The volcanic light gleamed against the Filipino's shirtless chest and glinted on his machete. Behind them the rising half moon silhouetted the tops of the trees. Soon the whole hillside—and Gavin and Maile—would be bathed in moonlight.

The Hawaiian stood rigid, studying the glowing hole, then shook his head and turned away. The Filipino jabbed his machete toward the skylight and muttered something so laced with heavy pidgin that even Maile didn't catch it.

"No!" the big man responded. "Something's not right here."

At that moment, a large bird flew out of the forest, swooping so low that the tall Hawaiian ducked, suddenly rattled.

"We have to find another place to do it," he announced.

The Filipino again thrust his machete toward the skylight. "Wha's wrong wit' dis place? We wen' use it before!"

"No. We go lower down." He pointed at some bright flows closer to the coast.

"Too risky! Tourists go dat side!"

"Not tonight," the Hawaiian replied, shoving past the smaller man, who followed him into the darkness, where they rejoined the procession. Gavin and Maile heard murmurs of heated conversation. Finally, the group continued downslope, disappearing into the steamy night.

"What was *that* about?" Gavin asked, standing up.

Maile gazed into the darkness that cloaked the departed procession.

"*Kanaka loko 'ino!*" she muttered to herself. Evil men! "Why are they doing their dirty business here?"

"Who are they? What's going on?"

"Never mind," she said firmly, striding up the hill toward the Blazer.

Gavin shook his head and followed.

They threaded their way back to the SUV in the first rays of the rising moon, not a word passing between them until the vehicle's moonlit windshield came into view.

"I'll drive," Maile decreed. "I know how to get us out of here." Having no choice without an argument, Gavin climbed in beside her. She sped down the subdivision road, zipping past its spooky ruins. Maile forgot to slow for the berm at the gravel road, and the Blazer leaped into the air with a jolt that knocked Gavin's head against the ceiling.

"Blast it all, Maile! What the bloody hell is going on!"

Maile, hunched over the wheel, glaring out the windshield, seemed not to hear him. When they passed the Kapu sign and pulled out onto the coastal road, she finally spoke, her eyes fixed on the dark pavement. "They're getting bolder."

Gavin knew better than to question her as he sat wondering what kind of serpent was loose in Pele's paradise.

6 Evil Afoot on the Sacred Volcano

M*ahina*, the moon, half-full like a weary, heavy-lidded eye, gazed down on the mysterious procession as they descended the devastated slope. The glowing skylight glittered far above them.

The chain of seven men passed a tiny island of trees and shrubs protected from lava flows by a crumbling stone ruin left from an ancient time few remembered. In fact, those stones had stood hidden in the brush since the island's earliest habitation, long before the great Tahitian priest, Pa'ao, with his warriors and clergy—and practice of human sacrifice—sailed to Hawai'i to overthrow the islanders who had lived peacefully in the archipelago for at least a thousand years. Towering above the ferns and 'ohi'a stood a single giant *koa* tree, so straight and tall that Hawaiians of another time might have asked the gods for permission to haul it to the sea and chisel it into one of their mighty voyaging canoes. Its pale leaves rustled in the lava-heated wind that moved down the volcano.

The procession stopped right below the island of vegetation, where a stream of red lava oozed from the rock. The molten flow crept steadily toward a deep pocket in the slope left vacant by the swirls and mounds of previous flows.

The Hawaiian leading the procession was six foot six, with enormous limbs and an oversize head. His was old ali'i blood, passed down through royal generations that had once selected mates for size and intelligence. He lumbered so heavily that his boots crushed the glassy crust of the still-cooling lava beneath his feet. His floral aloha shirt shone in the darkness as he moved, and a .45 automatic tucked into his khakis bobbed with each step. At his signal, the assembly formed a half circle in front of the hole, their faces maroon in fumy light.

The men watched the lava approach the hole, then ooze over its edge, a thick scarlet tongue reaching its rocky floor. The giant moved close to the rim and turned to his crescent of men. Volcanic light throbbed a harsh radiance, illuminating his beamy eyes, colossal nose, and thick black mustache. Behind him the red lava—bubbling at the bottom of the hole—crackled and hissed, and the hot wind moaned.

The giant spoke in a booming voice that left no quarter for the meek or ambivalent. The other six listened with strict attention, until a distinct rustle in the island of rainforest drew their eyes to the leafy gloom beneath the towering koa tree. Nervous glances flashed among the men, and the giant felt goose bumps erupt under his shirt. He searched the bearded face of the eldest man there, a Hawaiian kahuna known to recognize and understand things beyond the physical realm. But the kahuna's wooden expression revealed nothing.

The giant hesitated another moment, then barked an order. A young Hawaiian, slumped between two other men, was dragged to the front, his arms drooped over their shoulders. His rubber thongs slipped off as the bare tops of his feet scraped across the coarse lava. He seemed only half-conscious, and his head, soaked with sweat, hung limp on his chest.

With a huge hand, the giant cradled the captive's jaw and peered into his face. Purple bands of bruised flesh circled the young man's swollen eyes, and his broken nose sagged crooked, the nostrils lined with blood. One cheek was lacerated. He opened a puffy lid, revealing an eye that shimmered in the palpitating light from below. He blinked, and a tear—blood red in the glow—dribbled into the wound.

"You broke the rules, Kalama!" the giant accused. "You violated the protocol!"

"I followed *true* protocol," the beaten man replied wearily, the words mangled in his swollen mouth, ". . . the ancient rules."

The giant tightened his grip on the young man's jaw and jabbed his breast bone with a finger. "Those were your own rules, brah. You betrayed your *'ohana*!"

"'Ohana?" The young Hawaiian's eyes flashed. "Family . . . heart of all things in Hawai'i . . . now twisted by false loyalties . . . desperate schemes for a dying race." He struggled to shake free his head but the giant's grip was too powerful.

"We warned you, Kalama. You're too radical." The giant let the captive's head drop. "You've become dangerous!"

The young Hawaiian struggled to raise his face, gasping his last audible words. "Makaha . . . you . . . *kumakaia*!" Traitor!

The giant, Makaha, stared at the limp figure held before him and shook his massive head. "*Kamipulu hala'ole*." Innocent fool.

Shoving his big hands under Kalama's armpits, he yanked him from his men's grip and leaned the sagging body out over the bubbling lava. Smoke rose from Kalama's pant legs, and he started to swoon. The wind carried the sweet voice of his grandmother singing, and the crackling lava, the soft pluck of her 'ukulele. Facing death, regret had no hold on him, for never had Kalama felt so Hawaiian. He muttered an old native prayer and gazed at the last thing he would ever see—a column of flame leaping up from the edge of the flow, twisting and spinning, agitated in the wind. Then the giant let go.

Kalama's screams overwhelmed the other sounds of the night—the raspy breathing of the men, the moan of the hot wind, the hiss of the oozing molten lava. Then, as the echoes of shrieks faded into the rock and trees and moonlit haze, another scream resounded across the volcano's moonlit flank—the cry of an owl. The circle of men stepped back, cowering, their faces turned in the direction of the giant koa tree.

The body sizzled and popped, like a boar hung above a luau fire. The sharp odor of burning flesh rose from the hole, mingled with the nauseous tang of sulfur. Bandannas over their mouths, the men slowly rejoined Makaha at the rim of the radiant hole. A bright yellow flame danced wildly above the heart of the dead man, flashing on the contorted features of the murderous clan. Makaha noted each man's reaction in the log inside his head.

The bearded kahuna stepped out of the half circle, a blue plastic bag in his hands, and surprised Makaha by withdrawing from it a garland of dark green leaves. It was *maile*, sweet-scented vine of the upland forest, a lei reserved for very special occasions. The elder held it above the funeral pyre, muttering a litany of Hawaiian words, then tossed the lei onto the half-buried char of the young man.

Makaha turned to the group, the scented leaves smoldering behind him. "*Pau*!" he declared. Done! The kahuna threw the blue bag toward the smoking fissure, but the wind caught it, tossing it into the island of vegetation.

The giant turned to go and the others followed him back into the moonlit haze beyond the ruby glow. A new layer of lava was already covering the old one, forever concealing Kalama's remains inside Kilauea. But the winds sweeping over the devastated slope carried the vile stench of his death.

7 An Innocent Abroad

LATER THAT NIGHT . . .

Not far from where lava poured into the sea, a bespectacled young man, breath labored and face brined with sweat, pounded the screen door of a shabby little cabin near the shore. The racket echoed through the dark grove of coconut palms that had somehow survived the flows that buried most of the seaside village of Kalapana. The man banged so hard that the door wobbled against its sash and the resident tomcat leaped out a window and dashed into the jungle.

Sleeping only a stone's throw from the Pacific surf, Captain Jack Hemmingson had downed the better part of a bottle of whiskey before collapsing into unconscious doldrums induced by the sweet melancholy of a Friday-night gin game with the boys. In his deep slumber, the pounding outside intruded into his dream as a woodpecker tap-tap-tapping under the eaves of his long-gone North Woods cabin on Lake Superior. An earthquake would not have stirred him. Even the crushing surge of a tsunami would not have swept away the dream that haunted a man who had lived too long away from civilization.

"Anybody home?" the young man hollered. Hearing no response, he stepped inside to search for a phone and noticed an old man sacked out in the bedroom.

"Mister!" he shouted, dashing into the berth-size space. "I gotta use your phone! It's an emergency!"

"Huh?"

"The phone! Where is it?" He switched on the bedside table lamp and held it over the jumble of man and sheet sprawled on the bed.

"Are you deaf? Or *dead*? Or what?"

That comment about being dead registered somewhere in the old man's foggy brain, because he woke abruptly, with a wild, dazed look on his face. He blinked the speckled blackness out of his eyes.

"I need to call the police!"

"Don't have a phone, sonny," he mumbled.

"You've got to be kidding!"

"I never kid." Captain Jack pulled the covers up over his naked body, scrunched his eyes into little slits, and glared at the hovering youth.

"No phone?" the young man gasped. "Who *doesn't* have a phone?"

Mainlander, Jack thought.

"Well, then, where *is* the nearest phone?"

"In Pahoa."

"Can you drive me there?"

Jack peered through the round lenses of the young man's glasses to see what kind of eyeballs stared at him. "Listen, kid, it's the witchin' hour and I still have dreamin' to do." He let his eyes shut.

"Mister, I gotta get a hold of the police! Right away! My cell's got no reception down here! If you won't get your carcass out of bed, then at least let me borrow your car."

Carcass? Jack opened one eye just enough to display its fierceness. "Forget it, kid!"

The young man stepped back, wiped the sweat off his brow, and plopped down on the bedside table, knocking the latest issue of *Stars and Stripes* onto the floor.

"Someone's been killed. An hour ago, only a mile from here! I saw it with my own eyes!"

Jack cracked open his other eye. It wasn't the first time someone stumbled to his place after a fight or a tumble on fresh lava, what with his cabin being the only home left near the black sand beach. But no one had ever come to his door saying they'd witnessed a *death* down there.

He sat up. Tanned like a farmer, he was brown on his forearms and below his knees, with a patch of amber around his neck. The rest was ghostly white, save for a small blue tattoo, the letters *USN*, on his left upper arm. He swung his arthritic knees out from under the sheet and, moaning, eased his feet to the floor. He groped for his old Navy khakis crumpled up on the rug. His faded red aloha shirt—with birds of paradise on it—hung askew on a chair. He dressed while his visitor paced the room.

This Hawai'i trip was the young man's first solo adventure, and things had gone poorly from the start, beginning with a five-hour flight delay out of Minneapolis. By the time he'd finally made all his connections to the Big Island, Cheapo Rentals had given away his reservation—and the last car in little Hilo town. Undaunted, he'd hitched rides all the way to Kalapana so he could see the lava first thing. As he trekked to the molten flow, he felt "back in the adventure groove," but it wasn't long before he realized he was in a very foreign—and apparently dangerous—place.

"Relax, kid," Jack said, escorting the nineteen-year-old out to his *lanai*. "Pull up a chair and I'll be with ya in a second."

After a quick visit to the bathroom, Jack stopped at the old Frigidaire to see if there were any beers left. He found two—one to bring him back to life and the other to calm his guest. The old sailor paused at the screen door to study his visitor. A yellow bulb, peppered with dead mosquitoes, barely lit the scene. The young man, slumped forward in one of the dog-eared wicker chairs, held his face in his hands. Sweaty blond tangles poked out from under a red Twins cap, and a damp T-shirt clung to his trembling body. A nylon backpack, on which a photographer's tripod was strapped, lay heaped on the floor.

Jack swung open the squeaky door, startling his unbidden guest. He eased his bulk into the wicker chair opposite the visitor and offered him the beer.

"It was awful!" the boy blurted, absently accepting the bottle. "They murdered him in cold blood!"

A tingle crept up the back of Jack's neck. It was the familiar feeling he used to get during close combat or when howling typhoons threatened to hurl the ocean's waves through the bulkheads. Despite the feeling—or maybe because of it—he remained calm.

"Simmer down, m'boy," he said. "It's over now." Jack cupped a hand under the young man's beer and nudged the bottle forward. "Take a swig. I guarantee it'll help."

The young man didn't seem to hear him. "Can't we just call the police?"

"Listen, kid, if a man's already dead, your runnin' to the cops ain't gonna bring him back to life. Fill me in on what happened, and we can *both* go into town to fetch 'em."

"OK," he said, drawing in a long, deep breath.

"Just start from the beginnin'." Jack plucked his pipe out of the ashtray next to his chair and made it ready to smoke.

"Well . . . I . . . I was out on the lava flow, taking pictures—"

"Are you crazy? That volcano's dangerous, especially at night!"

"Mister, do you want to hear what happened or not?"

"Dammit anyway, yes! Get on with it." The old man lit his pipe and drew in a smoky breath.

"I'm a newspaper photographer with a weekly back home, and I came here to take pictures of the eruption. But I . . . I just saw something I wasn't supposed to." He fought back a sob.

"Go on."

The young man recounted his picture-taking hike from the coastal flows to a lava outbreak high up on the volcano. His skin flushed as he described the seven islanders emerge from the darkness and the heated exchange between the giant Hawaiian and the battered young victim in the light of the glowing lava.

"And you're positive they didn't see ya while all this was happening?"

"Well, pretty sure. When I first heard them coming, I took off downslope and watched the whole thing from behind a big mound of lava."

"They didn't see your flashlight?"

"Didn't use it. I was digging the natural light."

Jack shook his head. "You make out anything they said?"

"Not really, but then the wind changed and I caught one word from the victim—*kuma*-something, maybe like *kuma-ka-i-a*."

Jack shrugged his shoulders, then leaned way forward. "You didn't happen to take pictures?"

The question startled the young man, and he paused before answering. "Well, I thought about it—at first. What a choice opportunity—pictures of a native ritual up on the volcano."

"Whatdaya mean, ritual?"

"Well, it just looked that way—you know. Anyhow, I reached for my camera but then thought better of it. They'd have heard the shutter's motor drive." The old man nodded. "Somehow I knew they were going to kill him. I would have tried to sneak away, but I was scared they'd see me."

Jack puffed briskly on his pipe, his face warped in anticipation.

"So . . . I stayed. Then . . ." Another sob bubbled up in the young man's throat. "Then they threw him into the molten lava! I started to puke, but I made myself swallow it." The pale youth shuddered, then took a sip of beer. He fell silent, tugging the tangles of his hair.

Jack bit hard on his pipe, cracking the stem. "And after that?"

"This old bearded guy pulled a string of leaves out of a bag and started talking to the lava—I guess in Hawaiian. He tossed the leaves onto the flames. Then they all left."

The young man took off his glasses and wiped his eyes with his T-shirt, his face frozen in anguish.

"Terrible, m'boy! Terrible!" Jack got up and stepped to the rail of the lanai, staring at the red sky beyond the palms. The surf's boom echoed like thunder inside Jack's head, and he cursed under his breath.

"Now can we go to the police?" the boy asked.

"Let me think on that a bit." He puffed on his pipe, but the bowl was spent.

"What's there to think about? A man's been murdered!"

Jack walked back to his chair and tapped the remnants of his last smoke into the ashtray. "Going to the cops could lead to a lot o' trouble—for *both* of us."

"But—"

"Look, kid, I've lived in these islands longer than I care to admit—more than thirty years. Some things happen here that are best forgotten. Local business, if ya get my drift. It's *their* concern, not ours."

"I saw a man killed! You just heard the story! That makes it *our* business!"

"I guarantee you'll wish ya never saw what ya did. I already regret ya told *me*." He packed his pipe with fresh shag and lit up.

"Listen, old man, we have a *responsibility*—"

"Ya don't know what this is about, do ya, kid?"

"I know I witnessed a murder!" He grasped the wicker armrests and glared at Captain Jack with bright blue eyes exaggerated by his spectacles.

"But do ya understand *why* that man was killed?"

"Why? Why? Of course, I don't know why! Do you?"

"Whatever the reason, ya can be damn sure it was an *internal* matter, among the Hawaiians themselves."

"I don't believe this! Do you hear what you're saying?"

Jack nodded, puffing away on his bitter pipe.

"I don't get it." The young man dropped his glare and gazed out toward the thundering surf. A faint mist of moonlit sea spray drifted through the palms toward the cabin. "Are you telling me this was some kind of—of *sacrifice*?"

Captain Jack's poker face stared back. "I s'pose ya might put it that way."

"C'mon. I don't believe that for a second. Two hundred years ago, maybe. But this is the twenty-first century."

"Don't be so sure, my boy." He pulled the pipe out of his mouth and pointed its stem at the youth. "The killin's may be different, but human life is sacrificed nonetheless. There are new pressures on these people—the few o' them that's left. Now and again, ya hear about these murders. Nobody's gonna defend 'em, but most everybody says it's *their* business."

"I can't believe I'm listening to this!" He got up, grabbed his gear, and started down the steps. "I'm going into town and report this on my own!" He marched off toward the driveway, then stopped in the moonlit mist at the edge of the woods.

"Coward!" he shouted as he disappeared under the dark palms.

Jack slumped back into the wicker chair and relit his pipe. "Dumb kid reminds me of me at that age," he snorted. Drinking down the last of his beer—and finishing the departed's bottle as well—he gazed out at the waves and pondered the young man's fate.

8 ∫ The Resolute Dreamer

EARLY SATURDAY MORNING, JUNE 3, IN NORTH KONA . . .

American entrepreneur Robert Conway gazed at the sparkling waters of Kiholo Bay from his new golf course at the Royal Paradise Bay Resort. His bronze face was alight, handsomely lined with a look of determination. A morning sea breeze ruffled the open collar of his silk aloha shirt, a custom-made masterpiece of sailboat designs. Hands on his hips, the king-size man inhaled a deep, contented breath. He was only days away from the debut of his latest—and greatest—creation. So far.

Conway turned from the sea to marvel at the 1,400-room resort he had built atop a stark lava desert on the North Kona coast. Two ivory crescents of high-rise suites gleamed in the morning light above dozens of Polynesian-style thatched huts tucked into thickets of coconut palms, banana trees, ferns, and flowering shrubs. Conway had spent millions furnishing the King and Queen's Towers and the bucolic bungalows of his Hawaiian Village. The same attention to detail distinguished the resort's seven restaurants, nine bars, and three golf courses.

Sunlight glinted off the resort's artificial ponds, including two saltwater lagoons stocked with dolphins, manta rays, and tropical fish. Conway had spent $3 million on imported fish, birds, and animals for the resort's gardens—more than the wildlife budgets of all his previous resort projects combined. He had hired a full-time biologist just to take care of them.

The resort's most extravagant features resulted from Conway's need to find a practical way to shuttle patrons around the sprawling complex. An elevated monorail made every hotel suite, restaurant, and attraction just minutes away. For those interested in a more leisurely and romantic journey, Conway had constructed five miles of landscaped canals on which graceful little sloops would carry patrons to their desired destinations. From the architects to the upholsterers, Conway had spared no expense—$2 billion, making the Royal Paradise Bay the largest nonmilitary construction project ever undertaken in Hawai'i, and the world's costliest hotel outside Dubai.

Conway's gaze shifted back to Kiholo Bay, where he admired the resort's most unusual adornment, a life-size replica of the square-rigged ship used by British captain James Cook to discover the Hawaiian Islands. Although Conway planned daily tours of the 1778-vintage vessel, the ship satisfied a more personal goal—to honor the Western world's greatest seafarer, a man who had defied the limits of his day and died only thirty miles away at the hands of angry Hawaiians.

When his financial success had finally arrived, Conway overcame the long-standing prejudice against mainland haoles by converting his local detractors into business partners. They all made money. Conway's movie star charisma also made him a darling of the Honolulu social set, but no one really knew how he'd risen from obscurity to become Hawai'i's most prominent resort builder. Whatever path he had taken—and however he had raised the capital to get there—Conway had now built a resort that promised to transform the island of Hawai'i into a tourist destination rivaling Honolulu and make him an *international* figure.

Conway's reverie was interrupted by distant voices upslope, laughter emanating from one of his many grounds crews. He turned to look. High above the company of brown men, the cloud-covered summit of Hualalai towered over lava fields that stretched all the way from the mountain to his resort.

His cell phone rang. He almost didn't answer it, because he knew the desk clerk would be calling to announce the arrival of a visitor he did not want to see. Instead, it was Dusty Smythe, the golf pro who'd designed Conway's finest course, the beautiful Hualalai Mountain Links, phoning to confirm his participation in the grand opening two weeks away.

"I can't imagine what you did for publicity, Bob," he said, "but I've been getting inquiries about the course for nearly a year!"

"And what do you tell them?" Conway asked, beaming.

"That if Hawaiians had invented golf instead of surfing, King Kamehameha would have built a course like this."

Conway laughed heartily. "Can you imagine the reporters' faces when they discover real monkeys hanging in the trees at the dogleg on number three?"

"You never cease to amaze me, Bob, always pushing the envelope."

"And why not? The way I see it, we've got a new legacy to leave. You need something bigger—more dazzling—to attract people these days."

"Well, you may have just built the best golf course in the world. And I can't wait to play it!"

"The whole resort is like that, Dusty, no expense spared to do it right."

"I just hope you can fill it up. You're a long ways from Honolulu down there on the Big Island."

"Are you kidding? Almost all of our fourteen hundred rooms are already booked, and we have two weeks of reservations for tee times."

Buoyed by the conversation with Dusty, Conway decided to run down to the Royal Ballroom to see if workmen had finished installing the chandeliers. It was in that hall where most of Conway's dream resided. Conway hopped into his golf cart and sped back to the resort, leaping out at the pro shop, cell phone again pressed to his ear. He directed the concierge to send a sloop to meet him. An elderly Hawaiian man, half-hidden behind the cart he was polishing, eyed the haole chief, amused.

Conway glanced at his Rolex as a little boat approached up the canal. A muscular Samoan stood at the wheel with perfect posture and a smiling round face. He looked colonial in his matching whites—captain's hat, Bermudas, and knee-high socks. His shirt, still creased from its packaging, bore a gold nameplate buffed to a bright gleam.

"Don't bother to tie her," Conway told the boatman, leaping onto the sloop's deck as it passed. He stepped down into the cockpit, and the boatman pulled the lever that recoupled the craft to an underwater cable, then piloted the impotent wheel as if it actually steered a rudder.

"Sorry about the delay, Mr. Conway," the Samoan said, "I had to find my uniform. They only just arrived today."

"I appreciate your efforts," Conway said, reading his name tag. "Needs a little pressing though, Sam. Don't worry about it now. Just tell Winnie to make sure all sloop captains have pressed uniforms by tomorrow. I've got more VIPs dropping in before the grand opening and I want to be able to escort them by boat—with proper attire, of course."

"OK, Mr. Conway."

The usually chatty islander decided to leave himself out of Conway's world, and nothing else was said between the two as the sloop glided down the jungle-lined canal between the King and Queen's Towers. The boat then meandered through an orchard of breadfruit trees and into the main open-air lobby. The lobby walls were covered with South Pacific art—from the primitive to the sublime—including Gauguin's original sketch for his 1892 masterpiece, *Manao Tupapau* ("Spirit of the Dead Watching"), which hung in the center of the lobby (wired for security under weatherproof glass) above a Bösendorfer concert grand piano.

The sloop passed through the lobby just above the resort's largest waterfall, a roaring 100-foot plunge into the Great Ali'i Bath swimming pool, its mist speckling the cockpit windows. The boat soon reached one of the resort's most audacious attractions, the Crocodile Jungle. Most of the animals inhabiting the resort were tame and nonthreatening—peacocks and parrots, flamingos and dolphins, monkeys and deer—but here in the Jungle things were different. Guests could safely glimpse the man-eating reptiles from boats on the elevated canal or in the enclosed cars of the monorail. Conway frowned. The Jungle was his concession to an influential young investor from Texas who had insisted that something "more ominously exciting" be added to the animal collection "lest we all forget that it's survival of the fittest out there." Conway thought the idea was beneath his high standards, but he had gone along with the Jungle because he couldn't afford to upset a key investor at a critical moment in the negotiations.

The call announcing the arrival of Conway's unwanted visitor came just as he left the Jungle, but he was determined to visit the Royal Ballroom before their meeting. “I’ll be there as soon as I can,” he said, smiling at the thought that the governor’s aide would have to wait.

Conway beamed when the boat finally swung into the orchid-lined canal fronting the corridor leading to the Royal Ballroom, a broad hallway resembling the passage to a temple. A dozen replicas of feather *kahili*—royal scepters of the ali‘i—formed an arch of golden feathers above the smooth lava floor.

“Tie her up here,” Conway told the Samoan. The boatman lashed the sloop to one of the brass cleats as his passenger stepped out. Conway ambled down the stately corridor to the ballroom. Its wooden double doors stood three stories high from floor to ceiling and were carved with a giant image of Hualalai. Even Conway looked tiny next to them. He dug into his trousers and pulled out a ring on which a dozen keys dangled. He fingered the largest one, a brass key cut in the shape of a feather kahili.

He pushed open one of the doors, revealing a cavernous oval room three times the size of a football field. Thirty colossal chandeliers—each comprising thousands of sparkling crystals—hung around a dome of stained glass depicting an erupting volcano. Beneath the glass was a sweeping parquetry floor, lacquered to a polished gleam.

Conway sauntered across the vast room, dreaming of possibilities. “We’ll fill you up,” he murmured, “and bring Hawai‘i into the twenty-first century.”

“Whoa!” the boatman said, peering around the corner of the door. His exclamation was unintentional—he was just trying to sneak a peek. He hadn’t seen halls that big and fancy since his last Vegas vacation.

Conway might have been annoyed by the intrusion, but the Samoan’s awed expression made him chuckle. “We’re planning some pretty wild parties,” he hollered across the room.

The big door whooshed closed and Conway strolled back to the entrance, all the more certain his secret scheme was sound. That knowledge would help him tolerate the nuisance of dealing with the governor’s aide, who awaited him in the resort’s Golden Coconut

Saloon. Conway closed and locked the big wooden doors and got back into the boat.

Within minutes they arrived at the bar, and Conway spotted his visitor through the window. Conway took a deep breath and squared his shoulders as he opened the door.

9 ∫ The Governor's Weasel

No scratch or stain yet marred the bar of the Golden Coconut Saloon, and its polished native wood mirrored the white clouds above Kiholo Bay. At the bar's far end, two Filipino busboys joked as they unpacked a box of imitation Baccarat crystal. At the other end, shaded by an arbor of hibiscus, Andy Lankowski hunched over a bottle of Budweiser, smoking.

"Really sorry to bother you, Bob," Lankowski said as Conway sat down before a tumbler of Perrier left for him by his staff. "We know this is a busy time, what with the opening only two weeks away. But Calvin is nervous, nervous as hell."

"It *isn't* a good time," Conway replied, always put off by these encounters with Lankowski, a twenty-year veteran of statehouse intrigue and currently an aide to Governor Calvin Kamali'i.

Lankowski mindlessly curled and uncurled the corners of the purple napkin under his Bud, all the while smoking Vantage cigarettes. One dangled between his fingers while another smoldered at the filter in the crystal ashtray set before him. Lankowski's nerves were frayed from years of behind-the-scenes deal making with the sometimes saintly, but often unsavory, people who made their living in Hawai'i's politics. As far as Lankowski was concerned, it was the "saints" who made his job difficult.

Lankowski's boss was a big handsome Hawaiian who once entertained grand visions of reform for his native state. Calvin Kamali'i's idealistic debut had been a breath of fresh air in a political atmosphere rife with self-interest and corruption. He was not one of the "good old boys," a long line of politicians whose careers dated back before statehood—island haoles, *Nisei* Japanese, Chinese entrepreneurs, and a few Hawaiians who'd heralded the Americanization of the archipelago. When he spoke, looming above the podium with his beautiful hands outstretched, his deep voice booming pronouncements of change, he reminded locals—ethnic non-haole islanders—of Maui, the demigod who had fished the islands out of the sea with magical flair and the strength of his mighty will.

But Calvin Kamali'i's physical appearance and rhetorical skills belied his limited power. Not only was he was not one of "them," but he was personally weak and ineffective, unaccustomed to formal authority and too enamored with the trappings of office to effectively fight the long-established powers of Honolulu. Like most Hawaiians, he admired Hawai'i's last monarch, Queen Lili'uokalani, whom descendants of American missionaries, supported by US marines, had overthrown in an 1893 coup d'état, but the governor possessed neither her moral fortitude nor her political skill. After numerous battles behind the scenes, he had buckled, later rationalizing his "compromises" in a *Honolulu Star-Advertiser* interview as "reasonable concessions to modern economic realities."

What the governor didn't tell the reporter was that he had discovered an intricate—and intractable—web of political and business connections, some dating back to pineapple and sugarcane days, a few stretching all the way to the missionaries. Even though many locals held key positions in the entrenched establishment, its goals remained fundamentally haole: to wring money out of the islands.

Calvin Kamali'i's capitulations had kept him politically alive, but not without personal and political cost. His big brown eyes had taken on a melancholy cast, and his own people lost faith in him, some transforming their sense of betrayal into militant action by forming the Kapu Hawai'i movement, an effort to slow development by invoking the sacred tenets of Old Hawai'i.

At about that time, veteran infighter Andy Lankowski had shown up at the governor's door, offering his services on the pretense that an old hand like him might be useful in tempering the greedy powers that be and placating the Hawaiian traditionalists. But Lankowski's true loyalties lay with the haole, and he sensed—like the mongoose who knows when a nest is unattended—that eggs were available for the snatching. The governor, by that time weary of criticism—and feeling betrayed himself—gladly accepted the offer of a man who could prowl his way around the shadowed corners of the unseemly establishment.

"In two weeks," Conway explained to Lankowski, "this resort will be filled with people from all over the world. They're expecting to be impressed, and I've got to be ready for them." He tilted the tumbler against his heavy lips and swallowed deeply, then repeated his admonishment: "No, Andy, it isn't a good time."

"No, it isn't." Lankowski took a long drag. "But we thought you should know the latest, keep you up to date, so to say. I come with three items of interest—"

Despite his impatience, Conway tried to remain polite. He hated the intrusions of the politicians, shortsighted and cowardly as they were. They acted only when they had something at stake—money or votes or both. Vermin—that's what Conway thought of the bastards.

"Unsettling news, very troubling," Lankowski said, crunching up his weasel face as he slouched further over the bar. He had a hump on his back from years hunching close to the ears of those who made up his vast network of political and business contacts. His flesh was pale, always isolated from the Hawaiian sun inside drab rumpled suits, and he'd taken on the jaundiced hue of the fluorescent corridors he frequented. He looked unhealthy, malnourished on fast food, cigarettes, and coffee, and his graying black hair was a wild mess of unkempt curls. Lankowski shifted his shrewd black eyes from the ragged napkin to Conway's face. "We're concerned about that memorandum, the one on Hualalai," he said.

"I thought that was taken care of two years ago." Conway shuddered inwardly, recalling that just before the resort's groundbreaking ceremonies, US Geological Survey scientists at the Hawaiian Volcano Observatory had written an internal memorandum suggesting Hualalai might not be as peaceful as it looked. Supposedly that report had never found its way to the public or even to the island's Civil Defense agency, because, as Conway was told at the time, the USGS had determined that the memo's analysis was based on "questionable science."

"We thought it *was* taken care of," Lankowski said, "but somehow the thing has found its way into the hands of an eager cub reporter at the *Star-Advertiser*."

Conway's jaw clenched. "How is that possible?"

"Don't know for sure, but we think it got there through the Kapu Hawai'i Movement."

Conway bristled. "And of course, those radicals *love* to make trouble. They'd think nothing of distorting the truth to stir up public fear."

Lankowski's black eyes twinkled. "Interesting idea, the truth. What do *you* see as the truth, Bob?"

"I don't see that memorandum as containing anything but wild speculation." Conway's face reddened. "If USGS is really concerned about the safety of people on this side of the island, why don't they issue warnings to all those hotels farther up the coast at Waikoloa? They could get buried by Mauna Loa lava, and that's a volcano that erupts every few decades!"

Lankowski shrugged. "Anyway, you can see we have a problem." He crumpled his cigarette into the ashtray, dragging it through the butts already littered there.

"What's the newspaper story say?"

"Hasn't run yet. We're strong-arming the editor, Tommy Oshiro—as much as you ever strong-arm the press. It's delicate, you know, even when the guy's in your camp, which he is."

"So he might not run the story?"

"I didn't say that. He's sitting on it, that's all."

"Surely he understands the speculative nature of that memorandum, and he's aware of how people would overreact to its contents—"

"Yes, he is, he is. But he still *wants* to run the story."

Conway shook his head. "Typical. Questionable facts, but since it will sell newspapers—"

"Bob, it's not the Hualalai information that interests Oshiro. It's that USGS suppressed it for two years. No matter how speculative that memo was, somebody thought it needed to be hushed up—maybe to protect *your* pile of gold." Lankowski smiled cynically. "That's the story."

Conway wadded up his napkin.

“Big Islanders don’t want to know the dangers, Bob. They’re still building houses on Kilauea’s active rift zones. Nobody pays attention to the warnings until there’s lava in their backyard. That’s human nature. What *does* interest them is political shenanigans. That’s what they gossip about at Teshima’s Restaurant.”

“Andy, I’ve got investors—”

“And scandal can kill a project.”

“Progress running afoul of human nature,” Conway sneered. “All the busy little bastards picking away at the people trying to push ahead the world. So what’s to be done about this editor?”

“We asked him to hold off on the story, at least until after the grand opening. Oshiro’s a Big Island boy—born and raised in Hilo—and we tried to convince him that the future of the island’s economy lies in big-buck tourism, including the success of the Royal Paradise Bay.”

“And?”

“He didn’t buy it, says he thinks the resort is nothing but ‘a haole fantasyland,’ and that it’s going to rely too much on mainlanders for employees. Naw, he was pretty skeptical until,” Lankowski lit another Vantage, “until I told him the resort is just the beginning of something *really* big over here, the centerpiece of a major commercial and real estate venture.”

Conway grabbed his arm. “You told him that?”

“Had to. It was either that or see the story run before the grand opening—”

“That project was to be an absolute secret! Now you’re telling me the editor of the Honolulu paper is sitting on information no one is supposed to know until Calvin’s announcement at the grand opening.”

“That’s what I told him, that there’d be an announcement at that time and that we needed utter secre—”

“Damn you, Lankowski! You and your goddamn boss—” Conway forced himself to take a deep breath. Like it or not, Calvin Kamali‘i was Conway’s primary link to the good old boys, and while they required constant ego massaging and deference paid to their contractor friends, there was no other way to do development in Hawai‘i. Calvin and his operatives had been helpful in securing the land, changing the zoning ordinances, and expediting the environmental and archaeological reviews. Bumbling as they seemed, they were trying to keep this potentially damaging story out of the newspapers, even if only for their own necks.

"Sorry, Andy, but I've got potential investors out there trying to decide whether to jump into the real estate project. Some commitments are still shaky—at best. I can't afford any bad news, on the volcano or the project, until I get all the investors' commitments signed and sealed."

"Relax, Bob," Lankowski replied, exhaling cigarette smoke through his slit-narrow nostrils. "I *had* to tell Oshiro about the announcement. Otherwise he would have run the story on the GPS satellite information, and the governor and you and all your investors would be standing up there on the platform with egg all over your faces, looking stupid *and* corrupt."

"He gave you a commitment that neither story would appear until after the announcement in two weeks?"

"That's what Oshiro *said.*" Lankowski shrugged. "Wouldn't hurt to gear up your PR people for a response, just in case. Got another beer?"

Lankowski rather enjoyed being the bearer of bad news, especially to men with power like Conway and the governor. While his own life was intertwined with the big shots, Lankowski was less reliant on them than they were on him. They needed skilled operatives to do their dirty work, so his future was secure, regardless of who occupied the governor's chair or what the governor thought of him.

"You might also want to develop some PR to respond to the scientists' new assertions."

"What do you mean, *new* assertions?"

"Well, Bob, that's item of interest number two." Lankowski suppressed a mean little smile.

"The geologists got kinda jittery after the summit of Kilauea exploded last year—apparently took 'em by surprise. They think a lot more magma's welling up inside the island, and they decided they'd better reexamine some of their earlier surveys, including the one for Hualalai. Anyway, they have some new data and new conclusions. They say Hualalai is getting bigger."

Conway's mouth dropped. "You mean it might erupt?"

Lankowski shrugged. "Apparently they reinterpreted the data they gathered two years ago. The earlier GPS survey? That was pretty tentative stuff. They were still working out their system for detecting changes in these volcanoes from satellites in space. Well, they've done some new GPS surveys and compared them with that earlier data. Of course, they expected to find some changes in the more active volcanoes, Kilauea and Mauna Loa, but not in Hualalai. Now they say the old hulk is, ah—what do they call it—inflating."

"Inflating?"

"Yeah, they say the shape of the summit is different than it was two years ago, and that means something's happening inside."

"What exactly do they mean when they say it's getting bigger?"

"You know, a little taller here, a little wider there."

"How big is a 'little'?"

"About a tenth of an inch."

"A tenth of an inch! You've got to be kidding!" Conway's face turned as red as if he'd held his breath.

"No, and believe it or not, they're not kidding either. They say it might be, well, *significant*. With the current state of the art in GPS monitoring, it's possible to detect even tiny changes in the surfaces of volcanoes from satellites. Anyway, if they're right, that mountain behind your resort is growing."

"But how can a tenth of an inch matter?"

Lankowski paused to light yet another cigarette. "The guys at USGS don't want to get their butts burned if the mountain starts smoking. Calvin got a call from Congressman Yamashita yesterday. He says USGS wants to issue a statement about it, a technical bulletin kind of thing, just to get some reaction from other scientists in the field."

"Yamashita says this? How did he find out?"

"How does the happy face spider know when a bug's landed on its leaf? Anyway, our formidable congressman convinced the director in Washington to hold off until the grand opening is behind us."

"He said that? About the grand opening?

"Of course not. He simply asked to see the Hualalai statement before it's issued, and said he'd need two weeks to review it. The director, always eager to share responsibility for bad news, and not wanting to piss off Yamashita, agreed to show it to him. We should have a copy in a day or two, so we'll know what we're dealing with."

Conway got up and stepped out from the shade of the arbor. He stared at the sea, the back of his neck bright red. "What else?"

"Huh?"

"You said there were three items."

Lankowski drew heavily on his cigarette.

"It can wait. I'm going to meet with some Big Islanders who are closely watching what happens at Kiholo, people with their own long-term goals for Kona, if you know what I mean."

Conway knew exactly what he meant—Haku Kane and his underworld gang of the Hui, who had taken an unwelcome interest in his resort. Even a vague reference to those people made him uneasy.

Lankowski waited just long enough for two drags on his cigarette. "I'll get in touch if I need to talk to you before I fly back to Honolulu. Tomorrow, Monday at the latest. If you don't hear from me by then, don't worry about it."

Lankowski downed the dregs of his beer and slid off the stool. He wiped his narrow lips with the mangled cocktail napkin and tucked his shirttail back into his pants.

"Place looks beautiful, Bob," he said, a new cigarette wagging between his lips. "You've really outdone yourself this time."

Conway, still staring at the ocean, didn't reply.

Lankowski sauntered over the purple carpet with his peculiar swagger, as if one leg were shorter than the other. He paused in front of the entrance, a heavy wooden door on which was carved a rendering of a native woman holding a coconut. Lankowski looked back at Conway, standing erect in the shadow of one of his transplanted palms.

"You know what your biggest problem's gonna to be, Bob?"

Conway glanced over his shoulder.

"I just can't see how you'll ever top this one."

Lankowski leaned into the carved woman and slipped out of the bar. The door drifted back with a quiet whoosh.

Robert Conway scanned the empty tables of the huge lanai that in two weeks would hold the throngs celebrating his long-awaited triumph. He imagined chic women and elegantly dressed men, silver platters of gourmet food and crystal glasses brimming with French Champagne, admiring speeches and upbeat jazz. He pictured the amazed notables milling about—business leaders and investors, dignitaries and celebrities, TV cameras and reporters. Reporters . . .

A lump of anxiety gathered in his chest. Things could fall apart, as they had with that failed geothermal scheme he'd lost his shirt on way back when.

"Damn you," he muttered, grasping the front of his aloha shirt so forcefully he left a button dangling by a thread off the schooner plying across his breast pocket. "Damn the reporters, damn the scientists, damn the politicians! Damn the goddamn volcano!"

10 ∫ The Wary Sailor

SUNDAY AFTERNOON, JUNE 4, NEAR KALAPANA . . .

Captain Jack heard nothing more about the murder or his late-night visitor until two days later, when a story appeared in the police blotter of the Hilo Sunday paper:

MAINLAND PHOTOGRAPHER
CHARGED WITH TRESPASS

> James Anderson of Elbow Lake, Minnesota, was arrested at 2 a.m. Saturday after police received an anonymous tip that someone was prowling around the abandoned Royal Gardens subdivision above the Kalapana coast. The 19-year-old newspaper photographer was charged with trespassing in the lava-inundated subdivision after police found insufficient evidence to link him with several items missing from the abandoned Harold Yokoyama garage, including a lawn mower and several bags of potting soil. Anderson was also charged with disturbing the peace after using foul language and violent gestures during the police investigation. He remained in custody Saturday night, pending payment of several fines.

The news didn't surprise Jack. He'd spent enough years in the Navy to know this sort of thing happened. Still, he felt sorry for the young Minnesotan. If the kid was smart, he would fly to Waikiki for the rest of his vacation and leave well enough alone. Somehow Jack doubted he would, and sure enough, Jimmy showed up later that very day, having hitched a ride in a surfer's mufflerless truck, its rusty hood painted with fluorescent flames. Silver, the grizzled old tomcat, slipped through the door when Jack stepped outside to see who was disturbing the otherwise pleasant afternoon. It wasn't long before the young man, red-faced and scowling, was stomping back and forth across Captain Jack's lanai.

"Idiots!" he screamed, raving about "police incompetence" and "lack of due process." He trembled so hard that his wire rims nearly shook off his nose. Slouched in his old wicker chair, Jack watched with calm indifference—until the young man turned his rage on him.

"And if you hadn't been such a lazy coward!" he said, pointing his red ball cap at the old man.

"Hold on a minute, boy. Before ya start railin' at me without knowin' my motivations, tell me what happened."

"A few minutes after I left your place, a black Camaro with a blue beacon on top came down the road. Imagine my relief when a police officer stepped out—until he drew his gun and demanded I lean up against the car!"

"I tried to explain what I was doing over here, that I'd been up hiking on the lava flows, but he wouldn't listen. 'Tell it down at the station,' he kept saying, like a line from a TV show. He handcuffed me, shoved me into the back, and drove me to Hilo. I was pissed, but as we got closer to town, I began worrying that they believed *I* was involved with the murder."

"Ya don't really look like the killin' type," Jack said, chuckling at the rosy-cheeked young haole.

"Well, I must look like a thief, because that's why they hauled me in. I explained that I was up in that old subdivision to take pictures of the lava. I mean, I had all my gear! Same treatment down at the police station. That jerk of a sergeant just shut me up. He assumed I was up there doing a ripoff!"

"Kinda peculiar, all this," Jack said, rubbing his fleshy cheek, "since a fair number o' idiots come over here to see the eruption. And you didn't have the stolen stuff with you."

"They claimed I stashed it in the bushes. That's when I started thinking maybe they just didn't want me up in that old subdivision."

Captain Jack's eyes narrowed. "So what did ya tell 'em about the murder?"

"I *didn't*. The whole thing seemed fishy somehow, and after being tossed into jail for looting, I decided to keep my mouth shut."

Good instinct, Jack thought. He pressed tobacco into his pipe with a thumb. "Ya never said a word?"

"Nope."

"How'd ya get out o' jail, anyway? Escape?" Jack snickered as he lit up his pipe.

"I guess they realized they had no real evidence—after making me sit in a cell for more than two days!"

Just long enough to let the dust settle after the murder, Jack thought.

"They dropped the looting charge but insisted I pay a trespassing fine. They called it a fine but I think it was beer money—and I said so!"

Jack groaned.

"I got really pissed off and they charged me with disturbing the peace, which I guess means smarting off." The young man leaned against the lanai railing, shaking his head.

"Wanna beer?" Jack asked, waving his bottle at him.

"Guess I could use one, huh?"

"They're in the icebox. Help yourself."

Jimmy came back with a bottle of Steinlager and sat down across from the old man. "Thanks for the beer, mister."

"Now that ya've been to my place twice—both times uninvited—and you're helpin' yourself to beers outa my fridge, I think we oughta introduce ourselves."

"Yeah, I suppose so, my name's—"

"James Anderson, if the newspaper's got it straight."

"Newspaper?"

"Yeah, you're in this morning's police blotter." He handed him the *Tribune-Herald*. "Sorry, kid."

The young man's face got even redder as he went through the article.

"This is just like being back in Elbow Lake. They even print your name in the *Bugle* when you get a parking ticket! I love this bit about remaining in custody until I paid 'several fines.'" He tossed the paper onto the old telephone cable spool Jack had salvaged from the sea one winter to use as a table.

Jack saw intelligence in the young man's eyes, naive smarts maybe, but smarts nonetheless, and the old sailor was impressed by Jimmy's gumption, the way he'd told the cops that their "fine" was just a bribe, which no doubt it was. He appreciated spunk in a man, even in a foolish one like this kid.

"Jimmy, if ya don't mind my calling ya that, my name's Claus Hemmingson." He offered his hand. "But my friends call me Capt'n Jack on account o' my bein' an old Navy man, and 'cause I have a fool's fondness for whiskey."

Jimmy smiled for the first time since the two had met. "OK, Captain Jack." They shook hands. "Some vacation I'm having, isn't it?"

"Back in the Navy we had a rule, Jimmy. When you're in a foreign port, get into trouble if ya must—and ya do—but at all costs avoid the authorities. If they do get hold o' ya, plead ignorance, smile, and keep some fivers handy to slip into their palms."

"But this is the *state* of Hawai'i, not a foreign port."

"Don't be so sure, m'boy. These are still Pacific islands, and things operate different here."

"Is that why you didn't want to go to the police?"

"I'm willin' to take a chance now and again—maybe even to do the right thing—but not till I know for sure what I'm gettin' into. When ya showed up with that crazy story about a killin', I knew it was no time to step forward."

"You *still* want to forget the whole thing?"

Jack sucked his pipe calmly, with easy, measured puffs. "That's the idea."

"Look, I can see staying clear of the local cops but what about—"

"The dead man? I didn't know 'im, did you?"

"How can you just sit here and do nothing?"

"Experience, lad, experience in the islands. Like I said the other night, it's best *all around* to stay clear o' what doesn't concern ya, especially squabbles among the locals."

Jimmy glared at him, his eyes a brilliant blue.

"Drink your beer, lad, and let the whole thing settle a bit. Before we make a move I think we oughta try to find out a little more than we know right now."

"So you *will* help?"

"Maybe so and maybe not. Like I said, I gotta know what I'm gettin' into."

Jimmy leaned forward in the wicker chair, pushing his glasses back up on his nose. "That night you said the murder may have been, well, a ritualistic sacrifice."

"I didn't say that—not in those words, anyway."

"The airline magazine said that in Old Hawai'i the royalty sacrificed their enemies and slaves to appease the gods."

"That's true, but the sacrifices are different now. They're not to appease the *gods*, anyway."

"You're not being clear."

"I'm not sure I wanna be clear just yet."

Jimmy leaped up and paced the lanai like a dog crazy on a scent. Jack sank deeper into the wicker, eyeing the youth with dismay. He considered kicking him out right on the spot. Then he could forget the whole thing and deny to anyone who might ask—like the cops—that he'd ever seen the kid.

Jack went inside to get another beer and think over the situation. More than six decades had taught him how to forget certain things, but he also knew some things can *never* be forgotten, despite every effort to do so. He hoped this incident wasn't one of them. But the situation had tapped into his old reservoir of curiosity. While rummaging through the refrigerator, he decided to invite Jimmy to stay over until he could consult an island elder who, no doubt, would be out harvesting his favorite shellfish—*'opihi*—off the rocks in front the cabin the next morning. In the meantime, he could keep the kid safe from the people he feared had murdered the man.

Jimmy accepted the invitation, mostly because he didn't know what else to do. Jack decided not to tell him about his planned chat with the old Hawaiian until he had a better handle on the young man's character. He could see that Jimmy was full of starch, but whether the kid had any real fiber was yet to be determined.

Jack cooked up his favorite meal—fried Spam and eggs piled atop steaming heaps of white rice. The old sailor liked his with *lots* of chili pepper water, an island sauce made hotter than Tabasco with the virulent little chilies of the Hawaiian pepper plant. Jack dared the young man to try it. "Islanders don't bother with black pepper, 'cept the geriatrics. We eat our pepper *red!* If you're a local man, ya pour it on. But I might have some wimp pepper in the cupboard—"

"No thanks," Jimmy replied, vigorously splashing the amber sauce across his dinner. His face turned bright red after a few bites, but he cleaned his plate anyway.

After dinner Jack suggested that Jimmy "help out" with the dishes, while he took his tumbler of whiskey onto the lanai. Silver came with him, curling up under his chair. A long bank of moonlit clouds hung over the sea, and Jack watched a single mast light bob its way along the far horizon. He thought about how much he loved these islands—and how he didn't want anything messing up his reclusive retirement. As a young sailor he'd gone out of his way for adventure, but when he turned fifty—years ago now—he quit putting his butt in harm's way, even when he was tempted. Jack reached over to a weather-worn sea chest that served as his captain's cubby and pulled out a bottle of Jack Daniels. He refilled his tumbler and left the bottle handy on the wooden spool.

"Do me a favor, would ya, Jimmy?" Jack hollered through the screen door. "When you're done with them dishes, start up that tape in my stereo. And help yourself to another beer."

On his way back through the living room, Jimmy spotted the old boom box, with its bent antenna, duct tape trim, and a play button that fell off when he pressed it. The melody Jack waited for came on midsong—a melancholy rendition of "Younger than Springtime."

"What are we listening to?" Jimmy said, settling into the other chair.

"*South Pacific*—the 1949 Broadway soundtrack."

Jimmy rolled his eyes but kept quiet.

Jack sipped his drink, watching the restless waves assault the shore.

"Ya know, Jimmy, ya can learn a lot from the sea. All things come from it, and eventually everything goes back to it. People like to talk about leavin' a legacy, but in the end nature has her way. The sea'll take ya from here to there—with a little help from the trades—or she'll leave ya stranded in her dismal doldrums. Oh, sure, the big ships have the power to ignore all that, but if the sea wants her way, she'll disrupt them too. There's many a man who never made it back to the quay, thousands lost at sea. I knew a few of 'em. Seen some o' their ghosts too," he said laughing.

Jack finished his drink and poured another. "Yeah, the sea's unto its own," he continued, staring bleary-eyed at the wrinkled water beyond the surf. "Ya know, the big shots—the generals and the captains o' industry—they think they run the show, buildin' empires or tearin' 'em down, but it's the sea what forms the real boundaries that matter, the only ones nobody can change."

"I suppose so," Jimmy interjected, the dinner and beer finally relaxing him. "Lakes, on the other hand—"

"Hell, we thought we were gonna run these islands," Jack said, spitting out a laugh, "but we were wrong! The islands don't work that way—not in the long run."

"Bali Ha'i" played on the boom box, and the singer's voice wavered oddly, the old tape stretched from years of play:

Most people live on a lonely island,
lost in the middle of a foggy sea . . .

Jack's whiskey-soaked thoughts vanished beneath the moonlit waves surging and swelling and shattering against the rocky shore.

. . . If you try, you'll find me,
where the sky meets the sea.
Here am I, your special island.
Come to me. Come to me!

When the tape ended, the lanai fell silent, leaving only the murmur of the surf and the quiet chirp of a gecko under the eave eyeing the humans beneath him.

Jack looked over at the kid with bleary eyes. "What about lakes?" he asked, trying to make amends for being such a pompous—and drunk—old man.

"Huh?"

"What about those lakes, Jimmy, back there in Minnesota?"

"Well, you can learn a lot from them too—same things you were talking about. Not so many shipwrecks, of course, but still the bigger lakes show their power."

Jack was suddenly back on Superior's rugged north shore, where he'd spent much of his youth, before his first war. But he wasn't about to tell the kid that, not yet anyway.

"Yeah," Jimmy replied, "when the thunderstorms blow in from Canada, the lakes turn black, and the shoreline gets a drubbing from the waves."

"Power, boy! Power beyond us!" Jack raised his fist toward the ceiling, while his eyeballs sloshed back and forth in his head. "That's why ya came all this way, ain't it? To see the volcano's power," his words slurred.

"That's right! And to capture it on film! And I mean *film*, the old way—like Ansel Adams and Edward Weston—not with those digital cameras I use at the newspaper."

"So yer traditional?" Jack said, peering into the young man's face, but his eyes no longer focused. "I like that! Me too."

The old man's gaze drifted offshore. "The sea is a great teacher," he said. "Just stare into her blue depths. If ya look long enough, ya might even see yourself, reflected in the ups and downs o' the great swells way out there, or in the murky surf bangin' over and over again against the rocks. Maybe ya see more than ya really want."

The gecko cackled.

Jack downed his final drink and struggled out of the wicker. Jimmy reached forward to steady the wavering old man.

"There's a blanket in the closet on your way to the head. Help yourself, Jimmy. I'd say the couch is your best bet, but if the floor suits ya better, just steal the cushions from the chairs. Whatever ya please . . ."

He stumbled through the door, the big old tom in his tracks. Soon the cabin went quiet, except for the creak of the floorboards under the old sailor's weight and the distant rumble of the surf. Jack slipped off his clothes and collapsed into bed.

"Not a bad kid, really," he muttered as he sank beneath the waters of that same old dream, of a cast-off love, that had haunted him for decades.

11 ∫ A Meeting with the Elder

It had cooled off during the night, and a crisp morning breeze blew through Captain Jack's cabin. The ocean drummed a gentle beat that brought the old sailor out of his dream, accompanied by a hangover's throb. He stepped out onto the lanai to make a routine check of the sea. The tide was out and the waves curled gently against the shore.

Jack spotted a tangle of gray hair popping in and out of view at the edge of the rocks and heard the wheezy humming of Aka Makimo Kaikala. He also heard the deep, slumbering breaths of Jimmy, sprawled sideways on a wicker chair, and stepped back inside. While the percolator gurgled, he poured a bowl of milk for Silver, who showed up the instant it touched the linoleum. Jack brewed his coffee bitterly strong and took a cup with him down to the sea.

It took a few minutes to traverse the overgrown path and reach the rocky ledge where his old friend hunted for little black-shelled limpets called 'opihi. The old Hawaiian was hunched over the shells with his prying knife, his brown back ruddy under the dazzling sun. He'd grown fat over the years but was still fit from fishing, swimming, and tending his taro patch every day. Despite his age—a decade older than Jack—Aka could swim 200 yards beyond the breakers. Twists of muscle still contoured his legs, and he had the wide, callused feet of an islander who had spent little time cramped up in shoes. His rugged hands reflected a lifetime of gutting fish and mending boats, herding cattle, and crafting beautiful things of wood. Aka's thick beard and full head of hair were mostly gray now, but in his youth women loved to run their fingers through his jet-black mane.

He glanced up at the sea, and his eyes, half-hidden under fleshy lids, caught the sun—beacons shining from some inner shore. With a raspy chuckle, he thrust a big hand into his mesh ʻopihi bag and retrieved one. Using a cracked fingernail, he scraped the live meat out of the shell and tossed it into his mouth. As he chewed, Aka looked out over the waves and smiled.

The old man, now seventy-three, had been picking ʻopihi in front of Jack's place for years, even during the lava flows that buried most of Kalapana. Aka would slip past the Civil Defense barricades before the guards came on duty and then sneak back out during their lunch break. Jack wondered why a man would stick to a risky routine like that for no good reason, but that was Aka—honoring his own private rituals.

That was how the two had met. Jack, occasionally fishing off the ledge, would notice Aka picking ʻopihi, but at first they rarely exchanged more than polite hellos. Jack had assumed his being a haole made Aka wary, when in fact Aka was just respecting the sailor's self-imposed isolation. But the silence broke one morning when Jack cussed aloud about that day's fishing.

"How many fish have you taken from the sea since you've lived here?" Aka had asked.

"Plenty," Jack boasted.

"Then you have no right to start complaining now."

Jack knew it was true but kept right on grousing, which got them into a bigger conversation, and they'd talked story ever since—about fishing, the islands, and everything else under the sun. During these dozen years Jack learned more about Hawaiʻi than he had in the decades he was stationed on Oʻahu, catching glimpses of old Hawaiian ways that Aka knew because of his Kalapana upbringing.

"Mornin', Aka," Jack said, easing himself down onto the rock. "How's your pickin' goin'?"

"The ocean helps me today," he replied, without looking up. "Tide's way low and they're easy to reach." Although he rarely used pidgin English, Aka spoke with that distinctive cadence that makes islanders' sentences sing. "But you still got to surprise them or they grab the rock. They're trying to stay out of my bag, but I've snatched a few." He held it up so Jack could see.

"Cripes! Ya must have three or four dozen in there, a'ready."

"Take some," Aka offered, spotting yet another cluster of shells on a nearby rock.

"Sure. I can try 'em out on this young fella stayin' with me."

"You? You got company?"

"A kid from the mainland. Says he's from Minnesota, but he's as pushy as a West Coast haole, if ya ask me."

"What's his problem?"

"He's got that just-outa-high-school attitude, goin' gangbusters, like he never heard the word *patience*."

"Hmmmm. I think he's probably just like you were at his age. Only you were probably more trouble. I know I was." They both chuckled.

"Is he family?"

"Naw, jus' someone who needs a hand."

Aka pried loose a clump of three 'opihi.

"It's a long story, Aka, one I plan to tell ya. But I need to ask ya somethin' first. You heard about anything peculiar happenin' out on the lava or up in Royal Gardens?"

"Somebody broke into Yokoyama's abandoned shed," Aka said. "He's complained all over town, but that old lawn mower's been broke since the day his boy ran over a piece of tailpipe."

Jack pulled out his pipe and lit up the bowl. "Heard anything else? Anything *really* unusual?"

Aka withdrew his knife from the rock and looked over at his friend. "What are you fishing for, Jack?"

"I heard a rumor—a nasty one."

"That right?" He turned his back and resumed picking 'opihi.

"Listen, Aka, I'm not involved—and don't intend to be. I just heard somethin' I thought I oughta check out with you. Your clan knows everything goes on round here—and not all of 'em keeps their noses clean."

The Hawaiian laughed a high-pitched wheeze.

"Somethin' weird happened, Aka, and I can't figure out what it means."

"You think I can?" He tapped a finger against his temple. "Aren't you the one says this old coconut has been out in the sun too long?"

"Yeah, despite your obvious disability, I think you can help me figure out what's what—and what, if anything, we oughta do about it."

Aka looked up at him, but the Hawaiian wasn't laughing anymore.

"You *have* heard somethin', haven't ya?"

Aka pursed his lips and shrugged.

"Dammit, Aka!"

"OK, Jack." The old Hawaiian slid his body higher up the rocky ledge. "Something *did* happen, and I'm still trying to understand it myself. The other night, a *pueo* . . ."

"Pueo?" Jack knew that to Hawaiians the owl was an *'aumakua*, an ancestor god, the physical embodiment of relatives passed into the spirit world, an animal form that the living could also assume under special circumstances. To him, all that was superstitious nonsense, but he knew Hawaiians took the appearance of an owl seriously as an auspicious—or ominous—sign. Aka was of the owl clan; he *had* to pay attention.

Aka leaned forward, pressing into the bubble of space that Jack normally kept between himself and other people. His brown eyes were aimed right at his friend, but they seemed to glaze over as if he were gazing inside. "The pueo perched on the big 'ohi'a tree behind my house . . . He sat there all night long, never leaving, even to hunt . . . Last night he was there again . . . same limb . . . He was still there this morning, just sitting."

"So?"

Aka's eyes snapped back into focus. "In all my years, Jack, I've never seen an owl sit like that, all night long, two nights in a row. It's a message."

"Aka, what I'm gonna blab to ya must be kept between ourselves—for both our sakes."

"You know I can keep my mouth shut."

"What night was it that ya first saw the bird?"

"Friday, just after moonrise."

Jack nodded slowly. "And Friday night a man was killed out on the lava."

"Auwe!"

Jack lowered his voice to a whisper, glancing in all directions to make sure there wasn't a soul within earshot.

"Murdered."

"*Pepehi kanaka*?"

"That's right, Aka, if that means murdered. Burned *alive* in the lava!"

"Auwe! *'Ino 'ino!*"

"It was ritualistic, carried out by six men. Seems that most of 'em was Hawaiians." Jack leaned back and let the news sink into the old Hawaiian's head.

Aka's eyes went glassy again. "I heard the scream," he muttered.

"What?"

"Friday night—I heard the scream."

"Ya couldn't of. The man was killed more 'n two miles from your place."

"No, no. I heard the pueo scream in my dream! I guess that's what woke me, made me climb out of bed. I went to the window—my head all cobwebs—and a few minutes later I saw the owl land in a tree." Aka pressed his big hand over his forehead. "Only just now I remember I dreamed him first!"

12 The Community Lie

"Captain Jack?" Jimmy hollered, tearing down the overgrown path. "Is that you over there?"

"Well, ya got that right, anyway!" Jack replied, annoyed that the pesky kid would show up at that moment.

Jimmy strode over to the two old men. "I thought maybe you'd decided to head into town to report—"

"No," Jack interrupted. "I'm just talkin' to my friend." He turned toward the Hawaiian. "Aka, this is Jimmy, the young fella stayin' at my place."

Aka nodded and Jimmy forced a smile. Jack could tell the kid's sleep had done nothing to quell his antsiness.

"Jimmy, le'me finish up this conversation and then I'll put together some breakfast. After *that*, we'll figure out what's what."

"Spam again?"

"What's wrong with Spam?" Aka asked, as if it was a matter of local pride.

"The way *he* makes it—"

"Kid had his first taste o' chili pepper water last night."

"Pretty hot," Jimmy said, crunching up his face as if he'd swallowed rotten fish.

Aka wheezed out a warm laugh that made even Jimmy smile.

"Who knows how long that bottle's been in there fermenting?" the young man said. "I mean, we almost needed pliers to get the cap off!"

"Five years," Jack replied, "barely long enough to give it some punch." He pointed at Aka's 'opihi bag. "Hey, Jimmy, Aka here is pickin' 'opihi, a tasty little critter found only in Hawai'i. I'm sure he'd be glad to let ya try one—*if ya dare!*"

Aka took one from the bag and scraped the meat out with his knife. He handed it to Captain Jack, who gobbled it down. "Delicious!" he said with a smile.

Aka held his 'opihi bag open for Jimmy, whose blue eyes darkened at the sight of the raw, living limpets. But without a word, he plucked one from bag and thrust his hand forward to demand Aka's knife. He scraped out the rubbery meat, and without flinching, chewed it right down.

"Not bad," he announced, crossing his arms.

"The boy might do well in the islands," Aka said, looking disapprovingly at Jack, "if he's given half a chance!"

"They produce good stock back there in the Midwest," Jack said. "It's just o' matter o' what happens once they let 'em out on the range. Listen, Jimmy. Why don't ya go up to the cabin and have yourself a cup o' coffee. I'll be back in a few minutes and we'll rustle up some breakfast."

"OK," he said. "But I really need to talk with you—"

"We will, kid. I promise."

"Nice to meet you, Aka," Jimmy said.

"You have a good visit, Jimmy," Aka replied, stretching out his big hand. Jimmy leaned over and experienced the warmth of his first local-style handshake. "And don't let this old geezer get under your skin."

When Jimmy reached the edge of the trail, he looked back over his shoulder. "Hey, Aka! Thanks for the 'opihi!" he said, then disappeared down the path.

Both men chuckled, and Jack shook his head. He was struck again at how Aka, like lots of islanders, could shift his mood so easily. . . like when the kid showed up. One minute the talk was somber, caught up in the troubles of a man's life, and then, with little provocation, everyone would smile and laugh and chase away the gloom that moments before had everyone fretting.

Once Jimmy was out of sight, Jack again brought up the murder, filling Aka in on the key details of the eerie scene. "So what about that owl, Aka?"

"Our ancestors watch over our families," Aka said. "Sometimes they advise, sometimes they scold, and sometimes they warn us of danger. To dream of a pueo is significant. Then to see him two nights in a row!" He shook his head as a cloud passed over the sun, giving them a momentary respite from the heat.

"What's all that s'posed to mean, Aka?"

"Too soon to tell."

Aka pulled a squashed pack of Kools out of his shorts, put a bent cigarette in his mouth, and lit it. He sucked hard, drawing the menthol smoke deep into his lungs.

"Jack, how do *you* know that a man was murdered out there?"

"I'll get to that in a minute. The real question is, who killed him? And *why*?"

"Six men, you say? And Hawaiian?"

"I believe so." Jack relit his pipe, then recounted more of what Jimmy had said without revealing the source.

"Did you hear all this from one of the six?" Aka asked.

"Doesn't matter where I heard it. Let's jus' say I don't doubt the story, 'cause o' how it came my way." He sucked hard on his pipe, drawing out the bowl's last smoke. "I take it ya didn't know anything about it?"

"No, I didn't, but when the really bad things happen, nobody hears about it. That's the way they want it."

"*They* being—?"

Aka looked down the shore in both directions, then spoke in a low wheeze. "The Hui," he said, snuffing his cigarette on the rock.

"That's what I was afraid ya'd say. But when *they* kill someone, they usually do it so nobody knows."

"Unless they want to make a point of it."

Jack poked the weeds with his pipe stem. "Seems odd they'd do it with six men when one or two would do. Not a typical execution."

"Hmmmm." Aka's eyes narrowed. "Six murderers means six witnesses, so that puts them all at risk."

"Yeah, if anybody gives a damn."

"Ah, yes, that's a question. People have gotten used to these things—"

"The boy might do well in the islands," Aka said, "if he's given half a chance!"

"What's that?" Jack interrupted, hearing a rustle in the jungle along the shore. They both fell as silent as mice hiding from a mongoose. Again, the rustle! Jack noticed Aka check his breathing. The old Hawaiian rotated his head slowly, focusing his eyes on every bush and tree, like he was young again, stalking boar in the forests of Mauna Loa.

"Just palm fronds in the wind," Jack declared.

"I don't know," Aka replied, concern in his eyes.

"The only soul I see, other'n you, is that man throwin' net on the point."

The brown figure was well beyond earshot. Even so, Jack hunkered close to Aka. "What d'ya make o' that business about the lei on the dead man's grave?"

"I don't know. You never hear of these killings being done with ceremony."

Jack scratched his balding head. "Maybe it *wasn't* the Hui?"

"Who else would it be?"

"And what about that Hawaiian word blurted out by the victim?"

"*Kumakaia*? It means 'traitor,' and that's interesting."

They both gazed out over the Pacific as the drifting clouds veiled and unveiled the sun. After a long time, Aka spoke. "Who else knows of this?"

"Only one other—the one who told me the story."

"You know, Jack, this has nothing to do with us."

"That was my *first* reaction."

"You're thinking about getting involved then?"

"My head's against it."

"But your gut says something different?"

"Well, dammit, Aka. Haven't we all had a belly full o' the bloodshed?"

Aka stared at the sparkling water below the rocks. "It's true the Hui uses the most down-and-out Hawaiians to do its dirty work and survives only because the rest of us despair that anything will change. But, Jack, is there any other way?

"To keep the 'old boys' in check, you mean—flip 'em the bird now and again. Maybe even keep some o' your people at the table when the haoles and the Japanese cut their deals. Sure. But it's a sad day, Aka, when the only thing left for honest-to-God Hawaiians to control is whores, and dope, and gambling."

"You point your finger at the Hui, Jack, but look at who controls everything else in Hawai'i. And these are *our* islands." Aka's eyes misted over and the cadence in his voice wavered. "Now they just use us. Postcard pictures of half-naked girls, some of them just Orientals with tans. Hula shows at hotels where our people can't get the decent-paying jobs. Our precious artifacts displayed in their lobbies! So I can understand why people tolerate the Hui, even *support* the idea of Hawaiians hanging on to those few illegal crumbs. Face it, Jack, even haole politicians don't mess with the Hui."

The old Hawaiian lit another cigarette and smoked it in silence, watching the tide rise and the waves break across the lava ledge. "I don't know what's left for us," he said, gazing at the timeless erosion of the shore.

"What do we do, then?" Jack asked. "Keep our mouths shut? Not even bother to report the crime?"

Aka turned back from the sea. "I'm not a bitter man, Jack. All my life I've kept myself alive by building things, not tearing them down. I've raised my children and grandchildren, swam in the sea, laughed with my friends, and enjoyed—every day—the beauty of these islands. I've watched all the changes, more rapid in my life than in my father's, and more rapid during his life than in his father's time. But I see no way to stop this, what the haoles—and now many of our local people—call progress. At least the Hui gives Hawaiians a power base to protect *our* interests in what little is left."

"Corruption! That's what it is! All those years in the Navy I just looked the other way and let things pass. Kept my trap shut and my butt well outa the line o' sight! But now I wonder. Ain't there no way to do better 'n that?"

A scowl marked Aka's face, but sadness stained his big Hawaiian eyes. "For centuries our gods protected the islands, providing us with all we needed—food, shelter, each other, the stars. Where are they now? Did they feel abandoned and go away?" Aka looked back at Jack. "Your first instinct was the right one—to forget you ever heard about it. Maybe it is *wrong*, and in the long run bad for the islands, but we can't do anything about it. Besides, the victim was probably—"

"Deservin' of it?"

"I'm not saying that, but he was probably part of their whole rotten mess. Probably just stole from them."

"And we should find comfort in that?" Jack's face reddened. "Maybe I'm just goddamn tired of people pushin' people around. What about the innocent witness who stumbles into the middle of it by accident? Ya know what those crooks would do to someone who saw somethin' they shouldn't o'? Do ya? Huh?"

"Jack, you know someone who actually saw this?"

"What if one o' *your* grandkids was the innocent bystander!"

"Jack! Jack!" Aka shouted, grabbing hold of his arms. "Who're you talking about? Jack, are *you* in trouble?"

"Not yet, Aka. But I'm thinkin' about it!" He knocked his smoldering char onto the rock.

"Jack, who is it? Who told you the story?"

"The kid, dammit! That young idiot has no idea what he's into. He's so naive he thinks ya can just report this kind o' thing to our crooked island cops!"

"Auwe!"

"I've tried to cool him down, for his own sake—and keep him from messin' up my quiet, meanin'less life—but he's stubborn as a mule!"

"Have you told him of the dangers?"

Jack threw up his hands. "Naw, he wouldn't understand it! And even if he did, he's the type to throw all caution to the wind. He'd go out an' martyr himself without even knowin' it! Just look what happened when he ran down to the police. Sassin' 'em back till they slapped 'im with a bunch o' fines!"

"He's already gone to the police?"

"Yeah. But they were too busy worryin' about Yokoyama's busted lawn mower—or maybe they wanted to make damn sure the kid didn't go back to the place where the cops already knew a murder happened that night! Leave it to the kid to start complainin' about due process o' law, like he was talkin' to a cop from some quaint Midwestern town. Aka, ya know what'll happen to him if the Hui finds out he witnessed the murder? They'll cut him up and send him back to Minnesota stuffed in the pockets o' his camera bag—'specially if they think he mighta taken pictures!"

"Did he?"

"Says not, but who knows with a brassy kid like that?"

"Auwe!"

"Auwe is right! I better go back up there right now and get his head squared on straight, before he does somethin' stupid."

Jack got up from the rock—groaning as he straightened his arthritic knees—and limped back toward the path. Aka followed. They tramped through the jungle at a fast clip and were both wheezing by the time they got to the cabin's lanai. Silver sat wide-eyed on the railing.

"Jimmy!" Jack hollered, bursting through the door. There was no answer.

"Jimmy! Aka and me need a word with ya, about what happened on the lava." The living room and kitchen were empty. Aka checked the bedroom while Jack rushed back outside, smashing the screen door against the wall. "Jimmy! Jimmy!" he hollered into the jungle.

"No one in the bedroom, either," Aka said, joining Jack on the lanai. Jimmy's coffee cup sat half-empty on the arm of the wicker chair.

13 ∫ A Wise Old Owl Visits the Activists

TUESDAY NIGHT, JUNE 6, ON THE SLOPES OF HUALALAI . . .

A pueo sat on a fence post outside the tiny church, its brown feathers gently ruffled by the steady night breeze. The little owl blinked its orange eyes at the glowing stained-glass windows, listening to the muffled voices inside, then glanced up at the three-quarter moon rising above Hualalai.

Inside a contentious debate was under way. Wailani Henderson stood at the front of the chapel listening to the crowd of Hawaiians, many of whom, members of Kapu Hawai'i, had good cause for their latest outrage. They'd been forcibly removed from nearby Lapalapa Ranch. Wailani stood erect, her hands on the pulpit, the vibrant thirty-year-old presenting an ironic contrast to the agonized figure of Christ hanging on the wall. Spotlights accentuated her round eyes and toothy smile, features inherited from her Hawaiian mother. Her father's Scandinavian blood gave her a slender frame, wavy hair, and skin the amber color of mango. Delicate tattoos of sea waves circled her wrists, and a thick lei of green ti leaves hung above her colorful *pareu*. The membership of Kapu Hawai'i had chosen as leader a woman both strong and beautiful to guide them through the latest crisis.

"That *pilau* governor oughta make offerings and ask for forgiveness," hollered a woman in the crowd.

"Ku would never accept it!" bellowed 'Iolani Carvalho, who stood at the back of the church gesturing with powerful hands. Supportive laughter rose from the crowd, and he acknowledged it with a restrained smile. Living on the beach had blackened his skin, and his long ponytail was frizzy with split ends. Though not large, he was all muscle beneath his faded tank top and surfer shorts, and a gridwork of triangular tattoos covered his upper arms—warrior's symbols stained into his flesh with great pain.

"Governor Kamali'i wen' give his offerings to Congressman Yamashita, dat's why," said one of the men standing with 'Iolani. The crowd's bitter laughter resounded among the beams of the wooden church.

Wailani listened without comment. She knew almost everyone there, members of Kapu Hawai'i or the Holualoa Catholic Church. Most were under forty, young activists steeped in the Hawaiian sovereignty movement. The rest varied in age, from infants to old people. A few elders, more often involved in hula, lei-making, or canoe clubs, were also there. Some of the crowd had come out of curiosity, Wailani thought, but most were committed to the cause. She wished, however, that 'Iolani hadn't come. Seething with resentment, he was divisive, and he advocated militancy, even violence.

"All right, all right," Wailani said, still smiling. "Chill out, you guys."

"It's the governor who needs to chill out!" 'Iolani shouted back. "Or *we* ought to chill him out!" Many people laughed, but Wailani wondered if they realized that 'Iolani was at least half-serious.

Wailani threw her arms up against the tumult, trying again to quiet the room. "I need a *serious* proposal."

After much coaxing, the group finally settled down.

"Hoku," Wailani said, "would you pass out the article?"

A woman from the front pew handed out photocopies of a news story that had appeared in the Kona paper several days earlier:

HAWAIIANS EVICTED FROM DISPUTED LAND

Police and ranch security forcibly evicted twelve Hawaiians from Lapalapa Ranch on Hualalai, including outspoken Kona activist Wailani Henderson. Ignoring recent warnings by authorities, the Hawaiians refused to vacate their encampment on the controversial range land. Kapu Hawai'i has long claimed that the land, recently subdivided for "prestige estates" by Island Country Living Corporation (ICLC) of San Diego, Calif., was "swindled from the Hawaiian people" back in the 1860s. No arrests were made.

Ownership of the 3,000-acre parcel, originally leased to American shippers for sandalwood harvest, has long been in dispute. Early Hawai'i County land records have been lost and Hawaiians question the legitimacy of the current ownership. Hawaiians also claim the land contains important cultural and religious sites.

"We sympathize with the Hawaiians who believe they were wronged years ago," said Ken Addison, a spokesman for ICLC. "But we can't undo the past. After numerous hearings, the County has issued the permits to go forward with our project, and we want to get started."

"That's the only coverage we got," Wailani said as the people in the church finished reading the article. "It's clear the police are gonna be on our backs from now on. Tonight we have to decide what to do next. Any ideas?"

"Let's go back Lapalapa, make camp again," said a brawny young man, a bone fishhook dangling from his neck. "Call da newspapers. Make da cops evict us again. Make 'em look bad."

"But Koke, we hardly got any publicity last time," Wailani replied, "and nothing in the Honolulu papers. Was one big yawn!"

"We do 'em bigger dis time. One giant luau! Fill up da ranch with everybody in Kapu. Bring drums, build *choke* bonfires. Maybe get one searchlight. Let everybody know—TV too. Den, when da cops come, dey gotta arrest us for campin' on our own 'aina."

"Yeah, and we give the cops leis as they haul us off to jail," shouted a plump young woman with a red hibiscus in her hair. "They come with guns, we kiss them on the cheek. Aloha!"

"Radical, Keola!" said a woman sitting behind her.

A number of people shouted their support for the idea. But a husky, middle-aged man leaning against the wall said, "TV nevah come Big Island for politics, only when volcanoes blow. You want publicity, you gotta go Honolulu." He turned to face the crowd. "You wanna get TV? Don't camp Lapalapa, camp in da gov'nor's office."

"You may be right," Wailani said.

"Then we'll shower the governor with leis as the cops haul us away," Keola said.

"Give 'im flowers?" 'Iolani cried, slipping into pidgin. "Coconut sellout to da haole! I like punch 'im out!" The crowd laughed, but the tone grew ominous.

"Maybe we oughta arrest *him*," he continued, "Make da governor camp at Lapalapa."

"Boy Scout!" somebody said.

"Yeah, make him build the fires, do the dishes!" said another.

"Him and our *distinguished* Big Island congressman, Yamashita!" ʻIolani said with venom.

"Yeah, coconuts and bananas go good together!"

The crowd was in an uproar, comments from every quarter of the church. In the midst of the ruckus, an old man in a tall cowboy hat stood up in the corner. His ruddy face was barely visible among the much larger Hawaiians.

"What good is all this stink talk?" he demanded.

The unruly crowd quieted a bit, many straining to see into the back of the room. Even ʻIolani stopped to look over his shoulder.

"Why waste our breath on the governor here?" the old man said firmly. Recognition of the voice passed through the room like a silent wave, and the crowd hushed.

"Talk, talk, talk!" he went on. "We gotta hit that opportunist where it *really* hurts."

Every eye fixed on Sonny Makakoa Kiakahi, a seventy-five-year-old rancher from Kaʻu and one of Hawaiʻi Island's most respected elders. Wailani was surprised to see him. Sonny Kiakahi had always kept his distance from Kapu Hawaiʻi. Why hadn't she noticed him earlier?

"Calvin Kamaliʻi hates bad publicity," the old cowboy continued, "and I know a surefire way to make trouble for him in front of the TV cameras."

"Uncle Sonny, tell us more," said a man standing by the exit, tattooed arms folded across his chest. He was not Sonny Kiakahi's nephew, but part of a larger family—the Hawaiian community—and respected elders were always referred to in a familial way, as "Uncle" or "Aunty."

"Yes, Uncle," Wailani said, "tell us your ideas."

"In two weeks the Royal Paradise Bay Resort will hold its grand opening at Kiholo."

The mere mention of the resort caused groans throughout the church. Kona Hawaiians, even the young ones, remembered Kiholo as it used to be, with its sparkling ponds, the sacred pool, and the ancient ruins and petroglyphs—most of which had been sacrificed for parking lots and golf courses.

"That monstrosity is the most offensive hotel in the islands, and worse than that"—Uncle Sonny paused to search the faces in the crowd, trying to gauge its reaction to the information he possessed. But his gut sensed danger in the room, and he stopped himself from revealing it—"this hotel is the most rotten fruit on the governor's tree of tourism.

"There'll be plenty o' TV people at the grand opening, including mainland guys," the old rancher continued. "Sucking up all the BS." The crowd chuckled. "You can bet the governor will be there. He loves that stuff!"

Wailani motioned him to come forward, and the crowd whispered as Uncle Sonny moved up the aisle. Though small in stature, he emanated strong mana, the power Hawaiians attribute to the wise, the good, and the divine. He was fit from riding and roping on the Kapapala Ranch, and his face was lined from years squinting into the sun and laughing with his rugged cohorts. The hatband on his Stetson had long been replaced with a lei of tiny gold feathers. When he reached the podium, the room fell silent.

"The public is invited to the grand opening. Well, we're the public, aren't we?" He cracked a big toothy smile. "So, we go! As many as can. Dress nice, mingle, talk story, and bring the little ones—our *keiki*—so the governor can see what is at stake for us. Everybody bring a protest sign inside your beach bag. When the governor gets up to speak and the cameras start rolling, out come the signs. 'Return Lapalapa and Other Stolen Lands,' or 'Aloha 'Aina,' things like that."

"Kanaka Maoli Sovereignty!" someone shouted.

"Perhaps," Uncle Sonny replied. "But we take them by surprise—and then bombard them."

"Bombard them?" Wailani asked.

"With leaflets, the one you used at Lapalapa that tells the whole history—including how the governor buckled under the congressman's pressure and now champions developments that hurt his own people. The mainland reporters will eat it up."

'Iolani bristled. "After all that, just hand them a piece of paper? I think we should *take over* the lobby! Refuse to leave until the governor negotiates!" He thrust up a fist. "They can arrest us if they want!"

"No arrests," Uncle Sonny said calmly, staring at 'Iolani and the men around him. "No need. We're part of the public. Just being there will make them nervous, and when we flash our signs, and they send in security to get us out, we leave *peacefully*—but having made our point, and in front of the cameras."

"But Uncle Sonny, what good will that do?" someone asked.

"It's a warning," Uncle Sonny replied sternly, "that Hawaiians intend to speak the truth *everywhere* that they threaten the 'aina, even when—especially when—it's inconvenient for them."

"You mean be in their face!" said a young man standing next to 'Iolani.

"That's exactly what I mean, son. Pit our spirit against theirs. If we are persistent, how can we *not* win?"

People grew excited, buzzing among themselves as the old rancher folded his gnarled fingers into a fist. "Remember—all of you—we do not fight alone."

His eyes caught the blue-white patch of moonlight shining through the door, and he spoke his words with deliberate care.

"We have the 'aina—our homeland. And the *akua*—our gods. Our 'aumakua—our ancestors. They will guide and protect us."

A murmur passed through the crowd. Some faces seemed surprised, others uncomfortable, and some of 'Iolani's cynical cohorts shook their heads.

"Have they ever failed us before?" Uncle Sonny continued. "Perhaps *we* have failed *them*, but they have stood by our side through all the trials of our people." He stepped forward toward the crowd. "Are they not alive in all of you?"

This was an awkward moment for some of the Christians at the meeting, torn between their reverence for the old gods and their devotion to the church. Most in the room nodded their agreement, and the youngest of the group—offspring of the Hawaiian cultural renaissance—smiled their support.

Wailani stepped forward next to Uncle Sonny. Again he noticed what he once called her "old woman's eyes," deep pools leading directly to her soul, pained with sorrow for her people. Yet they were also incandescent with youthful hope and courage.

"To rebuild the Hawaiian Nation," she said, "we need *all* the gods, Christian and Hawaiian. If *we* can fight together side by side, why not our gods?" There was no way Wailani could appease the most devout Christians in the room, but her empathy soothed their concerns. At least their inner conflict was being accepted with compassion. The crowd applauded.

'Iolani and his small band of followers slipped out of the church before tasks for the protest could be assigned. By ten o'clock everyone else had left, and Uncle Sonny and Wailani talked in a pew.

"You ran a good meeting, Wailani," he told her.

"Thank you, Uncle, but it was you who provided a plan." She paused for a moment. "I was surprised to see you here."

He smiled indulgently. "You must know that I care as much about the 'aina as you and your band of radicals."

"It's just that you've always seemed so soft-spoken in your concerns."

"The struggle for our native rights didn't begin yesterday. I've been fighting in my own way for years."

"I know, Uncle Sonny. Aunty Keala says you single-handedly caused more problems for the crooks down at Hawaiian Homelands than anyone else."

He did not smile. "Too long they kept us off lands the law said they had to give back to us. I was the first to go to jail, back in 1962, for squatting on land that once belonged to my grandfather."

"You went to jail?"

"More than once, and beaten senseless as well." He pushed the brim of his Stetson high up on his forehead, revealing a long gash. "That's my reminder. A haole ranch hand with a whip."

Uncle Sonny pulled his brim back into place. "After a while—when you realize there's no point in losing your life—you decide to take a different trail. So I turned toward my community, the ranch, and Ka'u, and to my children and grandchildren. There I planted the seeds of change." A look of pain passed over his eyes.

"There were many others too," he continued, "fighting in their own way—on the plantations, at the docks, in their communities, and at home. Trying to keep what's Hawaiian alive."

"What made you come tonight?"

The old man paused as if reluctant to disclose all that he knew. "I've been watching Kapu Hawaiʻi. A bunch of naive hotheads—"

"Hey!"

"Hear me out. Hotheads, yes, but with pure hearts, most of you anyway. Yes, I was critical, but only in the way that a father criticizes his children, because I believed there might be some hope in your group. And we Hawaiians need hope." Uncle Sonny paused, looking deep into the young woman's eyes. "I'll tell you what really upset me. The sellout of one of our own, the governor. You know, I sent Calvin $500 when he first ran for office. At last, I thought, a true Hawaiian, not like that first sellout. The more I think about Calvin, the madder I get."

Wailani again sensed that there was something else on Uncle Sonny's mind, a sharper bur under his saddle. But whatever it was, he was not going to reveal it that night.

"Well, Uncle, I'm glad you came to the meeting. You gave us hope."

The old cowboy got up from the pew, and Wailani walked him to the moon-washed entrance of the church.

"Wailani," he said, "our beautiful island is changing faster now than ever, just like what happened to Oʻahu, Maui, and Kauaʻi."

"I hope we're not too late, Uncle."

He shook his head. "The time is better now than it has ever been. Hawaiians are beginning to move beyond their sorrow. Talk of our traditions has returned. I hear the old language coming from young mouths, words I haven't heard since my father's time. And lots of talk about sovereignty. But I see trouble ahead. A new bitterness among our people."

"I see that too, especially among some younger Hawaiians, like ʻIolani."

"Even the old, Wailani. Remember, we've *lived* the demise."

Uncle Sonny placed a hand on the young woman's shoulder. "What worries me is that their anger could turn to hatred. In Honolulu and on Maui this is already happening. We must not allow it to happen here. It is aloha that will save us."

"How can you say that after all you've been through?"

"That is why I *can* say it. We must call back to our deepest heritage, to that which we believe in most. Aloha is the strongest weapon we have against the greed of our opponents. They have money and the power of government. But they do not have aloha. Remember this. You must not let the darkness overwhelm us."

"Me?"

"You are a born leader, Wailani, but you must not let your own anger poison your following. Be a warrior, yes, but always remember aloha. It is what marks our people as unique in the world. That, and our way of time. Patience is a virtue if you trust enough to wait for the right moment."

"We—you—all of us—have waited too long!" she insisted.

"Listen to me, Wailani. When I was young, we hunted the wild boar of Mauna Loa. In those days we took only spears into the forest. We'd stalk the pig paths for hours, looking for signs of foraging. Then we would wait—again for hours—until a boar wandered down the trail. After all that waiting, we were eager for the kill! But remember, you have but one strike and in only one spot, behind the pig's thick armor. Sometimes the animal moved too fast, or was just too far away, and we would wait again—maybe for an entirely different beast. Maybe all day. Maybe all weekend! We learned patience to wait for the right moment. Otherwise, our spear would miss the boar or uselessly wound him, and striking at the wrong time could mean getting gored by his tusks. No, we waited, never losing our concentration until the boar was ours!" He grinned. "And what a great luau we had after the hunt, Wailani! A real feast!"

Patience had never been one of Wailani's virtues, and she didn't reply.

"The time to pounce is soon, Wailani. I can feel it. Remember our way of time and aloha, and the gods will guide you."

Uncle Sonny stopped short of telling Wailani that what he knew was more than just a feeling; that he had had a dream impelling him to come all the way from Ka'u to North Kona to play out his piece of the vision. Nor did he tell her what he knew of Robert Conway's secret plans for his resort at Kiholo. That he would reveal later.

Wailani glanced at the clock in the back of the church. It was almost 11:00.

"It's late, Uncle Sonny, too late to drive all the way back to Ka'u. You can stay at my place."

"No need," he said, stepping over the threshold and down the church steps. "The moon is up." He pointed at the glowing orb. "Mahina will light my way."

Wailani hugged the elder, kissing him lightly on the cheek. "Aloha, Uncle, and *mahalo nui loa*."

She watched the old rancher stride toward the street, but no vehicles were parked there. "Where's your truck, Uncle?"

"You had so darn many people here tonight that I had to park down the road a piece." He smiled and waved, then disappeared down the moonlit pavement.

Wailani stepped back into the church. While straightening up the pews, she realized she had not heard the engine rumble of Uncle Sonny's old pickup. Concerned, she walked across the churchyard and looked down the road. It was empty, but a lunar rainbow hung in the sky, a pure white arch looming over the slopes of Hualalai.

14 Mischief from the Snow Goddess

WEDNESDAY AFTERNOON, JUNE 7, IN HILO . . .

Maile Chow sat in her office, her back turned to the cluttered desk, staring out the window. Even the golden afternoon light shimmering atop Hilo Bay couldn't brighten her mood, fouled by hours laboring over the final draft of the archaeological survey for a new subdivision on Lana'i. She turned back to her desk and was sorting through her mail when Gavin McCall appeared at the door. Five days had passed since their encounter with the strange procession on the volcano, and Maile's mood still bore signs of that misadventure. Even Gavin's surprise visit didn't shake it.

"Look at this monstrosity!" she told him, holding up a glossy brochure that had just arrived with the day's mail. "Disgusting!" she declared, tossing it into the pile of clutter on her desk. It slipped over the edge, carrying with it the rest of her mail. Gavin leaned over to retrieve the items from the floor and set all but the brochure back onto her desk.

Gleaming off its front page was a sultry brown girl with long silky hair. A lei of white plumeria barely hid the curve of her young bosom, and a satiny thigh parted her grass skirt. Fern leaves adorned her head, ankles, and wrists, and she beckoned the reader with outstretched arms. At her side stood a shirtless native male with a toothy smile and muscles that rippled across the page. His loins were snugged into a green *malo*. Beneath the photo, in purple ink, the couple declared:

> Come! Live out your dreams at the Royal Paradise Bay Resort, where *fantasies become real*...

"That's what we're turning into!" Maile sneered. "The Disneyland of the Pacific!"

Gavin flipped through the pages until he came upon another portrait, this one of a haole couple. The sleek blonde's blue eyes sparkled beneath a drooping safari hat, and binoculars hung over her shoulder. Her good-looking companion wore a fashionably crumpled shirt, open to expose his chest. Beneath the portrait, the purple print read:

> Adventures happen at the Royal Paradise Bay Resort. Hunt wild boar with a native guide in the forests of Mauna Loa, helicopter to an inaccessible beach for a private picnic, ski down the snowy slopes of Mauna Kea or, guided by a trained geologist, venture on foot into the heart of an active volcano!

"What's happening here?" Maile said. "They're turning our island into a playground for people with more money than taste!"

Gavin heard Maile's words, but his usual verve was subdued after five nights working on the mountain. He scanned a fold-out photo of the entire resort complex.

"It's very fancy," he commented.

"It's obscene, that's what it is! Why did they have to build that thing *here*? They've already ruined O'ahu and Maui!"

Gavin flipped back to the cover photo.

"I wonder if there's even a drop of Polynesian blood in those models!" she said.

Gavin looked up at the real Hawaiian in front of him—the human embodiment of the dynamic land from which she'd come. She has the same energy, he thought, that pulses through the heart of the island. Even he had felt it the other night at the skylight, looking down on the primordial river of fire.

"Damn haoles!" Maile blurted. "Oh, not you, Gavin. You listen. I mean the OTHER haoles, the ones who can't see what's truly special about Hawai'i. I think you recognize the deeper beauty of this place."

"I'm starting to." A long, awkward silence hung between them.

"Gavin," she said finally, a heavy sadness in her voice, "why can't they see it?"

"It's greed, Maile. The great human frailty."

That's right, she thought, the word that expressed so much of Hawai'i's history, especially after statehood. But what happened to that other word—*aloha?* To Hawaiians it means "love." Now it appears on every tourist brochure and box of macadamias. Uttered inconsequentially on the steps of tour buses and in the foyers of hotels. Now it means little more than "hello" or "good-bye." Tears filled Maile's eyes. "And I did the petroglyph survey for that awful resort.

"I thought maybe my work would save the whole area. But that was just a rationalization for getting the job." She shook her head. "They didn't understand the carvings. They saw them as doodles from the past. Hundreds of petroglyphs ripped to rubble by bulldozers. Only a narrow band, containing one-tenth of the carvings, was saved—now stuck between the fairways of two golf courses." She dropped her face into her hands. "What must my ancestors think of me?"

"But Maile, you couldn't have known—"

She waved his words away. "I am responsible. It was my *kuleana*." My responsibility.

"Sometimes we're powerless, Maile," Gavin said softly.

"Maybe so." She smiled at the Australian. "Gavin, I'm sorry for my comment about the haoles. I don't really think you're like them."

"I think we already know each other better than that."

"Our day together on Kilauea was really nice—until the very end. Those men. Maybe that's why I'm so upset." Maile got up and moved toward the Australian. "Look, Gavin, I don't want that incident to spoil what we've started here. There's still so much I'd like to show you. I've thought a lot about you since the other night."

"And I, you. All these days I've been up on the mountain, I've been thinking of you, obsessing, and also worrying about what we saw out there. I'm certain those men were up to no good—and bloody grateful they didn't see us."

"It would *not* have been pleasant. There's a lot of vice in Hawai'i—drugs, gambling, prostitution. Some of it's petty—neighborhood cockfights, marijuana plants in the backyard. But much of it's organized—*well* organized and protected. The connections go all the way from patrolmen on the beat to some of the highest, most prominent political figures in Hawai'i—" She stopped, apprehensive about going on.

"So were those men connected to organized crime?"

"I don't know," she lied. She didn't want to talk about the Hui, a subject all islanders knew was kapu. Off limits. The Hui was known to retaliate for even harmless criticism. Acknowledging its power would expose Gavin to Hawai'i's subterranean culture of violence. Too many local islanders were connected to it in their sprawling extended families—a brother or cousin, an employer or fellow union member. Yet they hesitated to admit a corruption that would tarnish their view of the islands and mar the tourist trade that supported the economy. For some, including Maile, acknowledging Hawai'i's sinister underbelly would mean they would have to do something about it. "Let's just say they're people we don't want to tangle with," she replied.

"That night, on the way back to Hilo, you said they were getting bolder."

"They do their business in strict secrecy, so it was unusual to encounter them in the act." Maile shrugged. "Look, Gavin, let's just forget it. There's nothing we can—or should—do."

He nodded slowly. "I suppose you're right."

"How was your weekend anyway?" she asked, changing the subject.

"Bloody fog's still fouling up the works. There was even ice on the domes this morning. Morale's quite bad, what with few decent observations in more than a week."

"Hmmmm." Maile rubbed her cheek thoughtfully. "Poli'ahu must be in one of her moods."

"Another one of your gods?"

"Mauna Kea's snow goddess."

"Ahh," Gavin nodded. "What's *her* story?"

"Poli'ahu is one of the mountain's ancient deities. The upper slopes, close to the heavens, are her domain, and in her breast beats the heart of the mountain. Our stories tell of a goddess even more luminescent than Pele, and with powers to match."

Gavin grinned. "So you think there's something supernatural messing with the weather?"

Maile returned a knowing smile.

"I'm glad there's a reasonable explanation for our troubles." Gavin's eyes twinkled impishly. "Now all I have to do is try to explain that to me colleagues. Maybe we could all pitch in and make some kind of offering?"

"Wouldn't hurt."

"We did have a brief respite early Sunday morning—clear enough to make calibrations on our infrared camera. We're hoping to resume monitoring of Io this weekend."

"So when are you next scheduled on the telescope?"

"Not till tomorrow, weather permitting—"

Maile's face brightened.

"—but I *should* do a little preparatory number-crunching before then."

"Oh, that's too bad." Maile frowned theatrically. "I was hoping we could do some more exploring."

"Well, it won't take all that much time, just a few hours to reexamine the little bit of data we've got." A sheepish look then crossed his face. "To be honest, Maile, I popped in today just on the off chance you might be free to do something."

She glanced at the papers spread open on her desk. "What did you have in mind?"

"I was thinking of something more tranquil than our last outing, like an excursion to the beach."

Maile pressed her fingers against the marked-up draft report. "I should be finishing this thing, but"—she gathered up the pages and dropped them into her briefcase—"maybe I can look at it tonight."

"Super!" Gavin smiled broadly, displaying his dimples. He pushed open the door. "Is there a beach nearby? I'm a bit road weary after driving down the mountain."

She slipped past Gavin, lightly brushing against him. "I know just the place."

15 ∫ Family Knots

Gavin and Maile hopped into her Jeep and drove toward Keaukaha, the coastal settlement where the luau had been, in the heart of the Hawaiian quarter. Much of the area was designated Hawaiian Homelands in accord with federal law, but state officials had broken the rules over the years to build an airport, a sewage treatment plant, and a solid-waste incinerator. When the Jeep reached an area of spring-fed ponds, Maile turned into the small park on the seaward side of a coastal wetland.

Four Mile Beach, so named because of its distance from downtown, was a favored hangout for local islanders. The brisk saltwater lagoon, cooled by runoff from the springs, offered relief from the stifling humidity that often suffocated the island's windward side. The rock outcrops along the reef were perfect for fishing with throw nets, and the submerged reefs beyond the lagoon teemed with fish easily caught with spears. Locals felt comfortable at Four Mile; it was off the regular path beaten by haoles and whatever mainland tourists found their way to the rainy side and Hilo. For Hawaiians it was ancestral land; their parents and grandparents had bathed in these pools, fished off the rocks, gathered *hala* leaves for mat weaving, and surfed the offshore waves.

Gavin and Maile strolled down the path to a grassy spot near the shore. Robust trades blew off the ocean that afternoon, rattling the fronds of the coconut palms, and the surf thundered over the reef protecting the lagoon. An elderly man swam its wind-wrinkled waters while a Hawaiian woman sitting on the rocks watched her children play in a shallow bay. Far out to sea, under steel-gray clouds, a departing cruise ship approached the horizon. Maile eased herself onto the grass next to a thicket of yellow ginger, its sweet scent mingling with the salt air.

"Lovely spot," Gavin said, leaning against the swooping trunk of a coconut palm. "Now this feels more like Hawai'i."

"More like Hawai'i than what?"

"Than Mauna Kea. I mean, it's bloody austere up there—and cold! Beautiful in its own way, but not like this."

"You mean this beach is more like the Visitors' Bureau image of Hawai'i." Cynicism crept into her voice, a residual of their earlier conversation.

"No, it's like *my* image of the islands, of Polynesia." Gavin gazed out over the scene. "Palm trees and lagoons, islanders lazing by the sea, ships plying the waters between islands. But the volcanoes, now that was the unexpected part. Even here at the beach—bloody lava rock everywhere. Your goddess has been busy, eh?"

Maile smiled. "Go for a swim?"

"Too right! But what are you going to do for a suit?"

"Island girls don't need them," she said laughingly.

"Gawon! In broad daylight?"

"I'm just fanning the flames of your Polynesian fantasy. I often swim after work, so I keep a suit in the Jeep."

Gavin grinned. "Mine's in me duffel, on the backseat."

Maile bounded across the grass toward the parking lot, her hair bouncing in the wind. She returned a few minutes later, clad in a yellow one-piece suit with a pareu wrapped around her waist. A gust caught the flowered fabric, momentarily exposing her strong swimmer's legs. Gavin had already taken off his shoes and shirt, revealing a muscular chest blooming with reddish-blond hair.

"And where are *you* going to change?" she said, tossing him his blue surfer trunks.

"Behind the ginger, where else?"

"There's a bathroom by the—"

"No need to walk all that way," he replied, already maneuvering out of his pants inside a gap in the bushes.

As they strolled toward the shore, one of the freshwater ponds caught Gavin's interest. He stooped down and tossed a pebble into its crystalline water. A cloud of *'opae'ula*—tiny native shrimp—quivered in reaction. It was as if the pool itself had come alive.

"These ponds are amazing!"

"Yeah," she said. "So amazing that the Royal Paradise Bay Resort plowed them under for a parking lot."

"What a shame," Gavin said, watching the little shrimp congregate on the other side of the pond.

At the edge of the turquoise lagoon, Gavin dove in, and the cool water quickly stripped away his worries—the bad weather on Mauna Kea, his unfinished camera trials, and a subliminal anxiety about facing his grief over Annie's death once his Hawai'i project was over.

"Invigorating!" he exclaimed after surfacing.

"The water's cold here because of the springs," Maile hollered, dropping her pareu onto the grass. She positioned herself high on the rocky bank, aware that Gavin was watching her every move and clearly liking it.

"The water's warmer farther out," she said. "I'll show you."

Maile dove. Her yellow suit flashed through the water like a dart of flame, her hair a trail of smoke. She surfaced fifty feet away, near the edge of a rocky islet on the far side of the lagoon, her wet skin radiant.

"C'mon, it's nice over here!" she called. But before she finished her sentence, Gavin had already disappeared beneath the surface.

"Hey!" Maile shouted as something snatched her ankle, tugging her into the water. Gavin leaped up behind her, grinning.

"Scared ya, eh?"

"Sharks have been seen in these waters, you know!" she said.

Suddenly, something grabbed Gavin's legs and he struggled to keep his face above the surface. He kicked madly, and breaking the grip, regained his footing. A few feet away, a bearded old Hawaiian rose out of the water.

"Uncle Aka!" Maile called out.

"Watch out for sharks," he said in a wheezy voice. He pointed at Gavin, "Like this one here!"

Maile laughed. "Even at seventy-three, you're still *kolohe*." A prankster. "You're lucky he doesn't bust you up, Uncle," she teased, then turned to the Australian. "Meet my rascal uncle, Aka."

Aka was her mother's brother, and Maile's favorite uncle. In her teens Maile had often stayed with Uncle Aka's family and relished his retelling of stories passed on to him from his parents and grandparents. She often recalled their account of a visit made to Kilauea crater by Hawai'i's last monarch—Queen Lili'uokalani—and their sorrow when "Yankee haoles" overthrew her constitutional monarchy. Sometimes, under the spell of the potent local hooch, Aka would recite his grandfather's hatred of the sugar plantation tycoons as if it were his own, railing about how "they stole the land, tore out the taro, and flooded the islands with Asian foreigners." Ironically, Aka later fell in love with and married a Chinese plantation girl he'd spotted bathing in a mountain stream, a romance Maile loved to hear repeated. Although Aka's parents shared his grandfather's grudge about importing Asian field hands, their dismay about the plantations did not extend to the workers condemned to backbreaking labor under the blazing sun, and they gladly brought the girl under their big umbrella of aloha. Aunty Hua had also shared with Maile her own rich Asian heritage in ways that Maile's father—more interested in acting American than Chinese—never did.

"Pleasure to meet you, Uncle Aka," Gavin said. They shook hands, local-style.

"Day off?" said Aka, surprised to see Maile at the beach on a weekday afternoon.

"Playing hooky," she replied, stroking the water. "I'm glad to see you still get back to our old beach now and again."

"Whenever I get to Hilo. I came in today looking for a friend, but no can find him." He sucked in a deep breath and tugged his shorts up under his belly. "Well, I gotta get going, Maile. Watch yourself with this one, Gavin."

"Something wrong, Uncle?" Maile said, surprised by the uncharacteristically short visit.

"It's just that I need to check a couple more places for this young guy we're looking for."

"Somebody I know?"

Aka shook his head.

"Where did you last see him?" she asked, immediately assuming familial responsibility to assist if she could.

"Kalapana. I checked the beaches over there, but nobody's seen him. He's been missing since Monday."

"That's two days ago." Maile took Aka's damp arm. "Uncle?"

Aka shook his head as if to say, "Don't ask," and an awkward silence ensued. Gavin broke it. "Is the young bloke a relation of yours?"

"A friend of a friend," Aka replied. How could Aka explain to Maile his concern for Jimmy, a perfect stranger? And he didn't want to discuss the murder or the owl's visit. Aka slogged back toward the lagoon's rocky rim, Maile and Gavin following alongside. As Aka climbed out of the water, he noticed a bundle of ti leaves tucked into the frame of the lifeguard tower—a native sign of good luck.

"Good to have ti leaf when you're guarding other people's safety," he said picking up his towel and cigarettes from the rocks. "I hope wherever the young man is, the ti leaf is nearby."

Maile's eyes flashed. "Gavin, would you mind fetching our towels over there?"

As soon as he was gone, Maile asked, "How can I help, Uncle?"

"Better stay clear of this one," he said.

"You know I won't. You look worried about him."

Maile took Aka's arm and guided him to a patch of grass under the coconut palms. The wind had picked up while they were in the water, and the rustle of bushes and trees, pleasant earlier, now seemed raucous and unnerving. Black clouds hung low over the far coast and distant squalls whisked across the ocean, veiling portions of the offshore horizon.

"Weather's changing," Aka remarked, wrapping his towel over his shoulders.

"Who is this young man?" Maile asked.

"A friend of Jack Hemmingson's."

"I didn't know Captain Jack had any friends."

"Maile." His tone was disapproving.

"Sorry, Uncle. I just never understood how you could get along with that creepy old sailor. He's crass and opinionated, and he drinks too much."

"All true. But he's my friend. You'd be crass and opinionated, maybe even a drunk, if you'd been through what he has." Aka shrugged. "But we're not talking about Jack here. We're talking about a young one, barely out of high school, caught in the middle of something he doesn't understand, something that could get him into trouble."

Aka paused, considering whether to continue. It wasn't that he didn't trust Maile, and he knew she would give him good counsel. But Aka loved Maile like a daughter and didn't want to endanger her with something that might involve the Hui.

"Weather looks a bit nasty," Gavin said, walking up behind them. Seeing they were in a serious discussion, Gavin sat down a little to the side. Aka eyed him apprehensively.

"No worry, Uncle," she said. "Gavin's my friend."

"All right, Maile, maybe you can help me," Aka said. "If you had to lay low over on the Kalapana side, where would you go?"

"Oh, Uncle, not another of our young ones caught up in drugs?"

"I wish it was that simple. This boy's from the mainland, and I'm afraid he's on the run from the Hui."

Maile gasped.

"What's the Hui?" Gavin asked.

"The Hawaiian mafia," Maile said. "I didn't want to tell you, Gavin, but that's who I think those men were Friday night."

"What men!" Aka grabbed Maile's hand.

"I took Gavin to a skylight up near the old Royal Gardens road. We saw a strange procession of men checking out the lava flows."

Aka nodded his head slowly. "So that's why we met at our old beach today. *Mahalo ke akua*." Thank you, God.

Maile glanced at Gavin, certain that Aka's belief in the providence of chance might sound odd to him, but Hawaiians, believing the world worked that way, acted on it. When Maile described the procession to Aka, and the quarreling men at the skylight, he shivered. Those were two of the group Jimmy had described to Jack—murderers within arm's reach of his precious Maile! The owl's scream flashed into his mind.

The squall approached the shore, mist bleeding from the darkening sky. Aka stared into the grass, seemingly unaware of the drizzle splattering his face. "I don't want to talk here," he said, getting up.

"Come with me to Jack's. I'll fill you in on the way."

The couple rose and followed Aka down the path to the parking lot.

Maile squeezed Gavin's arm. "I'm sorry to get you involved in this. Uncle Aka and I will take you back downtown to your truck."

"No way, Maile. I'm coming along. It's getting far too interesting for me to bugger off now."

Just as they reached the parking lot, the sky unloaded a blustery downpour that obscured even the lifeguard tower. The few diehards left at the beach bolted for their cars or dashed into the picnic pavilion. Several coconuts blew out of the palms and thudded onto the grass.

Maile gave Gavin the keys to unlock the Jeep and ran over to Aka, who was already sheltered inside his rickety truck. "We'll follow you, Uncle, but I'm not sure I remember the turnoff to Captain Jack's."

Aka gently pulled her into the passenger seat. "I don't want to talk about this in front of the haole."

"Gavin was with me. He saw everything I did."

"How well do you know him?"

"Well enough."

Aka's eyes turned grave. "You trust him?"

"Yes."

"You two are . . . involved, then?"

"No."

"Not yet, anyway," he said.

She shrugged her shoulders.

Aka thought for a moment. "You say he can be trusted. OK, have him come too—in your Jeep. You ride with me so we can talk alone first."

"Gavin," Maile hollered through the rain, "I'm riding with Uncle Aka. You follow us, OK?"

"Righto. Just don't lose me. I don't know the roads."

He pulled up behind them, wondering if what Aka had said was true, that he and Maile had been called to this place to play out their roles in some larger puzzle and help find the young tourist in trouble.

16 ∫ The Dark Reunion

Passing through the ruined village of Kalapana only affirmed Gavin's feelings of dread as he followed Aka and Maile to Captain Jack's. Nothing remained of the town's center, save for a salvaged nineteenth-century church up on blocks and the melted remnant of a plastic drive-in restaurant sign. As Aka's old pickup wiggled down the long stony driveway toward the old sailor's cabin, Gavin maneuvered Maile's Jeep around thick tongues of lava that had spilled onto the road—vivid signs of the eruption that on the night of the murder made Jimmy wonder whether anyone actually lived down there. The rain, which no doubt still pounded Hilo, had played out a few miles beyond Pahoa, but the overcast sky and impending nightfall made the trip seem all the more ominous. Gavin noticed the eerie yellow glow on the coconut palms—from the cabin's lanai light—that had drawn Jimmy down the road that night. For a moment Gavin pictured himself safely back on Mauna Kea, perusing the latest issue of *Sky and Telescope* in front of the base camp fireplace, far removed from the mysterious undertones of an island culture he could never hope to understand.

He reached the ramshackle cabin just as Maile stepped out of Aka's truck, her face even grimmer than that night at the skylight.

"What's this? A friggin' surprise party?" said a disembodied voice from the dark jungle.

"Jack? Where are you?" Aka called out.

Captain Jack emerged from behind a clump of ginger at the edge of the yard, zipping up his khakis as he walked back into the light. "Jeez, a guy can't even pee in privacy anymore! Who's your entourage, Aka?"

"You remember my niece, Maile Chow."

"Oh yeah." Jack nodded indifferently.

"And this is her friend—"

"—Gavin McCall," the astronomer said, stepping forward.

"Aussie, huh?" Years of military travel had taught Jack to discern an accent from a single word.

"From Canberra, actually."

"Welcome to my humble dump. So, Aka, what's the occasion?"

"Jimmy wasn't the only one to see those men Friday night."

Jack scanned the somber faces of his three visitors. "C'mon up. I'll fetch us some beers."

Aka followed Jack into the cabin while Maile and Gavin propped themselves against the railing of the lanai. The old cat Silver scowled at the intruders, then set his head back down on the rail, one wary eye peering out beneath a furry lid.

"Gavin," Maile said, setting her hand on his arm, "the situation is much worse than I first thought. I appreciate that you've come along to fill in details of the story, but you don't want to get any deeper into this. As soon as we've finished telling them what we saw, I'll take you back into town."

Gavin should have felt relieved, but didn't. One thing was certain; if he bowed out now, circumstances could veer him and Maile away from each other, and Gavin wasn't ready for that. "No. I'm in this with you," he told her.

"I appreciate the sentiment, but this a serious situation. We could all become dangerously entangled."

ENTANGLED. He'd been avoiding all forms of entanglement since his wife's death. His stare fell into Maile's eyes, eyes so dark they seemed not to be orbs at all, but black pools. "I realize that. I don't care," he heard himself say.

"Gavin, think carefully. We don't know where this is going to lead."

"I'm in. That's all there is to it." The instant he said the words, his heart dropped in that way it does when a person approaches a precipice.

The jarring squeak of the screen door interrupted the conversation, and Captain Jack and Aka stepped out onto the lanai, Steinlagers in tow.

"Well, Maile," Jack said, "I see we have somethin' in common again—and another mess at that. She tell you what we've got ourselves into, Gavin?" he said, handing him a beer.

"Not exactly."

"Then what have you two been talkin' about out here, Maile? The friggin' humidity?" Jack plopped down in one of the wicker chairs. Aka watched mutely from the other.

"Shut up, Jack," she replied sharply, a response that startled Gavin.

"So ya ain't yet told 'im we're into murder."

"Murder?" Gavin glanced back at Maile.

"It's actually *worse* than that, Gavin, m'boy. Accordin' to the kid who witnessed it, they burned a man alive, threw 'im right into the volcano and watched 'im sizzle!" Jack took a long drink off his bottle and set it down on the floor next to several already emptied.

"Jesus—"

Maile reached over to take the beer offered by Aka. "I told you, Gavin, it's ugly."

Gavin walked to the far end of the lanai—where Jimmy had so anxiously stood on the night of the murder—and looked into the coconut palms, swaying silhouettes against a shrouded sky that throbbed red from the incessant eruption. Gavin turned to face the group. "Well, somebody had best fill me in, eh?"

Jack lit up his pipe. "A'right, I'll tell ya the story as told to me by the lad who saw it happen . . ." Aka sank deeper into his chair, and no one said a word as Jack recounted Jimmy's gruesome tale. ". . . And when Aka and me got back up to the cabin," the old sailor concluded, "the kid had disappeared without a trace."

"What about those tire tracks on the driveway?" Aka asked quietly.

Jack shrugged. "Hard tellin' how long they'd been there. Might o' been one of the boys from Friday's gin game."

"Jimmy disappeared Monday morning?" Maile asked.

"Yeah. Three days and no sign of 'im! And o' course, I got no phone so we ain't heard from him neither."

"We've checked every hotel," Aka added, "even the airlines."

"He ain't left the island, that's for sure, not unless he went by boat, and he ain't the type to run by sea."

Maile turned to Aka. "And you feel the owl scream in your dream was a sign?"

The old Hawaiian nodded.

"This weren't no ordinary murder," Jack said, the last of his beer gurgling in his throat.

"*Mohai*," Aka muttered, dread shadowing his face. "A sacrifice."

Gavin was shocked. "But surely—"

"Uncle, those practices died long ago."

He shook his head. "What about those angry young radicals? I've heard some of them Kapu Hawai'i people have been dabbling with the dark side."

"Kapu Hawai'i isn't into that kind of thing, Uncle. They're a political movement. I know some of those people."

"So do I, Maile. Some of the young ones idealize the old religion without really understanding its power. In the name of their cause, they would do anything, even bring back the evil of Pa'ao."

Gavin tapped Maile's arm. "Pa'ao?"

"A Tahitian priest who led the religious conquest of Hawai'i in the thirteenth century," Maile explained. "He brought slavery and human sacrifice to these islands."

Jack knocked the char from his pipe and started repacking it. "I say it was plain old murder, probably the Hui shutting somebody up. They figured they'd use the volcano to cover the evidence, but they must o' been mighty upset with that guy, to burn 'im alive and all." The old man lit his pipe. "Anybody want some whiskey?"

Maile shook her head.

"*'A'ole*," Aka said, lifting his beer bottle, still half-full.

"Yeah, I'd take a spot," the Australian said

Jack pushed his heavy frame out of the chair and disappeared into the cabin, leaving a trail of smoke in the doorway.

"Uncle, at the beach you said you thought it might be the Hui."

Aka shrugged. "If it was those crooks, then I don't think there's much hope of finding Jimmy. And Jack could be in danger too, if they think the kid talked."

Maile turned to the sea. The waves rolled in steadily, breaking on the rocks like booming drums at a native funeral. "But why the ceremony? And why at the eruption, where they might be seen? Why not just kill him in the usual way, on a tuna boat?"

"That's why I think it could be the radicals."

"Uncle Aka, the men Gavin and I saw were thugs, not activists. I agree with Jack. I think it was the Hui. I felt so at the time."

Jack blustered through the screen door carrying two tall glasses filled with ice. "I shoulda left this island years ago," he mumbled, handing a tumbler to Gavin. "It's been downhill ever since World War II." He pulled a half-empty liter of Jack Daniels out of his sea chest cubby, drowned his own cubes, and walked the bottle over to Gavin. "We should o' left these islands to the Hawaiians," he said, filling up the Australian's glass, despite Gavin's finger pointing only halfway to the rim. "But they probably would o' messed it up too."

"Whatever happened," Aka said, "we need to find Jimmy, if he's still alive."

"Where could he be hiding?" Gavin asked.

"There are lots of places on the volcano—deep forests, hidden valleys, caves—but in order to find them, Jimmy would have to know much more than he does."

"He doesn't know squat!" Jack blurted. "Idiot's probably gone back to the cops!"

"No," Aka said, "not after the way they treated him."

The old sailor grunted.

Aka pulled a Kool out of his pack and lit it. "Nobody around Kalapana has seen him. I also talked to my nephew, Kimo. He's a cop in Hilo—and I trust him."

"Aka's got relations in ev'ry nook and cranny of this island—not that it's gonna help us now!" A belligerent tone crept into Jack's voice as whiskey seeped into his brain.

"Uncle, what's to say that Jimmy didn't head back into the national park, even cross over into the Ka'u desert? Nobody would find him out there."

"Put yourself into his mind, Maile." Aka tapped his forehead.

"According to Jack, Jimmy is inquisitive, stubborn, and a little self-righteous."

"Now who does *that* sound like?" Jack said, poking his pipe stem at Maile. His speech began to slur. "Like your mother."

"She was never self-righteous!"

"Aw, she bought all that missionary bull, and you know it."

"Jack, I don't want to talk about this."

"Why not? What are you doin' out here anyway, disturbin' my peace?"

"Knock it off, Jack," Aka said in a stern, fatherly tone. "What's past is past. Right now we gotta find Jimmy."

Jack slouched into the deep sag of the wicker. "Yeah, right." He put the tumbler to his lips, threw his head back, and emptied the glass.

"Maybe he's gone back up to Royal Gardens to hide," Aka said. "There's a few old houses still standing."

Gavin jumped in with his analysis. "These people don't know Jimmy witnessed the murder. According to Captain Jack here, Jimmy said he kept himself hidden until all the murderers left. And as far as anyone knows, he never spoke a word of what he'd seen to anyone but Captain Jack. Not even the police."

"Hmmm. At least that's something to hope for," Maile said.

"Yes, if the story's been recounted to us accurately." Gavin looked over at Jack. The old sailor's eyes were unfocused and his head swayed as if tossed by the breeze.

"Well, then he's in hiding," she replied, "or he's left the island altogether."

"Tha's what he'd do if he had a lick o' sense in 'im, but he's dumb—spunky, but dumb!" Well into another glass of whiskey, Jack's murky blue pupils floated freely over his bloodshot eyes. "Dumb fool! Why *didn't* I leave while the leavin' was good, head back over to Superior, up there in those sweet Minnesota woods?" His whole upper body swayed. "I kept thinkin' things 'ill change, but she, she . . ." The rest was inaudible.

The three of them sat silently watching Captain Jack slip into delirium. Suddenly he grasped the arms of the chair and pushed his body forward in the wicker, pressing his face so close to Maile she could smell his sour breath.

"Wharishenow, Maile? Whar'dshego after yer dad died? Huh?"

Maile stared back at the pathetic old drunk, trying to reconcile what he had become with the strapping young sailor she remembered walking with her mother, arm in arm, on Waikiki Beach. That was back in 1969, when Maile was just a little girl.

"Isheawright, Maile? I mean, OK and all that?"

So he hadn't heard. He didn't know a heart attack had taken Maile's mother away that previous Christmas. Maile peered into his ruddy, tearstained face. "She's fine, Jack. She's happy now."

"T'ank God." He fell back into the chair, his arms limp over the sides. He reached down to pick up his glass but knocked it over. The whiskey seeped through the lanai planking, leaving little ice lumps on the floor. Silver looked up from the rail.

"Jack, I think you better go to bed," said Aka, rising to help his friend.

"Prob'ly right," Jack mumbled.

Gavin helped Aka ease the old sailor out of his chair. As they maneuvered him to the door, Jack looked over his shoulder at Maile. "Sorry, ev'rybody . . . carry on."

Maile walked up and placed her hand on his sweaty shoulder. "Good-night, Captain Jack," she said, and he nodded sadly.

Gavin and Aka walked him through the doorway. The screen slammed behind them, but not before Silver slipped inside to follow the old man to his bed. Maile retrieved her Steinlager from the railing and slumped into the wicker chair where Jack had been. She lifted the bottle to her lips and drank, then stared out into the eerie yellow glow that dimly illuminated the trees.

17 ∫ Pele and the Astronomer

"Sorry to drag you into all this, Gavin," Maile said, maneuvering the Jeep around a finger of lava jutting across Captain Jack's driveway.

"Actually, I'm the one who got us into this mess. If I hadn't asked about Pele . . ." Gavin glanced over at the crimson clouds above the volcano.

"Are you sure you want to go in there with me tomorrow?" Maile asked.

"Somebody's got to search for the kid. And you can't go alone."

"Yes, I can."

"I *want* to go with you, Maile."

Maile smiled, but the storm in her eyes was visible in the green glow of the dash. "I have a terrible feeling about this whole thing. Organized crime has a long history of brutality in these islands, protecting their vice operations and other interests, economic and political. This murder has all the earmarks of a Hui killing, and yet—the number of murderers and the ritual—it doesn't make sense. I wish we could talk to Jimmy. Maybe there were other ceremonial articles used that night. I'd like to hear his version of this, unpolluted by Captain Jack."

"Seems doubtful you'll get the chance."

She nodded solemnly, turning the Jeep onto the main road.

"You don't think this is something for the police?" he asked.

"Eventually maybe, but there's always the concern about corrupt cops. I agree with Jack on that."

"Speaking of Captain Jack—"

"I wish he weren't involved."

"And not just because he drinks, eh?"

Maile looked over at Gavin. "No. They were lovers at one time, he and my mother. For years I thought he was an uncle."

She paused, collecting her thoughts from the past. "My mother was innocent, I suppose like all islanders used to be. I remember his shore-leave visits, the way her face lit up when he'd tell his stories of all the exotic places he'd been, things she knew she'd never experience as long as she stayed with my father. She fell in love with the Captain. I didn't know that at the time, of course, but later I could understand the attraction."

Maile laughed bitterly. "Funny to think of him that way, especially after tonight. It's sad, really. My mother was very beautiful, and she inherited my grandmother's passion. Men sensed this, and years later I tried to convince myself that Jack just wanted her physically. Of course I was fiercely loyal to Dad, and I never forgave Jack for the strains he put on my family during their affair. But eventually I came to realize that the Captain really did love her. And she loved him—the handsome sailor with his stories." Maile shook her head and laughed. "Yes, Jack was *crazy* about her—we say *pupule*. Can you blame him? She was beautiful, intelligent, and true of heart."

"Just like her daughter," Gavin said warmly. The lights of a passing car passed over his handsome face, and Maile was tempted to pull over right then and there. Fueled by adrenaline from the night's events and stirred by his penetrating gaze, she wanted to kiss him.

"Maybe," she said, deciding it best to change the subject. "All this we're driving through is Pele country, the part of the volcano where her clan first arrived. Many legends take place here, and many Pele sightings—even now." She glanced over at Gavin for a reaction, but he was staring out the window.

"I was just thinking about Kalapana, how it's been marked by Pele's hand."

She looked away, remembering. "Kalapana was like something out of your imagination. A centuries-old fishing village fronted by a long sweep of volcanic black sand. That beach was famous all over the world. Under the moon, it was a fairy tale."

"She must be a cruel goddess to have destroyed such a place."

"Who's to say she didn't have a good reason? Some of the old Hawaiians say a kahuna reported that Pele had come to him one night to warn that if the sacred rainforest above Kalapana was torn apart to make way for subdivisions and a planned hotel, she would destroy the whole village and everything else on the coast. The forests were to be left alone for her people to hunt, pick maile vine, and gather medicinal herbs. The story surfaced when the county considered approving the first subdivision, Royal Gardens. And now the entire coast, from Kalapana deep into the national park—including Royal Gardens and two other subdivisions—is buried under tons of lava. And there are no more plans for a hotel."

Gavin stared at her in silence.

"You're having a hard time accepting Pele, aren't you?"

"I'm a scientist."

"So am I," she replied, "but lately I wonder—"

"What?"

"I wonder if maybe I've gotten too far from my roots. I know these spiritual ideas are hard to accept until you've been here awhile, until you see some of what happens."

"I understand the bit about Pele as a symbol, but this business about sightings. That's as hard to accept as those crazy UFO stories, even though I believe there is other life out there."

"Do you think *I'm* crazy?"

"No, and that's why I'm puzzled."

"Remember I told you that lots of different people report having seen Pele in one form or another? May I tell you the story about the astronomer?"

"Go ahead. Anything is better than talking about the murder."

She took a deep breath and began: "The professor was an older man, nearing retirement, a University of Hawai'i astronomer who'd spent most of his career studying Mars. He'd observed on Mauna Kea since the late 1960s, before there were any really big telescopes on the mountain. I'd met him once or twice over the years, at public meetings about the expansion of the observatories. He was your typical scientist—reserved in manner and cautious about his conclusions."

Gavin laughed lightly. "I know the type."

"About five years ago the professor showed up at my office without an appointment. He looked much older than I'd remembered, his face pinched with stress. He paced the room, constantly fidgeting with his beard. I soon realized it wasn't the intervening years that had aged him, but the previous twenty-four hours. His hands trembled as he told me he'd experienced something unexplainable the night before. He thought I might know what it meant.

"He said he was driving Saddle Road back to Hilo, flanked by Mauna Kea and Mauna Loa under brilliant midnight stars. Just as the road dipped into the forest, his headlights flashed across an old woman sitting beside the road. Encountering someone way up there, miles from town, took him by surprise, and he hadn't noticed a stranded vehicle. Exhausted from his nights on the mountain, the professor concluded that his truck lights on the trees must have tricked him. A glance in his rearview mirror was his confirmation.

"Imagine his surprise when a minute later his lights flashed across yet another old woman, sitting beneath a stand of ʻohiʻa trees. There *must* have been an accident, he thought, leaving two women stranded on the road. But where was the wreck? And why hadn't either woman flagged him down?

"He pulled over and slowly reversed the truck, but no one was there, only twisted trees silhouetted against the stars. He got out and checked farther up the road, but it was empty too. While returning to his truck, a strange chill spread over his body—what we call 'chicken skin.' When he opened the door, he found the same Hawaiian woman sitting in the passenger seat. She had long white hair and a face creviced with age.

" 'What are you doing way up here?' he asked.

"She smiled at him, staring with what he described as 'bizarre shimmering eyes.' Agitated, he asked her, 'Has there been an accident? Are you alone? Who is that back up the road?'

"She just stared at him and smiled.

" 'Damn it, woman! Speak to me!' he insisted.

"Her eyes flared. He said it was as if the pupils turned to flame. She shook her head and pointed toward Hilo. Unable to solicit any other response, he drove the truck down the winding road. The old woman just stared out the windshield, that strange glow in her eyes. Whatever reason for the encounter she kept to herself.

"Just above the city, near the old Kaumana caves, she tapped his shoulder and pointed to the overgrown entrance to the lava tube. When he turned back, she was gone. Only a few shards of lava remained, bouncing on the vinyl seat. His shoulder, where her fingers had touched him, felt hot all the way to Hilo, although there was no sear to be seen. The next day he came to see me. And shortly after that, he retired. I think he's on the mainland now."

Gavin exhaled loudly. "That's quite a story. What did you tell the astronomer his encounter meant?"

"I told him she was probably curious about this man who was always driving up and down the volcanoes. I also told him he did the right thing giving her a ride."

"Quite honestly, I don't know what to think, Maile. This whole place is so strange, so mysterious."

"Just stay open. You might surprise yourself."

"What time do you want to get started tomorrow?" Gavin asked, changing the subject as the lights of Hilo came into view.

"Early," she said. "You can stay with me if you'd like."

His face perked with surprise.

"It's late," she said, curling her lips into a smile. "I have a spare futon if you don't mind sleeping on the floor."

"All right. Thanks."

As Maile drove into town, Gavin studied her beautiful face. Her soft mango cheeks, framed by her magnificent hair, reflected the city's night glow.

"This could be dangerous," he muttered, the unbidden words a sign of his growing attraction to Maile—and the unresolved grief of losing his wife, Annie, in an accident that still haunted him.

Maile was excited to have Gavin come home with her, even if only as a practical solution to the late hour. She sighed quietly, pleasantly aware of a familiar hunger. It had been almost a year since she'd left her last boyfriend.

Maile's house was a short distance past Four Mile Beach. By

that time, almost midnight, the road was deserted except for a few Hawaiians talking story and drinking beer over the bed of a pickup. Maile pulled into a driveway, and her little bungalow came into view. It faced the ocean, its spacious lanai lined with flowering plants.

"Please, come in," Maile said, turning off the engine.

Gavin followed her up onto the lanai. "I'm bushed," he said, plopping into one of two chaise longues.

"It's been a full day, hasn't it?" Maile replied. "Would you like a drink or something?"

Gavin yawned. "If you are."

"Yes, I'm wired. Gin and tonic OK?"

"Gin, eh?" He cracked a twisted smile. "Is this part of the Pele thing?"

Maile laughed. "No, I just like gin."

Maile opened the sliding door into the house, but paused before entering. "You know, that story about Pele's love for gin is just twentieth-century lore. I suspect it began with the old Greek who owned the Volcano House hotel on the crater back in the 1920s. I think he started the myth to boost his liquor sales. But you can believe what you want." She grinned and disappeared inside the bungalow.

Gavin settled into the chaise longue. It felt good to put his feet up. The night sky was still overcast and a light drizzle misted the air. Dark waves broke along the shore, reminding him of the lagoon at Four Mile. Good heavens, was that this afternoon? His mind thought about all that had happened since he'd stepped into Maile's cramped office less than a week earlier.

"Here you are," Maile said, returning to the lanai with his drink. "I'll join you in a minute."

"Good on yer, mate," he replied as she stepped back inside.

He took a long swallow and stared out at the sea. But the alcohol did not ease his anxiety. It wasn't just the murder. Maile was drawing him into a primordial world—of jungle and volcanoes, gods and goddesses, animal omens, ancient rituals, eerie apparitions . . . human sacrifice. Tomorrow they would venture onto the active lava flows to search for signs of Jimmy. Had he lost his own bearings letting himself get drawn into all this intrigue? And what about the astronomy work he had come here to do? Gavin looked up at the cloudy sky. Jupiter was behind there somewhere. Just a star would have been reassuring.

Standing in front of the bathroom mirror, Maile saw how exhausted she was. What she needed was a quick blast of hot water to rinse off the day. In the shower, her mind spun a tapestry of thoughts about Gavin. She saw his dazzling eyes and heard him say, "I'm in this with you, Maile." What man—besides her father—had ever said that? She felt herself opening up, drawn to Gavin by both his spirit *and* his lean good looks.

But a voice of caution called up from within. Had she told Gavin too much about the island and her people's ways? Would he ultimately misconstrue what she had shared, like so many other haoles? And yet, the snow goddess had thrown them together, hadn't she, by covering the mountain with ice?

"*Maka'ala*," she said, turning off the tap. Pay attention and be careful.

She slipped into a colorful pareu and, as an afterthought, stuck a plumeria blossom from a bathroom bouquet behind her ear.

By the time she rejoined Gavin on the lanai, he was sound asleep, his drink gone. She tiptoed back inside and returned with a cotton blanket. Gingerly she removed his shoes and socks and covered him up. Crouching next to him, she watched him doze. His sandy hair was tousled, his skin sunburned from their afternoon at the beach, and his jaw bristled with a day's growth of beard. He has such a nice face, Maile thought—welcoming, open—then brushed her hand against his cheek and went inside to bed.

18 ∫ Back to Pele's Realm

EARLY THURSDAY MORNING, JUNE 8, IN KEAUKAHA . . .

"I want you . . ."

"Huh?"

"I want you . . ."

"What?" Gavin, befuddled after a deep dreamless sleep, lifted his head from the chaise longue cushion. He rubbed his face and gazed out toward the sea. No one there and still no stars. "Bloody warm tonight," he mumbled, kicking off the blanket. He dropped his head back onto the cushion, damp with sweat, and closed his eyes.

"I want you . . ." the voice echoed.

He bolted upright and peered into the rustling trees. Darkness was fading, replaced by a dull ruby glow.

"Where am I? The volcano? Captain Jack's?" He blinked the sleep out of his eyes. "No, I'm at Maile's house, in Hilo."

"Come to me . . ."

"Who's there?" he whispered. The surf thundered against the rocks. I must be dreaming, he thought . . . just the ocean. He began drifting off, but an awareness crept up on him—of something moving on the lanai.

"Come . . ." A rustle, behind him.

Slowly he turned over on the cushion and noticed that everything on the lanai was maroon, reflecting some aberrant light. Then he saw her, against the far wall, a throbbing scarlet figure with a golden aura that cast shadow and hue on floor and wall. The radiance overwhelmed her facial features, and long gilded hair blew wildly about her head. Her arms reached out, beckoning.

Gavin rubbed his eyes, then looked again. She was still there. In slow motion, he rose in the chaise longue and set one foot on the ground. His toes revolted against the cool cement. Where are my shoes? he thought. Glancing up, he saw the glowing woman slip around the corner of the house and disappear into the trees, her radiance shimmering. Then the bright light dissipated and the lanai darkened, leaving only a dull ruby glow against the wall.

Gavin fell back on the cushion and stared at the ceiling. "Weird," he muttered. He considered following the apparition into the yard, but that thought made him feel both nervous and silly. "I'm losing me grip," he said, shaking his head. He lay there trying to reconstruct what had just happened, but he couldn't put it together in his mind. He let his eyes shut and tried again, but sleep came first. When at last his eyes opened again, the lanai was as bright as day, and the woman standing before him was Maile.

"Good morning," she said in a robust voice. "How'd you sleep?"

"Fine, except"—how does one explain this sort of thing?—"I had a bizarre dream."

"I thought so." Maile leaned back on the lanai railing, her eyes dreamy. She was already dressed, in a T-shirt and jeans, and her hair gleamed in the morning light. "You were talking in your sleep. I came out to see if you were OK, but you were dead to the world. I made Kona coffee. Want some?"

Gavin pushed himself up from the cushions and set his feet on the floor.

"Did you take my shoes off last night?"

"Yes, but I didn't take any other liberties." Maile smiled impishly, and Gavin laughed.

"I really pooped out on you." He scratched his bristled face. "Sorry to be such an awful guest, and I apologize for waking you. You say I mumbled something?"

"Actually you shouted, something about the volcano."

"What time was this?"

"About an hour ago, around sunrise."

Sunrise? No wonder everything on the lanai was red. It was day breaking! Gavin spun around. There was the wall where he'd seen the apparition beckoning. A tall clump of potted red ti leaves stood trembling in the wind.

Maile peered into Gavin's puzzled face. "Are you OK?"

"Fine. Just fine. But your stories about Pele are getting under me skin." He pointed toward the wall. "I could have sworn she was standing right over there."

"Oh?"

"Enough of this bloody nonsense. How about that cup of Kona?"

"I'll go get it."

While she was gone, something else came to mind—a vague recollection that someone had touched him in the night. He looked down at his shoes, neatly set against the wall.

Maile returned with a steaming mug in one hand and an antique volume of Pele legends in the other. She held it open to the frontispiece. "She look like that?"

"Very funny."

Gavin felt more himself after two cups of coffee and a shower. The couple ate a quick breakfast and packed for their venture on the lava, and within the hour, they were headed back to Kalapana.

"I'd prefer not to talk to Jack," Maile said as they pulled into the old sailor's driveway.

"Righto. I understand."

The cabin came into view, but Captain Jack's old Dodge Dart was gone.

She parked the Jeep under the palms. Gavin wrote out a brief note and tucked it into the screen door. Meanwhile, Maile wove her hair into a thick braid to keep it out of her face.

"It's going to be a scorcher," Gavin declared, rolling up his sleeves. They each took a drink of water, replaced the bottle in Maile's backpack, and proceeded down Captain Jack's driveway to the flow field. Gavin helped Maile step up onto the lava from the remains of the road, and they gazed across the inundated coastal plain, black rock as far as the eye could see. A quarter mile away a giant steam plume marked the current lava flow's entry into the sea.

"You really think Jimmy's out here?" Gavin said.

"I don't know, but maybe we can find some trace of him."

"How do we even begin?" he asked. "We can't just stumble around out here."

"First, we find the murder place. We know from Captain Jack's account that it was upslope where lava was filling a deep hole. But the active flow and the terrain around it changes constantly, and that was almost a week ago."

"By now that hole is probably crusted over, and lava could be flowing in an entirely different area." Gavin rubbed his bristled chin. "It's easiest for me to think of it like an astronomy problem. You have this enormous black space, constantly changing, dynamic. But it contains features that explain the formation of the whole space—the lava universe, if you will—and what it might have looked like when Jimmy was here."

"OK. But how can we tell that?"

"Just like we do when we're looking for planets we think are there, but cannot see—by *inference*, by noticing how those unseen objects affect the things we *can* see, like the suns around which planets revolve. In the case of the lava, we examine today's flows, then hypothesize where they might have been a week ago by looking at the *pattern* of flows nearby. The more recent flows will be hotter and have a shinier, less weathered surface than the older ones."

"That makes sense logically," Maile said, looking upslope. "But in my culture, we would approach the problem differently. We wouldn't *think* our way through it. We would *feel* our way, using our *na'au*." Maile placed a hand on her belly. "We follow our instincts and pick up cues too subtle to discern with the conscious mind. Our na'au calls on what we already know from all our previous experiences, including those of our ancestors."

"Ah," Gavin nodded, "like the Aborigines, or for that matter anyone who lives in the bush. No doubt people in these islands are in touch with their instincts, but I'm no good at that. I have to think it through logically with step-by-step observation and analysis."

"I may be a little out of touch with my instincts too—but not completely."

"All right, Maile, you use your na'au, and I'll use my head. I suggest we start where Jimmy did—out there." Gavin pointed at the towering steam plume on the coast. "Then we look at the whole bloody place from *that* point of view, as he must have that night."

That felt right to Maile. They trekked past the burned remains of coconut palms, cars, and other debris from the once-thriving village. The lava grew hotter as they approached the sea cliff where the lava tube emptied into the sea. The whole landscape was buckled with tumuli—huge plates of lava thrust up by subterranean flows. Gavin moved right to the cliff edge, at which point Maile fell behind.

"What's wrong?" he asked, looking back at her.

"This is close enough."

Gavin stared at the fiery scene below the cliff, following it to where the sea fumed, its waves dotted with steaming hunks of fresh lava suffused with hot gas.

"Magnificent!" he hollered through the coastal wind. Maile smiled, but her eyes registered concern until Gavin stepped back from the cliff and returned to where she waited.

"All right, let's get started," he said, wiping away a brine of salt, sulfur, and sweat. "According to Captain Jack's story, Jimmy headed upslope from here—but in what direction?"

"He followed the tube," Maile said, surprising herself with her own certainty.

Gavin scanned the slope and noticed a line of fumy wisps venting out of fissures in the ceiling above the underground lava tube through which the lava river flowed. "That makes sense, because whatever lava outbreaks Jimmy saw that night probably came from excess lava pushed out of fissures along the tube." He pointed at the gas vapors leading up the pali. "So we follow the fumes above the tube and look for areas that are flowing now, as well as those that might have been flowing recently. Maile, where exactly were we the other night when you showed me the skylight?"

She pointed to a spot a mile up the pali, easily identifiable because of the massive black flow bisecting the forest near the skylight.

"Then if we follow a line between here and there, we ought to walk pretty much right above the tube."

Gavin bounded forward, but Maile hesitated. She peered across the fumy terrain, watching for a sign—a bird, the wind, an odd cloud.

"Gavin," she said involuntarily.

"What's wrong?"

Maile knew Gavin's plan made *logical* sense, but her gut told her to be careful. Was it just irrational fear? "Never mind," she said.

They pressed forward above the tube, stepping over numerous steaming cracks lined with yellow sulfur. Huge tumuli rose nearby, some as high as eight feet, and a few were flanked by recent flows whose crusts were still shiny and warm. Their boot soles seethed, and at one point, shelly lava under Gavin's feet gave way, collapsing a few inches. He examined the shattered crust. "It's just the surface," he reassured her—and himself. "There's solid rock underneath."

"But remember, Gavin, there's a river of molten lava under the rock we're walking on. In some places the ceiling above the tube might be only a few inches thick, and that river is 2,000 degrees hot."

"All right. We can parallel the tube, but we still need to stay close to it."

They moved about twenty feet to the right of the tube and proceeded upslope. Maile's concern took on a sharper focus. She felt as if someone or something was watching, and she carried this feeling with each step, her instincts on full alert. She stopped to gaze into the forest above the distant ridge, watching for movement among the trees. That's when she noticed an enormous koa tree standing high above the desolation far ahead. She made a note of it.

"Something wrong?" Gavin said, growing impatient with their halting progress.

"No, just feeling my way up the volcano."

But it was not long before Maile stopped again.

"Now what?" Gavin asked.

"Listen."

Far from the wind and wave noise of the coast, a new sound could be heard—the crackling of lava extruding from rock.

"Follow me!" Maile said, bounding upslope. Within minutes, a long low line of red came into view, lava oozing down the hillside.

"Righto!" Gavin exclaimed. "Our first surface flow. Let's go have a look."

Gavin bolted ahead of Maile's more cautious pace and soon stood at the flow. He watched the lava migrate downslope, filling in depressions. "Let's check all around here," he said. "Look for anything that could have been a large hole before the lava filled it up, a depression into which the murderers could have pushed the victim that night."

"Keep an eye out for signs of human activity too," Maile replied, "cigarette butts, film canisters, that kind of thing."

They split up and searched the entire area. Nothing. No hole—filled or otherwise—big enough to bury a man in, and no signs of human contact.

They continued upslope, still paralleling the tube, but Maile began having second thoughts about their course. Her sensation of being watched persisted. Along the way, they checked small outbreaks of lava but found no clues. With each stop, Maile's anxiety grew.

Near one outbreak, Gavin and Maile sat down to rest. The coast was far away, and the distant steam plume looked tiny. Far across the wasteland, Maile spotted the roof of Captain Jack's cabin in an island of coconut trees surrounded by black rock. Why would Pele spare *his* house? she wondered.

Further up the pali she saw the ruins of several houses and a burned truck. The skylight could not be far away. Again she noticed the giant koa tree towering over a forested island between flows, much closer now.

"This way," she said, abruptly climbing to her feet.

"But I think the tube heads to the left," Gavin protested.

"Maybe, but what we're looking for is over here." She left Gavin and the tube, following her feelings, which were stronger than ever.

Gavin didn't follow, and instead set his course so he could keep both Maile and the fumes above the lava tube in sight.

That's when she saw the hawk swoop over the pali. Was this the same ʻio they had seen a week ago at the crater? Her naʻau said yes, but was the hawk guiding her to her destination *or* warning her away? Maile moved cautiously in the direction of the bird. The hawk circled above the forest, then lighted on the tallest branch of the koa tree. Maile pressed on toward the bird while Gavin continued to check closer to the tube. The distance between them widened. A moment later, Gavin heard a scream.

He spotted Maile crouching next to a slowly moving lava flow.

"Maile!" He dashed across the rough terrain, but his shoe caught the raised edge of a crack, throwing him down. He leaped back up without inspecting the angry scrape on his arm. "Maile! Are you all right? I heard your scream."

"It wasn't me. It was him." She pointed at the hawk perched high on the koa, its head turned in their direction. "And look where he's brought me."

A few feet in front of Maile, a short distance from the fresh flow, was a charred tennis shoe half-buried under the lava. A camera lay nearby, its shoulder strap melted into the rock.

19 ∫ The Portuguese Lieutenant

THE NEXT MORNING . . .

"Still nothing 'bout a murder or a missing Hawaiian in the police blotter," Captain Jack said from his wicker chair on the lanai. He slapped the newspaper on the spool table, intentionally disturbing the old tom's nap. "I sure as hell hope that doesn't mean the cops are in on it."

"The Hui's good at keeping things like this under wraps," Aka said from the other chair. "If they planted an excuse for the guy being gone—'out fishing or gone to Honolulu'—his family may not even suspect yet."

"Or they're scared to death to do anything about it."

"It's been a whole week, Jack, and there aren't even rumors on the coconut wireless."

The old sailor scowled at his Timex. "What's taking the cops so long?"

"Things move slowly on this end of the island," Aka said, wishing he was down on the rocks picking 'opihi instead of waiting for the police.

"I sure wish we weren't bringing the cops in on this," Jack said.

"We went through all that last night, Jack. We have no choice, not after Maile found Jimmy's stuff on the lava. Even if he's not dead, what would we tell his mother? That we never even called the police?"

"Maile and that Aussie sure did butt out in a hurry."

"Listen, Jack. I'm the one that insisted she stay out of it now that the cops are involved."

"Now it's just you and me in this mess!"

Aka set his big hand on his friend's arm. "I know you're worried about Jimmy, and I know Gavin and Maile's discovery out there makes things look worse. But we did our best, Jack, all of us."

Jack's eyes moistened.

"We're just lucky my nephew Kimo got himself assigned to the case," Aka said.

"You think he'll come with Lieutenant Machado this morning?"

"Yes, but he'll be pretty cautious around him."

"He doesn't trust the Portagee?"

"Kimo hasn't been on the police force long enough to know yet."

Just then a gleaming black Chevy Tahoe topped with a blue police light drove into the yard. Aka squeezed Jack's arm. "Remember, no mention of Maile."

Lieutenant Vincent Machado, lean and dark, stepped out of the SUV. He plucked his hat off the front seat and placed it low on his head so the bill obscured the upper half of his sunglasses. His navy-blue uniform tapered nicely over his small frame, and his black shoes gleamed with high polish. Aka's nephew Kimo looked shabby by comparison. His uniform seemed a size too small, his shoes were muddy, and his hat was tipped back, exposing a big round face. He left his sunglasses on the dash.

"Jack Hemmingson?" Machado asked, ascending the lanai steps as Jack struggled out of his chair.

"Dead on," he replied, extending his hand to the officer. Jack sensed the policeman's probing gaze behind his mirrored glasses.

"Uncle Aka," Kimo said, stepping up beside Machado.

"Aloha, Kimo." Aka rose to put his hand out to Machado, and Kimo introduced them. The lieutenant shook the Hawaiian's hand less firmly than he had the haole's.

"So. Who's the missing person?" Machado said, standing ridgepole erect with police pad in hand.

"Jimmy Anderson's his name," replied Jack. "A young fella from the mainland."

"When did you last see him?"

"This past Monday morning."

"Long time."

"You know how kids are. Until yesterday, we thought he was just off carousing."

"How old is he?"

"About twenty," Aka said.

Machado jotted down the information and frowned. "You said on the phone you thought he got lost on the lava flow. What makes you think that?"

"We found a camera and a tennis shoe out there yesterday," Jack said.

Machado pushed his cap up with one finger. "You have these items?"

"The camera, yes. The shoe was stuck in the lava."

"You mean stuck in a crack?"

"No, buried in fresh lava. The camera strap too. We had to cut it to bring back the camera."

Machado glanced over at Kimo.

"Why'daya think we called you guys? We've checked all over for the kid—Hilo, Pahoa, Kalapana—you name it. Finally we went out to the flow, 'cause we knew he'd been out there the other day snappin' pictures."

Machado eyed the two old men. "You two went out there?"

"That's right," Jack said without flinching. "Real desperate we were to do it, too. Trekkin' ain't all that easy for a couple old derelicts like us."

"I imagine," Machado said, rubbing his clean-shaven chin. "When was this?"

"Yesterday."

"How far from here?"

"Couple o' miles, I s'pose."

Machado took a long look at the pair, and the old sailor wished he could see through those opaque lenses.

"No way you could do it again?" Machado asked, "to show us where you found the camera?"

Jack grasped his back with one hand, feigning discomfort. "I'm pretty lame. How 'bout you, Aka? Think you could get your old bones out there again?"

"I'd rather not."

"But we got a map for ya," Jack said, reaching into his pocket. He handed it to Machado, then grabbed his pipe from the ashtray. The policeman studied the scrawled directions.

"You guys draw this?"

"I did," Jack replied, lighting the remnants of his third morning bowl. He was glad he'd followed Aka's suggestion to redraw Gavin's map in his own hand.

Machado examined the paper. "This shows the location of the camera and shoe at an elevation of 750 feet and more than a mile inland. Add another mile from your place to the base of the pali, well, that's a long ways for a couple old timers—"

"Listen, Lieutenant, Aka and me ain't no spring chickens, but I spent a lifetime in the Navy, and Aka here has walked on lava since before you was born. If ya don't think ya can follow our map, we'll go with ya." He paused for emphasis. "And we'll make it, too."

Machado chuckled and Kimo smiled.

"OK. OK. It would be easier to have one of you with us, but we'll do our best with your map."

Lieutenant Machado refolded the paper, unbuttoned his shirt pocket, and slid the map inside. "Let's see the camera."

Aka picked it off the spool and handed it to the officer.

Machado's eyes narrowed at the sight of the fifteen-year-old Olympus. "Is this a joke? I haven't seen a rig like this in years."

Jack shrugged. "Kid's a fan of old-fashioned photography. What can I say?"

"Any film in it?" Machado asked.

"No," Aka replied.

Machado opened the back and peeked inside. "Odd. You'd think if he went out there to take pictures, there'd be film in here."

"Yeah, we thought so too," Jack said.

Machado shook his head. "C'mon Kimo, we better go check this out." The policemen stepped off the lanai and headed for the SUV.

"You guys stick around, OK?" Machado opened the door. "We'll be back in a couple hours." He got in and started the engine. Kimo stuck his arm out the window to flash Aka a shaka, and the Tahoe spun away.

"That wasn't so bad," Aka said as the pair returned to their chairs.

"Man o' few words, that lieutenant. I'm not sure what to make o' him. I wish I'd seen his eyes." He tapped the char out of his pipe and packed another bowl.

"I was afraid he'd realize Jimmy was the same person arrested for trespassing," Aka said, "and I wasn't sure how we'd handle *that*."

"Let's hope he doesn't figure it out."

"But Jack, if they don't find Jimmy soon, we're going to have to tell them about the murder."

"I'm still hoping that idiot kid'll show up and we can put him on a plane to Minnesota and forget this whole damn thing."

Aka knew in his gut that wasn't going to happen, but he didn't feel like the kid was dead. He thought back to the owl. Although he hadn't seen the bird in a week, he still felt his own destiny was somehow tied to the missing young man.

"That nephew o' yours is a real talker, ain't he?" Jack said sarcastically, lighting his pipe.

"He won't say anything around Machado, but he'll let me know what's going on."

The black Chevy Tahoe reappeared at about one o'clock. Jack went inside to wake Aka from his nap on the couch. The Hawaiian sat up dopey, his hair and beard a wild tangle.

"Look smart, Aka. We gotta be on our toes."

The two old men stepped through the screen door just as Lieutenant Machado and Kimo climbed the steps. The policemen were drenched with sweat.

"Did ya find the spot, men?" Jack asked.

"Yes and no," Kimo shrugged.

The lieutenant glanced at his patrolman with reproach. "We followed your map," Machado said, "but the place is being covered by fresh lava right now."

"Yer kiddin'. No sign of the shoe?"

Machado shook his head. "You guys *sure* about the location?"

"Absolutely."

"How good's this map?"

"I was in the Navy. I know how to draw 'em."

Machado grunted. "We searched the area adjacent to that island of vegetation. Big koa tree just upslope. That sound right?"

"Gee, I don't know," Aka said, trying to rub his face awake.

"There's a lot o' terrain out there, Lieutenant," Jack interjected quickly.

Machado pursed his lips. "It's a pretty distinctive feature. You really can't miss it."

"Sorry, I don't remember."

"Sure ya do, Aka. 'Member tellin' me, 'You check this side o' the trees, I'll check over here?' "

"Oh, yeah. Yeah, that's right."

Machado rubbed his chin and stared at the old sailor.

"The only thing we found out there was this." The policeman held up a small blue plastic bag. He reached inside and pulled out a tiny leaf. "Kimo says this is maile, you know, the plant used for leis. That mean anything to you guys?"

Neither one wanted to answer *that* question.

"Didn't notice it out there," replied Jack.

Lieutenant Machado shrugged. "Might not be anything, just a piece of trash." He replaced the leaf and carefully folded the bag, tucking it into his breast pocket.

"We'll need a description of the missing man. You can give it to Kimo."

The lieutenant radioed the police station from the SUV while Jack and Aka filled out several forms with what little they knew about Jimmy.

"Not much for go on, Uncle," Kimo said. "But I touch bases wit' you soon."

"*Mahalo*," Aka said, patting Kimo's shoulder.

"And Uncle, you got anything else—you know—anything you no want *da kine* to know." Kimo glanced toward Machado who was just signing off the radio.

"I'll call."

Kimo nodded with a quick uplifted brow. As he descended the steps, he flashed a shaka behind his back. His uncle smiled.

20 ∫ Murmurings

LATER THAT MORNING, ATOP KILAUEA . . .

The Hawaiian Volcano Observatory, known locally as HVO, overlooked Kilauea on a cliff named Uwekahuna—“the wailing priest”—commemorating one in a cadre of fourteenth-century kahuna sent to the caldera to challenge the power of Pele. They failed. It was also here that the ill-fated warriors of King Kamehameha’s rival cousin made offerings to the goddess before they suffocated on her ash during an explosive eruption.

A tower atop HVO’s drab government building housed the Crisis Center, a room of windows providing USGS scientists with panoramas of Kilauea and Mauna Loa, the island’s two recently active volcanoes. Their features were detailed on huge topographic maps under the glass top of the room’s conference table. A row of seismic drums along the windows recorded ground-movement data collected from remote instruments stationed on the island’s five volcanoes.

On this particular Friday morning, four scientists had spread themselves around the great table. The only one wearing a suit instead of aloha wear was Dr. Royce Harlan, USGS Administrator from the regional office in Menlo Park. He had just finished talking, and the others sat in stunned silence.

Gus Parker, a longtime HVO technician, clenched his bony fists. “There’s no way in hell I’m goin’ along with this—this—gutting of our report!” His younger Native Hawaiian colleague, Dr. Lelehua Chin, looked down at the table in embarrassment, but after years working with Gus, she knew there was no stopping him once he got started, especially when it involved public safety. Gus was a fourth-generation Big Islander of old missionary stock, and he could just as well have been Hawaiian when it came to respecting volcanic power. Dr. Joe Murdock, HVO's scientist in charge, listened calmly, glad it was Gus and Lelehua defending their draft report on Hualalai. Privately he agreed with Gus, and since Gus was saying it, he wouldn't have to.

"You mainland basta—" Gus caught himself, his gray eyes fixed on the pallid, complacent face of the USGS bureaucrat. "You fellas come over here from California, as on high, and tell us—who've been watching these volcanoes for years!—that our conclusions are—are—what was the word you used?"

"Overstated," Lelehua said dolefully.

"You know what's overstated?" Gus said. "*Your* credentials to judge *our* work!"

The administrator leaned forward over the table and frowned. His face remained calm, but his flexing jaw told Murdock that the bureaucrat was about to pounce on Gus with the only weapon he had—rank.

Murdock intervened, sliding his chubby arms forward over the southeast flank of Kilauea, his mountainous gut bulging against the table. "Let's take a break," he said, folding his plump fingers together. "I need to visit the restroom, and I think we're all ready for some coffee."

Gus grumbled as he raised his lanky frame out of the chair and followed Murdock down the tower stairs. Lelehua rose from her chair, swept the creases out of her blue flowered dress, and without a word headed for her office. Dr. Harlan remained at the table, drumming his trim fingernails on the draft report before him, *Hualalai Update: Results of Inflation and Seismic Studies*, by Lelehua Chin, PhD, and Gus Parker, geophysical technician.

"Those sonsabitches are trying to water down our findings, Joe," Gus said, standing next to Murdock at the urinals. "And they're doing it for politics!"

Murdock stared at the tile wall.

"If we hadn't bent over and let those bastards suppress that earlier memorandum," Gus continued at the sink, "we wouldn't be in this mess today."

"I had nothing to do with that," Murdock said, zipping up his trousers. "Wellsly was scientist in charge back then."

"That slimy egghead did his duty, didn't he? Now he's one of the GS-13s at Menlo."

Murdock held up his hand between the two of them. "Whether you like it or not, we work for them," he said.

Gus swung around from the sink and grabbed Murdock's chubby arm. "Damn it, Joe, we have a responsibility to the people of this island!"

"—not to panic them," Murdock replied, disentangling Gus's fingers, "at least not until we're sure there's real danger."

Gus stepped back, trying to regain his composure. He had grown up on the slopes of the Hualalai, and the people he was worried about were relatives and friends. "Sorry, Joe, but you know damn well there's a real danger. Hualalai has had two more years to get ready to erupt, two years while we went along with those Menlo Park idiots. Who knows how long the volcano was inflating before that? A year? Two years? *Five* years? We were willing to back away from those early findings because we were still getting our act together, but Menlo did it because they got pressure from Washington."

"That was also before the summit of Kilauea exploded," Murdock said, as if to justify Menlo Park's decision.

"Yeah, that even caught *us* blindsided, but Lelehua always suspected more magma was coming up from the hot spot. Now everyone accepts that there's at least twice as much magma welling up under the island than when we did those surveys. If Hualalai's still connected to that plumbing, Kona's in big trouble, Joe."

"*If* it's still connected to the hot spot, yes."

"I know USGS doesn't want egg on its face—no false alarms—but if Hualalai goes and we haven't at least *mentioned* the possibility to the public, we'll *all* be the laughingstock, with Big Islanders *and* our colleagues. And we'll have blood on our hands to boot."

Murdock turned on the tap and put his fingers under the water. "We've got to bide our time, Gus. Let's go with a more cautious statement now, and in a month or so we'll issue the one we know has to be made."

Gus stuck his narrow face between the mirror and Murdock. "What if we don't have a month or two?"

Murdock wiped his hands. "That's possible, but highly unlikely—"

"Unlikely, yes. *Highly* unlikely, bullshit!"

"We have no choice, Gus. If there's going to be an eruption on the Kona side—and we both know that's almost a certainty given what you and Lelehua observed over the past two years—we'll need strong support from USGS, at Menlo Park and in Washington, when we break that news to the public."

"You mean to the real estate agents and developers."

"*And* the politicians too. They've put a lot of eggs in their Kona tourism basket, including that huge new resort at Kiholo Bay."

Gus shook his head.

"I know it's frustrating, Gus. We're talking about a disaster that could kill more people and destroy more property than any previous eruption, much worse than Kalapana, what with all the Kona build-out during the last thirty years—the McMansions, the hotels, those mainland-style shopping centers."

"We've been talking about that disaster inside this building for just as long, Joe. We know that historically Hualalai erupts every couple hundred years or so, but did we really sound the alarm while they were building all that stuff?"

"We hazard-rated the entire island every year and made no secret of those reports."

"Nobody read them until Royal Gardens and Kalapana got destroyed, and then the real estate agents tried to sue us for ruining their market."

"This is a tangent." Murdock stepped to the door, then paused before opening it. "A few months' delay publicizing your data won't make any difference in preparing for the disaster, and we'll need that time to get our ducks in a row."

"Ducks in a row? Joe, you're starting to sound like *them*."

Murdock frowned. "Look, Gus, in your own paper you and Lelehua state that the most likely scenario is an eruption two to five years from now—"

"At the present rate of inflation, and *if* Hualalai acts like we think she will. But that's just theory. When she blew in 1801, there were no scientists here to watch."

"Can't you two just let this first analysis stand at that? Then add the bit about possible imminent danger to a later statement?"

"But, Joe, theoretically it could start erupting anytime—tomorrow. We've got to keep that in our report. After all—"

"I'm sorry, Gus. I agree with your analysis, but including that in this report is just not in the cards. It will have to wait."

"Goddamn politics," Gus said under his breath. "OK, Joe, you know the lay of *that* land better than we do. But I know these volcanoes, and my gut tells me we're making a big mistake."

"I get the message. What about Lelehua?"

"*She's* the one that drew up the scenarios, but you know Lelehua. It took her a long time to get to where she is at HVO, the highest-ranking Hawaiian on the staff. She won't make a stink in front of the big boys."

"Good. Then it's up to *you* to keep your mouth under control when we get back up there. OK?"

Gus sighed. "As long as I have your word that we'll come out of our corner and lay things out—the way they should be—once the political dust settles from . . . what should I call it? . . . our *preliminary* report."

Murdock extended his hand. "You have my word."

Gus took it. "Within the next month or two."

Murdock nodded. "We'll issue our full statement, and talk to Civil Defense, within the next two months. I promise."

Gus let go of his hand. "Get us out of this meeting as soon as you can, will ya, Joe? I wanna give my stomach time to recover before lunch."

They stopped briefly at the staff lounge to refill their coffee cups, then climbed the stairs to the Crisis Center. The mainland bureaucrat was still drumming his fingers against the draft. Lelehua had returned from her office with the stack of files that formed the basis of their report, along with a map of Hualalai highlighting HVO's expanded Global Positioning System satellite stations.

"We obviously have some disagreements here," Murdock said, plopping his weighty frame into the chair.

"Obviously," Dr. Harlan replied.

"The bone of contention," Murdock continued, "seems to be the report's assertion that, in addition to the likelihood of a Hualalai eruption sometime in the next two to five years, there is a slight possibility of something more immediate."

"*Slight* was not the word used," Dr. Harlan said. "The exact language, from the conclusions on page fifty-three, is more . . . provocative." He lifted the report off the table and read:

> These results clearly indicate that a major eruption of Hualalai is likely sometime within two to five years, ample time to prepare if proper steps are initiated in the near term. Further, there is a very real possibility that the volcano may erupt much earlier, in fact at any time. Because no scientific monitoring was done prior to its last eruption in 1801, its pre-eruptive behavior is necessarily assumed to be similar to that of the island's two active volcanoes, an assumption that may understate the immediacy of the impending eruption. Moreover, expanded satellite monitoring on Hualalai is relatively recent, and therefore incomplete, and may also understate these hazards.

Lelehua smiled. She had labored over that wording, trying to express credibly the real dangers of the volcano but in a way that people would grasp immediately.

"I have only a few minor alterations to suggest to the body of the report," Dr. Harlan said, "but that provocative conclusion requires considerable modification"—the authors' faces dropped—"changes that will *have* to be made before USGS approves its release."

Lelehua leaned forward over her heaps of data. "What are you suggesting?"

The administrator curled his lower lip. "Just a few wording changes. Here's what I suggest." Dr. Harlan slid the report over to Lelehua. Red ink heavily marked the paragraph. Gus leaped up from his chair and leaned over his colleague's shoulder to read the edited text:

> These results indicate that an eruption of Hualalai is possible sometime within five years, ample time to prepare for this possibility. Because no scientific monitoring was done prior to its last eruption in 1801, its pre-eruptive behavior is necessarily assumed to be similar to that of the island's two active volcanoes, perhaps erroneously. Moreover, expanded satellite monitoring on Hualalai is relatively recent, and therefore incomplete, and may misstate

the likelihood of an eruption. Continued monitoring may illuminate this possibility in the coming years.

Lelehua was floored and Gus was livid. With a few clever strokes of the pen, the administrator had knocked out all the paragraph's teeth.

"You gotta be kidding," Gus blurted. "Our report is based on good science."

"I agree, but in your desire to protect the public, you've crafted conclusions that go *beyond* the—ah—fine analysis contained within the body of the report."

Gus knew that bastard was well aware that only a few scientists would read the whole report, especially if the new conclusions didn't say anything! He strode over to Dr. Harlan, fists clenched, and loomed menacingly close to him. Lelehua watched in disbelief, and Murdock rose from his chair.

"Let's just talk about this," Murdock implored.

"What's to discuss?" Gus replied. "Our esteemed colleague from California thinks we've pushed the science a bit too far. Right, Dr. Harlan?"

"Precisely," Dr. Harlan said, meeting Gus's vitriolic stare.

"But I have all the data here," Lelehua said, pushing the heap of files toward the bureaucrat, "including new data that will more than substantiate—"

"Write it up," Dr. Harlan said coldly, his pallid face now pink.

"We'll do that," Murdock said, walking over to Gus. He placed his hand on Gus's shoulder. "Won't we?"

Gus slowly stepped back from the bureaucrat. "Yeah, we'll write it up!" Gus's words rode on puffs of steam.

"Can you guys have a draft ready in, say—"

"It'll be ready in a month, Joe," Gus said.

Murdock turned toward Lelehua. "In the meantime, will you two accept Dr. Harlan's proposed changes, so we can issue this preliminary report without further delay?"

Lelehua nodded reluctantly. Gus just waved his hand and turned toward Kilauea's fuming caldera.

"It's settled then," Dr. Harlan said, rising from his chair. "As soon as you've added my changes, mail me the final draft and I'll approve it over the phone."

"We'll *e-mail* it Monday," Gus said, scowling into the volcano.

Murdock put his hand out to Dr. Harlan, but the administrator turned away, stepping toward Lelehua. Without a word, he picked up her coffee mug and examined the artist's rendering of Pele on the side. He smiled contemptuously, then headed down the stairs. Lelehua slumped over her data.

"Damn you, Gus!" Murdock said after the cleated steps of the administrator no longer echoed in the stairwell. "You almost killed this report with your bluster. I wouldn't have been surprised if Harlan had held up its release until you two finished the follow-up study. That certainly would have delayed your public notice!"

"Hell, we'd just leak it then."

"Don't say that, Gus. Don't even *think* it."

21 ∫ Lankowski's Latest News

LATER THAT NIGHT AT CONWAY'S RESORT . . .

The windward clouds that had rained on Hilo for two days did not extend to leeward Kona. A full moon hung above Kiholo Bay and the Royal Paradise Bay Resort. Robert Conway sat alone on the vast lanai of the Golden Coconut Saloon. A tumbler of bourbon, half-drained, stood on the glass table before him as he waited for the governor's aide to show up.

Conway had already responded to the unsettling news Andy Lankowski brought six days earlier. A public relations campaign—complete with TV commercials and full-page newspaper ads—had been launched to offset whatever negative publicity might result from a news story about the suppressed USGS memorandum on Hualalai. He had also secured signed commitments from two more investors in the Kona coast land development scheme, as well as made a courtesy call to Tommy Oshiro, editor of the *Honolulu Star-Advertiser*. Conway had carefully avoided the topic of the memorandum, instead offering the editor a private briefing about the grand opening and inviting Oshiro and his reporters to stay at the resort during the festivities, all expenses paid.

The classic tremolo voices of Alfred Apaka's Hawaiian Village Serenaders drifted over the lanai from speakers concealed in the hull of a Polynesian outrigger canoe.

When she passes by, heads all turn and sigh.

There goes Kealoha.
She is just a hula miss from those isles across the sea . . .

Conway gazed at the moon-washed replica of Captain Cook's *Resolution* rocking on the gentle swells, but his mind was on another bay across the sea. He and his aging mentor, Helmut Gieselmann, had stood watching San Francisco's dazzling nighttime panorama from their penthouse office in the Transamerica Pyramid. The bourbon was poured generously that night, and the usually secretive Gieselmann fell into a nostalgic reverie, passing on to his apprentice his private entrepreneurial creed.

Conway was so lost in the past that he failed to notice Lankowski was late. A single patch of cloud passed over the moon, momentarily darkening Kiholo Bay. Conway laughed bitterly. Even now, after all the publicity about the Royal Paradise Bay, no one knew how he'd managed to become Hawai'i's most prominent resort builder. Not even Gieselmann knew the whole story.

Honolulu's most tenacious gossips had pieced together some details. Conway first appeared in the midseventies, arriving at the docks of Waikiki's Ala Moana Yacht Club, a strapping young Californian just finishing a stint as crew with the consummate yachtsman Helmut Gieselmann. Gieselmann had twice won the Admiral's Cup and taken home lesser trophies in greater races. His ruthless sailing style aboard the *Pirate's Ark* was notorious: He was a master at blocking the wind of competitors, sometimes threatening collision in order to gain advantage on the turns.

Conway had wondered how the renowned real estate tycoon knew to invest in all the right places at just the right times, until Gieselmann asked Conway to give up his internship as a trusted accounts assistant to join the ranks of his numerous informants secretly positioned in other investment firms downtown. During that year of covert employment, Conway became the older man's apprentice and confidant. Excited by Gieselmann's stories of capitalist opportunities in Hawai'i—what his mentor called "America's still-developing frontier"—Conway left the *Pirate's Ark* before its return voyage, staying on to seek his fortune and fame. He soon discovered it was easier to imagine his dream than to achieve it—no matter how capable he knew he was—and within a year he was flat broke after investing his entire savings in a novice Honolulu firm that planned to generate electricity by tapping into the extensive steam vents of Kilauea. Excited in the wake of the OPEC oil crisis, Conway had jumped on board before more conventional investors were willing to buy into an idea that only a decade later would be well under way. Conway had chosen the right investment but at the wrong time.

Conway then became so reclusive that even Gieselmann lost track of him. Occasionally he'd be spotted in the Harbor Pub, a smoky sailors' dive near Waikiki, or on O'ahu's North Shore, where he lived in a shabby bungalow amid the shanties of surfers and fishermen. Hence the island folklore that the millionaire builder began as a poverty-stricken beachcomber.

His days of poverty didn't last long. By the early eighties he was back on the Honolulu social circuit, after serving behind the scenes as a "catalytic go-between" among some international investors (mostly from then capital-rich Japan) who bought out faltering hotels and restaurants and infused them with new money, resurrecting them for Hawai'i's growing tourist trade. Conway later said that "sprucing up" those old properties was like "turning taro into veal," and he used an old trick learned as Gieselmann's informant: "find out what's cooking before it occurs to anyone else to even look in the kitchen." In each case, the investors—and Conway—made a killing. There seemed no end to his success as long as Conway's strategy stayed just ahead of Hawai'i's burgeoning economy. How he first came by the money to do all that remained a mystery.

By the mideighties Conway had made his first million. A few years later, he was worth ten, and his reputation for putting together "miracle" deals had spread beyond the islands, to San Francisco, Los Angeles, New York, and Tokyo. Now, with plenty of money in hand and his reputation on the rise, he was ready to tackle the project he hoped would make him an international figure.

Conway took a long drink, stared a moment at the moonlit ice cubes rattling in his glass, and set the cocktail back on the table. He was tired after another full day overseeing preparations for the grand opening, little more than a week away. The slight, pleasant buzz in his head didn't suppress his annoyance at again having to meet with the weasel Lankowski. He knew that good news from the governor's office usually came by phone, bad news in person. During his last encounter with Lankowski, Conway had allowed himself to get flustered and upset. That, he had decided, would never happen again. From now on, he would be ready and in control.

. . . She's a beauty from those isles,
She'll charm you with her wiles,
That dancing, romancing, entrancing hula maiden,
Kealoha . . .

"Remembering the good old days, Bob?"

Conway smiled as Mali'o Rivera leaned over the back of his chair and kissed him on the cheek, leaving a cool wet spot lingering on his skin. Her makeup smelled sweet.

"No, I was recalling all the struggles," he said, still gazing at the *Resolution.*

"But this sounds like a love song to me." She slipped her skirted bottom onto the table in front of him and crossed her shapely legs—blue stockings hissing.

"What? Oh that." He chuckled. "The boatman put it on to keep him company while he polishes the sloops. Says that 1960s *hapa*-haole stuff reminds him of Waikiki before—"

"So what are you doing out here all by your lonesome?" The sea breeze rustled Mali'o's long jet-black hair, and her teeth and eyes sparkled.

"Waiting for someone."

"Oh, really?" Mali'o leaned back on her palms, and her miniskirt hiked farther up her thighs. "Who is she?" she asked with mock jealousy.

Conway got up from his chair and leaned over the twenty-eight-year-old beauty. He kissed her on the lips, pulling back before getting entangled with her eager tongue. "It's a he, and he's a royal pain in the neck—Lankowski."

"Oh, *that* creep—the wimp governor's strategy man—brains packaged in sleaze."

Conway chuckled, always delighted by Mali'o's sharp wit and candor.

"I know what a headache those political types are for you, Bob. How 'bout a drink when you're done? I'll wait for you at the Mauna Lani."

"Why drive over there? I'll have something brought to you in my suite."

"No," she replied, patting the front of his aloha shirt. "You need a break from this place, from everything weighing on your mind here. Let's have a few drinks up the coast. OK?"

"OK."

Mali'o slid her petite frame off the table and into Conway's arms. He kissed her mouth, this time letting her tongue travel where it pleased.

"See ya soon," Mali'o said, breaking free. She scampered toward the door, the heels of her pumps clicking loudly across the tile, and was startled to see Lankowski sauntering into the room.

He smiled knowingly, a crooked grin. "Spry little creature, isn't she?" Lankowski said, pulling a pack of cigarettes out of his sports jacket. "She still the jazz singer at the Mauna Lani?"

"Yes, but she'll be working *here* soon. She's very talented."

"I imagine so." Lankowski's eyes gleamed. "Gives you a break from everything weighing on your mind."

Conway's neck tightened. How long had Lankowski been listening?

"So what's the urgent news, Andy?"

"Gotta beer?"

"Help yourself," Conway replied, in no mood to get up for this man. "First cooler on the right."

"Thanks," Lankowski said, returning with a chilled bottle of Budweiser. "It's been a long day, a very long day, indeed. For you, too, I'm sure. This is not what either one of us wants to do on a Friday night." Lankowski threw an obvious glance toward the door through which Mali'o had just passed.

"Let's make it quick then, shall we?"

"Absolutely, Bob, absolutely. In fact, I wouldn't have come unless it was really necessary. I bring both good and bad news. Let's start with the good, shall we?"

Conway remained expressionless as Lankowski tossed his spent cigarette onto the floor and smashed it with his toe.

"The good news—or *relatively* good news, anyway—is that HVO has modified their upcoming report on Hualalai. It still contains some pretty disturbing stuff, but at least they took out the things that would have created *immediate* problems for us."

"How did you accomplish that?"

"I'd like to take the credit, Bob, but I can't. Once again we are indebted to Congressman Yamashita."

INDEBTED. Conway hated the word, at least when it applied to him. Ironically, the more successful and prominent he had become, the more often that word seemed to come up in conversation.

"Yes, indeed. The congressman cleared things up over at USGS." Lankowski stuck another Vantage in his mouth and lit it. "Isn't it wonderful how things work in Washington?"

"So what does this report say?"

"In a nutshell? That Hualalai might blow sometime in the next five years, but that the data supporting that claim are new, incomplete, and may be erroneous."

"It says the mountain might erupt *in the next five years*?" I'll be damned if I'll be indebted for that statement, Conway thought.

"Don't look so disappointed, Bob. From what I hear, it could be sooner rather than later. The scientists backed off from what they originally planned to say—from what they still want to say. With that disclaimer about the data, we can fudge all over the place. 'Maybe it's five years, maybe it's ten.' See what I mean?"

"When can I get a copy?" Conway snapped. "I've got my public relations firm coming in this weekend to work up specific responses."

"I'll send it to you as soon as we have the revised version, but it probably won't be till early next week."

Lankowski knew a second HVO report, containing better data, would be issued within a month or two—one that would be much harder to "fudge" on—but he'd decided there was no reason to reveal that now, no clear advantage in doing so.

"What about the *Star-Advertiser* story?"

"Ah, yes. The *bad* news. I understand you've been in contact with the editor."

"Yes." How did the weasel know that? "But we didn't discuss the story."

"Very wise on your part, Bob. Very wise. It wouldn't have done you any good anyway. The story runs Sunday."

"No!"

"The saving grace is that the newspaper's going to focus on USGS's internal decision to hold back the memorandum two years ago and doesn't reveal any *outside* pressure on the agency. At least that's what our sources say. Focuses strictly on the bickering between HVO and their bosses at USGS. Actually, I'm not sure the newspaper *knows* about all the maneuvering going on over this."

"But it still points out the threat of an eruption on Hualalai?"

"Yeah, but that's not its main focus. Besides, next week, when the new HVO report goes public, everybody will know that anyway."

Conway got up and walked to the cabana. He poured enough bourbon to cover the half-melted cubes at the bottom of his glass, then returned to his seat. "Have *you* seen the HVO report?" he asked.

"Portions of it." Lankowski lit another cigarette.

"Andy," he said, peering into the weasel's bland eyes. "What's the actual truth about the volcano?"

"The truth?" Lankowski drew hard on his cigarette and a piece of ash tumbled onto his rumpled sport coat. "Of course it's going to erupt. But when? Next week? Next year? Twenty years from now?" Lankowski threw up his hands. "Even more uncertain is *where*. Above Kailua? Over here at Kiholo? Each time Mauna Loa erupts—every couple decades—it can threaten Hilo. Do we quit investing in the state's second-largest city? Why should it be any different on this side of the island? That's what I'd tell your investors, Bob."

The entrepreneur leaned back in his chair and gazed at the *Resolution*, its masts and rigging silhouetted against the moonlit sea. How would his hero Captain Cook make ready for such a storm? Cook's wits, courage, and exploratory triumphs were legendary. All three of his Pacific voyages were brave quests to pursue mythic places long dreamed about by Europeans—the Great South Land (later called Australia), where riches might be found; Terra Austalis (Antarctica), a huge land mass believed to counterbalance the Northern Hemisphere continents; and the Strait of Anian, the fabled northwest passage that if found could link trade between the Atlantic and Pacific Oceans. Against staggering odds, the tenacious and visionary explorer made numerous discoveries along the way—including Hawai'i. Would not that same kind of brave vision help Conway overcome the gales he now faced?

Lankowski noticed Conway's preoccupation. "The captain also had a few trials and tribulations," he remarked sardonically. "But then those Brits are starchy, aren't they? Stiff upper lip and all." He laughed.

"Cook faced years at sea," Conway replied sharply. "Hostile natives, treacherous reefs, storms, icebergs—and the unknown. With all that, his resolve never faltered."

"A symbol to us all, Bob," Lankowski said, taking a long drag on his cigarette. "But in the end, the Hawaiians killed him, didn't they?" Lankowski let the smoke escape his nostrils, then sucked it all back into his mouth for a second nicotine hit.

Conway stood up. "Thanks for bringing over the news."

Lankowski remained seated. "There's one more thing, Bob. Last Saturday I met with our friends up at Paliuli Estate," a reference to the headquarters of Haku Kane, kingpin of the Hui, high up the slopes of Kohala volcano.

Not *my* friends, Conway thought.

"They don't want to get drawn into any publicity, but they're willing to exert whatever pressure is required to keep things on track."

"That won't be necessary."

Lankowski got the message and stood up. "I've got an appointment at Paliuli mansion tomorrow night, to keep them abreast of what's happening."

"I'll be expecting that USGS report."

"Yeah, we'll fax it to you."

Lankowski headed for the door, accompanied by Conway, but he paused before opening it. "I haven't heard those romantic Alfred Apaka tunes in years. A little, well, old-fashioned, aren't they?"

Conway didn't reply. Lankowski shrugged and disappeared through the door.

Conway returned to the table and noticed a scattering of crumpled butts smashed into the slate tiles beneath Lankowski's chair.

"Bastard!" Conway muttered, then glanced warily back toward the door.

22 ∫ A Meeting with the Old Stones

SATURDAY, JUNE 10, ALMOST SUNRISE ON HUALALAI . . .

Beyond the turmoil of resort preparations, scientific debate, and political maneuvering, others with a keen interest in Hualalai followed the dictates of higher powers that be. Kapu Hawaiʻi leader Wailani Henderson and her aging mentor, Aunty Keala Huelani, stealthily trekked the volcano's flank in a chill left from the night winds blown down Mauna Kea. The upland jungle was steely gray in the dull light reflecting off the sky, and the vegetation, drenched with overnight condensation, still hummed with crickets. A white speck high above them—an ʻio—circled close to the heavens.

Traveling before dawn was a solemn time, but it was essential that no one detect the two intruders on the now heavily secured Lapalapa Ranch. Both had blood roots to the land upon which they now trespassed, and the elder—two generations older than her companion—knew all of its secrets. She had the knowledge Wailani lacked, but the younger Hawaiian was willing to honor her ancestry with action, and together they made up for the middle generation absent on the trek—thirty years of Hawaiians made impotent by their vain efforts to fit into the world foreigners had brought to the archipelago.

Wailani carried a special parcel under her arm, and Aunty Keala guided the way. Twigs and grasses cracked under their callused feet on an overgrown path that few had traveled during the past five decades. Passing jungle-covered cinder cones, they descended the slope to the hidden place.

The night before, in the glow of campfire embers, Aunty Keala had recalled her first trek down that path, guided by a family elder now long dead. Secrecy was even more important then, right after statehood, as societal scorn for "pagan" practices was harsh. Aunty Keala had shared with the young activist tales of social and political repression each time someone new took over the islands, and the quiet heroism of each clandestine resistance. Despite those hardships, Aunty Keala explained, a few Hawaiians always maintained the link to their ancient past and secretly tended the sacred places to honor gods disgraced in the eyes of the Americans who now controlled the islands.

"If memory lives," the stout, graying woman had said, "the politics of the day don't matter." Smiling, she reported that the ancestral chain of memory for this area had never been broken because someone—under the protection of darkness—had always traveled to the ancient stone shrine to keep in touch through prayer.

The elder had said much in the firelight, but she did not reveal the deepest meaning of the place. That, she knew, Wailani must discern with her own na'au—her primal instincts—aided by ancestral memories in her blood passed down from family members who had walked this path before.

As far as Aunty Keala knew, no one besides her had made the trek for at least two decades. But now, the stone shrine—even the forest in which it stood—was in peril. Within a year, the old ranchland would be a subdivision, urban sprawl on the commuting edge of Kailua-Kona. So, one last time, they of the blood must visit in secret, making their offerings and exchanging knowledge with the ancestral stones.

23 ∫ Wild Boar

THAT EVENING ON THE SLOPES OF KOHALA . . .

The last light of day lit up the western face of Kohala, the island's only extinct volcano, but dark clouds blown in on trades shrouded its windward side. A blue Pontiac climbed the volcano's sunny flank and stopped on the shoulder just this side of the rain. Andy Lankowski emerged from the car's smoky interior, a cigarette drooping from his mouth, and slouched against the hood. His polyester sports jacket carried a whole new set of wrinkles after the hour-long drive from Kona.

Lankowski looked out from the high ridge. Miles away, a dozen giant observatories on Mauna Kea's cinder summit caught the sharp evening light—each having been a golden egg for Hawai'i's always-hungry construction industry, Lankowski recalled. Beyond Mauna Kea stood Hualalai, also aglow, presiding over the Kona coast. The governor's aide smiled.

A strong gust blew down Kohala, sending a shiver through Lankowski. He flicked his cigarette off the ridge and got back into the car. A few miles up the road he turned onto a gravel drive leading farther up the volcano. Open range gave way to dense forest, and sunlit views disappeared as the rented Pontiac penetrated the windward clouds. Dense, rainy fog engulfed the car, and Lankowski switched on the headlights.

Lankowski's thoughts sped along as well, working up strategies, considering tactics, thinking through political intricacies. During the tedium of long drives, interisland flights, and interminable legislative hearings, Lankowski's mental state was akin to that of a professional poker player who constantly catalogs cards laid and calculates the odds of turning up winning combinations. At times like this, he chain-smoked vigorously, sometimes lighting another cigarette while one, half-smoked, still smoldered in an ashtray.

Lankowski reached across the dash to search the glove box for a fresh pack. His fingers found one amid the crumpled wrappers of spent packs, but he couldn't quite grasp it. He thrust his hand deeper into the compartment, inadvertently pushing the cigarettes farther away. "Damn!" he said, letting go of the wheel just long enough to grab them.

At that same instant, he noticed an enormous black boar straddling the foggy road, its white tusks flashing in the headlights. Lankowski jammed on the brakes and grabbed the wheel, but too late to avoid jerking the car off the gravel and into a tree, smashing one headlamp.

"Shit." A hairline crack angled up the windshield. He looked back at the road; the pig was gone.

"Son of a bitch!"

The forest darkened suddenly and a downpour pummeled the car.

Lankowski felt a rage coming on, a temper he'd learned to control in front of others. He ripped open the pack of cigarettes with his teeth and, in the same manner, withdrew one. Too impatient to wait for the car lighter to heat, he lit up with matches he'd picked off the table at Conway's resort and inhaled greedily. Lankowski jammed the car into reverse and punched the accelerator. The car pulled away from the tree, and the wheels turned without hindrance. The engine seemed to run as before.

"Thank God," Lankowski muttered. He would still make it to the meeting with Haku Kane. This was too critical a time not to check in with the underworld agenda. Of all the wild cards in the deck, the ones played by the Hui were the most predictable—unless something went wrong. Then Haku Kane might do anything. And the Hui was the only player in this game with the power to change the rules. Legalities were of little concern. They acted in secret with no public image to worry about and could always force their agenda using the most primitive tactic—violence.

Looking over his shoulder, he guided the car back onto the road, but now the same boar blocked his rearward path!

"Out of my way!" Lankowski screamed at the top of his lungs, leaning on the horn, but the huge brute just stared at him, his eyes, teeth, and tusks glowing red in the brake lights.

"OK, you asked for it!" Lankowski pushed the gas pedal to the floor. The pig disappeared with a *thunk* and the car lurched upward. Lankowski leaped out, immediately drenched in the downpour, but he didn't care. He wanted to see the bloody carcass, relish its demise. He marched to the back of the car and stuck his head under the bumper.

But there was no body. Instead the car rested on a big lump—a cold, hard lava rock jammed under the axle. He searched either side of the rock. No boar! He examined the bumper for blood and hair. Clean! He looked up and down the road. Not even pig tracks in the muddy ditch. Soaked and disgusted, Lankowski plopped back into the driver's seat and slammed the door. How could he meet the crime chief in this condition? There was no way to reschedule with Haku Kane. Lankowski looked at his watch: 7:03 p.m. He was already late.

"Damn!"

Lankowski jockeyed the car back onto the road, then ran back to the trunk to retrieve his overnight bag. At least he had a dry shirt and trousers in there. He grabbed another carton of cigarettes while he was at it and changed inside the cramped Pontiac, smoking the whole time. Those few minutes gave him time to calm down. Now and again he thought he saw a shadow move among the dark trees, but he ignored it.

He sped through the rainy forest and soon spotted the lights of Paliuli Estate. A tall security fence surrounded Haku Kane's fortress, but it wasn't necessary. Everyone knew the place was off limits. Even the hunters who frequented the forest kept a safe distance from the estate of Hawai'i's most powerful criminal.

The Pontiac pulled into the oval patch of light in front of a huge iron gate. A beefy Samoan in a black poncho stepped out of the guard shack while two pit bulls paced behind the fence. Lankowski rolled down the window, and the guard peered in with a flashlight. "OK," he said, recognizing the governor's aide. He walked back to the shack, and a moment later the gate swung open. Lankowski proceeded through the woods, and about a quarter mile up the road, the mansion came into view.

The three-story manor stood perched on a rise in a grove of royal palms, with a sprawling lanai wrapped around the entire first floor. Invisible in the dark was the precipice upon which it was built, a sheer cliff above Waipio Valley. A waterfall gushed directly out of the rock below the house, dropping 1,300 feet to the jungle below. Built from the riches of Haku Kane's illegal empire, the mansion towered over a deep gorge once occupied by the most powerful kings to rule the archipelago.

A guard lumbered down the steps of the lanai to meet the car. Lankowski got out and another broad-beamed Hawaiian accompanied him to the door. Lankowski wondered where Haku Kane got these huge men for his security force, formidable even without their rifles and revolvers.

Visitors were usually taken to the Hoʻolauleʻa Room, a large ceremonial hall where Haku Kane held court against the spectacular backdrop of the valley. Lankowski was instead guided to the Hui chief's private den. It was not his first time there. The room was dark and windowless, paneled with koa wood harvested on the property in the 1890s. A well-worn leather sofa and several overstuffed chairs encircled a coffee table in front of an enormous lava rock fireplace. On the rough-hewn mantel stood several sea-worn stones passed down through generations of Kanes, a menacing wooden *tiki*, and a box of Cuban cigars (never opened for Lankowski's benefit). Affixed to the fireplace above the mantel was a collection of three ancient war clubs lined with sharks' teeth. Small lamps glowed on the walls, but most of the room's illumination came from the blaze. The flickering light revealed an antique feather kahili, royal scepter of the aliʻi, in a dark corner of the room.

Waiting for the crime chief, Lankowski wandered past a wall of photos—Haku Kane with politicians, business luminaries, and Hawaiian music celebrities—and plopped down on the sofa across from the fireplace. He lit a cigarette, tossing the match into the fire. The heat felt good against his chilled body.

Haku Kane, now the undisputed leader of Hawai'i's underworld, liked to think of himself as the most powerful Hawaiian since the overthrow of the monarchy in 1893. Like many of the ancient chiefs (and earlier underworld figures), he had acquired this prominence through force of will and violence, and by forging temporary alliances with foreigners—now the haoles and the Japanese Americans who dominated Hawai'i's halls of power. In the decades after statehood, various underworld leaders had staked out their own turf—in prostitution, drugs, gambling, and extortion—but their influence waned in the twenty-first century, when economic and political opportunities for young Hawaiians improved. Haku Kane had stepped in to keep those lucrative illegal activities alive, creating his new Hui by consolidating remnants of his mentors' old ventures and political associations, but managing them with a personal charm and sophistication that his brutish forerunners had lacked.

While the underworld's former grip on the islands' profitable entertainment business had also weakened in recent years, Haku Kane took over what remained, forcing many Hawaiian performers to publish their albums and book their concerts through Hui-connected recording companies. And like earlier underworld figures who'd used real estate and development as convenient activities for laundering vice money during the post-statehood boom, Haku Kane kept his hand in those pies too. As always, ample kickbacks secured the cooperation of business and political leaders, and just enough killing and other violence made it clear to the public that meddling with—or even criticizing—the Hui was dangerous, so its power, widely acknowledged in private, was seldom openly discussed. Fear made people keep a safe distance from Haku Kane, just as they had from the royal ali'i of ancient times who could put to death any commoner unlucky enough to have the shadow of an ali'i pass over them.

Lankowski's eyes wandered the room, pausing on another set of photos depicting Haku Kane with his prize-winning thoroughbreds, his smiling face always shadowed by a broad-brimmed hat. But the most prominent picture in the room was a large oil painting of Haku Kane with his wife, mother, and five children.

"Family man," Lankowski chuckled under his breath. A nominal Christian—though steeped in his own cultural myths—Haku Kane was known to be faithful to his wife and devoted to his kids. Lankowski found these kinds of contradictions hilarious, and he was ready to exploit them for political advantage when necessary. "Find their buttons and push them," Lankowski liked to say, "then watch the fun begin."

"Looks like you had a little mishap on the way over," Haku Kane said, strolling into the room, dressed casually in an elegant black turtleneck and blue worsted pants. Although of only medium height, his erect stance and large, muscular hands conveyed a powerful presence. Yet his manner was almost always affable and disarming. An old underworld rival once said, "You never fully feel the sting of Haku's knife, because you're dead before recovering from his smile."

"What's the other car look like?" he asked.

"About the same," Lankowski replied, rising from the sofa. Haku Kane motioned for him to stay put as he walked across the room's antique Persian rug toward the liquor cabinet below the portrait.

"Drink?" he asked.

"Sure, sure. Whatever you're having, Haku."

"Bourbon."

"Sounds great. On the rocks if you please."

Haku Kane looked older than in the painting. He was thinner now, and gray streaks had invaded his thick, shiny black hair. But his Hawaiian features were still stately—a heavy brow, firm jaw, and full lips. His smoldering brown eyes were arresting, but one was misshapen, allegedly from an encounter with a bull when Kane was a young cowboy on the Lapalapa Ranch. Haku Kane's men had learned to watch that eye carefully because it twitched whenever adrenaline flowed, never in fear, usually in anger.

"What happened, Andy?" Haku Kane asked, tossing several ice cubes into each crystal glass.

"Some idiot pulled out of a parking lot without looking. Happens all the time, I guess, but never to me. Naw, I been lucky, until today. Real lucky."

"Hmmm," Haku Kane replied, his dark eyes gleaming. "Looked like a tree bash to me."

"Just a fender bender," Lankowski said, feigning disinterest.

Haku Kane drenched the cubes with bourbon, his voice smooth and amiable. "Cracked window too. That's too bad."

"They don't make 'em like they used to," Lankowski said, wondering why Haku Kane persisted with this.

"My road's tricky on rainy nights." He handed Lankowski his drink. "I need to widen it."

Lankowski didn't reply. He knew that getting caught in even a silly lie was a serious tactical error.

Haku Kane eased into one of the overstuffed chairs. "Where'd you say this happened?"

He senses a weakness, Lankowski realized, beginning to perspire. "Kailua, this morning, before my meeting with Robert Conway." He tossed his cigarette into the fireplace and lit another.

Haku Kane sipped his bourbon, eyeing the rattled aide. "Andy, that road's bad enough without having to come up here on only one headlight."

Lankowski's face reddened, and Haku Kane smiled. "How is Bob?" he asked.

Finally off the hook, Lankowski took the cue. "Anxious, I'd say. Yes, indeed. See, there's a barge load of bad publicity about to wash up onto the beach."

"Oh?"

"Yeah, we tried to squelch it, but you know how newspapers are."

Haku Kane knew well. Reporters had repeatedly tried to expose his empire, but he had covered his tracks by letting underlings do the dirty work and by threatening fatal consequences to anyone who spoke against him. Despite this success, he still deeply resented the media's intrusion into his affairs. Lankowski sometimes wondered if Haku Kane had come to believe that his thousand-acre estate, with its deep forests and sweeping macadamia nut orchards, had been built with legitimate income. What had irked Haku Kane the most was when a tenacious *Star-Advertiser* reporter tried to interview his wife and children at a Waimea coffee shop. He wanted the reporter's head, but being more savvy than his mentors, he held back his thugs, instead browbeating the reporter's editor by brandishing the threat of a lawsuit. Lankowski was curious how Haku Kane would react to the latest newspaper story.

"Two years ago USGS suppressed a memorandum about a possible Hualalai eruption," Lankowski said. "The *Star-Advertiser* plans to run a story on it. I mentioned the memorandum at the time. You remember?"

"Vaguely."

"Well, it's going public tomorrow. Apparently the article focuses on infighting between HVO and USGS. Keeps the rest of us out of it, anyway."

Haku Kane leaned forward. "So what's the bad news?"

"Tomorrow's story will also say that scientists are worried about an *imminent* eruption of Hualalai."

"Really," he scoffed. "I wonder how many people will believe that."

Lankowski tamped his cigarette into a silver ashtray, relishing a chance to now knock a little bark off Haku Kane. "Hard telling. Most people avoid the truth, even when it's staring them right in the face, Haku, especially if it's a thing they can't afford to know."

"What are you saying, Andy?" Haku Kane stood up. He pulled a pack of Kools from his pants pocket and walked to the fireplace. "That Hualalai might actually erupt?"

Lankowski lit up another Vantage and inhaled deeply.

"What does it matter, Haku? The Royal Paradise Bay is done. As long as the volcano doesn't erupt before the real estate around the resort is sold, who cares? Another year or two is all we need."

Haku Kane withdrew a cigarette from the pack. He lit it with a hefty gold lighter. "What exactly do the scientists say?"

"That Hualalai could erupt sometime in the next five years. But"—Lankowski tapped the ash off his cigarette—"maybe they're wrong."

Haku Kane's misshapen eye began to twitch. "What information do you have on this?"

"Just what they're going to say in their official report next week."

"A public report?"

"You seem surprised," Lankowski replied nonchalantly. "I told you last week something might hit the newspapers."

"Volcanic threats haven't stopped a single project on this island,

Andy. Government officials don't know what to think when they hear geologists speculate."

"My feelings exactly, Haku. Absolutely. Fact is the archaeologists—and the radicals—disrupt more building projects than the volcanoes do."

Haku Kane stepped close to Lankowski. "The radicals?"

"You know what I mean, Haku, the Hawaiian throwbacks, people like Kapu Hawai'i."

Haku Kane frowned.

"So I wouldn't worry about the newspapers," Lankowski continued. "Let Conway do the nail biting."

"I'm not sure I like your attitude. Do I take it that the governor is just sitting around on his duff doing nothing to keep this sort of thing out of the newspapers? Dealing with those vultures is *your* job—"

"And we've been doing it," Lankowski said, trying to come across as unruffled. There was something more than just the press coverage eating at Haku Kane, and Lankowski wanted to find out what it was before going back to Honolulu. He had a pretty good idea too, based on a rumor he'd heard about the Hui's real interests in the resort. "Haku, if I told you what *might* have come out had we not intervened, you'd understand," he said, his tone a tad haughty.

Haku Kane's eyes blazed. "Don't talk to me that way, Lankowski. I don't need to know all the scientific details—that's your job. Am I to assume that the governor has suddenly lost sight of our interests in this project?"

"Not at all, my friend. Not at all. Yours are among the concerns we keep ever present in our minds. I'm just surprised you'd worry about a little news story that—" Lankowski paused with theatrical flair. "Wait a minute. You're not actually worried about a future eruption?"

"Not if it doesn't happen before we get our contracts for the developments adjacent to the resort." The Hawaiian sat back down in the overstuffed chair and took a long sip of his bourbon.

"Haku, is there something the governor and I ought to know?"

Haku Kane dragged his spent cigarette back and forth through the ashtray, as if weighing the consequences of a possible disclosure. "We have a longer-term interest in the Royal Paradise Bay Resort," he said finally. "Beyond the subdivisions. Something we've worked out with Conway."

Lankowski was not surprised—but he was annoyed. A wild card. A Hui wild card played under the table. Lankowski lit another Vantage even as the previous one smoldered in his ashtray.

"I'd planned to talk to Calvin about it soon," Haku Kane continued. "But the public push will have to come from Conway. Once the Royal Paradise Bay is opened—with all the publicity—he'll be just the man to spearhead it. I'm sure Calvin will agree."

"What are we talking about here, Haku?"

Haku Kane stared into Lankowski's rodent face, watching the aide puff away like an excited animal, then placed his hand on the coffee table and curled his fingers as if squeezing an imaginary ball. "The mango," he said. "Sweetest fruit of the whole operation."

24 ∫ The Unraveling Begins

SUNDAY MORNING, JUNE 11, AT THE RESORT . . .

Robert Conway stepped shirtless onto the lanai of his private suite, his silk pajama bottoms catching the cool wind off Hualalai. Beyond the shaded streams and pools of his artificial jungle lay Kiholo Bay, as blue as the cloudless sky, and the hull of the *Resolution* glowed in the morning light. Conway grimaced.

Mali'o snuck up from behind and wrapped her arms around him. Her soft bosom felt warm. She kissed his shoulder.

"You shouldn't be out here naked," Conway said, turning out of her embrace.

"Oh, shush!" she replied, slipping around to his chest. "There's nobody here to see us." She stretched up on tiptoes to kiss him, but there was no warmth in Conway's lips. Where's Lucio with that Sunday paper, anyway? he wondered.

Below them, netting leaves in one of the pools, an old Hawaiian groundskeeper noticed the couple's embrace. He shook his head and turned away.

"Let's go back to bed," Mali'o urged, sensing Conway's preoccupation.

"Not now. I've got things to do."

"And I've got things I want to do to you." She slid down his body onto her knees.

"Not here!" Conway pulled her back to her feet and ushered her inside.

Someone knocked on the door. "It's Lucio, sir, with your breakfast."

"Just a minute," Conway replied. Mali'o skipped into the bathroom to retrieve her kimono while Conway opened the door.

"Good morning, Mr. Conway," said the young Filipino, rolling the silver serving cart into the room. Amid its elegant food trays and coffeepot were neatly folded copies of the *San Francisco Chronicle* and the *Honolulu Star-Advertiser.*

"Good morning, Lucio," Mali'o said cheerfully, knotting the sash of her satin kimono, a shapely leg still exposed. The attendant smiled back obligatorily, shaking his head as he left the room.

Conway grabbed the *Star-Advertiser* off the cart and went out to the lanai. Mali'o leisurely poured coffee and began assembling two plates of food.

"Oh, my God!" Conway exclaimed.

Mali'o stepped outside to see what was wrong, shocked to observe Conway so shaken. His tanned face had actually gone pale. She grabbed the paper. A bold headline appeared below the masthead: *USGS COVERS UP HUALALAI THREAT*, and in smaller type, *Agency Bows to Development Pressure*. Her boyfriend's picture was among those next to the article.

HVO technician Gus Parker strolled down his driveway to the newspaper tube. The damp morning air carried the volcanic fumes of Pu'u 'O'o, a few miles away. He exchanged waves with a passing neighbor and withdrew the Sunday paper from its tube. "Oh, wow!" he exclaimed, almost bumping into a giant tree fern along the drive. A broad smile spread across his ruddy face.

Islands away in the governor's mansion, Andy Lankowski was breaking the news to his boss. "Looks bad, Calvin," he said, consuming his fifth cigarette of the morning. "Not at all what we'd expected, no siree, not at all."

Governor Calvin Kamali'i leaned over his enormous desk on which the front page was spread, a Kool Light smoldering in an ashtray nearby. "Who gave them this information!" he demanded, grimacing as he scanned the line of photos above the article—Congressman Yamashita, Robert Conway, and his own likeness, a file photo taken two years earlier at a union fund-raiser. He hated that picture, with that stupid disingenuous grin on his face.

Lankowski shrugged. "No idea, no idea at all. I'll bet the congressman's as surprised as we are. He knew they were going to reveal that two-year-old memo, but nobody expected all this stuff about the Royal Paradise Bay." He sucked his cigarette ponderously. "I thought Yamashita was a friend of the editor."

Kamali'i grabbed his cigarette and walked to the window. He gazed across the lawn of the governor's residence toward Diamond Head crater and the hotels of Waikiki. "Yamashita's getting old. His contacts aren't what they used to be."

"Maybe the editor lied to the congressman."

"Oshiro wouldn't dare," Kamali'i replied.

"Sometimes I think Tommy Oshiro is a closet Republican. He doesn't mind embarrassing the Democrats now and again, especially you."

"Why me?" Kamali'i seemed almost hurt at the suggestion. "I've always gotten along with Oshiro—with everyone at the paper, as a matter of fact."

"You know the press is two-faced, Calvin. Don't you think Oshiro would relish making you look stupid? They don't really approve of Native Hawaiians, you know."

Kamali'i knew exactly who *they* were, the same Japanese American establishment that fought his nomination three years earlier and only shifted their allegiance when a campaign-finance scandal made his opponent look too vulnerable to survive the election. Kamali'i bristled at the thought of those people double-crossing him, especially after all the kowtowing he'd done to get where he was.

"Get Haku Kane on the phone!" he commanded.

Lankowski, who had been wandering the room, plopped down on a leather couch in the farthest corner from the phone. "Why?" he asked, but he already knew the answer—Calvin wanted to talk to another

Hawaiian, to spill his guts, look for sympathy, enlist the aid of his Hui friends to fight the damn Japanese.

"I want to get his reaction to the story."

"To what end?" Lankowski asked nonchalantly, lighting up yet another cigarette.

"Andy! Just get Haku on the damn phone."

The Hui chief sat at his breakfast table overlooking the deeply shadowed gorge of Waipio Valley, reading the Sunday paper. His fingers grasped the front page so tightly that the newsprint wrinkled in his hands.

USGS COVERS UP HUALALAI THREAT

Agency Bows to Development Pressure

Special Report by Lisa Choy

KAILUA-KONA. After almost 200 years of quiet, Hualalai may be getting ready to erupt. "Recent data suggest that the volcano will erupt sometime during the next five years, possibly earlier." That was the alarming forecast made two years ago by the Hawaiian Volcano Observatory, a forecast never made public due to pressure placed on the US Geological Survey by some of Hawai'i's most prominent political and economic figures.

Today Hualalai sits quietly above the Big Island's famous Kona coast, one of the fastest-growing areas in the state. But for how long? Two years ago, an internal memorandum written by HVO scientists revealed that its summit region had expanded, indicating that magma was on the move inside the volcano, which last erupted in 1801.

"We've known for many years Hualalai would erupt again, but these data were our first real indication of something in the near term," said Dr. Joseph Murdock, HVO scientist in charge, during an interview yesterday.

According to knowledgeable sources, that data was withheld from Hawai'i County Civil Defense and the public after a hasty series of phone calls and meetings took place between USGS officials, Hawai'i Gov. Calvin Kamali'i, US Rep. Harold Yamashita, and hotel developer Robert Conway. At the center of this activity was Conway, whose luxurious Royal Paradise Bay Resort was just beginning construction at the time of the HVO discovery. The $2 billion resort is scheduled to open Saturday at Kiholo Bay.

"There's no question that the Royal Paradise Bay is critically important to the future economic health of the Big Island," Kamali'i said yesterday at a groundbreaking for the new Waianae Ritz-Carlton on O'ahu. Asked to comment on the potential eruption of Hualalai, Kamali'i laughed. "As a Hawaiian, I have good standing with the lady in charge of Big Island eruptions," he said, referring to the volcano goddess Pele. "There's nothing to worry about, I'm sure."

Neither Yamashita nor Conway was available for comment, but phone records acquired by the *Star-Advertiser* show a flurry of calls made between Conway's office in Honolulu and various political figures in Hawai'i and in Washington—all during a five-day period immediately following USGS receipt of the internal memo. Most of the calls were made to Yamashita's office. Congressional phone records indicate several calls from Yamashita's office to the US Secretary of Interior (which oversees USGS) and USGS offices in Reston, Va., and Menlo Park, Calif.

A USGS official confirmed that Yamashita was the only public official to receive a copy of the secret memorandum. "Our staff keeps in routine contact with USGS because there's always the threat of volcanic eruptions and earthquakes on the Big Island," said an aide to the congressman. "Our interest in this particular report was nothing unusual," she said. But sources intimately involved in the effort to suppress the memorandum suggested that Yamashita, a senior member of influential congressional committees, "strong-armed" USGS to kill the HVO forecast, threatening the agency with "funding woes for years to come."

In the two years since the memorandum was written, additional GPS data has been gathered on Hualalai. An HVO report containing that data, which Murdock said "will vastly improve our ability to forecast a Hualalai eruption," is expected later this week. Murdock declined to give further details until USGS makes the report public . . .

Haku Kane heard a muffled ring elsewhere in the manor, and he glanced at the enormous gold watch strapped around his wrist. 10:15. Well, somebody else has just read the story, he thought. Conway? No. He likes to think he's free of us, prefers to *answer* our calls or work through Lankowski.

Who then? Haku Kane smiled, as if playing a little game while waiting for one of his men to announce the call. His apish hands crumpled his pack of Kools as he withdrew a cigarette and stuck it between his lips. He lit it with his notorious gold lighter engraved with a silver shark, his family's ancestral spirit. Maybe that mongoose, Lankowski, he thought. That sly, self-serving cynic was constantly insinuating himself into everybody's business, all the while trying to strengthen his own hand in whatever game was being played. But Lankowski never lined his pockets, instead living off his meager state salary, and that worried Haku Kane. A man who can't be bought is dangerous.

There was a knock on the door. "Come!" Haku Kane said, folding up the newspaper. A big Hawaiian stepped into the room, his head barely clearing the doorway. "Governor Kamali'i on the line," he said, handing his boss the cell phone.

Haku Kane smiled. This will be much easier than talking to Lankowski. "Kane," he said.

"Haku, it's Calvin. Did you see the *Star-Advertiser* this morning?"

"Yes, I did," he replied coldly, unfolding the newspaper.

"Tommy Oshiro really put it to us, don't you think?"

"Oshiro didn't *write* the story. Who is this"—he scanned the byline—"Lisa Choy?"

"I don't know, but Lankowski's checking on it."

"Lankowski told me—just last night—that this story would only cover some in-fighting between HVO and USGS. He wouldn't lie to me, would he?"

Calvin's aloha shirt suddenly went damp. "Haku, how can you say that? We've been totally—"

"—misinformed then. You need new sources, Calvin," his voice was thin as steel.

Lankowski grimaced as he watched the governor squirm in his leather chair. If he'd been looking for a consoling ear, he'd called the wrong man. Lankowski might have found humor in the governor's discomfort had he not also been privately disgusted with himself. How could he have so misinterpreted the information he'd received from Yamashita's office and his informants at the newspaper? Or had he? Who else outside USGS knew about the memo, or that its squelching was done to protect Conway's project? Lankowski ticked off the names: Robert Conway, Haku Kane, Yamashita, the governor, and himself. None of them would leak it, so it had to come from inside USGS unless . . . Lankowski tapped the filter of his cigarette against a temple.

"Maybe we do need some more reliable sources," Kamali'i admitted, "but right now, Haku, we have to come up with a response."

"I've already read *your* response."

"Huh?"

"That dumb Pele comment."

Kamali'i flushed. "I was just kidding," he whined.

Haku Kane grunted. "Have you talked to Conway yet?"

"Well, no, I—"

"Don't you think that would be a good idea?" His voice was as cold as snow.

"But you're in this too. I thought maybe—"

"*My* name's not in the article. You and Yamashita are the talk of the town today."

"But—"

"You messed in your own corner, Calvin. You clean it up."

"But Haku—"

"*Ai kukae*," he replied calmly, then hung up. Eat shit.

The governor sat dumbfounded, the receiver humming in his hand. Lankowski couldn't help but smile. Haku Kane really knew how to play the game, he thought. Why shouldn't the eel move back into his hole until it was safe to strike again? The Hui could afford to put their interests on hold—play later, after they see whose heads roll—and keep their activities out of sight.

Lankowski lit another cigarette and ran the time frame back through his mind. He'd left Paliuli Estate at about 8:30 p.m. Would that have given Haku Kane time to have someone call the reporter? It would have been too late to smother the fire, but not to redirect it—and keep Haku Kane hidden in the resulting smoke.

25 ∫ The Owl Returns

LATER THAT SUNDAY NEAR KALAPANA . . .

Captain Jack sat on his lanai staring at the evening cumulus piled high over the horizon, unaware that Aka's truck had just rattled up the drive. The old sailor's bloodshot eyes were glazed. He mumbled softly, then laughed—a cynical outburst. He lifted his fifth of Jack Daniels and drank straight from the bottle.

As Aka ambled up the stairs, he noticed his friend's state. "Worried about the kid?"

Jack nearly dropped the bottle. "Christ a'mighty, Aka!"

The Hawaiian eyed the whiskey. "That won't do any good, Jack."

"Whatda *you* know?" He took another long drink.

"I know a few things, Jack. I know that Jimmy's pure heart busted through that old crust of yours and that he reminds you of yourself years ago, a gutsy Minnesota boy eager to taste the bigger world—the kind of son you would have wanted if you'd had one."

"C'mon," Jack scoffed, waving his hand through the muggy air as if brushing those thoughts away.

"And I know you aren't of any use to Jimmy like this."

"I ain't no use to him anyhow, Aka, so wha' diff'rence does it make?"

"Listen, Jack. I talked to Kimo this afternoon. The police are checking all over the island for him."

"Don't matter, Aka. The boy's gone." Moisture coated his eyes. "And I didn't help him when he needed me. I was jus' protectin' my own carcass, goddammit! Same cowardice I resigned myself to in the Navy, all so I could retire comfortably on the sunny coast of Kalapana—and now it's nothin' but lava!"

"Pull yourself together, Jack. Now is when Jimmy needs you most." Aka turned to leave.

"Hey, where ya goin'?"

"I'll be back tomorrow, later tonight if need be."

"Whatcha gonna do?"

"Something my gut says I have to do. I'm going to tell Kimo about the murder so he can really help us."

The Hawaiian drove to the end of the Old Kalapana Road where lava had blocked it. He sat on the tailgate watching the stars while he waited for his nephew.

A few minutes later Kimo zoomed up in his black Chevy Camaro, absent the blue police light it wore during the day.

"Howzit, Uncle," Kimo said in a somber tone, sliding onto the tailgate. The old pickup sagged rearward.

"Mahalo for coming, Kimo. Any news of Jimmy?"

He shook his head. "Machado goin' up in da helicopter tomorrow, search dis whole side of da volcano."

"That's good," Aka said.

"So, Uncle, you got information for share."

"Yes, but you can't give it to Machado."

Kimo sighed loudly. "All right, Uncle, I jus' hope I no end up in hot water."

They lit cigarettes and Aka began. "It all started about a week ago, when the pueo came to visit." Aka raised his eyebrows to punctuate the statement.

Kimo raised his too. He knew his uncle still thought ancestors visited in the spirit form of animals, but nothing in his own life had encouraged him to adopt those beliefs.

"Two nights the owl sat in the big ʻohiʻa tree behind my house. All night long, Kimo—all night! And on that first night—Friday—I woke up to the owl's scream in a dream." Aka leaned his face close to his nephew's so Kimo felt the gentle pulse of his breath. "At that same time—shortly after midnight—a man was murdered out there."

"Not!"

"And Jimmy saw the whole thing."

Kimo leaned back and whistled softly. Aka proceeded to tell all that he knew of the murder, but without revealing Maile and Gavin's involvement. When he divulged his suspicions about the Hui, Kimo slid off the tailgate and began pacing the road.

"Dis too heavy, Uncle. I t'ink we beddah tell Lieutenant Machado."

"You trust him?"

"I hope so, but I nevah know."

And at that moment the owl returned. The bird swooped low over the truck and glided onto a dead tree at the edge of the flow.

"Whoa!" Kimo jumped to his feet.

Aka slid off the tailgate and walked slowly to the end of the road, never taking his eyes off the owl's silhouette against the starry sky. Kimo heard his uncle talking to the bird in their native tongue, asking for guidance. When Aka took a step closer, the owl flew off to a fallen palm well in from the road.

"Jimmy's out there," Aka said matter-of-factly. "The pueo wants us to follow him."

Goosebumps rose all over Kimo's arms. His blood bond to his elder was immutable, but still he hesitated. "Even if Jimmy out dere, why not wait for Machado to find him wit' da chopper?"

Aka turned to face his nephew. Even in the dark, Kimo could see his uncle's disappointment. "I sorry, Uncle, but—"

"Then I go alone."

Kimo ran his fat fingers through his hair and sighed. "OK, Uncle, but jus' a little ways."

Kimo stepped to his car and opened the trunk. He pulled out two flashlights, handing one to Aka, then strapped on his holster. He tucked his badge into his pocket, threw his binoculars over his shoulder, and closed the trunk. By the time they climbed up onto the flow, clouds had begun forming over the slopes, obscuring half the Milky Way.

The owl took off again as they approached, lighting on a charred fencepost higher up the volcano. They followed, keeping the bird in sight with their flashlights, and each time they grew near, it flew to another perch—a remnant pole, a distant tree—farther up the rugged terrain. The night grew darker with the gathering clouds, but the owl seemed always to alight upon something still silhouetted by brilliant stars.

"He just hunting," Kimo said feebly.

" 'A'ole,"Aka said, pushing on. Not.

The long trek was difficult for Aka, yet his old bones took on new strength from some dormant inner reserve. Kimo was in better shape, but not that much better. More than a year had passed since his rigorous police training, and he now spent most of his time patrolling from the seat of his Camaro while munching Piggy Puffs and popcorn. Eventually they passed the oozing red outbreaks that had drawn Jimmy up the pali to the edge of the island of dense vegetation marked by the single towering koa tree.

"Hey, Uncle," Kimo said, his big eyes filled with trepidation, "you got chicken skin?"

Aka nodded. He peered into the dark sliver of jungle and waited. Within a minute he knew. "There's something in there," the old Hawaiian wheezed, easing himself onto a nearby rock. Kimo took his uncle's cue. He drew his gun and walked deep into the dense vegetation with his flashlight.

The owl screeched.

"Uncle," Kimo called out from the jungle, "you sure dis OK?"

"Keep going! See what's in there!" But with those words came an onrush of misgiving and the feeling that he should have gone in too.

"Uncle! Uncle!" Kimo's voice trembled with alarm.

Chicken skin covered every inch of Aka's broad back. "Get outa there, Kimo!" he hollered, instinctively stepping toward his nephew's light, its beam jiggling with Kimo's hasty retreat. Kimo exhaled loudly when at last he broke free of the jungle. Aka's eyes were now as wide as his nephew's.

"Got one heavy shrine in dere, Uncle! I wen' nevah seen one li'dat—old, dat's why, real old."

Aka, suddenly realizing where they were, grasped his nephew's shoulders. "Did you disturb anything?"

"I no t'ink so."

"Did you see . . . you know . . . anything else? And I'm not talking about Jimmy."

Kimo shook his head slowly. "I not see anyt'ing li'dat."

Kimo may not have seen the spirits, but Aka felt them. He picked a sprig of red lehua blossoms off an 'ohi'a, and struggling through the dense vegetation, carried it into the shrine. He reemerged from the jungle a few minutes later, calmer and with a deeper resonance in his voice. "I had always heard that our oldest ancestors built a shrine up here," Aka said. "Now I know."

Aka scanned the sky and landscape until, some distance away, they heard the owl call again. "Let's keep moving," he said. They followed the sound, angling far upslope. Later Aka looked back at the sliver of jungle isolated on the decimated slope, and tears formed in his eyes.

"What's wrong, Uncle?" Kimo asked.

"It's many, many years since anyone visited that shrine," he said, shaking his head. "Too many years."

A quarter mile farther up the pali they passed a half-burned house and a charred truck. It had been well over an hour since they'd begun the trek, and Aka was tired. He eased his aching body onto a smooth chunk of pahoehoe lava and gazed at the reddened steam plumes down at the coast, which looked tiny in the distance. Kimo squatted next to his uncle, his body streaming with sweat. The owl flitted onto an uplifted rock nearby.

"You OK, Uncle?" Kimo asked, flicking off his flashlight.

"I don't know how much farther I can go," Aka wheezed back.

"Where dis owl taking us, huh?"

"Royal Gardens," Aka replied, sliding a Kool into his mouth. He lit it and offered one to Kimo.

Kimo took the cigarette and stared at the dark remnants of the ravaged subdivision. "No more people up here," Kimo said, but the anxiety in his voice belied his statement. "I t'ink dat bird wen' take us on one wild goose chase."

"Jimmy is up here somewhere," Aka replied.

"You mean Jimmy's body."

Aka snubbed his cigarette into a crack and pushed himself up from the rock. "Let's keep going."

Kimo sighed. He stood and yanked his trousers up over his belly. As he stepped out ahead of his uncle, Aka noticed him unhook the safety strap on his holster.

The owl flew off the rock into a distant section of forest missed by the flows. The two men followed but the canopy of clouds made it impossible to track him.

"I've lost the pueo," Aka said, shining his light up into the trees.

A scream issued from deep within the forest, and they followed the owl's calls through the thicket of jungle until at last they reached the widest of the old flows that had destroyed most of Royal Gardens. Rain began drizzling from the sky, and a soft rumble issued from the clouds.

"He's out there," Aka said, squinting at the dark lava. "I can feel it." He switched off his flashlight and instructed Kimo to do the same. As his eyes adjusted to the dark, Aka noticed a slight movement on the ground. Just fifty feet away, the crouching owl peered at them. As soon as they spotted the bird, it took flight, soaring far out over the pali—screaming, screaming—its silhouette visible against the throbbing red clouds above the coast.

"What you make o' dat, Uncle?" Kimo said as the bird vanished in a distant steam plume.

"I'm not sure, but keep your flashlight off."

Kimo walked to the spot where the pueo had been while Aka leaned against a dead tree at the flow's edge. His leg muscles trembled and his lungs ached. Whatever power had gotten him there had faded, and he suddenly felt his seventy-three years.

"Uncle, look!" Kimo said, pointing toward the jungle on the other side of the vast swath of lava that lay before them. There, blurred in the drizzle blowing across the devastated pali, was a single flickering light.

26 ∫ A Trek inside Hualalai

THAT SAME EVENING AT THE ASTRONOMERS' BASE CAMP . . .

I'm afraid the news is bad."

Gavin McCall looked up from his lasagna as his Australian colleague, Donny, sat down across the table.

"Sorry to interrupt your dinner, mate, but I knew you'd want to know right away. The infrared camera's shot," Donny reported.

Gavin had expected as much. For two days they'd struggled to get data, but each time the summit cleared enough for them to observe, the camera wouldn't respond to commands from the computer.

"I've confirmed the problem with one of the chaps from the NASA day crew," he continued. "Apparently some soldering cracked on the timing board."

"Nuts!" Gavin gazed out the dining room's wall of windows where Earth's largest volcano, Mauna Loa, took up half the view, the giant blue-gray in the day's last light. No clouds cloaked *that* mountain, he noticed, but even if the sky above Mauna Kea's domes cleared up, it wouldn't matter. Gavin's eye on Io's volcano was blind.

"You're the instrument expert, Gavin. What do we do now?"

"There's another timing board at the Canberra lab. We send for it—post haste." Gavin looked at his watch. "Still only midafternoon in Australia."

"Problem is, it's Monday over there, mate. Everybody's probably at that conference downtown."

Gavin pushed his plate away. "The weather, and now this bloody instrument problem! Our whole week buggered! We haven't accomplished a thing, and I'm already exhausted from our futile efforts."

"Why don't ya take a day off, g'down to the beach or something? I'll take care o' the call, eh?"

"But you haven't been off the mountain all week."

"Ya want to know the truth, mate? I love it up here. No phone ringin' every ten minutes, no department head jabberin' 'bout university politics, no students draggin' their papers in a week late. On top o' that, we get three squares and a warm bed. Mauna Kea's a little less than halfway up into space, but that's close enough to heaven for me."

Gavin turned back to the window. A purple twilight gathered over Mauna Loa, and Jupiter, high in the southeast, sparkled against the darkening sky. "Being in a wild place like Hawai'i—far from the routines of home—can put things into perspective, eh?"

"Yeah," Donny replied softly, rising from the table. "Well, Gavin, if the summit does clear, I can use that telescope time for me own pet project—comet dust, ya know."

"Might as well."

Gavin, his appetite gone, slid open the glass doors and walked out onto the lanai. The brightest stars already shone above Mauna Loa, including the Southern Cross. No doubt Polynesians used those, he thought to himself. Long before Magellan, Drake, and Cook, those islanders, without chart or compass, had crisscrossed the Pacific using stars as guideposts, brave men and women exploring remote constellations of islands in a vast, watery universe.

Night fell with the suddenness common in the tropics, and Gavin noticed a red glow to the east, the fumes above Kilauea's distant Pu'u 'O'o cone. Why hadn't he noticed it on previous nights? Had it been masked by clouds, or were his perceptions changing because of his experiences with Maile? Even his volcano on Io seemed imbued with new mystery. Out of these musings emerged yet again that vivid picture of Maile at the luau, her face and figure etched in gold against the dark jungle. Yes, her Polynesian ways intrigued him, and more than that—he missed her.

The glass doors suddenly slid open and a bold Hawaiian face emerged. "There's a phone call for you," said the camp's senior cook.

"Thanks, mate."

Gavin stepped inside to the phone. "G'day, this is Gavin McCall."

"This is Maile."

"Extraordinary. I was just thinking of you."

"Oh, I like that." Her voice was warm. "You were on my mind too, so I thought I'd call. Going up tonight?"

" 'Fraid not. Our instrument's buggered. I'll be twiddling me thumbs till new parts arrive—a couple days, anyway."

"May I make a suggestion?"

"OK."

"I'm taking pictures of an archaeological site on the Kona side tomorrow. Would you like to come along? I'll be driving over the saddle, passing right below the base camp. I promise we'll avoid high adventure."

Gavin laughed uneasily. "Yeah, right."

"I think you'll find the site interesting."

"Quite honestly, Maile, I'm ready for a respite from this bloody mountain."

"Then it's a date."

"Indeed it is. What time do you want to pick me up?"

"One o'clock OK?"

"Righto. I'll look forward to it, Maile."

"Me too. Aloha."

Maile arrived at the base camp the next afternoon at about 1:30. The usually locked door was propped open to let in some fresh mountain air. She stepped into the lobby, a vaulted space lined with flags from the dozen countries operating telescopes on the mountain. Gavin sat alone in front of the fireplace reading a copy of *Sky and Telescope*. He leaped up from the sofa, the delight on his face so obvious that a passing housekeeper threw them both a smile of encouragement.

"Aloha," she said, kissing Gavin on the cheek. "I'm sorry, I got delayed picking up some documents at the university."

"Where are we off to?" Gavin asked as they settled into the Jeep.

"A rich and mysterious site," Maile said, pulling the vehicle out onto the road, "one that development will soon disturb. That's why I need to get some pictures."

"Sounds intriguing."

"By the way, did the summit ever clear?"

"Now and again. Last night we had freezing fog till well past midnight, but there was too much moisture left in the air to open the domes. Imagine it, Maile—a brilliant sky full of stars, and no way to look at them."

"You could use your eyes." She smiled.

"So we're back to our lessons, eh?"

"Well, we can't let that good-looking astronomer from Australia waste a moment of his precious time here, EH?"

They laughed heartily.

The hour-long drive to Kona began with the austere saddle between the two high volcanoes. Colossal cinder cones stood on one side of the road, where thousands of years earlier Mauna Kea had spewed forth fiery fountains—incandescent torches that illuminated the inner flanks of both mountains. On the other side lay the raw rugged lavas of Mauna Loa, the most recent from 1984.

"Few Hawaiians made the trek over the top of the island," Maile said, "but those who did recognized the power of this upper realm. Mauna Kea—highest and most sacred summit in the Pacific, where oracles ascended to consult the gods. Mauna Loa—Pele's fiery alpine home, so revered none visited without due purpose. Hualalai—on whose slopes sixteenth-century stargazers constructed a sprawling temple to serve as their observatory. And Pohakuloa—the vast mysterious region between the three mountains, dotted with religious shrines and crisscrossed with trails linking every region of the island.

"In the high country," Maile concluded, "stand Hawai'i's oldest temples, monuments to a time before the Tahitians brought their royal order. It must have been a peaceful age," she said wistfully, "when navigators—rather than warriors—were held in the highest esteem, and aloha—not royal decree—ruled the land."

"Love fares poorly against power and greed, eh?"

Maile didn't answer, but her eyes burned.

"Hawai'i seems to have two distinct faces," Gavin said. "I saw them both at the luau that first night. One is of aloha. The other—obvious in those young men who wouldn't talk to me—is deeply bitter. I can appreciate the former, but the latter is still a puzzle to me."

"I can tell you the story, but it may jeopardize your romantic view of Hawaiʻi."

"I'd rather hear the truth."

At that moment they passed a sprawling compound of military buildings, vehicles, and helicopters enclosed in a high steel fence topped with barbed wire. An armed soldier guarded the entrance gate.

"Pohakuloa Training Area," Maile said sullenly.

"Way up here?"

"For desert and mountain combat, in places like Iraq and Afghanistan, with tanks, artillery, and helicopters."

Gavin shook his head.

As the Jeep descended Mauna Kea's long slopes and approached Hualalai, Maile recounted Hawaiʻi's sad history of conquests—the Tahitian takeover and the intergenerational clan wars that followed, the Christian missionaries' religious and cultural intolerance, the Americans' land grab and militarization, and the "old boys'" commercialization after statehood. When she finished, tears stood in her eyes.

"Sorry, luv," he said, touching her shoulder.

"I've always considered myself thick skinned, like my Chinese father, but lately my feelings seem just beneath the surface."

"Perhaps your heart is opening up, eh?" Gavin offered, his rugged face soft with compassion. Maile peered at him so intently that he felt as though she was looking *into* rather than *at* him. "Mind the road, eh?" he said, breaking her gaze.

A few minutes later, she turned off the highway into the heart of a subdivision still under construction on the slopes of Hualalai. They parked in front of a row of tidy tract houses with trim lawns and groomed flower beds. The development reminded Gavin of suburban Canberra.

"What're we doing *here?*" he asked.

"Looking for history," she replied, grabbing her backpack from behind the seat. They took drinks from a water bottle Maile kept in the vehicle, then trekked through a grassy field plotted with survey flags.

"Here we are," Maile said, stopping in the waist-high grass. Gavin was puzzled. She pointed at a rock cairn hidden in the grass, then led him down a gentle slope to a barely visible ridge of exposed rock. A narrow crevice marked its face.

"I found this cave during the archaeological survey for the subdivision," Maile said, piling her locks atop her head and securing them with a barrette. She pulled two large Maglites out of her pack and handed one to Gavin.

"Be careful," she said, slipping inside the opening. "There are fallen rocks all over and the ceiling's low."

Gavin squeezed through the crevice. Only a narrow sliver of sunlight illuminated the rubble inside. He switched on his flashlight and caught Maile's face in the beam. As he moved toward her, she took his hand, easing the overwhelming darkness. "C'mon," she said.

As they moved well beyond the rubble of the collapse into the main body of the cave, Gavin looked back. The small patch of light at the entrance was no longer visible, and the air was stale and weighty. Scanning the defunct tube with his flashlight, he noticed its tunnel shape and many tiny basalt stalactites hanging from the ceiling.

Maile gently pulled Gavin toward her. "This cave carried lava to the sea during the 1801 Hualalai eruption." She pointed her flashlight down the cavern's descending slope. "That way goes toward the ocean. And, if it hadn't collapsed where the entrance is now, the other side would continue up to the craters of Hualalai. Some lava tubes go for miles, and it's easy to get lost because they branch off along multiple routes. Now and again you hear of someone disappearing."

"I imagine that's led to a few island legends, eh?"

"Hawaiians used these caves for shelter and to collect freshwater dripping off the ceiling. Warriors, runaway slaves, and others fleeing hid in them. Caves were also used for burials. In fact, King Kamehameha the Great's bones are said to be hidden inside a lava tube somewhere along this coast."

"What's so special about *this* particular cave?"

"Follow me. I'll show you."

They trekked for several minutes down the dark tunnel to a place where the tube angled to the left. Maile stopped abruptly.

"Gavin, look behind you."

He shone his light on the dark passage.

"We came from there, right?" Maile asked.

"Righto."

"You're sure?"

"Of course, I'm sure. You see how it slopes upward in the direction of the entrance."

"Now move your light a little to the right."

"Good God! *Another* tube."

"Exactly. Now, which one did we take?"

"Damned if I know! I hope you do."

"The one on the right."

"Jeez, I wouldn't have even *noticed* that one on the way back out."

"There are dozens of branches like that—in *both* directions. So you have to keep constant watch all the way down the tube. Otherwise—"

"I take it *you've* been keeping track."

"As best I can," she teased.

"How much farther do we go?"

"Not too far," she said, turning to proceed.

"I bloody hope not!"

"By the way, Gavin," she said over her shoulder, "lava tubes are not good places to be during earthquakes."

Gavin glanced up at the cracks in the ceiling. He followed Maile down various bends of the tube, aware that she was constantly checking both sides of the cave with her flashlight. The dank air tasted as if it hadn't been breathed for ages. Gavin grew uneasy, but he wasn't sure why. He'd explored much more confining caves in Australia. Maile seemed to know exactly where she was going, yet Gavin felt as if he had stepped over some invisible line of safety.

"Look at this," Maile said, stopping in a spacious chamber of the cave. She slowly cast her light across the left wall. Dozens of pecked carvings shone in the light—figures of men and women, drums and canoes, fish and birds, rainbows and shamans. "Some of these petroglyphs may date back to just after Hualalai's last eruption."

Gavin, awestruck, said nothing.

Maile turned her flashlight to the opposite wall, revealing scores of petroglyphs there as well. The carved figures seemed to Gavin like messages from another time, when a Polynesian way of life still dominated. Maile stepped close to the Australian, letting her shoulder rest against his as they stared at the wall in silence. Despite the wonder and intimacy, Gavin still felt uneasy.

Far in the distance, in the ambient light of her beam, stood a tall pear-shaped stone. Sea-worn smooth and placed upright, it stood like a sentinel guarding the rest of the cave. Gavin's gut clenched at the sight of it.

Maile set her light on a ledge, illuminating both walls of carvings, then moved about the chamber taking a series of flash pictures. After documenting the petroglyphs, she sat down on the floor and gazed at the entire display. Intrigued as Gavin was by it all, he was glad when they finally headed back up the tube.

The return seemed to take forever, and Gavin's anxiety was fueled by concern about whether they were following the right branches back to the entrance. As the minutes dragged on, Gavin became convinced they had passed several tubes not met on the way in.

Finally, they reached a collapsed ceiling and ascended some rubble that Gavin hoped was where they had earlier entered the cave. They got to the top, where the ceiling hung low, but no light was visible. Gavin distinctly remembered that this whole area had been illuminated by sunlight through the opening. Where was it now? He cast his flashlight in all directions, struggling to get his bearings. When he turned back, Maile was gone.

27 ∫ The Cave of Fear

Gavin stood alone in the dark, silent cavern.

"Maile?" he whispered.

"Maile!" This time shouting. "Where are you?"

A shaft of light passed over his face, momentarily blinding him. "Out here."

He blinked the dark-vision back into his eyes and saw a flashlight sticking straight out of the wall.

"The opening's right here."

He followed the light through the crevice and was surprised to discover that the sun had set. A thin purple line lay across the horizon beneath the first evening stars. The lights of Kailua town twinkled along the distant coast, and the nearby houses glowed under orange streetlights. Had they really been down there that long?

"Weird," he said, shaking his head. "I feel as though I've just emerged from another world."

"You have," she said, reaching up to unfasten her hair. She shook her head, and its great mass of locks tumbled down her back.

"How long were we in there?"

Maile looked at her watch. "Almost three hours."

"Incredible. Time just disappeared."

"Yes." She peered into Gavin's face, the luminescence of her eyes softer in the faded light, revealing a more subtle intensity.

"That is an extraordinary place," he said, returning the gaze. "What do the carvings mean?"

"They're still a mystery. Usually petrogylphs are in the open, on stretches of lava with ample smooth surfaces for pecking. So this cave must have had special significance."

"Was it considered sacred?" he asked, recalling his wariness.

"If not, why conceal the carvings? And why so far down the tube?"

"Maile, when we first met, you said that some places were off limits, that they were—"

"Kapu, that a taboo had been placed on them by the chief or, under his direction, by a kahuna. Religious sites, or burials."

"Might this cave have been one of those tabooed places?"

"Maybe."

Gavin sensed that Maile was not telling him all she knew about the cave. He flashed her an inquisitive look.

"There's still a lot of debate about petroglyphs," she replied, suddenly more academic in tone. "One theory is that they document the history of particular families, because you find them where *piko* ceremonies took place, where the umbilical cords of newborns were placed. Another is that they mark special places where other ceremonies were held. Some archaeologists assert that they're just ancient graffiti, but I don't believe that. What's interesting is that Hawaiians don't usually talk about them, a sure sign of their importance."

"And what did you make of that upright stone?"

Maile's face darkened. "Oh, you noticed that too?"

"I know this sounds weird, but I had a strange feeling about it."

She glanced back toward the cave, the low entrance barely visible in the twilight. The cool breeze off Hualalai sent a chill through her sweaty body.

"It looks like a protectorate stone, to guard the rest of the tube."

"What do you think might be down there?"

"Hard to guess. Maybe some local Hawaiians placed the stone there to make sure people know it's kapu."

"If a place is kapu—for whatever reason—might you be able to, well, *feel* it?"

"Oh yes, many places in the islands are like that—you just *know*. Why? Did *you* feel something?"

"I know this sounds crazy, but I had the distinct feeling I wasn't supposed to be there."

"That's not crazy. For Hawaiians, such feelings are a gift. It means you are in touch with your na'au, your core instincts. Tell me what you felt."

"Well, the deeper we went, the more anxious I got. It actually became difficult to breathe, like someone was sitting on me chest. Amazing as those carvings were, I really didn't want to linger."

Maile took his arm, her expression suddenly grave. "If you ever get that feeling again, wherever it is, pay attention to it."

"Did you feel anything, Maile?"

"Well, it was *different* than before—but then, I was busy taking pictures." Her face lightened a bit. "I was also distracted by my companion."

A smile crept over his face.

"Gavin, those feelings also mean that you're beginning to connect with the island." She smiled. "You sure there isn't some Aboriginal blood somewhere in your background?"

To Gavin's way of thinking, all this was hokum, yet his gut told him otherwise. His experiences with Maile seemed to tap a source deeper than his mind. Even on Mauna Kea he had begun to *feel*—not just think about—the wonders of the universe. Astonishingly, they were familiar feelings, like those he'd had as a child during nights stargazing under dark southern skies. Maile was awakening something long ago put to sleep.

Gavin stared at her. She stood in the hip-high grass under the twilight glow, her skin luminous, long hair tossing in the breeze. Gavin slid his fingers into her palm; she took them willingly. Passion surged in each of them. They drew so close that Maile's breasts brushed against his chest and she smelled his scent, musky after penetrating the cave. Maile pressed against him, and Gavin buried his nose in her hair. Its feel and aroma excited him. Lightly, he kissed her head, face, and neck, at last finding her lips. Moist, she tasted like earth—tangy, fresh, new. Their kisses, fierce at first and full of hunger, eventually eased into a gentle flow of lip brushing lip, furtive tongues touching. Twilight faded as they clung to one another in the windblown field. Stars rose above the dark summit of Hualalai while others dropped into the sea. When at last their lips parted, Maile exhaled into Gavin's mouth and gently grazed his nose with hers, the traditional Polynesian kiss.

Gavin opened his eyes, now burning through the darkness. "Maile," he said, gently sliding two fingers under her jaw. "I've thought of kissing you since the very first day we met."

"You waited a long time then." The passion in her eyes turned dreamy.

"Well, once ignited, fires can easily run out of control."

"Yes, they can," she replied, again pressing herself against him. "That's one of the things I like about fire."

Maile brushed her lips against his, teasing his tongue into her mouth. She felt her heat rise. Gavin pulled her even closer, his whole body burning. Reality fell away, and he pictured the two of them as companion suns in deep space spinning around their mutual orbit. Then, like a comet flaming in from his subconscious, a memory flashed across his mind—Annie, shirt open to the breeze on a sunlit mountain in the Kimberleys. The blaze left a streak across his consciousness that sobered him back to reality. Maile's eyes were still closed when he removed his mouth from hers. Her hair was tousled, her lips swollen, her tongue poised to receive his.

"How about some dinner?" He whispered, gently breaking free.

Maile opened her eyes and stared at him. "What?"

"I need a bit of a breather, luv."

With a flash of disappointment, the focus returned to Maile's eyes.

The couple started out across the field, wordless, each picking a detail of the landscape on which to rest their eyes while their minds sifted—Maile, the running lights of a sailboat slowly making its way home, and Gavin, headlight beams speeding down the Queen Ka'ahumanu Highway. When at last they stepped into the yellow glow of a street lamp next to Maile's Jeep, she let go of Gavin's fingers to unlock the door. But he retrieved her hand and spun her around to face him. He pressed her gently against the door and cupped her broad face in his hands.

"Maile," he said, his handsome features lined in deep shadow. "I'm afraid you've swept this Aussie away."

"*I'm* not afraid. I'm glad." She was *in touch* again, with everything—this man, the island, her Hawaiian self. It had been years since she had felt that way, maybe as far back as high school.

"Kiss me again," she demanded, parting her lips in anticipation. He kissed her roughly as she clung to him. His hands explored her body while she pulled up his shirt and stroked his back. A gecko called out from the tall grass. The brooding hulk of Hualalai towered over them, beneath a dazzling splash of Milky Way stars.

Finally, many minutes later, they pulled apart.

"Nice," she said, smiling up at Gavin. Her gold necklace gleamed inside her half-open shirt.

Gavin, flushed, stepped back as if searching for ground on which to place his feet. "I suppose we ought to be off to that restaurant before we create a public spectacle here, eh?" He tucked his shirt into his pants.

Maile laughed, reaching up to rebutton her shirt. "There's an old Japanese hotel not far from here. They serve the best tuna fillet on the coast."

Gavin smiled dreamily. "Sounds good."

Maile drove the Jeep through the coffee country high above coastal Kailua. They passed through the quiet town of Holualoa, but neither Gavin nor Maile paid much attention. Both were absorbed with anticipation of what lay ahead.

Gavin placed his arm atop the back of Maile's seat and lightly caressed her neck. Sexual energy throbbed between them. "I must admit," he said, studying her face in the amber light from the dash, "I didn't expect something like this to happen."

"Hawai'i is full of surprises," Maile said softly. "It's foolish to come here with any expectations. Fate too often intervenes."

"Maybe that isn't such a good thing, in this particular case."

Maile flashed him a puzzled look. "There isn't a Mrs. McCall, is there?"

Not anymore, he thought. "No."

"A girlfriend then?"

"It's not that, Maile. Let me be honest with you."

"Please do."

"From the first, I was drawn to you. It makes me a tad nervous."

"So? That makes two of us. Though I'm not surprised. Even when you first came to see me, I wondered what might happen between us."

Gavin's eyes were ambivalent. "I guess we're destined to find out, eh?"

He knew, and it shook him. He hadn't felt this way about a woman since Annie. Four years had passed since her death, and yet she still invaded his dreams. "Soul mates," Annie had called them, a term he hadn't really understood until he lost her. Infatuated young students—she a bird biologist and he a budding astronomer—they had married in graduate school, each pursuing their field with zeal and wonder. More interested in sharing adventure than rearing kids, they set up their "vagabond shack" outside Canberra, a rustic cottage on the Molonglo River that served as love nest, library, and expedition headquarters.

During their twelve-year marriage, Gavin felt a deep sense of well-being, but the true source of this happiness had remained a jumble in his mind. Oh, he knew he loved Annie—compelled by her intellectual brilliance and country good looks—but he was often preoccupied with his own professional explorations. Then she died, on a field study of African gray parrots in the Congo, a project she had long dreamt of. A deadly boomslang bit her after she'd stepped on the snake while photographing in a tree, and the remote location made it impossible to reach a hospital in time. Gavin never recovered from that African phone call. Eagerly anticipating their weekly conversation, he was instead informed that he would never hear her voice again.

The emptiness of that long winter alone in their cottage dissolved his earlier confusion; he realized it was their love that had made everything worthwhile. The decision not to have children left him all the more alone, with no genetic remnant of his soul mate to remind him of her gifts—or distract him from his profound grief. The antics of her own Australian parrots could not lift his spirits either, their presence in the cottage just keeping the terrible memory of her death alive. Eventually he gave the birds away. He had tried dating, but no new spark could overcome his sorrow. He allowed his teaching load to grow as a way to fill the days, and over time his noted curiosity dulled, along with his interest in the astronomy research projects that used to inspire him.

Then, two years after Annie's death, when he'd reached his emotional rock bottom, he bought a new Dobsonian—the first amateur telescope he'd owned since retiring his childhood five-inch in the pursuit of professional astronomy. Although he regularly observed for the university at Mount Woorat, he began spending weekends alone under the clear skies of the Australian bush, staring at the beautiful objects that had given him most of his joy before Annie.

Maile looked over at him, her eyes so big and dark that for an instant Gavin lost track of the face around them. "You know," she said, "I'm not in the habit of falling in love with haoles."

"And I dare say, I've never fallen for a Polynesian either."

"And yet, I feel we're connected by something inexplicable that transcends our cultures."

He flashed on the image of a star being sucked into a black hole, a vortex so powerful even light itself cannot escape its grasp. Everything about Hawai'i challenged Gavin's sense of personal control—the volcanoes, the islanders, the spirits and legends, the mountain weather, this woman. Even the island's overwhelming beauty was unsettling, so stunningly primordial that it evoked a frightening sensation of surrender, as when a man falls in love with his fantasy of a woman, only later to discover that the distortions of his imagination have put him in peril.

"There's some reason," Maile continued, "that you and I have been thrown together at this time."

Reluctantly, Gavin nodded.

28 ∫ Love at the Hayashi Hotel

Maile parked in front of a homely wood-frame building, its two stories adorned with a lofty false front and an illuminated art deco sign—"J. Hayashi Hotel." Built in the 1920s on the island's old circle route, the roadhouse accommodated the Big Island's first significant wave of tourists. Later, to meet the burgeoning trade after statehood, Joe Hayashi Jr. added a wing of modern rooms with stunning views of the famous bay called Kealakekua, "the pathway of God." On its rocky shore Hawaiians had killed Captain James Cook after he stole their temple god images to use as ship's firewood, killed a popular chief, and then attempted to kidnap the island's king to compel the return of a stolen boat.

Maile led Gavin into the lobby, where the elderly son of the original proprietor was hunched over an antique desk, scanning his account books. "Can you handle two more for dinner, Mr. Hayashi?" Maile said. The old Nisei glanced up through half-moon glasses.

"Ah, Maile Chow." His furrowed face abruptly transformed into a boyish, smiling countenance. "Of course. Of course."

Mr. Hayashi popped up from his chair to escort the couple into the dining room, a homey little space with an open kitchen issuing tantalizing smells. The place was packed, mostly with islanders.

"Whoa. You're really busy tonight," Maile said. "I'll bet you haven't an empty room in the house."

"Yes. Yes. Many visitors from Honolulu this time of year. I'm afraid we're booked solid." He bit his lip in mock shame. "Sorry, Maile. If you'd just given me a call."

"Oh, we were planning to drive back to Hilo tonight."

"Tonight?" Mr. Hayashi looked at his watch. "It's almost seven-thirty."

She shrugged. "It's always difficult to start back when you're in Kona."

"Yes." Mr. Hayashi smiled.

He seated them at a small table near a window, bowed, and scurried away. Maile leaned over to smell the fresh ginger blossoms adorning the Formica table while Gavin studied the room. Dusty prints of seascapes hung on the walls along with a menu board spelling out the dinner fare in plastic letters. A fat gecko lounged on the window frame above their table, its big eyes blinking every time the waitress approached.

The family-style dinner began with potent gin and tonics and a platter of Japanese appetizers, followed by more cocktails and the main meal of fresh tuna fillets, steamed okra, and huge bowls of white rice. The serving tempo was unhurried, and the waitress, part of Mr. Hayashi's sprawling extended family, chatty and warm. Although the proprietors and menu were Asian, the feeling was the same as at the Hawaiian luau in Keaukaha—relaxed, convivial, island-style.

"This is first cabin!" Gavin said, spooning another helping of rice onto his plate.

"The tuna is *'ono*, yeah?" Maile said, setting a shred of fish in front of the gecko with her chopsticks. The lizard eyed the morsel noncommittally, then snapped it up with his tongue.

"If that means 'tasty,' then yes."

"This whole day has been wonderful," Maile said, intertwining her fingers with Gavin's. "And yet"—the liquor had made her introspective—"our times together are having a peculiar effect on me. In trying to explain Hawai'i to you—the real truth of it—something inside has surfaced that I don't quite know what to do with." She searched his eyes, hoping—trusting—that it was safe to tell him these things. She tightened her grip on his fingers. "I'm angry, Gavin, and getting angrier by the minute."

"Why?"

"Those thugs we saw on the volcano are part of a larger disease sickening the islands, a plague even more virulent than the missionaries' measles that killed so many of us." Maile's dark eyes misted over. The gecko croaked softly. "And in facing that anger, I realize that I've played a part in the demise by doing the surveys for the developers."

"But, Maile, you couldn't—"

She threw her hand up between them. "Yes, I could. How many things have I conveniently forgotten about my culture so I could live a comfortable middle-class life in Hilo? Think about it, Gavin. I own a bungalow right on the beach. Few Hawaiians can afford that. Instead, they risk arrest by 'squatting' on old ancestral lands at the outskirts of town where they can fish and grow taro next to their beloved sea. They live under blue tarps while I—"

"Maile, don't—"

"Using the excuse that I'm helping my people, I take the money of developers like Robert Conway who have no real sentiment for Hawai'i. They could build anywhere for all they understand the place."

"Maile, it's just the downside of progress."

"Progress? How can the destruction of the island's beauty and way of life be progress?"

Gavin shrugged.

Maile withdrew her fingers from his hand and picked up her chopsticks. She poked around the food on her plate, thinking.

"You know what else, Gavin? When they need surveys done in really sensitive areas, they hire me. Because Maile Chow is such a fine expert?" Bitterness crept into her voice. "No, because using a Hawaiian buys them credibility."

"Maile—"

"Why don't I refuse? Why don't I tell them what they're doing is wrong?" A tear rolled out the flooded corner of her eye. "Because I want to live the haole lifestyle, like the other Chinese and Japanese in Hawai'i—like my father—safe, secure, and prosperous." She stared out the window.

"Now may I say something, Maile?"

She turned back from the window and nodded, tears streaming from her eyes.

"When we were kids, knowing what was right and wrong was easy. We had no real involvement to taint our view of things. It takes a long while to get back that knowledge of right and wrong. And it takes guts." Gavin reached over and took Maile's hands into his. "You've got them."

Maile shook her head, gently pulling her hands away, her eyes full of storm.

"Hear me out," he continued. "It takes guts to follow your instincts. This business on the lava—at every step you've led the way. It was your courage that made me come along to Captain Jack's that night, and to search for Jimmy the next day. And now, right here, Maile, at this table, I'm shaking in me boots. I know the world you're trying to show me is where great meanings lie. But to venture there takes guts."

Maile peered into Gavin's empathetic face; he seemed more handsome than ever. She leaned forward, placing her hands on his.

"I wish they had a room available," she said.

A jolt jagged through Gavin's body, made of both heat and agitation.

"Aye," he replied, climbing into her dark eyes.

The gecko laughed.

At that moment, Mr. Hayashi stepped briskly to the table. "Excuse me, Maile, some visitors from Boston just turned down their reservation," he said indignantly. "Apparently the room is just 'too rustic' for their tastes. So it's yours, if you want it—up on the third floor, a wonderful ocean view."

Startled, neither knew what to say.

"Give us a minute," Maile replied.

"OK, but let me know as soon as possible. That room will go quickly."

"We will. Thank you, Mr. Hayashi." The little man hustled back out of the dining room.

Gavin and Maile stared at each other as if peering into an abyss.

"Gavin, I think we should take that room."

"I don't know," he replied, not meeting her eyes.

The gecko opened his mouth a crack and blinked.

"What does your na'au say?"

Frustration rose inside him. "Damn it, I can't do it that way! Not yet."

The gecko crept into the corner of the sash and curled up with its head resting on its tail, watching.

"It's OK, Gavin," she replied weakly. "You have to do what feels right."

He squeezed her hand firmly. "That's just it, Maile! It *does* feel right!"

She stared at him in surprise. Her face softened, and her gathering tears dislodged, streaking each cheek.

"Listen to me. I'm going to call the mountain to make sure I'm clear of my responsibility. If I don't have to go back tonight, then I'll know this is the right time to find out where all this is leading. Can you live with that?"

Maile nodded.

Gavin's Australian cell network couldn't reach the remote mountaintop, so he found a pay phone outside the hotel entrance. Standing in the golden glow of the neon sign, he made the call, the whole time nervously tapping his sneakered foot against the wall. The answering telescope operator called Gavin's colleague to the phone.

"Good heavens, Gavin! Back at base camp already?"

"No, still down in Kona. What did Canberra say?"

"No problem. They—" The line crackled, the connection fading in and out.

"I can't hear you!" Gavin shouted into the phone.

"I said, they've located the part and it's on the way."

"So we'll be able to observe tomorrow night."

"Not a chance. Turns out there's no overnight FedEx to Hawai'i. Express takes at least two days. And that's not the half of it. We're in the middle of a big fog. Everything's coated with ice and we've got gusts up to seventy miles an hour."

"It's clear as crystal down here."

"Apparently the whole island's clear except the summit of Mauna Kea."

"That's weird."

"It *is* weird, but Dave says it happens. The satellite reports on the Web show a big storm forming just off the Big Island. Dave thinks it might screw up the next *few* nights, even if we do get the instrument working. Sorry."

Now the whole observing stint was in peril. But Gavin faced an even more difficult challenge, a riddle more confusing than the missing dark matter of the universe. Yet, oddly, he felt relief in losing the option to escape.

He hung up the phone and stepped back into the lobby. Maile sat in a big green vinyl chair, staring out the street-facing windows.

"Well, are you going to tempt fate, or not?" she asked, holding the keys to the Jeep in her hand.

"All work has stopped on the mountain. It seems your snow goddess has intervened." He walked over to Maile and took her hand. "Frankly, I'm glad for it."

Maile led them past the hotel's lovely old bonsai garden and up the third-floor staircase. They found the room and Gavin latched the door behind them. It was small, clean, and simple, with a double bed, a chest of drawers, and a bedside table on which were a Bible, a book of Buddhist teachings, and a radio tuned to the local AM Hawaiian music station. Maile slid open the glass doors leading to the lanai, and the sweet scents of ginger and plumeria poured in. The sky was a brilliant display of stars, and the Southern Cross hung like a compass needle pointing to the mythic South Sea isles. Far below the pali lay Kealakekua Bay, a dark patch hugging the shore. Murmuring voices emanated from other lanais.

Gavin stepped up behind Maile and wrapped his arms around her. "It's lovely," he whispered in her ear. "*You're* lovely."

She revolved inside his embrace, placing her arms around his neck. For one stark moment they caught—and held—each other's eyes. They kissed. Conscious thought dissolved, leaving only instinct, their bodies signaling, it is time. It is time. It is time! Mouths and hands went wild—lips caressing, fingers grasping—all to the jangle of Maile's gold bracelets.

Breathless, Maile broke free. She stepped back and without a word, unbuttoned her shirt. A thud of energy hit Gavin's chest when Maile opened her blouse and slipped it off her shoulders. His eyes fell to the deep gorge between her breasts, where her golden necklace rose and fell with each weighted breath. She shed her brassiere, exposing her bosom, the nipples stiffening in the cool breeze coming off Mauna Loa. Her eyes never left his face as she slid off her jeans and stood naked before him. At that moment the moon rose over the volcano, bathing Maile in blue-white light. Gavin reached for her, but she stepped back and held up a hand.

"Undress," she said softly, curling the corners of her mouth ever so slightly. She leaned back against the lanai railing and watched Gavin strip off his clothes, her gaze following his progress. Naked, he stood before her, hands outstretched, eyes gleaming. She felt the ache of yearning rise within her, the dampness between her legs. Her eyes feasted on his strong, lean body. His were not the muscles of a carpenter or mechanic, bulged from years of lifting or laboring with tools. They were subtle curves, honed while swimming and hiking. His fleecy torso tapered at the waist above a distinct tan line and the pleasant arc of muscled thighs. The rest showed nature's artistry—full, plump, hung between his legs like fruit on a tree. Her eyes rested there a moment. She caught her breath as a mixture of apprehension and desire stabbed her.

Maile leaned back, her sumptuous arms outstretched upon the rail and her marvelous hair cascading down her back. Moon shadows accentuated the round contours of her breasts and the delicate splay of hair running down the middle of her torso, ending in the dark patch that held her treasure.

Gavin grabbed Maile and pulled her to him. She moaned gently as his lips grazed her throat, her chin, the lobes of her ears, then pressed down in hunger on her willing mouth. Gavin slid down her body, kissing her breasts, lightly biting her nipples, licking her navel, brushing his cheek against the soft hair between her legs.

"You're a stunning creature," he said, looking up. Maile gazed down at his face, half-shadowed by the moon. She spread her fingers through his hair, opened her legs, and pulled him hard against her. His tongue carried an electric charge. With a deep exhalation, she dropped her head, covering them both in her magnificent hair. Vaguely aware of people stirring on nearby lanais, she restrained her moans, but occasionally a hushed cry escaped.

She did not want to explode out there, or in that way, and after a few minutes, she eased him to his feet. "I want you inside," she said breathlessly, pushing Gavin into the room. They fell upon the bed and she opened herself to him, arms flung out in abandon as he entered her. Maile's physical strength surprised him, yet there was tenderness in her response. Moving, rocking, rising to meet his thrustings, she muttered sweet unintelligible things, coaxing him into a wild fervor he had almost forgotten. As his thrusts grew more frenzied, she groaned with joy. Near crazed, he added his moans to hers, both crying out as if heralding the universe to witness their mating.

When the final eruption came, they shook savagely, pressed together in unified embrace. After it was over, they rolled apart, panting, smiling, stretching their sweaty limbs. They rested, hands clasped and legs entwined, and laughed about how they were probably heard through the old hotel's thin walls. Gavin knew that whatever protective membrane had sheltered his heart after the death of his wife was now stripped away.

An hour passed before they resumed their night of lovemaking. There were lengthy, unhurried interludes of dozing and conversation, laughter and long gazes at one another, accompanied by easy, aimless fondling. At times they became frenzied, almost desperate to bring each other to climax. Then a cool mountain breeze would blow into the room, diluting with the sweet fragrance of citrus blossoms the sharp aroma of sex. By midnight, damp linens lay tangled on the floor and moonlight poured over the naked sleeping couple. Neither had said "I love you"; he, because he was still afraid of the words, and she, because she assumed it was self-evident.

29 ∫ Gavin's Dream

It's hot, dark . . . *stifling.* Gavin's collapsed on the cavern floor, suffocating in the stale humidity. He's gone down too deep, beyond daylight and fresh air, trapped inside the fuming volcano, alive but in hell. *Why did I let her take me here?* He opens his eyes. A ruby glow illuminates the stick figures etched into the wall—six men in a circle facing the one standing apart with his arms raised to the sky. Above them is an adze-scrawled bird, beak agape as if screaming.

Gavin, too weak to move, panics as dazzling orange light streams into the cave. But it's not lava. A magnificent flame floats down the tube, slowly spinning into the shape of a woman. Haloed by fire is a face of unspeakable beauty—incandescent eyes, flared nostrils, and red lips curled into a warm smile. She moves toward him, wisps of fire leaping up between her toes.

A wave of sweltering heat envelops him. Certain he'll be consumed, he tries to close his eyes, but the lids don't work. He cannot escape the vision before him.

She reaches into her breast and pulls out a fiery heart that throbs in her palm. She unfolds her fingers and the burning heart drifts slowly toward him, resting inches from his hot, sweaty face. Her smile broadens, revealing a golden glow inside her mouth. She turns and walks back up the tube, disappearing around the bend. The cave darkens, leaving only the radiance of her heart pulsing against his cheek.

Gavin finally manages to shift his body, but something presses down on his chest and covers his mouth with hot breath! He tries to roll away, but a sweaty limb restrains him. He cries out!

"It's OK, Gavin. It's just me."

He opened his eyes. The hotel room was awash with harsh daylight, and Gavin squinted to see Maile. She eased herself off his body and lay down beside him. The fire in her eyes faded, replaced by a look of puzzled concern.

Gavin sat up, dazed, glancing randomly around the room. "Bloody dream." He dropped back down on the damp, twisted sheet and stared at the ceiling, trying to reconstruct the details of his nocturnal encounter.

Maile tried to calm him by stroking his chest. "Tell me about it."

He shook his head, his green eyes distant. "You're taking me to places I'm not sure I ought to go, places very foreign to a bloke like me."

"Is that so bad?"

Gavin brushed the back of his hand against her cheek. "I guess we'll find out, won't we?"

"Something's happened to me too," she said. "When I was just a little girl, my mother told me that love unshutters windows you never knew were there, that if you open your heart completely, your *mind* opens too, and you can see things you've never seen before."

"But you've got to have the courage to look."

"It's well worth it, don't you think? Is there anything better than this?" Her serene smile almost melted his fears.

Maile rose to kneel beside him, her body stunning in the morning light. She turned to the sea view out the window. "My mother fell in love with a haole too."

"Captain Jack, eh?"

"The thing between them was special." Maile sighed. "But my mother was raised in Catholic schools and was heavily influenced by two beloved but very devout aunties. Out of their own fears of a changing world, they put Christian guilt into her Polynesian heart."

"That's sad."

Maile looked back at Gavin "Yes. She denied who she was."

"And what about your father? Where does he come into all this?"

"In the middle of it. You see, Mom and Jack fell in love *before* she was married, midway through the Vietnam War. It was a whirlwind romance, and then Jack was gone—for two tours of duty. That was a long time, and although they tried to stay in touch, Mom met Dad—a steady, prosperous man—and he persuaded her to marry. He knew that when Jack returned from the war, there might be trouble, but he underestimated the old bond between them. They really couldn't help themselves, you know, and the affair went on for months. It was rough on everyone. In the end, though, Dad was right—Mom came back, and stayed."

"And Jack hit the bottle?"

Maile nodded. She stroked Gavin's leg, noting the contrast of her dark hand against his hay-colored skin. "I guess you never know when, where, or how love will show up," she said.

"I can sympathize with Captain Jack, poor bastard. I once lost someone dear to me heart."

Following the Hawaiian custom of not prying, Maile did not ask for details but waited in silence.

"I guess you may as well know. My wife died in a tragic mishap in Africa. It's taken me a long time to heal."

Maile sensed his heartache, and her eyes moistened. To Gavin they looked like two wet obsidian stones.

"Still, I wonder," she said. "Isn't it better to have loved like that than to have never experienced those deep feelings?"

"I dare say, but—"

"I've never had that," she interrupted. "It's not easy to find the right companion when you're hapa." Half-half. "And not just being half-Chinese. It's about living in a modern world while an ancient one resides in your blood. Like other Hawaiians, I live with conflicting values—the Polynesian ones handed down through generations and the transient ones of today. Should I seek the material symbols of America or the island values of family and place? Do I listen to the logic of my mind or the wisdom of my na'au? Do I trust what's in the *palapala*—books and newspapers—or the stories of my elders?" She shook her head. "All this confusion comes up when thinking about choosing a mate."

"You know, Maile, there are very few cultural 'purebreds' anymore, no matter where they live or what color skin they have. The world's isolations are all but gone, and I don't think that's bad. Life is far richer for it, even if confusing. Your dilemma is everyone's, really. Fact is, I think you've worked it out fairly well."

Maile laughed. "That's what it looks like on the outside, but inside I'm only just beginning to come to terms with it." She paused and looked at Gavin, who was gently stroking her arm.

"You know what's strange? That in meeting you—a haole—I'm getting more in touch with the Hawaiian in me. From the very beginning, I wanted you to really *understand* my island. I've had to stretch within myself to reach cultural touchstones I'd nearly forgotten, bridging stones that lie beneath the surface of my day-to-day life."

"Is that so strange? Don't they say that you never really know your own hometown till you show someone else around?"

"But that doesn't explain why I bothered, why I felt it important that *you* understood. Gavin, there's something deeper going on here."

"Destiny's a difficult concept for me."

"I'm convinced you and I have been thrown together for a reason, maybe more than one." Her thoughts turned inward and her eyes grew distant.

He sat upright and took her hand. "Well, I'll tell you one thing, pretty Maile. If there was some grand reason, OK, I'll try to open me mind to it. But right now I'm satisfied to know I'm damn lucky to have met you, even if everything you are challenges my little mind." Gavin ran a finger along her torso, then lightly touched the undersides of her breasts. She shivered pleasantly.

"I'm in love with you, mate," he said, pulling her forward, his mouth ready for another exchange of breath.

30 ∫ Clues from the Turtle Man

TUESDAY, JUNE 13 . . .

At breakfast Maile listened intently to Gavin recount his dream.

"Hawaiians pay close attention to what comes to us in the night," she said, "and some dreams are considered visions. But it's hard to say what yours might mean."

"I'll tell you what it means. Bloody indigestion from that pickled *daikon* last night."

Maile smiled sympathetically. "That's what you believe?"

"Unfortunately, no."

"This is the second time Pele has come in your sleep."

A shiver traveled Gavin's spine as he recalled the glowing apparition on Maile's lanai.

"She must be nearby," Maile said.

Gavin shook his head, at some level worried Maile was right. He grabbed a newspaper off a nearby table and skimmed the headlines. Maile sipped her coffee, deciphering the rugged lines of Gavin's face.

"Says here they had earthquakes near San Francisco last night, temblors all along the San Andreas fault. And fierce storms across the Midwest."

"Earth's rebelling," Maile said, downing the last of her coffee. "You can't abuse the planet endlessly without some response."

Gavin slapped the newspaper on the table and stretched his arms out with a yawn. "I wish I didn't have to go back up the mountain tonight," he said, taking hold of Maile's hand.

"What time do you have to be there?"

"Around dinner, I guess, so me colleague knows I haven't vanished altogether."

Maile's face brightened. "We've got some time then. Let's drive back the south route, past Kilauea."

"Pele country, eh?" he chuckled.

"I can show you the part of the island where I grew up."

Little was said—with words—during the drive, but there were smiles, affectionate glances, and relaxed touching. In their dreamy state, their worries dissipated as the landscape flew by. What little talk they had included warm references to the night before, each carrying a hint of erotic intimacies to come.

Rounding the southernmost part of the island, Maile noticed a hawk circling high above the road. The ʻio remained visible for many minutes, following them all the way to the district of Kaʻu and the black sand beach at Punaluʻu. Gavin, marveling at the scenery, didn't see it.

Maile parked next to the dark strand of volcanic sand. Above the beach, atop a lava outcrop, stood the ruins of an ancient temple, now marked by a wooden altar upon which recent offerings of fish, fruit, and taro had been laid.

As the couple got out of the Jeep, Maile immediately noticed an old Hawaiian man sitting on the sand in a badly frayed lawn chair. It was Joseph Polehulehu Kai, known to Kaʻu people as "Honu Man," the Turtle Man. Although Maile often swam at Punaluʻu, she had not seen this elder of her childhood for two years and had assumed he was ailing. Honu Man had always been a keeper of ancient knowledge, particularly about fishing and things of the sea. He was also known to see things before they happened, including several Mauna Loa and Kilauea eruptions. In 1975 seven dolphins swam up to the beach to warn him of an earthquake whose tsunami washed away the village, but he was tending a dying aunt in Hilo and missed the message. In recent years, people said he had lost part of his mind, sometimes slipping into delirium. Maile hoped this wasn't true.

Honu Man sat under a spreading *kamani* tree near the far end of the beach, watching sea turtles forage among the rocks, his back to the parking lot. As Maile stepped from the Jeep, he abruptly raised his head as if struck by a windblown nut from the tree. He turned and flashed his rusty eyes right at her. Maile waved, and the elder nodded. Gavin followed her across the beach.

The old Hawaiian peered at the Australian with one faded brown eye, barely visible beneath his sagging lid. "Who da *malihini*?" he asked. The stranger.

"A friend of mine," Maile replied.

Honu Man pointed his bony finger toward a busload of Japanese tourists taking pictures at the other end of the beach. "Bettah send him down beach, haole side, then we talk story."

"Whatever you say, Uncle." She shrugged at Gavin sympathetically.

Gavin left the two Hawaiians under the tree, and Maile eased herself onto the sand. She looked youthful next to Honu Man, his face deeply wrinkled and ruddy black from the sun. But like the younger fishermen stalking the reef with their nets, he was lean, his leathery flesh tight against his ribs.

"You look good, Uncle. Healthy."

A crooked smile crossed his face. "Prayer and herbs," he said, nodding.

Gavin strolled to a thatched curio hut where a Filipino girl hawked wooden tikis, shell leis, and grass beach mats—all manufactured in the Philippines. He put four quarters into a vending machine for a can of Coke and gazed out across the beach. A little haole girl in a plastic "grass skirt" her father had just purchased showed off her ballet steps along the water's edge. Nearby an older gentleman strolled the beach in swim trunks patterned after the American flag while his wife read a murder mystery atop a beach towel declaring "Hawaii Is Paradise!" Gavin cringed, suddenly aware that his perspective had changed. He ambled away from the tourists toward a ramshackle pavilion where an old Hawaiian man played guitar and a teenage boy strummed an ʻukulele.

"What you doin' wit' dat haole, Maile?" Honu Man asked. "Plenty local boys fo' pick from. Like Kea dere."

A paunchy young man, his thick arms covered with tattoos, strolled by and flashed a wicked smile.

"Looks like trouble to me."

The old man cackled, revealing his missing teeth. "Why you no marry yet, find one good man, settle down?"

She bristled. "I'm too busy, Uncle."

"Some *kane* could use one good *wahine* like you—strong, smart." He brushed his rough hand across her cheek. "Ugly too."

Maile smiled. No Hawaiian of his generation would tell another of their beauty—that was bad luck—so his comment was a compliment.

"You not even looking?"

"Uncle, I've got work to do."

"Work. Work. Dat's da *Pake"*—the Chinese—"in you."

"Someone's got to protect the old stones, Uncle, our history."

"Ahh. Da *pohaku.* Old, old pohaku. Dey very important, Maile." He patted her knee with his bony hand. "Dey see t'ings, you know—dey remember. Why, just da uddah day, my friend from da ranch—Sonny—he heard dem talking . . ." Honu Man's voice trailed off, his head nodding, eyes distant.

"And what did the stones tell Uncle Sonny?"

He shook his head and shrugged. To share that was up to Sonny.

"Good you protect our pohaku, Maile, but . . ."

"But what?"

Honu Man laughed. "Don' fo'get about da kane. Git one wit' brains."

"Uncle!"

"You too smart fo' *dees* local boys. But da haole, dey don' know not'ing. Dey don' know how fo' treat wahine. Dey don' know how fo' treat uddah peoples. And dey don' know how fo' treat da island. Dey takers, you know."

"Gavin is different." Maile felt defensive, but she was cautious about contradicting the elder. He had lived long and had many reasons to be bitter about white men.

"Uh! No more dis *shibai.*" Bull. The old man waved his gnarled hands in front of his face, as if swishing away mosquitoes. "Now we talk *serious* business, Maile. I knew you coming Ka'u, ya know. I as' da gods' help fo' bring you."

"I saw the hawk."

"Aye." He scrutinized her face, and for the first time since she had arrived, Honu Man's eyes were sharp and luminescent. "Somet'ing weigh heavy on yo' mind, yeah?"

"Yes."

"So why you here, Maile?"

"Uncle, you called me."

The old fisherman slapped his hands on the lawn chair's arms and shook his head vigorously. "No. No. No. No!" he growled.

"Uncle, it's hard for me to understand you when you talk in riddles."

"'Io called you! 'Io been wit' you for many days." His eyes narrowed. "Lissen to yo' na'au. What does it tell you?"

"That you have information for me." The words came before thought.

He nodded.

"That you know something about . . . about . . . the murder?"

"Yes!" Slowly he opened his eyes to their full width, revealing the red birthmark next to his left pupil. "Go on, Maile," he said, placing his hands on hers. They were hot.

"It's bigger than the murder, isn't it?"

"Aye."

"What do you know?"

Honu Man pointed at a cluster of Hawaiians standing near the curio hut. "Dey t'ink I *lolo*." Crazy. "Dey t'ink Honu Man lose his mind." He shook his head slowly. "Noooo. I know many t'ings go on round here."

"I know you do, Uncle. I don't think you're crazy."

"Good, Maile. Mahalo." The elder rested his bony hand on her head for a moment. "I tell you a little of what I know, but you gotta help. We work togethah."

Maile stared at Honu Man's weathered face. "Do you know the young man who died?"

He closed his eyes and nodded. "Kalama. From Hamakua."

"Why?"

"Because he was a warrior."

"Was it the Hui?"

Honu Man nodded.

"Why?"

"I told you. He was a warrior. And dey cowards!"

"What do they want?"

"Dat's all I know, 'cept one uddah t'ing. Dere's some reason you involved, why you saw what you did."

"There's also a reason for Gavin—the haole—isn't there?"

He shrugged his sun-scarred shoulders. "Maybe."

The old man took a deep, raspy breath. "Bad stuff, dat, Maile. Be careful." He looked away, fixing his eyes on the turtles offshore. Maile waited for more.

"Honu soon lay eggs," he said eventually. "I watch'um all da time. I know dere ways. Dey my 'aumakua." My ancestor spirits.

"Yes, Uncle, but—"

Honu Man turned to face her, his eyes black pebbles embedded in his craggy face. "Da mango sweet, but hard fo' get off da seed, yeah?"

"Mango?"

"You remember da story of Pele and Kamehameha? When da king took too many breadfruit, too much fish fo' his own self? Pele git angry."

"Yes, I remember. Hualalai. 1801."

"Too many forget."

Maile couldn't connect the story with anything. "What's that have to do with the Hui?"

Honu Man turned away, again resting his eyes on the waves. "Maile, you play blackjack?"

"What? No, I don't."

"No need learn," he said, suddenly breaking out in laughter.

Maile was perplexed. Maybe his mind *was* gone.

"Uncle, what about the Hui?"

"Strange," Honu Man interrupted. "Yesterday, no honu—all day. Vanished." He swept his muscled arm over the beach. "Dey confused, know somet'ing. Honu act strange couple time last week too."

"What do you think it means?"

"Could be one o' da volcanoes belch inside, honu feel rumble. Maybe one earthquake coming. Eh, maybe Pele upset."

"The volcano? Honu?"

"Honu can, you know. Honu smart." The old man turned back to Maile and tapped a crooked fingertip against his temple, its long nail cracked down the middle. "Dey know dees t'ings."

"What about the Hui? What do *they* know?"

"Same. Wanna keep'um quiet. Shhhh." He pressed his finger against his ruddy lips.

"Why?"

"Da kine—money, riches. No can build if Pele upset."

"Why does the Hui care?"

"Shhhhhhh! Dangerous fo' talk story about da Hui."

Maile peered into Honu Man's face, trying to decipher the riddle of his words. He gazed at the turtles popping in and out of view in the sparkling water.

"One minute, Uncle," Maile said, rising on the sand. "I'll be right back."

She walked to the curio stand, turning his words over in her mind. A few minutes later, she returned, a newly purchased pack of Kools in her hand. The old man spotted the green label out of the corner of his eye and grinned.

"You always bring me," he said, recalling the old days when their contact was more frequent. "What if Honu Man switch brands?"

"It'll never happen," she laughed, handing him the pack.

He tore off the cellophane and let the wind take it from his fingers. He opened the pack and withdrew a cigarette. "Maybe you no mess wit' dis, Maile," he said in a calm, fatherly tone. "Let Pele take care of it."

She nodded, unsatisfied. But the old man had given her something to go on, fragments to consider: Mango sweet, but hard fo' get off seed—honu know—Pele angry—could be volcano belch inside—shhhhh!—Hui wanna keep'um quiet—no can build—bad stuff. Remember Kamehameha. But what did the old stones tell Uncle Sonny? And which old stones?

"Fo'get trouble, Maile," Honu Man said, gently tapping her leg. "Enjoy da kane." He tossed his head toward the pavilion where Gavin was standing.

Maile smiled and leaned over to light his cigarette. "Aloha, Uncle," she said, kissing him on the cheek.

"Aloha, Maile," he replied, coughing a little on the menthol. "Remember, shhhhh." Smoke all around his finger. "Shhhhhhhhh . . ."

31 ∫ Enlightening the Haole

He doesn't have much aloha for haoles, does he?" Gavin commented as Maile sat down on the sand next to him. The little jam session continued inside the pavilion, several others from Punaluʻu now lending their voices to the Hawaiian song.

"Sorry about that. Honu Man's bitter."

"I can understand that," Gavin replied, "I just hate being judged by the godawful things me fellow white men have done. God knows the Aborigines back home have cause for their feelings too—I had a childhood mate who could tell you all about it—but *I'm* not responsible."

"We all share the kuleana—the responsibility—for things our people do. If a Hawaiian acts hatefully, or with prejudice, that reflects on me as a Hawaiian, don't you think? That's one reason why Uncle Aka and I are worried about Jimmy. As custodians of the island, we have a responsibility to protect an innocent if we can."

"I see your point, yes, but what can *I* do about the sad history of the Aborigines?"

"That's for you, as a white Australian, to figure out."

Gavin nodded, filing the comment away. "What does *haole* mean, anyway?"

"A deeper meaning lies in the pieces of the word—*ha*, the 'breath' and *'aʻole*, 'no' or 'none.' Literally, 'no breath.' "

"I don't get it."

"When we Hawaiians greet each other, we embrace, touch noses or kiss, and exchange our *ha*. This is an expression of love, an exchange of the breath God gave us. It's an intimate thing, a sharing of mana, of divine spirit, a recognition of our relatedness. When we say *aloha*, we're saying, 'I share with you the breath of my life.' It is something to share with *all* people. When the first white men came, they kept their distance, greeted without exchanging their breath, and so they became, literally, the ones without the breath of life."

"Fascinating."

"It's important."

"You had a good conversation with the elder?"

Her face darkened. "He knows about the murder."

The dreaded word hit Gavin like a bucket of cold water. "How?"

"I'm not sure, but there's an amazing communications network among Hawaiians. Believe me." She glanced over at the old man still perched in his chair, staring at the waves. "And Honu Man has special abilities."

Gavin shook his head, unsure what to think. "I hate to ask, but what did he say?"

"It's not important right now." She leaped up off the sand. "Let's take a swim!"

Gavin, though still curious, let it go. The company of his beautiful companion made that easy.

Gavin finished changing first, so he sat down inside the pavilion to listen to the music. Several Hawaiians caught his eye and smiled. "Aloha," said the boy with the 'ukulele. "G'day," Gavin replied cheerily, but a knot formed inside his chest. After getting to know Maile and her island, he could now hear the sad notes in the Hawaiian melody.

Maile darted out of the bathroom and down the beach, relieved at the prospect of immersion in the waters of Punalu'u. In an instant she was gone, her yellow suit flashing beneath the waves. Gavin, too self-conscious to run, ambled to the water, then dove in. Maile, well offshore, seemed unaffected by the bay's strong currents. Gavin worked hard to catch up, but even then, she was lost in her own world. Occasionally turtles popped their heads above the water, and Maile addressed each with a friendly greeting. She was in her element here, in the waters she loved so well.

After the swim, they warmed their bodies on the hot black sand. Maile stared at the white clouds drifting overhead, her limbs tingling from exertion. Gavin leaned over and kissed her firmly on the mouth. She pulled back, smiling, "Not here, Gavin. Let's find some privacy—and soon!"

They changed into dry clothes, Gavin into a pair of shorts and a T-shirt, and Maile into a yellow pareu wrapped loosely over her body. They drove up from the dry palm-fringed coast into the green uplands. Acres of remnant sugarcane and their replacement crop, macadamia nut trees, lined the road as they passed the town of Pahala.

"I grew up here," she said, pointing at the little plantation settlement nestled into the slope.

"I'd like to see it."

Maile laughed. "No ways, bruddah!" she said, slipping into pidgin. "I drive up there and my family sees me, we gotta stop, talk story, all da aunties, da uncles, da cousins. Stay for drink beer, den luau. We nevah get back alone, brah!"

Gavin buckled over in laughter, his ease with Maile greater than ever. She, too, was perfectly relaxed. It was as if the waters of Punalu'u had washed away any thoughts of Honu Man, the murder, or Gavin's responsibilities on Mauna Kea.

"All right," he replied, "but I'll expect a rain check, eh?"

"OK." She smiled, deeply pleased by his interest.

A few minutes up the road, the cane and macadamia nut trees gave way to a vast expanse of rugged volcanic terrain—the Ka'u desert—on the foreboding southwest rift of Kilauea. The road ran along the edge of the desert just below the forested slopes of Mauna Loa and eventually entered Kilauea's rainforest.

A few raindrops splattered the windshield. "Say good-bye to the Kona sunshine," Maile said, switching on the wipers. "We're approaching the wet, windward side of the island."

Gavin shook his head. "First desert, now rainforest! Marvelous!"

Maile dropped her hand inside his thigh and flashed a vampish look. "You were awesome last night," she said. "I wish you'd stay with me tonight."

Sexual voltage aroused Gavin. "I'd love that."

"Can't you just call the mountain and tell them you'll be up *tomorrow*?"

For the first time all afternoon, Gavin's responsibilities on Mauna Kea intruded into his mind. At stake were months of preparatory work and many thousands of dollars in research funds dedicated to this single observing stint. And yet, almost without guilt, he had nearly forgotten the reasons his department had sent him to Hawai'i. His perspective was gone, his priorities shifting. It was confusing enough before he and Maile had gone to bed, but now!

"I really should begin to acclimate to the altitude," he said unconvincingly, "in case we get a chance to observe tomorrow night."

"That's a shame."

He leaned toward her, meaning to kiss her cheek, but she tossed back her head, exposing her throat. Lifting the gold chain aside, Gavin brushed his lips along her neck. She moaned quietly, sliding her hand over his loins. He slipped his fingers under her pareu. Their fondling became so fervent that Maile was unable to concentrate on the road.

"I know a place," she said breathlessly.

She turned off the highway onto a narrow road zigzagging up the wooded slopes of Mauna Loa. She hid the Jeep in the brush near an old, seldom-used trail that she had once explored alone. They dashed through the forest, eager, excited, as if encouraged by spirits in the trees. The afternoon shower on the highway had not yet reached Mauna Loa's higher slopes, but rafts of clouds flew over the wooded path.

Maile guided Gavin to a meadow beneath a grove of ancient koa trees, where she sat down on a thick bed of grass. She unfastened her pareu and leaned back. Her brown skin gleamed in the emerald light filtering through the canopy of leaves, and her hair blew about her face. Gavin slipped off his shorts and shirt and knelt before her. He caressed her legs while she stroked him.

"You belong with nature," she said, admiring his amber skin and taut muscles. "You belong in me."

"Yes," he muttered in a deep voice, pushing her down onto the grass. She gave a small cry as he entered her. A cool gust blew over them, cooling their heated flesh. The forest darkened as the clouds thickened, and patches of fog slipped through the trees like spirits dashing about for better views of the entangled lovers. They moved together, their passion rising until at last it was freed. Wild animals, they screamed into the forest.

For many minutes they sprawled side by side on the grass, spent. Maile curled herself against Gavin's back and dreamily ran her fingers through his chest hair. "It's a wonderful world, this one we're in," Gavin said. "I don't want to leave it."

They dozed until some time later when more clouds arrived—dark and full of rain. They dressed and returned to the Jeep, just as the clouds unloaded their burden. Intoxicated with lovers' passion, they snuggled all the way back to Hilo, chatting about the islands, the stars, the rain—nothing in particular. All their concerns forgotten until they reached Hilo.

"Mind if I stop at my office for a minute before taking you back up the mountain?" Maile asked as they pulled into town.

"Not at all," Gavin said, squeezing her hand.

"I'll only be a minute," she said, hopping out of the Jeep.

As she stepped into the office, she noticed the flashing red light on her answering machine. "That can wait till tomorrow," she muttered, sitting down at her desk. She searched a pile of archaeological reports for the Kona cave study she intended to reread that night—consciously ignoring the blinking light. Report in hand, she stepped back into the hallway. As she locked up, the flashing red light glowed diffusely through the frosted window of the door.

"Not now," she said, and hurried down the hall.

32 ∫ Maile's Message

It was well after 6 p.m. when Maile finally reached her neighborhood. A few people still enjoyed the lagoon at Four Mile Beach, but most were packing up to head home. Stiff from the long drive down the mountain, Maile decided to stretch her limbs with a quick dip. She bobbed about the cool water, gazing up at Mauna Kea. The afternoon showers had blown out to sea, and all but the summit—still capped with frothy white clouds—was visible in the fading light.

Maile imagined Gavin sitting in front of the base camp fireplace. She recalled his firm kisses in the parking lot, strong arms wrapped around her, and his green eyes shining with affection. She wished he was with her, that they could make love again tonight. Maile slowly backstroked across the lagoon, gazing up at the sky, recalling their two days together. A short while later, the sun disappeared behind Mauna Kea, and the evening land breeze carried the mountain's chill. It was time to go.

Back at her bungalow, Maile showered and cooked a bowl of instant *ramen*. After eating, she lay down on her rattan couch to reread the report on the petroglyph cave, but her curiosity about the message on her office answering machine distracted her. She even considered driving downtown to listen to it, but fatigue won out, and she dozed.

The phone rang.

Maile, startled, fumbled for the receiver on the table next to the couch.

"Hello?"

"Maile! Where in hell you been?" A gruff male voice, guttural, the words slurred. "I been callin' yer office for two days!"

"Who is this?" she said, still not fully awake.

"Jack Hemmingson, for Chris'sake! Damn nuisance too, havin' to drive all the way to Pahoa for a phone. Finally, I got yer home number from Aka's kids."

"Captain Jack?" Maile sat up. "Why are *you* calling?" Her tone was frigid.

"Aka's disappeared."

"What?"

"Him and his nephew, Kimo."

"When? How?"

"Musta been Monday mornin'—so say the cops."

"The cops?"

"The cops! The cops! They think Aka and Kimo were out pickin' 'opihi—"

Maile's heart dropped.

"—that they got washed out to sea."

"No!"

"But that don't make sense, Maile! If Aka and Kimo were goin' pickin', he'd o' parked right in my yard, not down at the end o' the road!"

She glanced out the glass doors to the lanai and, fighting rising anxiety, took a deep breath. "Calm down, Jack," she said, as if that would help her do the same.

"Dammit, woman! Don't tell me to calm down! Aka's disappeared!"

"Start at the beginning, Jack. Please."

"Aw'right. Aw'right. Yesterday afternoon I walked down to fetch the newspaper, and there's Aka's truck and Kimo's car parked at the end o' the road. I thought, well, maybe they went out on the lava to watch the helicopters search for Jimmy. But why wouldn't he stop by my place first?" He paused to swallow hard, liquid bubbling in his throat.

"Are you drinking?"

"Damn right I'm drinkin'! Wouldn't you?" His voice cracked. "Aka's my best friend!"

A lump rose in Maile's throat.

"Meanwhile, 'bout the time I spotted the cars, Aka's kids were gettin' worried 'cause they couldn't reach 'im, so they come down to my place, and we put two and two together. They called the cops on their cell. Everybody in town's been checkin' all along the coast. But it don't make sense to me."

"Then where are they?"

"Up on the lava flow, that's where! Don't ask me how Aka ever got his old bones out there, but he musta gone with Kimo."

"Did you tell the police that?"

"Those idiots! Yeah, I told 'em. But Machado's miffed. Says Kimo wouldn't investigate without official clearance. Why wouldn't he just wait for the helicopter search, set for that same morning?"

"Hmmm—*if* it was that morning. You said you saw Aka Sunday. Could they have gone out to the flow that night?"

"I s'pose they coulda, but why?"

"I don't know, Jack. It's all so confused."

"You ain't telling me anything. Ya know that owl Aka made so much fuss about? Well, he's been hangin' round my place since Sunday night. I seen him a hundred times if I seen him once, up in the trees or flying along the coast."

The feelings in Maile's na'au started taking shape.

"You there, Maile?"

"Yes, Jack. I'm just thinking."

"Well, while you're thinkin', tell me this—why didn't Aka tell me he was going out onto the flow when I saw him Sunday night?"

"Maybe he didn't know. Maybe something happened. What are the police doing?"

"They called in the Coast Guard. Searched the waters from Kalapana to Halape. But they called it off tonight. Figure they're gone."

That comment might have dropped Maile's heart, but it didn't. Her instincts told her Jack was right: Aka and Kimo had not gone out to pick 'opihi. They were on the volcano, maybe looking for Jimmy on their own. But why?

33 ∫ Maile Connects with Her Ancestors

LATE THAT NIGHT . . .

A gecko straddled the limb of a guava tree above the freshwater pond, alert to the rustle of Maile coming down the jungle path. Passing beneath the lizard's perch, she stood at the edge of the pond. Maile stared at the mirror of dazzling stars and recalled that in glassy pools like this, young Hawaiian navigators had studied the positions of the stellar beacons they used to find their way back and forth across the Pacific. If only these stars could guide her through the stormy seas she felt herself foundering in.

A gentle breeze ruffled her pareu and tugged the delicate petals of the plumeria lei draped over her bare shoulders, moon-white blossoms plucked that night from trees in her yard. Beneath the lei was an ancient talisman, a lizard of bone on a sennit cord. This was only the second time it lay upon Maile's chest. Eighteen years earlier, on the sixteenth birthday of the woman-child, her mother had placed it there. "This is not jewelry," she had cautioned her daughter. "It carries the mana of generations of women in our family, including that lodged in the bone of a seer in the line. It will give you protection when you need it, and insight if you have the will to accept it." Maile had recognized its power immediately, for it tingled that day upon her breast. Too powerful for a girl uncertain of her identity, a child not yet proud of her Polynesian blood. She might just as easily have been given a jade pendant, ancestral symbol of her Chinese heritage. But at that time, either would have been too potent for the young

Maile. She had placed the bone talisman in a fine wooden box and tucked it away in her chest of private things.

Some years later her mother and father gave her a gold necklace and a "Hawaiian heirloom" gold bracelet engraved with island foliage and her name, a high-priced, modern status symbol to island women of all ethnicities. These Maile wore with pride. Over the years she received more heirloom bracelets from her family, including those that had been worn by her mother. Engraved in the stylized characters of Victorian England, the gold bands also held personal meanings, and for some invoked sentiment for Hawai'i's last monarch, Queen Lili'uokalani, who'd been given one by Queen Victoria. Before coming to the pool, Maile had removed the bracelets and replaced the necklace with the bone talisman.

In the distant windows of a condominium built above the ponds, blue television screens flickered, and the black hulk of Mauna Kea loomed over the twinkling sugar towns far up the Hamakua coast. The surf roared, its frothy combers pummeling the jagged coastline just beyond the ponds.

Maile looked up at the spray of sparkling stars spread across the sky—the Milky Way, *kua mo'o*, the backbone of the lizard. She began a chant stored in her memory since childhood:

O na 'aumakua wahine me na kupuna wahine ali'i,
Na 'aumakua wahine i ka hikina, a i kaulana a ka la,
Na wahine i ka lewa lani, i ka lewa nu'u . . .
O female 'aumakua and ancestral chiefesses,
Female 'aumakua at the rising and setting places of the sun,
Female spirits in the firmaments of the heavens and of the clouds . . .

Maile's eyes gleamed in the starlight, and her voice sank into a rich tremolo not unlike the reverberation of the distant waves.

. . . Owau nei o Kiha ka pua keia i ke a. Homai i mana.
This is I, Kiha, your descendant in this world of the living. Give me mana.

Maile peered into the pool and pondered the great serpent of stars moving across it. She lifted the lei from her shoulders and set it on a prominent lava rock next to the pool. Then she loosened the fabric knot beneath her arm and dropped the pareu onto the grass. The breeze felt balmy against her nakedness, and the skin beneath the talisman tingled. Maile stepped down the bank and slipped into the brisk water. Only her face and great spray of hair were visible against its dark surface.

Her ancestral line was the *moʻo*, the lizard, many of whom, according to legend, lived in pools like this. She discovered at an early age that she would lose her center—become distracted or confused—if she did not get into the sea, the pools, or the mountain streams at least once every few days. Here was communion with her ancestral spirits. But she need not be in water to receive their guidance. They often visited her home or office in the form of geckos, little striped lizards who perched on window sills or hung from her lanai beams. Their silent presence or a soft chortle were taken as signs of affirmation, but a cackle meant it was time to pay attention, and when on rare occasions they leaped onto her shoulders or scampered directly across her path, she knew something was seriously amiss.

Maile's grandmother taught her to ignore the bad reputation moʻo had among some Hawaiians, islanders who accepted ancient aliʻi legends that portrayed lizards as evil or cruel. Those stories had been passed down by royal descendants with an historical ax to grind—many of her moʻo clan had resisted the Tahitian takeover of the islands and the dark priest Paʻao.

The cold water helped Maile focus her mind—on Aka and Kimo's disappearance; on the missing photographer, Jimmy; and on the grisly murder on the molten flank of Kilauea. With intense concentration and traditional prayer, Maile requested assistance from her ancestors. She stayed in the pool for many minutes, treading water so gently that she remained almost still. The stars of kua moʻo blurred into a hazy vision, and the roar of the sea spoke to her as ancestral voices—distinct, loving, and wise. The inner voice of her naʻau translated the messages. At last, as her body began to tremble, she knew what she must do.

Maile pulled herself up onto the bank. She lay for a moment in the cool grass, naked to the elements, then knelt beside the glassy surface of the pond. She gathered up the garland of plumeria from the rock and for a moment buried her nose in its sweet blossoms. She gently pushed the lei out onto the water, an offering of gratitude for the strength and guidance she had just received.

34 ∫ The Damaged Warrior

WEDNESDAY MORNING, JUNE 14, IN THE RUINS OF ROYAL GARDENS ESTATES . . .

Quiet!" the big haole said, slamming the butt of his M16 on the kitchen table. His ashtray skipped an inch down the Formica.

"They'll find us eventually," Jimmy blurted, wriggling against the nylon cords binding his wrists to the kitchen chair. Jimmy's blue eyes, magnified under his wire rims, flashed with anxiety. Aka and Kimo, lashed to the other chairs, said nothing.

"Shut up, kid, or I'll stuff a papaya in yer mouth!" Jake Bluestone said, turning back to the window. The ex-soldier's icy blue eyes darted back and forth, alert for other intruders coming up the hardened lava flows below his cabin. His face, furrowed from years of grimacing, made this child of the sixties look older than his fifty-nine years, his blond ponytail now streaked with gray. Only his strong, athletic body—conspicuous under a faded tank top—hinted at his former youth. Ready for combat, Bluestone had exchanged his surfer shorts for jungle fatigues. Over six feet tall, he stood erect, his Army-issue boot perched on the room's only unoccupied chair. "Nobody out there today," he announced. "They've thrown in the towel on you guys."

The tension in Bluestone's body had reminded Aka of an animal stalking its prey, but as the morning wore on, he realized the opposite was true. Here was a cornered beast waiting to be preyed upon. This, Aka thought, is when animals are the most dangerous.

Jake Bluestone had been running from civilization for decades, ever since the day he'd nearly choked his wife to death. Terri's face had turned blue before finally he stopped on that stormy Chicago afternoon when the sky exploded with lightning and Lake Michigan turned black. The waves had threatened to wash away their lakeside confectionery stand, but it was the Coast Guard helicopters that really set Jake off. He'd felt the demons rising inside him as the first howling gales blew in from Canada, but when the choppers appeared offshore and tiny Terri tried to pull him away from the windows, her anguished face suddenly held the familiar features of the enemy. Terri loved Jake before Vietnam and after—perhaps she still did—but that incident forced her to abandon him and get on with her life.

"Missing in action. That's what you guys are! The helicopters won't be back!"

Jake set the rifle on the table and snatched the half-smoked joint in the ashtray. He lit up, inhaling so deeply that his shirt rose, revealing Kimo's service revolver stuffed into the waistband of his fatigues. Jake held his breath, eyes closed, letting the marijuana permeate his lungs.

"I know they haven't abandoned us," Jimmy said, his tone desperate. He had, after all, been holed up with Bluestone for more than a week. At first the little cabin had been a sanctuary, and the ex-soldier Jimmy's guard against adversaries. Someone *had* come snooping around Captain Jack's place that morning when Jack and Aka were down on the rocks—hence the fresh tracks they'd noticed in the driveway. Jimmy dared not chance that the young local with a shotgun cradled in his pickup's back window was linked to the murder, so he bolted, making his way across the lava toward Royal Gardens, hoping to find a hiding place where he could rest and reconsider his options.

Bluestone immediately recognized a fellow refugee and let the young man in. They shared a common need to hide, and neither had allies in a world that had put them both at risk. Jake offered to drive Jimmy to the Hilo airport when he next made his regular supply run into town.

The lonely veteran had seemed a gentle, if wounded, soul and proved to be an affable and loyal companion. Together he and Jimmy harvested Jake's extensive food garden, chatted over homemade soups and stews, and gathered mangoes, guavas, and avocados from throughout

Royal Gardens. They followed an extraordinary map pinpointing all the subdivision's fruit-bearing trees, drawn with the precision of a soldier who had once executed search-and-destroy missions in the jungle. Jimmy occasionally accepted Jake's nightly offers to get stoned on his own "Gardens-grown gold" and enjoyed watching the dropout's childlike enthusiasm as they observed Kilauea's volcanic displays from the cabin's lofty lanai using Jake's Army binoculars. It had been Jake's idea to divert people away from the cabin by planting Jimmy's camera and tennis shoe in the distant fresh flow.

But Bluestone got rattled during one of their jaunts to the fruit trees when he spotted Gavin and Maile snooping around on the lava. The next day the police came, wandering about in the tracks of the pair, and the sight of blue uniforms so close to his marijuana crop kindled Jake's paranoia. Then, on Sunday night, Jimmy spotted two flashlights slowly moving up the lava-decimated slope. When the intruders approached the cabin, Jimmy assisted Jake with an ambush, only later realizing that the bruised and battered pair were Aka and his nephew coming to help. Things might have been OK had Jake not discovered Kimo's police badge in his pants pocket. He tied them up, and Jimmy's protests only heightened Jake's paranoia, making him suspicious of the young man too. When the Coast Guard helicopters started a search for the missing pair the next morning, Jake snapped. Suddenly back in Da Nang, he was protecting the perimeter of the air base.

"I know they'll find us!" Jimmy shouted.

Aka admonished the young man with his eyes, and Jimmy fell silent. For several minutes they watched Bluestone scan the horizon with his binoculars and smoke his joint to the end.

"My wrists hurt, Jake," Jimmy finally said in an even tone. "Can't you untie us just for a little while?"

Bluestone swung around slowly. The tension in his eyes had subsided, the cannabis already calming his nerves—and blurring his judgment. The soldier grasped Jimmy's shoulder, close to his throat, and the young man stiffened.

"Punishment, loud mouth. Two days ago you were free as a bird inside this jungle cage." Bluestone scowled at the two Hawaiians. "Jimmy said we were safe here, that no one would find us." The pitch of Jake's voice dropped, as though echoing from a deep chamber. "He lied."

Never had Aka heard two words carry such disillusionment.

"Jimmy said he had no real friends here. Then you two showed up." He glared at Kimo. "One a cop!"

Bluestone pushed Jimmy out of his grip and picked up the M16. He turned back to the window and surveyed the steep slopes of Royal Gardens. This was to have been his sanctuary after six years of wandering following his divorce from Terri. Hawai'i was as far away from Chicago as Jake could get and still be in America. Back then, in the early '80s, he could easily set up a simple life in the woods, growing *paka lolo* ("crazy weed") to supplement his Army disability checks. In 1981 he bought five acres in a remote section of the Gardens and soon replaced his Army bivouac tent with a small cabin overlooking the Kalapana coast. By that time, Big Island jungles were filled with vets, some with damaged bodies or ravaged souls, a few even more phobic than Jake.

Two years later, Kilauea volcano disrupted his peaceful retreat. Overnight the Gardens crawled with people, residents hauling out belongings and scores of uniformed men—Civil Defense, National Guard, and county police—helping with the evacuation. Helicopters crisscrossed the sky. To stay calm, Jake left for long periods, rooming with acquaintances in Pahoa—hippies, marijuana growers, and other war vets. He kept thinking his cabin would be overwhelmed by lava, but the flows always stopped just short of his property. Jake couldn't believe his good luck, especially after the savage things he'd done under orders in Vietnam.

Months later, with utility poles down, a hundred homes destroyed, and half the streets blocked by lava, Civil Defense announced they would not reopen the subdivision access road if it was inundated again. Almost everyone packed up and left, but Jake stayed, figuring that once that road was blocked he would finally have the isolation he longed for. Just before the final inundation, Jake parked his pickup in Kalapana so he'd have wheels "on the outside" (for getting supplies and peddling his crop), then hot-wired an abandoned van inside the subdivision (to tend his marijuana patches and harvest his network of fruit trees). Over the years, the flows chased out the last die-hards—some dope growers, a couple of flower children, and an old Filipino who'd spent his life savings building his home. Jake alone remained in the Gardens.

"There's nothing out there," Jake said, peering through his big binoculars. "Only an owl hunting for rats."

"Dey be back," Kimo said, with feigned hope. He looked sadly clownish with his round cheeks, swollen nose, and blackened eye. "Dey jus' regrouping."

"I'll kill anyone who comes within a hundred yards of my post," Jake replied.

Aka, gut still throbbing from a blow inflicted by the butt of Bluestone's rifle, shook his head, silently urging Kimo not to provoke the man.

"When dey come, dey wen come wit' reinforcements," Kimo continued, despite his uncle's admonishment. "If I was you—if I no more want company—I'd let us go before da big-time trouble hit the fan."

Jake took the binoculars from his eyes and set them on the table. He marched over to Kimo, grabbed him by the collar, and punched him in the face.

"Jake!" Jimmy hollered. "Jake, stop! These are my friends!"

But the veteran wasn't listening. He wasn't even there. He was off in a jungle of the past with the enemy. Kimo struggled to pull his face away, but Jake held firm, pounding him mercilessly. Kimo's lip split open, and blood splattered onto the others.

"Stop! Stop!" Jimmy screamed, dragging his chair toward Kimo. Bluestone was oblivious.

Aka closed his eyes and began chanting:

Na 'Aumakua mai Kalahiki a Kala'akau
Mai ka ho'oku'i a ka halawai . . .
Na 'Aumakua . . .

He was calling on the gods and his ancestors for help, well aware that ancient chants also have a potent effect on the living. Once, when a fleet of Tahitian war canoes had come to take over the little island of Moloka'i, the outnumbered islanders gathered on the shore and chanted. Pa'ao's warriors were so unnerved that they left, having never landed, and Moloka'i's inclusion in the ali'i regime wasn't completed until generations later, through royal marriage.

'O Kiha i ka lani
'Owe i ka lani . . .

The elder's speech took on a peculiar resonance, as if containing voices of the very spirits it summoned, and the tiny room reverberated with an eerie tremolo. It seemed only to further provoke Bluestone, who just kept hitting Kimo, tearing the flesh below his already blackened eye.

A blood-curdling scream resounded outside, over the pali. Bluestone stopped punching. He cocked his head, still clutching Kimo by his bloodied shirt. Aka saw the owl fly past the window. The pueo screamed again, this time right above the cabin. Jimmy sat dumbfounded, unsure of what he was witnessing. Bluestone let go of Kimo and unslung his M16. "Stop it!" he kept hollering, as he dashed through the cabin's tiny rooms, emptying the rifle into the ceiling. "Stop it!"

Then the earthquake struck.

35 ∫ Seismic God

The quake also rattled the ground under the Hawaiian Volcano Observatory. “Six or better,” Gus Parker said to Lelehua Chin as they scurried down an HVO hallway.

“Five point five is my guess,” Lelehua replied, her bare feet slapping on the white linoleum. She glanced into the offices along the way, noticing pictures askew, books and papers on the floor, and in one room a computer that had slid precariously close to the edge of a desk. She dashed in to nudge it toward the wall, then sprinted back into the hall to catch up with Gus, who had reached the stairway to the Crisis Center. A small crowd of scientists was already in the tower checking the row of seismographs for data from across the island.

As Lelehua entered the stairwell, a second shudder rattled the building, tossing her against the wall. It was smaller and shorter in duration than the first, which had rumbled for almost twenty seconds. Lelehua joined the group huddled in front of the instruments. Outside, visible through the tower windows, wisps of steam drifted up from Kilauea’s quiet crater, catching the morning light.

“Aftershock,” said one of the new summer interns, a busty brunette from Stanford. Everyone nodded in recognition of the obvious.

“East Rift,” announced Murdock, hunching over the seismic drum that recorded activity from that part of Kilauea. Its needle scratched the aftershock’s signature across the paper. “Probably a flank shift.”

“Meaning what exactly?” asked the intern.

Murdock glanced up at the young woman in her brand-new jeans with Vasque hiking boots so bulky they looked like Mickey Mouse shoes.

"Volcano shift, Debbie," Murdock replied. "The whole east flank of Kilauea just sagged toward the ocean."

"How far?" she asked.

"Several inches anyway. We'll know for sure after we send a crew out to measure it."

"At least it's not Mauna Loa," said the scientist responsible for monitoring the island's biggest volcano. With Mauna Loa almost fully inflated, there was worried expectation that one day soon it would erupt—and that *always* meant disaster.

Murdock stepped over to the develocorder—a large metal cabinet on the far wall—and peered at the series of horizontal lines on its glass screen. This machine automatically registered how long each quake continued to shake in key locations across the island—as it vibrated first through Kilauea, then Mauna Loa, Mauna Kea, Hualalai, and lastly, Kohala. Using a small ruler hanging on a cord off the cabinet, Murdock measured the lines, then compared that figure with the reference chart above the screen.

"Six point one on the first quake, five three on number two," Murdock declared. "That's the preliminary estimate."

"Where was the epicenter?" the intern asked, leaning over the drums, her brown eyes cast with sober intensity, an affectation learned in graduate school.

"Probably between Puʻu ʻOʻo and the coast," Murdock said, walking over to the huge table map. He rested his plump finger on the Royal Gardens subdivision. "Somewhere around there."

"Good thing nobody lives up there anymore, except a few mongooses," said the other intern, a bespectacled young man with a perpetual grin of excitement. As usual, Richard wore long baggy shorts, an oversize T-shirt, and black high-top basketball shoes—all a ruse to counterpoise his crisp analytical mind.

"Yeah, there's probably some more buildings off their foundations," Gus replied, recalling a 1989 quake that tossed several homes off the pali.

The building shuddered again, this aftershock smaller than the last but strong enough to shake pencils off the glass tabletop.

"Madam Pele's restless today," Gus said, winking at Debbie in an attempt to shatter her supercilious manner. "She must be angry." The intern looked back at him blankly. Richard chuckled.

"Lelehua," Murdock said, "will you assemble a field crew to investigate?" She nodded and motioned to the two interns to head downstairs for a reconnaissance briefing.

The scientists dispersed, all except Gus, who was still comparing the seismic records on the various drums. By that time, there had been a dozen aftershocks, most of them imperceptible save for some jags across the Kilauea and Mauna Loa drums. Gus stood up and stretched his back, slowly revolving his head to loosen the muscles in his neck. He heard a distinct scratching sound—the needle on the Hualalai drum.

"What's this?" Gus muttered, "another aftershock?"

The needle jerked up and down, leaving a wildly jagged—but shallow—line across the paper, indicating a small magnitude of 1.0 or less. The seismograph sending the signal sat on Hualalai's northwest rift, near the summit, above the Kona airport. Gus glanced at the Kilauea and Mauna Loa drums, but their lines were virtually flat. Whatever was happening on Hualalai was not related to the Kilauea quakes.

Gus watched the needle for almost a minute before it stopped moving. A tiny swarm of quakes? That would mean magma moving inside the volcano. Gus took out his pocket magnifier and knelt before the drum to take a closer look.

"Praying to the seismic god for a little action on Hualalai?" Murdock said, standing at the top of the stairwell.

Gus didn't laugh. He was studying the line so intently that he barely noticed the comment.

Murdock tried again. "Searching for data to justify all that BS in the *Star-Advertiser* last weekend?" he said, still stinging from the grilling he'd received from Menlo Park after the exposé.

"Come here, Joe," Gus said, ignoring the implication. "Look at this."

Murdock laughed cynically. "You gotta be kidding."

"I'm not." Gus stood up and offered his boss the magnifier. Murdock waved it away and ambled over to the seismic drum. He lifted his glasses off his nose, resting them upon his forehead, and squinted at the record.

"Hmmm," he grunted, looking at Gus for an explanation.

Gus shrugged. Given Murdock's mood, he had best let the scientist in charge speculate first.

"Aftershocks?"

"It's beneath the wrong side of the island to be aftershocks," Gus replied. "And it happened ten minutes after the other quakes settled down."

Murdock sighed heavily and stood up. "Well, then, it could only be one thing." He pulled his glasses back onto his nose and peered into Gus's gray eyes. "Some hiker's tramping around up near the Hualalai seismic station."

Gus's face flushed. "Jumping up and down you mean! For a whole goddamn minute!"

"I don't want to argue with you, Gus. I'm tired and frustrated—"

"You're not the only one."

"Then get off this Hualalai bit. I'm fed up with it since that stupid leak." His words carried an accusatory tone.

"I didn't have a thing to do with that story!"

"I never thought you did," Murdock said sarcastically. "The article quoted *'knowledgeable'* unnamed sources."

"If they'd called me, I'd have told them a helluvalot more than was in that article!"

"Oh really?"

Gus didn't reply. A survival instinct overrode his anger. Even private words among colleagues had become potentially dangerous. Gus had always trusted Murdock, but with the pressure on, he now wondered.

Murdock slumped over the Hualalai drum and stared at the subtle jag of lines. His neck tightened.

"I'm sorry, Gus," he sighed. "I wish we'd been able to issue your updated report on Hualalai *before* the newspaper ran the exposé. Then we'd have an easier time finessing a public warning. Now we're stuck debating USGS's cover-up of that two-year-old memorandum instead of two years of new Hualalai data."

Gus was taken aback. "So that's why you went along with Royce Harlan and the Menlo Park boys?"

"Exactly. I figured we'd lost the battle on the first report, but once your update came out, we could ease people into a discussion of the real dangers. Then you and Lelehua could bring in all the new data, including what you've collected over the past few months."

Gus suddenly felt guilty for adding to Murdock's troubles. He could never do Joe's job, he thought; the politics would drive him crazy.

"How soon will the revision be ready?" Murdock asked wearily.

"Lelehua planned to recheck my changes this morning, so we could run it by you this afternoon. But now she's going out with the field crew to check the quake."

Murdock rubbed his balding head. "I want that revision on my desk today, so we can issue it tomorrow. I'll ask Lelehua to look it over before she leaves." He stepped toward the staircase.

"Joe," Gus said, pointing at the Hualalai drum. "What do we do about this?"

"Nothing, not until that report is out, so we have some kind of leg to stand on." Murdock turned to descend the stairs.

"We could still mention it in the report, before it goes out tomorrow."

Murdock didn't look back. "And catch hell from Menlo Park? Not on your life."

Gus leaned out over the stairwell. "Not even a short sentence buried in the body of the report?"

"No!" Murdock growled, but then stopped on the last step and looked up. "You and Lelehua prepare a statement on this morning's Hualalai earthquake swarm, and check the latest GPS data in case there's any evidence of further deformation. We'll issue the warning on Monday, after we've had a few days of public reaction to the report. In the meantime, keep an eye on that Hualalai drum."

"But Joe—"

"Yeah?"

"What if she blows over the weekend?"

"Then we'll all start looking for new jobs."

36 ∫ The Young Activist's Dream

THAT SAME WEDNESDAY MORNING . . .

Still asleep in her little Kona seaside apartment, Wailani Henderson is dreaming. She bobs in water far offshore, spear in hand. Hualalai, shadowed against the pink predawn sky, looms above a palm-lined beach. Wailani knows it's risky to enter the shark's domain before sunrise, but her hungry family waits on the beach. She dives down the submerged cliff, its coral-studded ledges strangely empty. "You're too early," says a watery voice. "The *mano* still lurks in the shadows."

She ignores the warning and dives again, this time well below the ledge, and spots a large creature moving slowly up the submerged cliff—a turtle surfacing. "Leave before it's too late!" A shadow passes overhead, the wings and tail of a manta ray silhouetted against the leaden waves above them. "Leave now!"

Warnings from the two passing animals? Rising to the surface, Wailani slides the dive mask up off her face and sees even more people on the beach—friends and neighbors and their families too, every one of them staring out, awaiting her return with the catch. How can she possibly feed them all?

Wailani inhales the biggest breath she has ever taken and dives almost forty feet down the cliff. "Don't be foolish!" says the voice. "You will bring mano out of his dark domain."

"I have no choice! My people . . ."

Wailani frantically searches for the schools of fish she knows must be there. Surely Kanaloa—wise god of the sea—would not allow her people to starve. Down, down into the depths she goes, hugging the submerged cliff, peering under every ledge. The water grows dark. Her lungs ache, limbs quiver. At last she spots a plump parrotfish munching a coral pod protruding from the wall. Wailani maneuvers close and releases the spear, its usual *zing!* indistinct because of depth pressure ringing in her ears. The spear tears through the fish's body. Wailani sets the prongs with a jerk and, dropping her head, kicks furiously toward the surface, the waves an eternity away.

Far below, an enormous shark glides up through the cobalt depths. With dizzied perception, Wailani watches the beast approach, then devour the parrotfish at the end of her line. She breaks the surface, exhausted, and gasps for air—sweet, life-giving air—just as the shark slams her torso, shredding her with razor teeth. The last thing she sees—the horrified Hawaiians waiting on the beach—dissolves in a dark-red swirl.

Slowly the dream's fragments dissolved in the sunlight pouring into the room. Her side ached. She rolled over, nauseated, and stared at the ceiling, trying to recapture details of the nightmare, then got up, too fast for the pain, and limped across the room. Sitting naked at her desk, she scribbled everything she could remember. An accurate recounting would be essential so her mentor Aunty Keala could make sense of it. With all that Kapu Hawai'i faced, it was vital to know.

Many years earlier, Keala Lulu Huelani had taken Wailani under her wing, teaching her Hawaiian traditions to help Wailani translate her love for the island into political action. To support her efforts, Wailani lived a frugal life, working half time as a bookkeeper on her uncle's Kona coffee farm. She ran Kapu Hawai'i out of her cluttered little studio in the old Tiki Beach Hotel, the last "affordable" surfers' dive on the ocean side of Kailua-Kona. This once-scenic village was now a busy "tourist destination," with huge hotels and dozens of condominium complexes. Wailani's love of the ocean kept her there despite the ever-rising rent.

Wailani was a relative newcomer to the forty-year-old Hawaiian rights movement. Her involvement had sprung from personal outrage, provoked at a community meeting where a proposed resort development at Waipuna Beach was being justified by Tokyo developers, local

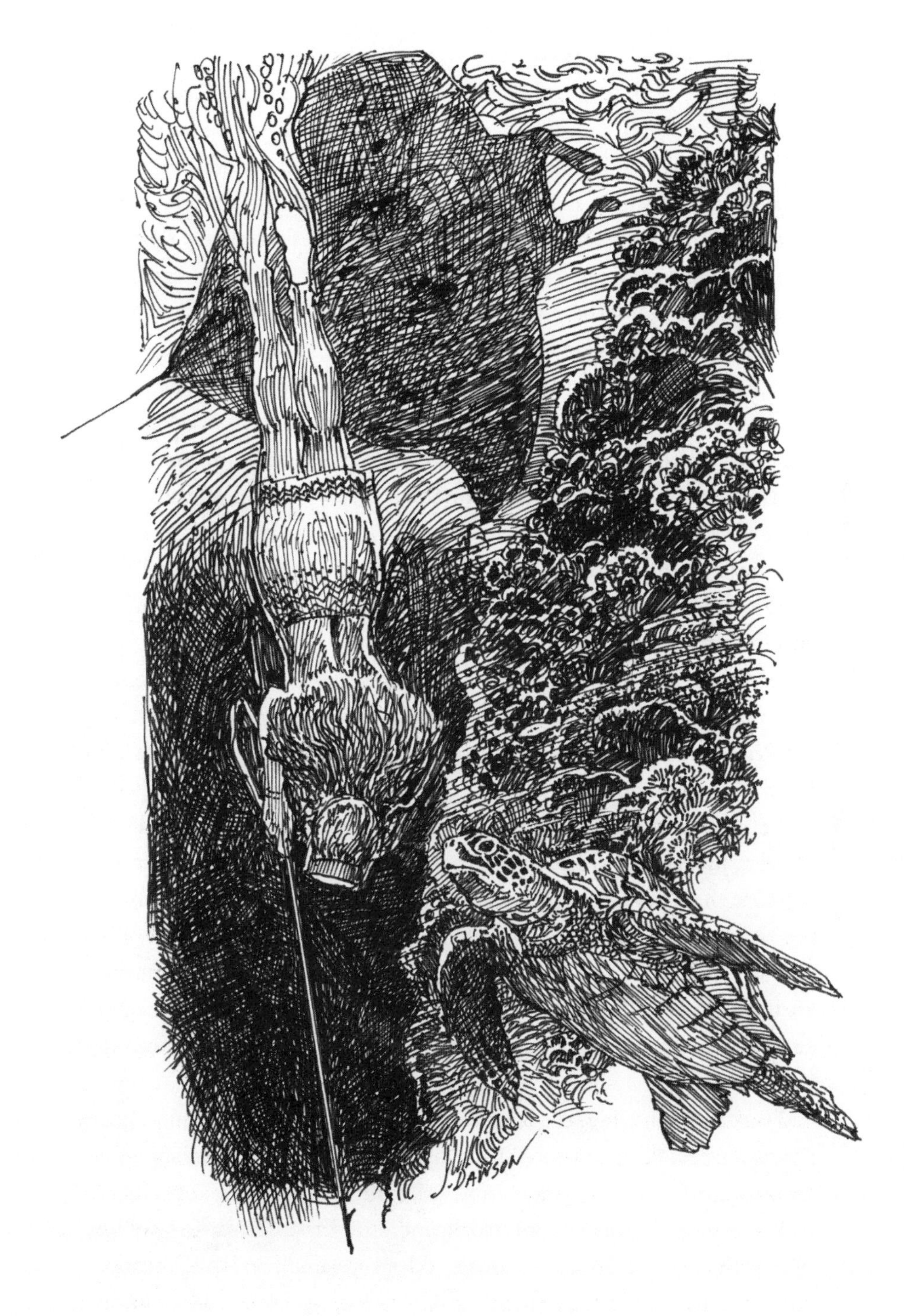

"Leave before it's too late!"

real estate agents, and politicians. Wailani had visited this lovely strip of white sand at the base of Kohala volcano since she was a baby, camping with her parents in full view of four of the island's five volcanoes. She did not believe the developer's assurances that it would "build with sensitivity"; islanders had heard that fiction many times before. She also knew that Waipuna's "improvements" would bring more tourists, that strict rules and regulations (like "no camping") would be imposed, and that eventually the visitors to Waipuna would be as white as the sand. This had happened to every great beach in Hawai'i.

Wailani had not intended to speak, but when the planners and developers droned on about their "environmentally innovative development designs," "mitigative measures to ameliorate negative impacts," and "critical economic variables" that justified the development, the young Hawaiian stood up in the middle of a county planner's presentation.

"I understand what all these complicated words mean," she declared, "and I can help translate them. They mean you want our beach, and you intend to get it no matter what we say at these so-called public-involvement meetings. I've been coming to Waipuna since I was a child, and as far as I'm concerned, its magical sands are sacred." Surprising even herself, Wailani pleaded with the county board: "Please don't let them desecrate our altar."

Before anyone could respond, Aunty Keala, an influential cultural activist, had stood up and said, "This child spoke more truth in fifteen seconds than did all those 'professional' experts during the past two hours."

The crowd roared its agreement, and the county board, unnerved by the outbursts, adjourned for the day to reassess their strategy. After the meeting, Aunty Keala invited the young woman to come see her anytime she wished.

Months later, when the county board approved the Waipuna Magic Sands Resort, Wailani visited the elder to seek comfort from someone who would understand her grief. Wailani had come unannounced, not realizing that as one of the keepers of the ancient knowledge, Aunty Keala was extremely busy—assisting her son's hula troupe, advising the State Department of Education on language programs for Hawaiian children, and providing spiritual guidance to a cadre of

Hawaiian rights activists working for the return of disputed lands. She was also in the center of a protracted controversy with London's British Museum, demanding the return of Hawaiian bones displayed in the museum's Polynesia exhibit.

Even so, the elder spent the entire afternoon consoling Wailani, and during their conversation, she recognized that the young woman had attributes that could someday be important to her people—if properly developed. Guided by aloha and a deep concern for the ʻaina—the homeland—Wailani had a natural ability to string words together straight from her naʻau—that deep, gut-level knowing. The two felt an immediate rapport, and the headstrong young woman, usually skeptical of others' suggestions, accepted at face value the elder's advice. Twelve years of mentoring, on everything from politics to spiritual matters, had made Wailani an effective and enlightened leader, utilizing the talents Aunty Keala had recognized in her that day.

Wailani finished jotting down the details of her dream and got up from the desk, her side throbbing. She wrapped herself in a blue-and-white pareu and stepped out onto her tiny seaside lanai. The water seemed dark and foreboding. Was the warning in her dream related to Kapu Hawaiʻi's planned protest at the Royal Paradise Bay Resort? And who was the shark that would come after her? She looked forward to Aunty Keala's insight on the matter.

The elder's 1920 coffee shack stood high on the slopes of Hualalai, near the village of Holualoa, and Wailani's old hatchback strained to make the climb. Still shaky from the pain, Wailani ambled to the little green house flanked by banana trees. The grazing chickens made a ruckus as she passed Aunty Keala's garden of vegetables, herbs, and *kava* bushes. "Aunty, it's Wailani," she said, stepping onto the lanai.

"In here, darling," said a robust voice through the window of the elder's office.

Wailani passed through the living room. Old koa wood furniture stood before a stone fireplace, on whose mantel sat several ancient tool blades from the quarries on Mauna Kea, a poi pounder Aunty Keala had inherited from her mother, and bone fishhooks from her Kiholo fishing clan. In the corner was an altar of three tall lava rocks draped with leis of ti and maile, standing beneath a 1922 photograph of Mauna Kea, Mauna Loa, and Hualalai, all capped with snow.

"Aloha, Aunty," Wailani said, stepping into the cramped office. She handed the elder a bag of fresh-picked Kona oranges she'd purchased on the way up.

"Aloha, Wailani," replied the stout woman seated at the computer, her small plump hands resting on its keyboard. "Mahalo for the oranges."

One of the few full-blooded Hawaiians left on earth, Aunty Keala had a large, open face with bold features—a broad nose, full lips, and skin as dark as chocolate. Her face was virtually unlined, reflecting her inner contentment and aloha, and her graying hair was piled high atop her head.

Wailani leaned over and kissed the elder on the lips, and Aunty Keala returned the greeting with a warm hug that pressed a little too hard on Wailani's side. She winced.

"What's wrong, child?"

"It's nothing, really. I'll explain in a minute."

Aunty Keala switched off the computer. "Let's go out to the lanai."

Wailani followed the old woman through the house, the elder walking with a dignified waddle, shifting her weight from one sturdy leg to the other. On the lanai, Aunty Keala eased herself into the largest of the chairs, a koa rocker with a wide seat and tall back, made for her by one of her sons. Wailani sat down next to her.

"What's happened?" asked the elder in her typically direct manner.

"I had a dream this morning. I wonder what it means."

"Tell me about it."

Wailani pulled the notes out of her shorts pocket and read to Aunty Keala, adding details as they occurred to her. The elder listened intently, her eyes closed.

Aunty Keala gently touched the young woman's side. "And your *'opu* still aches?"

"Yes, but much less now."

"You should have that checked."

"It's just sore from muscle strain—from the terror of the dream."

"I don't think so."

Aunty Keala gazed out to sea and noticed wispy clouds gathering far south of the island. Wailani tapped her wrist. "What did I see, Aunty?"

"You've had a premonition, Wailani, and not a happy one." She turned to face the young woman. "You must now be very careful."

Aunty Keala's grave tone startled Wailani. Never before had the old Hawaiian seen such ominous portent in one of her dreams.

"Listen carefully. You must think only positive thoughts until that ache goes away."

Wailani nodded.

"You have been given a warning. The shark in your dream is evil. He represents dark forces among our own people. You must retreat a little now—"

"Retreat?"

"Just for a little while, until your health returns."

"But, Aunty, I'll be fine."

The elder shook her head. "You are being visited by the negative. But evil spirits cannot overwhelm one who knows she cannot be conquered. Do you accept this to be true?"

"Yes."

"Believe it! Your dream warns that dark forces are gathering to stop those who work for the true benefit of our people. You are a target because you are now the most visible of Kapu Hawai'i's leaders. Be wise. The attack will come from within your own ranks."

"Who would do that?"

"That I cannot say. You will have to dream some more—and so will I." The elder turned from Wailani and again stared at the horizon. The clouds that had been visible far to the south were moving in on the island. After a minute or two, Aunty Keala turned back to the young woman. "Wailani, dear, take a few days off from all this. Go to the beach or the mountains, and rest. Draw in all the strength you can from these places."

"But, Aunty, the protest at the Royal Paradise Bay is Saturday. The governor will be there and we—"

"I have given my advice."

Wailani sighed with frustration. "Just let me do what needs to be done for Saturday. Then, after the protest, I'll take a week off and do absolutely nothing. I promise."

Aunty Keala shook her head. "Stubborn woman! At least stop for the rest of today. And I want to know when the pain is gone."

As Wailani drove back down the volcano, Aunty Keala sat for a long time studying the gathering clouds. She knew something big was about to happen, a response to bad things that had built up over the years. Today's events were but a confirmation of knowledge passed on to her when she and Wailani made that secret morning trek to the ancient Hualalai shrine. She was less certain about Wailani's ailment. Was it meant to keep the young leader from helping prevent the imminent calamities—and the death of innocents—that Aunty Keala sensed? The elder would have to wait for more to unfold before she would know.

Aunty Keala went into the dense forest behind her house to find what she would need for an offering. That night she would drive to the big temple at the foot of the island's oldest volcano, Kohala. Wailani now needed more than her mentor's help. Aunty Keala would have to summon the gods.

37 ʃ Progress

THAT SAME WEDNESDAY MORNING . . .

A few hours before the Kilauea earthquakes shook the HVO scientists, an unusually thick veil of that volcano's fumes hung over Kona, blown around the island on prevailing winds. The brown haze masked all but the very summit of Hualalai, and the mountain cast a shadow over the coast. Robert Conway, his face crowding the tiny window of the private charter, paid no attention. His gaze was fixed on his vast resort below the plane. Sprawled across hundreds of acres, it outscaled everything else on the coast. Even he, who had lived for years with its image in his head, was impressed.

Most pleasing were the thatched huts of the Hawaiian Village Suites nestled along Kiholo Bay. The eighteenth-century-ship replica added to the picture of the past—Captain Cook sailing in to refresh his men with sweet water, fresh food, and the legendary delights of the island women. Conway laughed aloud at the thought of the erstwhile explorer marching into the Golden Coconut Saloon to order a pint of rum.

"Anything I can get you, Mr. Conway?" offered the young flight attendant, a comely blend of Filipino and Hawaiian blood that reminded Conway of Mali'o, whose gig at the Mauna Lani resort had kept her from accompanying him during his two-day trip to San Francisco.

"No, thanks."

The stewardess smiled, then sauntered back up the aisle. Conway watched her slide into a seat near the pilot's cabin and imagined his girlfriend. His libido, like his lust for life, pulsed a vital beat inside him. A handsome and charismatic man, he found that beautiful women always showed up to take care of his needs. But Mali'o had proved different from the rest—brighter and more ambitious, a dreamer in her own right. During their two years together, she had made herself integral to his quest, and her loyalty was deep and abiding.

He looked back as the plane arched over the sea to make its landing at the Kona airport. More than the view gave Conway heart. He returned to Hawai'i with commitments from two more investors in his massive real estate development next to the resort—one from Sacramento, the other from Tokyo. He was also relieved that the Hualalai memorandum scandal, which had received widespread coverage in Hawai'i, had barely made the mainland press. The *San Francisco Chronicle* had run a two-paragraph Associated Press summary of the story, but that's as far east as it got. Only the American investor had asked about the incident, but he wasn't concerned; Californians had long ignored warnings of earthquake hazards, and he scoffed at the idea that a volcano might disrupt Conway's resort. Nor had the USGS's suppression of the HVO memorandum surprised the investor, who remarked that hushing up troublesome data was standard practice in California. The Japanese investor would certainly have been concerned, given his own country's devastating earthquakes and volcanoes, but the story hadn't reached the Tokyo newspapers.

Conway's buoyancy was a welcome relief from the mood he had carried *to* San Francisco. Anxieties had nagged at him all the way there, spurred by the *Star-Advertiser* exposé. Not only was his own money riding on the resort (although others had risked the vast majority of dollars), but he'd also begun worrying about his larger—secret—scheme. While it would transform Kona into a world-class destination, Conway now realized it would also mean more intimate dealings with the Hui, associations he thought he'd left behind years ago, and Haku Kane was already staking out more and more Hui territory. But Conway's deepest anxiety was a fear he had long lived with—and ignored—most of his career, that his dreams might get derailed through circumstances beyond his control. He could maneuver around financial and political pitfalls, but the whims of a volcano were beyond his influence. Would he someday be cast up as the fool who built on the slopes of a volcano? He imagined the hushed whispers of his social companions at the Moana Hotel as he passed through the lobby: "There goes poor old Conway, the builder of that disastrous resort on Hawai'i."

All of that was forgotten in the glories of his successful trip, and as the plane touched down, his excitement to see what his staff had accomplished since Monday grew. He strode across the tarmac, scanning the open-air gate for his personal assistant, who was working on break from the UCLA Business School. Lawrence wasn't there. Conway glanced at his Rolex: 9:15 a.m. The young man had been instructed to always run ahead of his boss's schedule—thereby never making him wait. Conway's jaw tightened. He called the resort on his cell phone and, incapable of stillness, paced as his hotel manager tried to explain Lawrence's absence.

Andy Lankowski observed all this from the lei stand at the far end of the gate. When Conway put his phone away, the governor's aide strolled over.

"Looking for me, Bob?" he said with a disingenuous grin.

"What business is it of yours to send my driver away?" Conway replied sharply.

"Only trying to save us both a little precious time. I just flew in myself—carrying some fresh news for you—when I noticed your driver at the curb. I thought, 'Gee, why not kill two birds with one stone?' Handle our meeting while I take you back to the resort."

Conway didn't reply.

"Your man wasn't too keen on the idea, but I assured him that you would appreciate the arrangement." Conway frowned, and Lankowski lit a cigarette.

Just then Lawrence raced up in Conway's bright-red Range Rover. He leaped out onto the curb, his face flushed. "Sorry, Mr. Conway, they just relayed your phone message—"

"Listen to me," Conway said, pressing his finger into Lankowski's rumpled suit. "I don't care who you work for. Nobody jacks my schedule around without my permission."

Lankowski was startled by the entrepreneur's unusually charged response. "Hey, I'm sorry, Bob, I was just trying to—"

"Forget about it, Andy," Conway interrupted, walking toward the

SUV. He knew this was just another of Lankowski's petty power games, and he wasn't going to stand for it, especially in front of his staff. "I can't return to the resort with you. I'm due in Kailua in ten minutes." A lie, but it would do. Conway opened the door of the Range Rover.

"I see," Lankowski frowned. "Maybe later in the day?"

"Might work," Conway said, handing his briefcase to Lawrence, who had already retrieved his luggage from the baggage carousel.

"Bob, it's *bad* news—"

The word pierced Conway's tough demeanor, instantly draining his strength. Lankowski waited for a reaction, but Conway refused to show it. He slid into the seat.

"We'll talk about it later," Lankowski said, crouching next to the open door, the smoke from his cigarette drifting inside. "Let me just mention that Governor Kamali'i may not make it Saturday."

Conway turned toward Lankowski, his blue eyes icy.

"It's complicated, Bob, but there's some heavy politics coming down and he might have to pass on the grand opening."

Conway, his back rigid, looked straight into the weasel's steady eyes. "That *is* bad news. I thought Calvin would relish the international attention, say nothing about the local political capital gained from the creation of *thousands* of new jobs." He slammed the door.

Lankowski's face collapsed in puzzlement. Conway was usually at least shrewdly diplomatic. "I'll, ah, call your secretary . . . and see if an appointment's possible?"

"Two o'clock this afternoon!" Conway replied, then motioned his assistant to drive away.

"Two it is. Yes, indeed. See you then . . ." The rumble of the vehicle overwhelmed Lankowski's words as it whisked the entrepreneur away.

Conway leaned back in the plush seat and sighed. What could possibly keep the governor from attending the grand opening?

"I'm really sorry, Mr. Conway. Mr. Lankowski was very pushy."

"Never be intimidated by politicians," Conway said, privately wishing that he himself had mastered it better. "Remember, they depend on us as much as we do on them."

"Because we bankroll their campaigns?"

Conway looked into his assistant's naive eyes. "Something even more important. What people want from politicians is assurance they will get, and keep, their little piece of the American dream. It's not much really—a job, a house, a car or two, maybe a college education for their kids—but to get it means keeping paychecks coming. Politicians always claim credit for economic growth, but they know we're the ones who deliver it."

"In school we're taught that government is the *adversary* of business."

Conway laughed. "The rivalry is just posturing, Lawrence, for the public. Anyone who's actually played the development game knows that government and business sleep together all the time. In Hawai'i, it's a goddamn orgy. And that's why you never let anyone—even if he's the governor's aide—intimidate you."

"I understand."

"Besides," said Conway, resting his big hand on Lawrence's shoulder, "Lankowski is an asshole." They both laughed, easing the tension.

On a rise in the highway the shining hotel towers of the Royal Paradise Bay came into view, and a few minutes later the Range Rover turned into its palm-lined drive. The landscaped entrance, finished while he was away, pleased Conway. A bronze-sculpted replica of a kahili, feather scepter of the royal ali'i, stood on each side of the road, and a black slate sign announced the resort in gold letters:

THE ROYAL PARADISE BAY
Where fantasies come true. Dream!

Conway imagined his own dream—condominiums and homes, shopping centers and restaurants, a massive development that would eventually cover this whole wasteland, spreading across the highway and up the side of the volcano. Those last two investors were all he needed to safely announce the larger scheme at the grand opening—including its secret element.

"Drop me off at the lobby," Conway commanded, eager to walk in as his guests would on Saturday. Lawrence pulled up under the spreading white portico. Two more kahili—these topped with real golden feathers—flanked the lobby entrance. Conway stepped out onto the Italian tile and watched his reflection in the polished stone as he passed into the lobby. The roar of the waterfall filled his ears as morning sunlight filtered through the spreading arms of the giant banyan.

Conway smiled at the impression conveyed, then walked over to the registration desk. Above a long koa-wood counter hung a series of brass chronometers indicating the time in ten cities across the globe. An oil painting of the entrepreneur hung on a side wall; its brass plaque, which read "Robert Conway, Hotelier Extraordinaire," was engraved with a quote from his groundbreaking speech: "Progress is a state of mind."

"Good morning, Mr. Conway," announced the pretty blonde behind the counter. "We're almost ready for Saturday." Her blue eyes sparkled.

"Yes," he replied, nodding his head thoughtfully, "I think so."

"What can I do for you?" she asked with that feigned enthusiasm everyone in the tourist industry is taught, the impression that they're as excited about your vacation as you are.

Conway stepped behind the counter. "Where do our bookings stand at the moment?" he asked.

"Let me check," she said, still holding her toothy smile. She clicked a few computer keys and looked up, beaming.

"We're full—all fourteen hundred rooms."

"And the VIP list for the grand opening?"

She swiveled the screen toward Conway. "The ones with an asterisk are staying overnight."

Conway examined the names—a who's who of Hawai'i business and government, including the mayor and other Big Island officials, the state's legislative leaders, six members of the powerful Board of Land and Natural Resources, and the US congressional delegation (including, of course, Representative Harold Yamashita). Numerous prominent citizens also appeared on the list, not the least of which were representatives of the old *kama'aina* families who still controlled most of the land in Hawai'i, along with some important Hui names, including Haku Kane. This last made Conway cringe, but overall he was pleased. The governor should see that list, he thought; then he'd think twice about not coming.

"Is there anything else, Mr. Conway?"

"No, that should do it." He glanced at the gold nameplate above her perky bosom. "Good job, Brook." He patted her hand like a lord praising his subject.

"Oh, thank you, sir."

Conway unlocked the brass door of his mailbox under the counter and pulled out a stack of messages, faxes, and hard copies of his e-mail. He nodded at Brook as he strode back into the lobby. Her smile was still in place.

Conway stepped up to the monorail where a brawny man of Portuguese blood proudly polished the chrome trim of the train. He didn't recognize Conway but smiled anyway, his exquisite teeth glistening beneath a thick groomed mustache.

"This thing running?" Conway asked tersely.

"Fo'sure," the man replied with pride. "But I can't carry jes' anyone—not yet—not wit'out proper authorization. Only VIPs, dat sorta t'ing."

"I'm Robert Conway."

He nodded. "I'm Manuel Silva," the first name pronounced "Man-yo."

"I'm Robert Conway," he repeated.

Manuel shrugged his shoulders and smiled.

Conway frowned. "This is *my* resort."

Manuel's face dropped, suddenly aware that he *had* seen this guy before, on the painting behind the counter in the lobby.

"Sorry," he said, turning amber. "I didn't recognize you, Mister, Mister . . ." He still blocked the name. "You wanna ride?"

"That's the idea. Suite number one, the King's Tower." Conway turned, walked to the first car, and stepped inside. Manuel shook his head and stepped up into the train engine. Only recently trained to operate the monorail (the chief engineer came on later in the day), he carefully engaged the controls. A moment later a chime rang in the lobby, the electric doors whirred shut, and the train sped away. Conway leafed through his e-mail printouts as the resort's lush scenery flew past. Suddenly the cabin lights flickered, then went out, and the train moaned to a stop, stalled on an elevated track fifty feet above a manmade island in the Crocodile Jungle. Irritated, Conway leaped out of his seat and strode to the front of the car.

Manuel looked back through the window separating them and shrugged his thick shoulders. Conway stepped over to the exit, waiting for the driver to open the door.

"No can wit'out power," hollered Manuel through the glass.

"There must be a way!" Conway shouted back.

Manuel stared down at the control panel. He tried a couple of buttons but the doors remained sealed.

"Le'me try unlock 'um manually." While he searched the various knobs and levers in the engine, concern replaced Conway's annoyance. The grand opening was only three days away, with VIPs arriving as early as Friday morning. What could be wrong with the monorail?

Parrots and cockatoos fluttered about the palms next to the train, and a monkey on a *kamana* limb puzzled over the stalled machine. Two crocodiles yawned from the muck at the edge of the island, and several groundskeepers, having noticed the trouble, gathered on the walkway next to the lagoon. "Manuel," shouted one of the groundskeepers. "Try grab da emergency release above da door."

Manuel found the latch and pulled it. The door thudded open. He stepped out onto the narrow catwalk beside the train and inched his way to the next car. Conway stood inside, fuming. The train's cool conditioned air had quickly dissipated and his face streamed with sweat.

"I couldn't hear him," Conway shouted through the glass. "Where's the emergency latch?"

"Next to da kine," Manuel replied, nervously glancing down through the catwalk grating.

"What?"

Manuel stretched his big hands across the steel skin of the train to steady himself. "Next to da kine," he shouted, removing one hand to point inside Conway's car.

"Where?"

"Above da kine," Manuel said again, distracted by the crocodiles lounging below.

"Speak English, you idiot!"

"ABOVE THE DOOR, CONWAY!" shouted one of the groundskeepers.

Conway finally noticed the latch and reached up to pull it. But he was suddenly thrown back against the seats as the train jerked forward. Out of the corner of his eye he saw Manuel fall away from the window. The lights flickered on, and the train hummed its way down the track.

38 ∫ Accumulating Troubles

After a quick shower and a potent cup of coffee, Robert Conway met with his young resort manager, Cyrus Bond, to discuss the monorail mishap.

"The whole resort was without electricity," explained Bond, "because of an earthquake."

"What earthquake?" Conway sat down opposite Bond's desk, stunned.

"On the other side of the island, under Kilauea's south flank," Bond said, adjusting the Oxford knot of his necktie. "Hawai'i Power Corp. says they lost part of their load when a six-point-one earthquake knocked out the generators at the Puna geothermal plant. Apparently, it's quite a mess over there—steam explosions, sulfur dioxide emissions, the works. Anyway, over here we were blacked out for about five minutes."

"But we're on the priority grid," Conway said. "The county building and the schools are supposed to shut down before we do."

"I complained about that, but HPC says that's only during *planned* outages. With the earthquake, there wasn't time to switch us over."

"Goddamn coconut power!" Conway said, all too aware that resorts on the outer islands had to build atop the decrepit infrastructure of the old plantation economy.

"If it's any consolation, our backup generators should be up and running in about three weeks," Bond said.

"I also want those emergency door latches on the monorail clearly marked with signs at eye level."

"I've already ordered the stickers. They'll be posted by Friday."

"Good," Conway grunted, impressed with the aggressive young Chicagoan trained in that city's finest hotels. Conway had stolen the thirty-five-year-old from the Rockefeller-built resort up the coast, offering him ten grand more per year plus his own suite in the King's Tower. Bond was a superb administrator with a nouveau riche style perfect for Conway's target clientele. He accented his conservative Brooks Brothers shirts with avant-garde ties and drove a white Mercedes sporting an island bumper sticker that urged "Chance 'em!" Offbeat imagination leavened Bond's keen economic sense, especially with PR (like ordering the slick *Vanity Fair* and *New Yorker* ads showing a taciturn couple on a desolate beach being spied on by an impish Polynesian phantom) and his staff protocols (including employee seminars on "The Cross-Cultural Wow Experience," by a black Sausalito psychiatrist). Most importantly, Conway's "first mate" was a materialist and utterly loyal to the man who signed his paychecks.

Bond's confident demeanor eased Conway's agitation, but the entrepreneur still seethed over having been trapped on the moving monorail for almost an hour before someone finally figured out how to stop the train.

"This was a real fluke, Bob," Bond said, resting his manicured fingers on the edge of his desk. "I can't imagine another case where the train would ever run without a driver on board. Even so, I've sent a memo to all senior employees telling them the location of the master panel downstairs."

Conway nodded.

"And I've asked the manufacturer to come up with a system of emergency stop switches for the passenger cars."

"We'll see what that'll cost when the time comes, but if there's any criticism as a result of the accident, don't hesitate to mention the possible modification."

Conway got up and stepped to the door. "Good work, Cyrus."

"Thank you, sir."

Conway paused in the threshold. "By the way, how is the driver?"

"Back luck, sir. They think his neck may be broken."

Conway felt a serpent bite his gut. "That's terrible."

"Yes," Bond replied, casting his eyes to the floor. "He also lost a foot to one of the crocodiles."

Conway shook his head, disgusted with himself for giving in to the investor's insistence there be wild reptiles in the Jungle.

"Send the family some money, will you? With a card from me." Conway paused, glancing at the Gauguin in the lobby. "Say, $10,000, to help with his medical expenses. OK?"

"Yes." Bond nodded, affirming the prudence of the figure. Even so, a lawsuit was inevitable.

"Thank you, Cyrus," Conway said, turning to leave.

"I'm afraid keeping it out of the papers will be difficult," Bond added.

Conway looked back over his shoulder. "What do you mean?"

"The driver isn't out of danger yet. He's still in surgery at the Kona hospital."

Conway sighed and Bond's eyes returned to the floor.

"Keep me posted."

"I will."

Conway stepped into the lobby, passing two police officers waiting to see the resort manager about the accident.

"Why *now?*" Conway muttered under his breath.

Conway decided to walk rather than ride back to his suite. He took an indirect route to avoid the scene of the accident, but the image of Manuel Silva's stunned face falling away from the window pressed in on his mind. He swapped the terrifying recollection with a comforting thought: any great endeavor involves risks. How many died sailing with Captain Cook or building the Golden Gate Bridge? Even so, the serpent gnawing Conway's gut continued to distract him, and twice he got lost in the labyrinth of elegant hallways, lush jungle paths, and art-filled corridors leading back to his suite.

An unbidden admonition from his mentor came to mind. "Disaster visits boats plagued with multiple difficulties," Gieselmann had said one wintry cruise off San Francisco. "Troubles accumulate piecemeal, and suddenly the craft's in jeopardy." Conway could see his troubles building—changes in Hualalai, the *Star-Advertiser* exposé, Haku Kane scheming behind the scenes, the monorail mishap, and now the governor backing out on Saturday's festivities. A sense of ill fate took over his mood.

When at last he reached his suite, Conway escaped from his business suit and shrugged into a pair of cotton slacks and a polo shirt. Uncharacteristically fatigued, he drifted into the bedroom, thinking maybe he could nap before his meeting with Lankowski. A pink envelope waited on the pillow atop his enormous bed:

Lover Bob,

Sorry I couldn't go with you to SF. The gig went real well—lots of tips and applause. Call me when you get in so we can make up for lost time . . . I'm "hungry." How about you?

XOXOXO!!!!
Mali'o

Conway lay down on the bed, thinking about Mali'o. He finally dozed, uneasy in his sleep. He still felt drained when the call from Brook woke him, announcing Lankowski's arrival.

"Send him over to the Golden Coconut. I'll be down in a few minutes."

"Yes, sir," Brook replied with a cheerfulness Conway now found hard to bear.

Conway left a message for Mali'o at the Mauna Lani, then retreated to his opulent bathroom. He splashed cold water on his face and stared into the mirror, noticing some new wrinkles. "There was a cost," he muttered, "but I've created a paradise on earth out of a wasteland."

Conway studied the self-made man before him. "Self-made?" He snorted, recalling the deal compelled long ago with the Hui. The thought of Haku Kane's name on the VIP list turned his stomach. "Gotta get out from under . . ." He blinked and left the bathroom.

With false bravado, Conway strode through the swinging doors of the Golden Coconut Saloon. Lankowski was hunched over the bar next to a bottle of Steinlager and an oversize crystal ashtray.

"Hi, Bob," he said, lifting the bottle. "I helped myself. Hope you don't mind."

"Not at all," Conway said, appalled at the gall of the weasel. He sat down kitty-corner from his unwanted ally.

"Before we get started," Lankowski said, crushing his cigarette into the ashtray, "let me apologize for my faux pas this morning. What a mistake!" He laughed. "Yes, indeed. *Way* out of line. But I hope we can get back on a positive footing this afternoon. Whatdaya say, Bob?"

"Let's do that."

"Yes, indeed." Lankowski offered his bony hand, but Conway pretended not to notice.

"I've got to keep moving, Andy. What's the news?"

"Yes, indeed. News, news, news. I regret to say the governor is having second thoughts about coming to the grand opening. We're all quite excited about the celebration and the announcement of the big development plan, but some new problems have gotten tangled up with the resort."

"New problems?"

"Yes. The natives are getting restless, so to say. The activists of Kapu Hawai'i are planning a surprise protest."

"At the resort? Why?"

"As you know, they have a long-standing feud with the state over disputed lands, lands they claim were stolen back in the olden days. They've been bugging Calvin for support and, you see, being as he's one of 'em and only the second native governor ever, they had *big* expectations, which—fortunately—he hasn't met."

"What does any of that have to do with my resort?"

"Seems they found out the governor is playing a prominent role in the grand opening, so they've decided to come over on Saturday and raise hell with him."

Conway clenched his jaw. "Kapu Hawai'i here? Isn't that the group that squats on other people's property?"

"Uh-huh. 'Course, they think the property is theirs."

"Grumblers, holding up progress!"

"Grumblers?" Lankowski rubbed his chin thoughtfully. "I think they're more of a problem than that. They've got lawyers now."

"You can't stop progress, even with lawyers. Not in America."

Lankowski nodded. "Yes, yes, indeed. But, frankly, Bob, they have some pretty strong legal arguments, what with decades of Native American case law on their side."

Conway was surprised to hear such talk from Lankowski.

"See, there's some pretty nasty skeletons in the state's closet, and we can't control those federal judges like we can our state ones."

"So that's why Calvin and the congressman give lip service to their sovereignty proposals."

"That's part of the reason, no question about it. But even that won't keep them from taking us to court." Oddly, Lankowski seemed genuinely concerned. "Could screw up a lot of plans. Even affect Hawai'i's balance of power."

"You're not serious."

"I am, actually. They're after the old crown lands—properties of the monarchy ceded to the state in 1959 when Hawai'i joined the union." Lankowski tapped the ash off his cigarette. "It's more than half the state, Bob."

"And how does the governor's office respond to all that?"

Lankowski laughed. "For being one of 'em, Calvin's not doing too good, and scandals in the Hawaiian Homelands program aren't helping. Yeah, the Hawaiians are pretty much against him, and that could hurt us at the polls."

"They're such a small group. I find that hard to believe."

"Yeah? At least a quarter of the people of this state have some Hawaiian blood. And don't underestimate the folks who sympathize with the underdog. If all those people ever vote together, we're done."

"None of this has anything to do with my resort."

"Nothing *directly*."

"How do you know they're planning to raid the grand opening?"

"We have contacts inside the movement." Lankowski smiled.

Conway shook his head. Why was everything going wrong?

Lankowski saw the entrepreneur's mood darken. "Hold on a minute, Bob. The governor's still thinking about it. He *wants* to be here."

"He was going to make the announcement!"

"And he still wants to. But we aren't sure his presence will be good for *any* of us, if that means Kapu Hawai'i will show up."

"Look at this, Andy," Conway said, handing him a copy of the VIP list. "Virtually all the powerbrokers are coming to the opening, except Calvin. If he doesn't show, he'll look foolish."

Lankowski shrugged and lit another cigarette.

Conway gazed out at the *Resolution*. "When will Calvin decide?"

"By tomorrow. We're expecting more intelligence on Kapu Hawai'i's plans. If we think we can defuse them, he'll come. But you've got to realize the governor has worked hard for months to avoid a confrontation until after the November election. Besides, we don't want that conflict to spoil the good things happening at Kiholo Bay."

"Even if Calvin doesn't show, what makes you think they won't protest anyway?"

Lankowski shrugged. "Calvin says he's the target, not you."

Conway recognized the sense in that, but he still didn't like it. "Keep me posted," he said, rising. "If the governor can't come, we'll have to make other arrangements."

"We thought the lieutenant governor might make the presentation."

Number two man, Conway thought. The idea disgusted him. "Let me know."

Lankowski rose and stepped toward the door. "Oh, by the way, Bob, sorry about the accident."

"What are you talking about?"

"I just heard it on the car radio. Terrible tragedy with the monorail. The poor man had six kids."

"What?"

"Oh, hadn't you heard? He died on the operating table."

Conway's head began to swim.

39 ∫ *Aftermath of the Earthquake*

THAT SAME AFTERNOON ON THE SOUTH FLANK OF KILAUEA . . .

Look at this!" shouted Debbie, as the young HVO intern placed a bulky boot on either side of a deep crack. Even from fifty yards away, geologist Dr. Lelehua Chin could see that the rent in the volcano's flank stretched almost a hundred feet along the upland slope.

"It's similar to the cracks we found at the coast," she replied.

"There's more over here!" Richard, the other intern, hollered, kneeling beside a deep fissure.

"It took a lot of force to break this rock," Lelehua said, joining Debbie.

"There was a whole lot o' shakin' goin' on," Richard said, pretending to dance the twist as he ambled over to the two women. Lelehua chuckled and Debbie scowled.

"The quake also collapsed the underground tube system," Lelehua said, "forcing lava to the surface." They could see the massive red flows creeping down the black hillside.

Lelehua sketched the cracks on the blue orthophoto fastened to her clipboard. Murdock was right; the volcano's flank had slumped into the sea.

"The leveling crew will have to figure out how much the island shifted, but I'll be surprised if it isn't half a foot or more."

"What do you suppose happened up in the subdivision?" Richard asked.

"Let's find out," Lelehua replied, slipping the clipboard into her pack.

It took half an hour to reach the remnants of Royal Gardens. They crossed hour-old lava to get there, and the cracks beneath them glowed iridescent orange. Debbie found this unnerving and worried about melting her new $300 boots. Richard, on the other hand, was elated: "I can't believe I'm walking on the newest land on Earth!" Debbie rationalized his bravado as naiveté. Besides, the dweeb's boots were Army surplus, issued free by HVO.

The deserted subdivision unsettled both interns. Buried homesteads, abandoned vehicles, and charred street signs put a human dimension on their detached scientific inquiries. Lelehua duly noted the new cracks on the ortho, now covered with a web of jagged lines.

The team eventually reached a portion of the subdivision where quake damage was even more apparent. Several houses, once propped on stilts to afford spectacular sea views, slumped against the slope, their backs broken in the fall. One of the tumbled homes belonged to Jake Bluestone. The ex-soldier's cabin lay shattered below eight splintered posts that had held it aloft. Bluestone's sparse belongings—a few sticks of furniture, his TV and boom box, and some kitchen appliances—lay strewn about the yard amid shattered glass. The three geologists succumbed to the morbid curiosity that attends all natural disasters, unconsciously increasing the distance between them.

Bluestone lay motionless behind a bent solar panel, M16 at his side. He watched the three intruders explore the ruins of his precious retreat. Their presence wasn't the only thing making him angry. His prisoners were on the loose. When the first temblor hit, Bluestone had bolted out the door. Halfway down the steps, he heard the cabin posts snap and noticed the building sag. Inside Jimmy was shouting, "Jake! Jake! Don't leave us in here to die!"

Perhaps the quake had knocked Bluestone back into reality, or maybe it was the memory of his slain buddy's last words in that burning village on the Mekong Delta, or just basic human instinct, but Bluestone charged back up the steps to save the three captives. He had managed to cut away their cords and bolt down the teetering staircase before the house collapsed, but a falling timber knocked him cold. By the time Bluestone came to, a long shard of glass in his thigh had already emptied a fair bit of blood. Using his T-shirt as tourniquet, he bound his leg to stanch the flow, then limped about the fallen walls searching through the debris for his prisoners. All he found was his M16. Bluestone—now a kidnapper—had a whole new set of reasons to be on the run. His strength sapped, Bluestone passed out in the shade of the solar panel, waking to the voices of the three approaching geologists.

He could have killed them easily, but two were women—he had already done too much violence to women—and the other was a scrawny wimp. No threat there. Bluestone lay quietly among his broken things and waited for the trespassers to move on.

"It almost looks like someone lived here," Richard hollered, holding up a Tupperware container half-full of cookies. Bluestone tightened the grip on his M16, his eyes burning with contempt.

"Not as far as I know," Lelehua replied. Richard shrugged and rejoined her at the edge of the property. "We've got a long hike back," she said. "Where's Debbie?"

Richard and Lelehua scanned the area. "Debbie, let's go!" Lelehua hollered. Only the wind in the trees answered.

"Debbie!" Richard shouted. "We gotta go!"

"What's the fuss?" Debbie finally replied, emerging from behind a heap of wreckage. "I'm right here."

The geologists headed back toward the coast, noting new cracks along the way. Halfway down they stopped to rest in the shade of a giant koa tree towering over an island of vegetation.

"Look what I found at that collapsed house," Debbie said, holding up the brass badge of a Hawai'i County police deputy. The three scientists speculated on the significance of her find, unaware of the pale figure hovering in the foliage a few yards away.

40 ∫ Mali'o Shares Conway's Secret

LATER THAT EVENING AT THE ROYAL PARADISE BAY RESORT . . .

Feeling better, Bob?" Mali'o asked, looking up from pillows at the head of the bed with a smile like the Cheshire cat's. She was naked, save for a black pearl dangling from each ear and a delicate gold chain around her ankle. Robert Conway withdrew from her petite body and rolled over beside her.

"Much better," he replied, winded from the effort required to keep a twenty-eight-year-old woman satisfied.

Mali'o propped her head on an elbow and sighed, keenly aware of how vulnerable this powerful man was to her affections. She brushed his gray-blond hair back into place, excited that a man like Conway was in love with her. She had slept with powerful men before, muscled guys with machismo (rough and domineering in bed), politicians (always eager to please), and Hui men (who didn't give a damn about the women they were screwing). Conway was different. His power derived from confidence and intellect. When he extolled his dreams, Mali'o found him irresistible.

Mali'o Rivera could not have come from a more different world than her lover. She grew up in the former sugar town of Honoka'a, daughter of a Filipino plantation mechanic who married a Hawaiian woman with offspring from two other men. None of the seven children had any education save for the carpentry classes her two brothers had received as inmates at Kulani Prison. But Mali'o possessed raw intelligence ("You one quick girl," her father would say), and that drove her to seek more in life than just adding her own brood to her vast extended family. Before she met Robert Conway, Mali'o had been off island only three times—twice to visit Honolulu members of her clan and once to audition for a cabaret act at a Waikiki hotel.

But she and the entrepreneur had two things in common—a heady ambition to make something notable of themselves and a love for the limelight in which they thrived. Like many islanders—especially those as beautiful as she—Mali'o chose entertainment to fulfill her aspirations, building on a natural singing talent she had developed at family luaus and in the choir of the Honoka'a Catholic Church. The Mauna Lani Hotel was a choice Big Island venue, but it wouldn't lead anywhere—not even to Honolulu, where island performers could make real money and sometimes find statewide fame.

Mali'o had deftly steered clear of working for Hui-controlled talent agencies and entertainment establishments, but she still had ample opportunities to associate with Hui men of money and influence. Their luster wore off when she realized they were too far down the Hui ladder to matter, especially the musicians. The ones with real money were the most entangled with the underworld, constantly fearful of losing their place in the Hui's fierce pecking order. Besides, there was a part of Mali'o that needed *real* love and adoration more than applause for her beauty or bedroom performance, the kind of affection that criminals seemed incapable of giving. So she began to pursue men with greater independence—the haoles.

Singing at the Mauna Lani gave her opportunities to meet such men. Some were attractive, like the middle-aged Californians on respite from jobs as stockbrokers, doctors, lawyers, and the like. She got involved with a few, but her instinct for seeing people as they really were showed her that many of these well-to-do were just high-paid serfs of the corporate kingdom, as caged as the Hui men she'd known.

When Robert Conway walked into the Mauna Lani's Lava Lounge two summers earlier, Mali'o was struck by how different he was from the other successful haoles she'd seen there. He carried his tall frame with a vitality that was neither grandiose nor haughty, and his striking good looks made him instantly stand out. That night he had been seated at a table near the stage with a pretty, young blonde. At first, he was very attentive to his companion, looking into her eyes, touching her hand, and listening carefully to what she had to say. Here was a man who loved women! But Mali'o watched Conway lose interest as the blonde frittered away her opportunity on small talk and petty flirtations. When the pair left early, Mali'o was certain they would not end up in the same bed that night.

The next time Conway came to the Lava Lounge, he strode in alone. He had watched Mali'o's performance with interest, charmed by her dazzling personality, clever patter, and the silky voice she'd inherited from her Hawaiian grandmother. During the break, Mali'o stopped by his table and, sensing that Conway would appreciate an assertive woman, hustled him aggressively. This was Mali'o in true form, the way she was most happy with herself. She knew she needed a confident man who would not be threatened by her willful nature and intelligence. To Conway, these attributes and Mali'o's exotic good looks were more than compelling.

Over the next weeks, Conway became a regular patron of the Lava Lounge, always chatting with Mali'o on her breaks, and before long he asked her to dinner. After one more date, they were in bed, two ambitious and self-assured people dedicated equally to pleasing themselves and their quest. Two years later, they were still ensnared.

"You see," she said, propped up on her elbow, "Mali'o knows how to relax her man." She slid her long fingers over his spent genitals.

Conway smiled, scanning her teak-colored body. Petite, with firm little breasts high up on her chest—"mangoes," he called them—she offered a youthful profile. A small umbilical knot adorned her taut stomach, which Conway loved to kiss like a third nipple. Rigorous hula training as a child had superbly contoured her long legs, and tiny nails formed a perfect line across her toes.

"You are a *crazy* good lover," she said for the hundredth time.

Conway, aroused again by her words and fondling, moved back into position above her, but she slipped away and hopped off the bed. She had learned at a young age that it's always best to leave a man hungering for more (assuring an energetic effort later on his part). She ambled to the window and stretched her limbs, fully aware she presented an erotic silhouette against the purple twilight outside.

"Let's go for a drive," she suggested, looking out at the sea.

"Tonight?"

"Yeah, you need to get your mind off all these resort hassles."

Her words abruptly broke the respite their afternoon lovemaking had provided. The monorail driver's face falling away flashed across Conway's mind, and his jaw tightened again.

"Yeah," Mali'o said, pivoting away from the glass. "Let's drive up to Kohala. The coast below the volcano is so beautiful at night."

Conway sat up on the side of the bed. "I don't know."

She moved toward him. "We could get the kitchen staff to make us a picnic supper. Cheese, fish, wine."

Conway knew getting away for a few hours was a good idea, yet he held back. Was he beginning to fear the island, that world outside his manmade reality? "I just don't want to have to deal with anything."

"I know a private little cove"—Mali'o crouched in front of him, grasping his knees with her long fingers. She dropped her head and gently brushed her luscious hair across his lap—"with a beach perfect for lovemaking."

"Well, then . . ." he agreed, his eyes burning.

While driving them up to Kohala in her sporty red Miata, Mali'o tried to steer the conversation away from the resort, but Conway needed to vent first—with the one person he could share his feelings with. Mali'o's was a loyal, sympathetic ear, and her intelligence often yielded sound solutions far different from his own. Conway railed against the governor and Lankowski, and the bad luck that had killed one of his employees. He might have complained about Haku Kane, but the Hui entanglement was too painful to bring up, and that rage remained submerged.

By the time they reached the slopes of the island's northernmost volcano, Mali'o had Conway refocused on his vision for the resort. "Think of all the incredible things you can do in that marvelous Grand Ballroom!" she said, gleefully peering through the windshield as if it were a magic mirror on the future. "Concerts, dances, theater productions, huge conventions! And once it's turned into a casino!"

He shook his head. "I told you, Mali'o, not a word about that."

She slapped him gently on the arm. "C'mon, sweetheart, it's just you and me alone in the Miata. I grew up with gambling, and I think it's going to be great! My father ran cockfights for years, and everybody loved it. Besides, people need jobs now that the plantations are closed. What you've done at Kiholo is so beautiful and exciting that I'm certain the legislature will take their cue and finally make gambling legal."

"I love your enthusiasm, Mali'o, but I don't want to talk about the casino until after Saturday."

"That's silly!"

Conway grabbed her arm and shook it. "Look, Mali'o, with everything that's happened, I don't want to jinx that too!"

Conway was sorry to be so strident with Mali'o, but he was uncomfortable talking with her about his secret. He had revealed it to her just two months earlier—but only after the heady intoxication of some all-night lovemaking following a cocktail party at the governor's residence. The resort, with its Disney-like attractions, phenomenal room capacity, and huge ballroom, was designed to be the Flamingo Hotel of Hawai'i. The real estate development adjacent to the resort—all that land painstakingly acquired over the past decade—would be the beginning of a whole new city: a place of blackjack and roulette, slot machines, and big-name entertainment. Conway envisioned Kiholo surpassing even Honolulu as Hawai'i's main attraction. With Japan and the US so close, it might even outdo Vegas.

Ever since the 1920s, there had been talk of legalizing gambling in the islands, but opponents killed every legislative proposal. First it was the missionary descendants and other old kama'ainas who questioned its moral character or saw it as antithetical to Hawaiian traditions. In later years, as gambling swept the mainland, the underworld (and its political allies) joined the opposition because legal gambling would jeopardize their own illicit trade. Now things were different. The old kama'ainas had been overwhelmed by a flood of mainland newcomers indifferent on the issue, and the shaky post-sugar economy had defused other public opposition. As the twenty-first century progressed, high-buck tourism designed for the wealthier classes had to compete with what Florida and the Caribbean had to offer. Las Vegas and California had modernized—some would say fantasized—their hotels while Waikiki grew a bit shabby and overcrowded. The "old boys" began thinking that casinos were the only thing that would restore a lucrative tourist trade in Hawai'i.

Haku Kane had seen the writing on the wall. How he found out about Conway's casino plans remained a mystery, but the Hui chief called in an old debt he claimed the entrepreneur owed from his desperate days after the geothermal fiasco. As soon as Conway's secret casino plan was announced at the grand opening, Kane's people would turn up the heat on their legislative allies to legalize gambling. The most cooperative politicians would also get a piece of the action—tip-offs of potential real estate windfalls and the usual under-the-table payoffs. In exchange—and without any choice on Conway's part—Kane would control the games through a dummy state commission. Under this scheme, the resort and its casino would stimulate all kinds of additional development, including other casinos. To keep the commission politically viable, Kane would allow some non-Hui casinos to operate at Kiholo but never to challenge those associated with the Royal Paradise Bay Games and Entertainment Corporation. Of course, the Hui would continue to control Hawai'i's other vices, greatly expanded with the stimulus of gambling.

For Conway—still ignorant of the full scope of Kane's scheme—the casino was simply a means to two ends. He would finally get free of Kane's claim on him, at the same time becoming the founder of a whole new city on the far edge of America: Kiholo, *his* frontier.

Conway gently patted Mali'o on the cheek. "After Saturday's announcement, you can tell anyone you want."

Mali'o smiled impishly, her teeth glistening between peach-painted lips. "I'm so excited! I find it hard *not* to talk about it."

"You haven't told a soul, have you?"

Her face changed abruptly, the smile vanquished. "Not really."

"What does that mean?"

"I only mentioned it once—to my family."

"Your family? All five hundred of them, no doubt." It was a familiar tease, but this time it carried real apprehension. "What did you tell them?"

"I was vague about it."

She thought back to her indiscretion, a family luau in Honoka'a after the men returned from cockfights behind the Enriquez place. It was more of a coy quip than a full disclosure. Her brother, Rufino, had said, "I don' know why dey don' build one beeg casino Waikiki. Make some jobs fo' Hawai'i, fast like." The other men, drunk on Budweiser and their winnings of the night, had chimed in their agreement.

"What's wrong with this island?" Mali'o had replied. "Why not over in Kona?"

"Dat what your big-shot boyfriend gonna do at Kiholo?" said Rufino.

"I'm not telling, but if I were you guys, I'd save up my chicken winnings for some real gambling!"

This had greatly excited the group, all except her Hawaiian cousin, Kalama, a local musician with ties to the Hui. Like many island performers, Kalama relied on a Hui-run company to distribute his albums and dole out his gigs. What Mali'o didn't realize—in fact, what no one in her family knew—was that Kalama had become interested in the Hawaiian sovereignty movement and had recently paid membership dues to Kapu Hawai'i.

"Legalize gambling and that'll be the end of anything Hawaiian in these islands," he had declared. "The place will change overnight."

Upset with Kalama's remark about her lover's dream and knowing his Hui connection, Mali'o had privately scolded him, mentioning that Haku Kane, himself, was involved. She thought the disclosure would stir in him some local pride, but Kalama's reaction was quite the opposite.

"That makes me even more upset. The Hui doesn't care about Hawaiians any more—if they ever did!"

"Don't forget you work for them."

"Only because there's few other ways people like us can get into the music business. So far you've been lucky." He had clenched a fist and held it up between them. "But someday—*soon*—it will all be different!"

At the time, Mali'o had dismissed the comment as nothing more than local bravado fueled by beer. Like Conway, she hated to acknowledge anything negative about either of their dreams. For this reason, and because her lapse in judgment embarrassed her, she had never mentioned the incident to Conway.

"I'm sorry, Bob," she said, as the car passed a tiny harbor town below the volcano. "I can't imagine my family knowing makes any difference."

"Let's hope not, but damn it, you've got to be careful with what I tell you."

"I am, Bob—really," she declared, eager to move on. "Look, with or without gambling, a ballroom like that could finally draw world-class shows to the Big Island. And then," she playfully poked him in the ribs, "you could invite *me* to be the opening act!"

She laughed like a naughty child, and Conway found himself smiling.

"Have I told you I've got a fantasy about that boat of your famous Captain Cook? I'd like to dance the deck for you under the stars, Polynesian-style—naked!"

Conway laughed heartily, and Mali'o was glad to see him buoyant again. That was the Robert Conway she'd fallen in love with.

41 ʃ Ancestral Prayer

Near the island's northern tip at Upolu Point, at the end of a long cinder road, Mali'o tucked the red Miata under a grove of thorny *kiawe* trees. Stars dazzled through wisps of high cloud, the far edge of the gathering storm over Kona. On a rise above the shore stood the shadowed ruin of the Mo'okini temple, which according to some oral traditions was built in one night by thousands of slaves hauling stones from a valley nine miles away. Beyond its rugged walls, also shadowed by starlight, was the extinct volcano, Kohala.

Mali'o guided Conway down a stony path to the cove, following bits of white coral marking the trail. She spread a blanket on the sand between two coconut trees and the couple settled in for their picnic. They might have toasted to the Royal Paradise Bay, but Mali'o thought it better to honor "the dreamers of the world," among whom she included herself (though Conway assumed the toast was to him). Finishing her glass, Mali'o stood up, unknotted her pareu, and dropped it on the sand. Naked, she flashed Conway a smile, then dashed into the water.

Conway downed his wine, stripped off his trousers and shirt, and followed her into the gentle surf. He dove into the cool water and immediately felt the tension in his limbs dissipate. He emerged next to Mali'o, who was floating face up, staring at the stars. He was about to kiss her when a freakish wail broke the quiet of the night.

"What the—!"

"Shhhh," Mali'o said, pressing her fingers against Conway's lips. "We're not alone."

"I don't see anyone."

"Over there, at the far end of the cove."

Conway blinked the salt water from his eyes and peered through the darkness.

An old woman, her face to the heavens, chanted atop the lava promontory that bordered the cove's north side, protecting it from wind and waves. A yellow pareu covered her weighty body, and a long garland of green maile vine hung over her bare shoulders. Her head was ringed with fern. Next to her, on a boulder washed up during some extraordinary storm, sat a large bundle enfolded in ti leaves. Behind all this the temple loomed.

"*O 'Aumakua . . .*" she called as the ocean lapped her ankles.

"What's she doing?" Conway asked. Mali'o put her slender hand between them and shook her head, cocked to catch the words pouring from the old woman's mouth.

"*O Na Akua . . .*"

Conway watched with astonishment as she chanted on and on. Suddenly, from the direction of the temple came a brisk wind that fluttered the old woman's pareu and rippled the waters of the bay. Conway shivered.

"I recognize that woman," Mali'o whispered, her eyes shimmering. "I think it's Aunty Keala Huelani, a *kahuna nui* from Kona—"

"A what?"

"Kahuna nui—very important priest. They say she's a *kaula*—a seer."

"Do you know what she's saying?"

"I've forgotten much of the Hawaiian I knew as a child, but I'm catching a few words. She's summoning the spirits of her ancestors. Also the old gods."

Mali'o's face froze in concentration. "She seems to be asking for some kind of help..." Mali'o's eyes opened wider than Conway had ever seen them. "What? The *'ana'ana*?"

"Ana-what?"

"Shhhh!" Mali'o waved her hand vigorously in front of his face. "One of the things she's asking for is help to counteract a curse placed on a friend. I didn't know anyone still practiced the dark sorcery." Aghast, Mali'o listened until, many minutes later, the chanting ceased. Now both she and Conway were shivering.

Stepping down a series of small ledges beneath the water, Aunty Keala stood waist deep on a submerged shelf. The ocean swelled against the old woman as she lashed herself to the boulder with a rope she had carried into the water. She reached back to retrieve the green bundle, and with outstretched arms, held it above the sea. Again, she chanted.

Surge by surge, the sea climbed well above her waist, until at last a set of towering waves washed over her. She pushed the offering into the waves.

Clutching the rope, Aunty Keala watched the green bundle bob away on the backwash, then disappear with the receding waves. With trance-like concentration, she searched the windswept waters beyond the cove for a message or a sign. She did not notice the couple's heads protruding above the rippled waves; her eyes instead tracked a distant object moving steadily toward shore.

Mali'o pressed her eyes into slits.

Eventually, a dark triangle came into focus, a huge dorsal fin silhouetted against the stars.

Conway instinctively pulled Mali'o toward shore, but she resisted. "Stay absolutely still," she whispered.

As the shark angled close to the rocky point, its full dimensions became apparent. It was the length of a yacht with a dorsal fin as big as a sail.

"Good God!" Conway exclaimed at the sight of the whale shark, its spotted back visible at the waterline. Mali'o gently placed her hand over Conway's mouth. In shivered silence they watched the enormous beast move in on the old woman lashed to the rock, the shark's sheeny eyes just visible above the swell rushing along its flanks.

Aunty Keala leaned forward against her lashings, arms outstretched. With a quick flip of its tail, the shark slowed its approach, then gently nudged the elder with its snout. The kahuna patted the shark's mammoth head, muttering to the creature as it gently rocked in the ocean waves. Slowly it moved forward, its smooth skin passing

"Mahalo," Aunty Keala called after the whale shark.

beneath her hands. When the shark's broad back was directly in front of her, Aunty Keala lifted the long garland of leaves off her shoulders, knotted its ends, and tossed the green hoop over the top of the dorsal fin. The kahuna continued her low mutterings as the shark eased itself away from the shore and angled back out to sea. Aunty Keala watched its giant dorsal fin—now adorned with maile vine—recede from view.

"Mahalo," she called after it.

For several minutes, the shark's fin remained visible as a dark jag on the horizon. When at last it disappeared beneath the waves, the wind died and an uncanny stillness settled over the cove. Aunty Keala untied the rope and climbed back onto the promontory, where she sat down to rest. She removed the ring of ferns from atop her head and tossed it into the sea. "Mahalo," she said again. A few minutes later, she got up and trudged back through the thorny trees to the road.

"Let's get out of here," Conway said, when at last the taillights of her truck bounced down the road. But Mali'o was distant, as if in a trance.

"Come on!" he exclaimed, tugging her shivering arm. "I don't want to be out here when that thing comes back."

"Don't worry," she said quietly, still absorbing all they had witnessed. "He has other things to do now."

42 ∫ Wailani's Portentous Dream

THAT SAME NIGHT . . .

Lights flashing and sirens screaming, the ambulance roared up to the Kona hospital. Paramedics flung open the back doors and wheeled the gurney into the emergency room. Wailani Henderson, numb from excruciating abdominal pain, was unconscious, her thoughts still tangled in the dream. She had followed Aunty Keala's advice to stay home, but hadn't rested, instead organizing details for the protest. Her condition worsened, and by evening the pain and nausea had driven her to bed. She passed out around seven o'clock, talking on her cell to a Kapu Hawai'i member. When the phone thudded to the floor, he called 911.

Wailani isn't aware of anything happening at the hospital. She is back in her earlier nightmare, being pulled into the depths by the tiger shark that had attacked her. She travels for hours in agonizing pain, surrounded by a cloud of her own blood. Gradually the mano releases his grip, then vanishes into the black depths. Wailani is suddenly alone, suspended in cobalt sea, no longer bleeding. She feels the presence of Kanaloa, wise ocean god, embracing her with warmth and aloha. She hangs in the serene emptiness, absorbing these gifts.

After a timeless interval, a dozen shadows approach from below, but she is no longer afraid. A pod of playful dolphins glide up to join Wailani and she follows them to a place where sunshine streams into the water. The creatures leap through the ceiling of glassy waves, but when Wailani breaks the surface, there are no dolphins, no islands, only the great expanse of sea.

A chill gust blows over her—a powerful wind from the west—and she turns to see an angry cloud forming on the horizon, advancing at tremendous speed. As it grows nearer, the cloud sucks into itself, darkening further, and when it's almost upon her, it compresses into the distinct form of a double-hulled canoe with a black sail.

Four Hawaiians occupy the craft, one of whom Wailani recognizes. 'Iolani Carvalho, her tattooed nemesis in Kapu Hawai'i, points at her from one bow with the same hostile look he'd flashed at her as he stomped out of their meeting at Holualoa Church. A much older man with a bearded face and waxy eyes sits in the other bow. An ominous talisman peeks out beneath his black shirt and a stone god rests in his lap. Kahuna. The third Hawaiian, his haole business suit draped with a tattered bolt of traditional tapa cloth, sits on the canoe's suspended deck, looking backward. He glances forward a moment and Wailani recognizes Governor Calvin Kamali'i, his cheeks drenched with tears. The last man—firmly at the helm—wears a cloak of golden feathers and a broad-brimmed hat that obscures his face. A fishnet bulging with bleached human bones lays at his feet.

The canoe close now, Wailani spots something dragging in the water behind the craft, suspended by a rusty chain locked to the stern. The brine-bloated body of a naked haole breaks the surface of the swell, and she recognizes Robert Conway, his lifeless blue eyes staring up at the sky.

Wailani tries to swim away, but 'Iolani yanks her aboard and covers her mouth. As the canoe races forward, an island appears, first as a speck on the horizon, then as a line of mountains rising out of the sea. Wailani recognizes Mauna Kea and Mauna Loa, with Hualalai between them—all three capped with snow. Rivers of fiery lava pour down Hualalai's face.

Transfixed by the spectacular sight, the four men don't notice the enormous dorsal fin rushing the canoe abeam. The whale shark, much bigger than the canoe, strikes with the force of stone, lifting it up and over. Wailani lands in water far from the wreck. The men struggle to keep afloat on scraps of broken rigging, while the shark rams the canoe over and over until only debris marks its former place on the sea. Then, one at a time, the beast crushes each man in its monstrous mouth, pulling them into the depths. Rejected by the discerning shark, the corpse in towage is left to sink on its own.

Finally, the giant fish turns toward Wailani. The great mano slides beneath the young woman and raises her onto his broad spotted back. "I'll take you home," he says as she grasps his sturdy fin. The shark dives—down, down, down—into the cobalt depths where Wailani had earlier felt the presence of Kanaloa, where she had known peace.

43 ∫ Aroused from a Drunken Dream

THE SAME WEDNESDAY NIGHT . . .

Wailani wasn't the only one dreaming. Captain Jack, slumped drunk in the wicker on his lanai, dove deep into his own turbulent seas, waters murky with unresolved emotion. Maile's mother, Alana Chow, stands on the quay near a broken lifeboat, keel torn from the hull. The anguish in her beautiful face sets Jack's gut afire, and he squeezes the ship's rail, choking back tears. They had said many good-byes at that Honolulu dock, but this would be the last. His lover waves her shapely arm in final farewell, removes her garland of flowers, and tosses it into the wake. As the blue sea expands between them—one more time separating his ship from her island—Alana buries her face in her hands.

It was the same dream that had haunted him on and off for years, but that night, Jack could feel the sweat inside his Navy whites and taste the bitter tears. Seeing Maile Chow must have brought it on, that and all the booze he'd consumed to drown his fear that his friend Aka was dead.

The dream of Alana's last good-bye dissolved into a vivid picture of Aka, now the only person about whom Jack really gave a damn. He saw his shining eyes, broad smile, and aging whiskered face—and on his shoulder, an owl, its big yellow eyes just as discerning as the man's.

"Aka," he said, reaching out to his friend.

"Jack."

"Who is that with you?" Jack mumbled, turning a bit in the old wicker.

"You'll never guess."

"Who?"

"Jack. Jack, wake up."

Aka shook his head. He picked up the empty bottle off the lanai floor and tossed it into the waste can. This roused Silver, who was dozing under the old sailor's chair, and he bolted into the ti plants lining the cabin. "He's out, fellas," Aka said. "Must have hung one on tonight."

Kimo, his face still swollen from Jake Bluestone's thrashing, smiled. Jimmy shook his head, recalling the first time he'd met Captain Jack—in exactly the same condition.

"Jack," Aka whispered, gently shaking his friend. Jack's eyes raced back and forth under his lids.

"Still dreaming," Aka told the others. "Let's get something to eat and wake him later."

Jimmy and Kimo nodded, and they all stepped into the cabin.

"See what you can find, will you, Kimo?" Aka said, collapsing onto the living room couch. His old bones were stiff from their anxious escape back down from Royal Gardens, and his leg muscles quivered from countless steps over lava.

"I'm starving," Jimmy declared, switching on the kitchen light.

Kimo peeked inside the old refrigerator and searched its almost empty shelves. "Gee, dis guy's fridge is bad as mine. No more nothing."

"You're kidding," Jimmy groaned.

"Wait!" Kimo exclaimed, pulling out a shiny blue can hidden behind the mustard. "Aw'right! Here's one-half can Spam." He grabbed a saucepan off the lower shelf, removed the cover, and sniffed it. "Some old rice too," he announced. "Onions, garlic," he said, probing the produce bin.

"Fried rice," Aka mumbled sleepily. "Good enough. Wake me when it's ready."

Kimo began preparing the first meal they'd had all day. The smell of fried pork—even if it was Spam—drove Jimmy wild, and his hunger couldn't wait. He plopped down at the kitchen table with a box of stale saloon pilots, spreading each cracker with a generous blob of butter.

The same sizzle of Spam that lulled Aka to sleep invaded Jack's subconscious, and he woke abruptly, suddenly aware of people inside his cabin. His perceptions distorted, Jack reached inside his captain's cubby next to the wicker and pulled out a service revolver hidden there in the event of intruders. Kimo was just plucking a big chunk of hot Spam out of the rice when Jack burst through the door.

"Freeze, you dumb shits!" he hollered, brandishing his pistol at the blurry figures before him.

"Hey, don' shoot!" Kimo shouted, "It's us!"

But it was too late. Jack had already fired a bullet into the kitchen. It blasted the box of crackers right out of Jimmy's hand and penetrated the oven door with a loud *zing-thud*! Jimmy and Kimo both flew under the table. Aka, sound asleep with exhaustion, didn't stir, but the rhythm of his snore broke with an obscene *stuh-hunk* that drew Jack's attention. He aimed his gun at the man sprawled out on his couch.

Jack blinked his eyes back into focus. "Aka, is that you?" He jammed the pistol into his pants and grabbed his friend by the shirt.

"Aka?" he asked again, shaking him wildly. "You alive?"

The old Hawaiian opened his eyes and smiled. "We're *all* alive."

44 ∫ Ugly Truths Revealed

THURSDAY MORNING, JUNE 15 . . .

Wailani Henderson slowly opened her eyes. An Asian man robed in white loomed above her, a shiny object dangling from his neck. Talisman?

"Where am I?" Wailani muttered, trying to focus in the dim room.

A warm hand grasped her palm. "At the hospital," said a woman's voice.

"Aunty Keala?"

"Yes, I'm here."

"We removed your gall bladder last night," said the young doctor with a kind Japanese face. He pulled the stethoscope off his neck. "You had a wicked gallstone stuck in there."

"How long will I have to stay here?" she asked.

"It was a simple laparoscopic procedure," he replied, "so you can go home this afternoon—but you *will* have to rest. You're a tough young woman. You were obviously in extraordinary pain." The doctor nodded and withdrew from the room.

Aching all over, and woozy from painkillers, Wailani eased herself up against the pillows. "Aunty, you knew there was something wrong, but I didn't want to believe you."

"Your nightmare convinced me." She leaned her face close to the young woman. "This was more than a medical problem. It was ʻanaʻana. Someone used the evil sorcery against you."

ʻAnaʻana was believed to bring illness, insanity, loss of particular bodily functions, or even death to those against whom spells were cast.

First brought from Tahiti in the thirteenth century by the conquering priest, Pa'ao, the practice went underground when Christians arrived in the 1800s, but kahuna 'ana'ana continued the "black magic" in secret, passing on their skills to their offspring. Wailani had heard of its occasional use, but assumed that nowadays it was just a way to scare people.

"Even after Dr. Taguchi removed your gall bladder, you still lay on your deathbed—though he didn't know it. As your condition worsened, I called my cousin, a *kahuna pale*, and she did what was necessary to counter the spell."

Aunty Keala stared into Wailani's dark eyes. "And you are not the only one. The worst hit Uncle Sonny. He had a stroke last night. He's alive, but can no longer speak."

"No!" Wailani moaned, picturing the old cowboy as she had last seen him, standing in the doorway of the Holualoa church.

"We don't know yet if he'll survive. Sonny is a man of great mana, so whoever did this must be a powerful kahuna. It is evil—this silencing—and those with the skills to respond are doing what they can to counter the curse and expose the culprit." Aunty Keala placed her hand on Wailani's. "Sonny only recently took his beliefs back into the political realm, and they tried to kill him. He came to harm because he was not prepared for the attack. Now *you*, Wailani, must prepare." Her mentor firmly squeezed her hand. "Do not let your fears weaken you against the dark side. Aloha is your protection. Believe this. Know it. Do not forget it. That is what the ancient ones taught, and it is true. The immediate danger has passed, but you must pray to your ancestors and ask them to walk beside you for protection against those enlisting the dark side."

Wailani had long felt her ancestors' presence—an acute sense of being in the company of family—but never more than now, when she was fighting for the 'aina, her homeland.

"Of course," Aunty Keala continued, "most evil comes, not from the spirit realm, but from the physical world, from people who cannot abide the goodness that aloha brings. And if I trust what I have seen in my vision—as I must—an innocent young Hawaiian has been killed—a young musician from the town of Honoka'a named Kalama Ho'eha'eha. His sense of personal sovereignty was so recent, yet profound, that he placed no prudent limit on his zeal for change. Secret information about the Kiholo resort came his way, dangerous information in the hands of one so inexperienced, and the kind of knowledge that could be fatal to possess alone. That's why I sent Kalama to see you two weeks ago."

"He never came."

"I know. No one has seen him since June second. I fear the Hui has silenced him for good."

Aunty Keala lumbered over to the window and peered into the sliver of ocean visible beyond the buildings. The waves were dark, churning. "He was a bright-eyed child, always with guitar in tow and ready to sing in that high sweet voice Akua had given him. Like many of our young men, Kalama wondered where his place was on an island of dead plantations and American hotels. He didn't want to go to Honolulu, so he stayed in Honoka'a, and like too many young ones, drifted into Hui activities—first selling paka lolo, then hard drugs."

Wailani, eyes moist, shook her head.

"I suppose he was looking for a sense of belonging, of being part of some special Hawaiian brotherhood," Aunty Keala continued. "But those kinds of ties bind the truly spirited, and eventually Kalama distanced himself from the Hui's illegal activities, instead turning to his musical gifts and the old songs he'd learned from his grandmother. Singing professionally made him feel more independent, but he soon discovered he was again webbed in by the Hui, who insisted on controlling his bookings and the distribution of his recordings. So he joined Kapu Hawai'i as a more constructive way to identify with his brethren and foster real change.

"But then he got a phone call from his booking agent, telling him, 'Everybody's performing at a big flashy political fund-raiser headlined by Governor Kamali'i, and we want you there too.' He should have been pleased, but instead said no—'Screw Kamali'i!' to be exact—and the second call, from a voice he didn't know, asked whether he'd rather have his fingers broken instead."

"An all-too-familiar story," Wailani said, her eyes finally brightening, but from ire.

"So Kalama said he'd perform, but there was something in that

Ho'eha'eha blood that could not surrender. Perhaps his ancestors were great warriors, or religious men of high ideals, because Kalama felt the kind of courage that drives heroes into battles they cannot win. He decided to fight for his freedom, with information that had come through his family, information he knew would damage the Hui with other Hawaiians. He came to me first, thinking I would know what to do with it."

Aunty Keala turned from the window and returned to the edge of the bed. "Kalama had discovered that the Royal Paradise Bay Resort is being built to house Hawai'i's first gambling casino."

"What!"

"He also told me Haku Kane himself is involved."

"Of course." Wailani's jaw tightened.

"The Hui must have something on Robert Conway, because Kalama found out that Conway's been forced to give over control of the games to Haku Kane."

"Their evil influence runs deep, doesn't it, Aunty?"

"Not just down, into the Hui slime, but all the way to the top."

"You mean the governor."

"Perhaps even higher." The kahuna's face filled with dismay. "But I'm not certain yet, and I fear the Hui caught wind of Kalama's inquiries."

"Could he be hiding?"

"I thought so at first. He told me he was going to see Uncle Sonny."

A light flashed inside Wailani's head. "Auwe! So that's why Uncle Sonny came to our meeting in Holualoa! Kalama told him about the casino! Uncle Sonny said he wanted to embarrass Governor Kamali'i, but I'll bet he was also planning to expose Haku Kane's role in it."

"I think Haku Kane has silenced both men," Aunty Keala said with a sigh. "It falls to us, the Hawaiians, to protect the island from evil. In the old days, it was simpler because the threats were fewer, and working together we could do what our homeland required of us. Sometimes we had wise chiefs and chiefesses to guide us—caring ali'i like Queen Lili'uokalani. But now the intrusions are so great, and we are so marginalized, that I fear the gods—perhaps even the island itself—will respond to protect what is sacred with actions that may harm innocents too."

Wailani noticed a weariness fall upon Aunty Keala's face as the elder pondered all this in the chair next to the bed.

"It is a time of change," Aunty Keala said finally, "a *huli* time, when things turn upside down. It is not surprising that in the confusion some in the Hui would fall back on the dark sorcery." Aunty Keala glanced over her shoulder to make sure the door was closed. "But the transition is well under way, Wailani. In the long run, everyone living here, even non-Hawaiians, will be better for it—despite the immediate troubles ahead. After more than a generation of effort—bringing back the language, the dance, the prayers, and offerings—our gods have returned."

"Our ancestors have come back too, haven't they, Aunty?"

"They never left, Wailani. It's just that so few of us called upon them for guidance. We broke their hearts."

"I feel their presence, stronger than ever. And my dreams come more often."

"Many of our people are dreaming again, as they did in former times."

The kahuna stared into Wailani's face, knowing that this young warrior must be told something of what was ahead. "We have always understood that certain acts of nature were signs, but generations have passed since they fit into such a clear pattern as now marks our time. I think it started in '69 with the eruption of Mauna Ulu."

"The warning about Royal Gardens?"

Aunty Keala nodded. "Pele came in spirit form to warn the Kalapana elders, and they, in turn, carried her message to a public hearing: that if the forest, long frequented by Pele's clan, was ever disturbed, she would bury the entire coast—including Kalapana. Of course, the County Council scoffed. Royal Gardens was started, even plans for a seaside resort were drawn up. Then the five-year eruption began. Pele buried nearby national park lands—an acreage bigger than Honolulu—but stopped short of any inhabited areas. Then, to make her point, she shook Kalapana so violently that the whole coast slumped into the sea and was flooded by a tsunami."

"I heard about that, Aunty. My grandfather's house tumbled off its foundation, and my mother knew the fisherman who vanished in the wave."

"Her first warnings." Aunty Keala shook her head. "And then a terrible thing happened, but at the hand of man—the killing of that wonderful young singer from Maui."

Wailani knew the story well. Hawaiian performer George Helm was an activist trying to force the US Navy to return the island of Kaho'olawe to Hawaiians after decades of shelling it for bombing practice. Through his music and clandestine island landings to conduct traditional ceremonies, Helm and his cohorts inspired a generation of young Hawaiians. When elders heard his angelic voice sing the old songs, they, too, were inspired, and after generations of submission, joined the fight. And then Helm and his compatriot, Kimo Mitchell, vanished off the coast of Maui while returning from one of their island "occupations." Police said the sea had taken them, but some Hawaiians suspected the sinister hand of the underworld.

"So then came the hurricane," said Aunty Keala. "1982. It took Kaua'i ten years to reconstruct what Hurricane 'Iwa destroyed in a single day—the island's hotels ruined. How appropriate to name the storm after a bird who steals food from another by forcing them to vomit what they have in their bellies."

"While Kanaloa set things right on Kaua'i, Pele waited patiently for a response to her Mauna Ulu and earthquake warnings. But the deference once paid her never came. Houses continued to be built in Royal Gardens, and the forest behind the subdivision was further assaulted by geothermal development—despite Hawaiians' pleas. Then that next January, there was another eruption, just above Royal Gardens, right on top of the geothermal test wells—now buried deep beneath Pu'u 'O'o."

"You saw the fireball, didn't you Aunty?"

"You mean the *akua lele*," she corrected. "Yes, in 1984. It scorched across the night sky from that towering cone of Pu'u 'O'o to the summit crater of Mauna Loa, and Pele's fiery heart erupted from both volcanoes. I was at Kilauea that night with my hula *halau*, dancing on the rim at Wahine Kapu, and we watched lava rivers pour down the slopes of Mauna Loa toward Hilo. Scientists—those not there to witness the event—said the fireball must have been 'space junk' entering the atmosphere, but I notice that the HVO geologists who *did* see it never talk about it."

Aunty Keala rose from her chair and moved again to the window. "Pele loves her people," she continued, "and because of our vigorous prayers, she stopped short of taking Hilo. Only by a few miles and almost too late, but she stopped."

"But eventually Pele lost her patience?" Wailani asked.

"Yes, and Royal Gardens, Kalapana, and more miles of park land suffered for it. Meanwhile, the rest of the gods waited and watched—for almost ten years—but the signs were ignored because too few knew how to read them. Even as Hawaiians danced, prayed, and made more offerings, the exploitation continued, with new developments on Oʻahu, Maui, Kauaʻi, and even this, the most sacred of our islands. Forests were ravaged, streams polluted, beaches 'acquired' like property. Worst of all, more sacred places were disturbed, in spite of supposed legal protection."

Aunty Keala seemed to age as she recounted each incident. "Despite their indignation, the kahuna prayed and prayed, this time aided by kahuna who'd kept their skills hidden out of societal fear. But they couldn't convince the gods to stop the rampage." More tears fell from Aunty Keala's eyes. "*ʻIniki*, 'the pinching wind,' came, and more destruction."

Wailani nodded. "I have family on Kauaʻi who lost everything."

"All the rebuilding after Hurricane ʻIwa was for naught. And something else happened that year—and this I saw in a vision—*before* the sharks began to attack. Four decades had passed since mano took anyone in the waters of Hawaiʻi, and then two dozen innocents were taken, all from the islands of Maui and Oʻahu—those little colonies of mainland culture where aloha is as hard to find as undeveloped land. Then came that rash of helicopter tour accidents, killing dozens. And the Paramount movie crew that crashed inside Puʻu ʻOʻo."

"But Aunty, why did she spare *those* men?"

"As examples. One of them, his lungs permanently scorched from Pele's breath, claims he saw her inside the cone—and so he told the world. And still no one listens."

The women shook their heads.

"So more were taken," Aunty Keala went on, her face flushed with grief. "On Kilauea alone, another seven, including the innocent couple mysteriously scorched from the inside out. Three workers died in a fire while building yet another observatory on our most sacred Mauna Kea. On O'ahu, four H3 Freeway construction workers were crushed when a beam mysteriously collapsed . . . which the engineers could never explain. Eight died at a Sacred Falls landslide. More helicopter crashes. And then the recent Kilauea explosions at Halema'uma'u, sending Pele's choking fumes all across the state. A final warning?"

Wailani stared at the kahuna. The picture was beyond belief, yet her na'au knew that what the elder described was true.

Aunty Keala walked back from the window and slumped into the chair, exhausted. "It is a huli time, Wailani, and more is to come. I have seen it." Tears streamed down her cheeks.

There was a long pause, and finally Wailani spoke. "Aunty, after I passed out, I dreamed again."

"I know," she replied. "You lay still as a corpse, but your eyes darted beneath your lids. Tell me what you saw."

Wailani recounted the dream. The kahuna was especially interested in the image of Hualalai crowned with snow and convulsing between the two other snowcapped mountains.

45 ∫ Alpha Males

THAT THURSDAY AFTERNOON . . .

Cheryl Tokunaga, the governor's receptionist, glanced up from her computer, startled by the wall of brown blazers crowding her desk. Three huge Hawaiians towered over her tiny Japanese frame.

"Yes?" she said in a tough little voice perfected during thirty years at the capitol.

"I'm here to see Calvin," said someone behind the blazers.

"I'm sorry, the governor is not available," she replied, rising on three-inch heels, her face even with their breast pockets. But she *was* tall enough to notice two more men behind them, pulling shut the big koa doors to the governor's outer office.

"Hey, you can't—"

"Sorry, Miss," said the voice behind the blazers. "Is Calvin here?"

"Do you have an appointment?" the words so tart her lips puckered.

The jackets parted and the face of Haku Kane loomed forward, his big hands grasping her desk. "No, I don't." He smiled, his left eye quivering ever so slightly.

"Just a minute." Mrs. Tokunaga turned on her heels and slipped inside the governor's office.

"Haku Kane," she announced, startling Calvin Kamali'i, who was reading the afternoon paper over a deli sandwich and a Styrofoam tub of poi. Mrs. Tokunaga clutched the door handle behind her, determined that no one—not even the king of organized crime—would get past her gatekeeping.

Calvin took a big bite from his sandwich and gobbled it silently for a moment. Haku rarely came to his office, never midday, when citizens and reporters were in the hall. Calvin stood up, still holding his little tub of taro pudding, and stared wide-eyed at Mrs. Tokunaga. "Can you stall him?"

She shook her head. "They've already closed the public entrance. They can't do that, Governor, no matter who they are."

"Get Lankowski! *Wikiwiki*!" Quick! "Stall them as long as you can!"

But Calvin barely had time to clear away his lunch before Kane strolled in.

"Aloha, Haku! Good to see you."

"Cut the crap." Ignoring Calvin's outstretched hand, Kane sat down in the visitor's chair opposite the governor's desk. He stared into Calvin's face as if waiting for something, a reply, an explanation, a justification for his existence.

Calvin just stared back, waiting for Kane to define the territory of the discussion.

"Why didn't you return my calls?"

"I just got back to the office."

Kane's eyes narrowed, the left one struggling to remain still.

"I was going to phone you right after lunch."

Kane grunted.

"Lankowski's on his way," Calvin said, praying that Cheryl had been able reach him.

Kane grunted again, shifting in the chair, and decided to proceed without the governor's aide. "We have a problem."

That morning the *Honolulu Star-Advertiser* had run a story about the USGS Hualalai study just released by Hawaiian Volcano Observatory scientists. It was the same HVO report Gus Parker and Lelehua Chin had watered down to comply with the Menlo Park restrictions. A small sidebar reported the previous day's quake over on Kilauea, but contained no mention of the tiny Hualalai swarm. Gus Parker and his boss Joe Murdock were still keeping that one to themselves.

On his way home, Murdock had put the Hualalai study directly into the hands of the paper's Hilo stringer. This, he figured, would give the public one more day's notice—just in case Hualalai started rumbling again—and gave the reporter the impression the report had some urgency. Following the proper USGS chain of command, Murdock had received Menlo Park's approval on the revised report—but he wrote the press release on his own. In it, he implied that the study had shocked scientists (despite its gutted conclusions) and that immediate steps were being taken to get additional data. The newspaper responded predictably—cranking up the story yet another notch, thereby giving Kona readers something close to the right level of anxiety. Murdock would be in the clear when it came to Menlo Park; he could just blame the coverage on media exaggeration. The article—headlined "After 200 Years, Kona Volcano Ready to Blow?"—included the following provocative paragraph:

> Even though the report concludes that a Hualalai eruption is only *possible* sometime in the next five years, scientists are scrambling to beef up their monitoring. Just this morning HVO dispatched a team to Hualalai armed with GPS and other technology to determine possible changes within the volcano.

Apparently the reporter had located the island's mayor late that night, after the public servant had downed more than a few nightcaps. The reporter read him the main HVO conclusions over the phone, and the mayor, never missing an opportunity to get his name in the Honolulu papers, offered a quote:

"I always wondered when that old powder keg would blow. The timing really stinks, what with all our recent development over there. But I can assure the citizens of Kona that in such an emergency everything will be done to minimize the loss of life."

By the time the morning television programs picked up the story, they had dramatized it even further, prominently displaying the mayor's "loss of life" quote while showing old footage of the Royal Gardens and Kalapana disasters, including shots of houses bursting into flames and a kid's tricycle being buried by lava. The afternoon paper read pretty much like the morning edition, but now included quotes from Lelehua Chin and Gus Parker. Lelehua reaffirmed her confidence in the science, "These data are *more* than solid," while Gus tried to rile up his fellow citizens: "Well, in geological terms, the Big Island is a dangerous place to live. Only one of our five volcanoes is dead—and it's not Hualalai." God knows what the TV stations would do with the story by evening broadcast time.

The governor folded his fingers in front of his nose. "Of course, Haku, the scientists are exaggerating. We just need to knock their HVO report around a bit. Beat it up, so to speak."

"It won't be that easy."

"I think you're wrong, Haku. Besides—" Calvin stopped mid-sentence, suddenly aware of his visitor's scowl and wildly twitching eye.

"I've had enough of this!" Kane rose and walked menacingly around the governor's desk. "I've decided you're gonna have to go, Calvin." He reached deep into his sports jacket.

Calvin shot up out of his chair. "Go?"

Kane pulled out a pack of cigarettes and, facing the windows, lit up. "You're gonna have to go to Conway's grand opening." He snapped shut his big gold lighter, the silver shark on its face glinting in the sun.

A wave of relief passed through Calvin's body. For a moment he thought his knees wouldn't hold him up.

"Lankowski told me you were planning to skip it," Kane said, his back to the governor.

Calvin skittered away from his chair, widening the distance between him and the crime king. "Well, the protests, you know."

"Big deal. Twenty or thirty people in a resort as big as Disneyland. Who's gonna notice them?"

Calvin, now standing awkwardly in front of his desk, shoved his hands into his pockets. He wished he weren't sweating so much. "The press."

"If you're smart, you'll control that," Kane replied, turning back from the window. He was a silhouette against the sunlit glass, the smoke from his cigarette a dark serpent crawling through the air.

"Calvin, I know *deep down* you sympathize with our Hawaiian brothers and sisters. So do I. But these protests aren't going anywhere." He fed more smoke into the serpent. "All this talk about getting back the land, it's too idealistic. These islands are part of a bigger economic picture. What Kapu Hawai'i wants will never happen. It *can't* happen. The land is too valuable to give back to taro planters and fishermen."

The governor bristled. Beneath all the compromises—and there had been many—he was still Hawaiian. "Look, Haku. I'm a realist too. I know we can never go back to the old days, not even to the way it was before statehood. But I like to recall the reign of our last king, Kalakaua. He resurrected hula and the old chants, made Hawaiians feel proud again!"

"Yeah, right. The haoles poisoned him in San Francisco, then brought in US Marines to take the country from his sister."

Calvin, silenced, dropped into the chair vacated earlier by the Hui chief.

"Look, Calvin, all that cultural stuff is important for our families and communities, but there's no real power in it. Money is power! Land is power! And control over money and land is power over people! That's sovereignty. I, for one, don't intend to be a powerless *kanaka*."

A cloud covered the sun and the room suddenly grew dark. Kane ambled along the windows behind the governor's desk until he reached Calvin's empty chair. He placed his big hands on its tall back and squeezed the burgundy leather.

"It's idle sentiment, Calvin," he said. "We have bigger fish to fry. And the one at Kiholo is a very big fish. You gotta be there to stand up for the resort, *especially now*, to reassure everyone in Kona—and our investors—that Paradise Bay and the North Kona Development Project are the future prosperity of the Big Island and Hawai'i."

At that moment, the door opened and Lankowski strolled in. As always, he was a mess, his hair tousled, his suit rumpled, and his face as pallid as ever. But his eyes shone like diamonds. "Now isn't this interesting," he said, scanning the scene.

Calvin immediately rose up out of the chair, intent on retrieving his desk, but Kane didn't budge.

"Great work with the press, Lankowski," Kane said stony-faced, tamping his cigarette into the governor's coffee mug.

Lankowski dropped onto the sofa at the back of the room and lit up a Vantage. "You're right about that, Haku. We were taken by surprise."

Kane grunted his disapproval.

"Well, now, just listen a minute, Haku," Calvin interjected, still standing *futless* by the visitor's chair. "The actual report doesn't say anything all that provocative. It's almost exactly what we expected—"

"You're not making sense, brah," Kane said, dropping into the governor's swanky chair. Lankowski puffed his cigarette, waiting for Calvin's reaction, but it was nothing more than a pout.

"It's just media hype," Lankowski said, "but now we've got a PR problem."

"Worse," Kane replied. "Some of my money guys are getting jumpy. I got two calls this morning from inside the Hui—important men concerned about the casino."

"How jumpy?"

"Very. These two guys—from the Maui operation—always had second thoughts about the Conway deal. The way they see it, why put our operation inside a legal structure if we don't have to? They're worried we could lose control of the State Gaming Commission."

"And what do you say?" Lankowski asked, crushing his cigarette butt into a crystal ashtray. "Are you changing your mind too?"

Kane leaned forward over the governor's desk. "Obviously I'd prefer to keep things the way they've been, but with the state government's financial problems, even a few of our legislative allies think Hawai'i's *got* to legalize it. Sugar's gone down the tubes and tourism's dragging. Without new income, there's nothing to fund state building projects—and we *all* need those contracts."

"Green blood keeps the system alive," Lankowski muttered. "But it's not just the economics, Haku. Hawai'i and Utah are the only states where gambling is still illegal. Everybody knows why Utah won't do it—the Mormons. But it's starting to look a little suspicious when Hawai'i refuses to legalize, especially when the politicians who've been against it are friends of yours."

Kane chuckled. "What things look like never used to matter."

"But they do now," Lankowski said, another cigarette wagging in his mouth. "Hawai'i's changing. These aren't unquestioning plantation workers anymore. And a few of this new generation of legislators actually see a political advantage in exposing corruption. Some are even giving lip service to the Hawaiians."

"That's what I told these two Maui boys. If it's gonna be legalized with a commission we control, I say do it now while we still have political influence in Honolulu and Washington. Like I told them, the Conway project is a perfect lure to get the legislature to bite."

"Yes, indeed," Lankowski agreed, smoke trailing from his mouth. "Disneyland with class. Mickey Mouse in a tuxedo."

"But I have to control that commission," Kane said in a dark tone, his eyes flashing on Calvin, "including governor's appointments to put my people on it."

"Don't worry," Calvin replied distractedly, still bewildered at being displaced in his own office but relieved that Lankowski was dealing with Haku Kane.

Lankowski looked up at the ceiling, rotating his head as if studying its ornate stucco. "What amazes me is that Conway went along with all this."

Kane smiled knowingly.

"I know he's always wanted to build something big and flashy over here, so I can see how he came round to the casino idea. But how did you ever get him to agree to letting you control the games?"

A smile crept into the corners of Kane's mouth. "Conway knows that to realize his dream he has to work with the powers that be. He just doesn't know the extent of our role in the future."

Lankowski, still gazing at the plaster curls, shook his head. "Yeah, but—"

"Why don't you ask the governor? He's the man who will ultimately take credit for all this."

Calvin, back in the visitor's chair, didn't respond. Staring at the clouds outside the window, he had fallen into a reverie. He was a young man again, back on bomb-riddled Kaho'olawe. No one was even supposed to fish near its shoreline, but people did, and one New Year's weekend, on their way back with their catch, Calvin and his buddy, "Cookie" Nanikula, had pulled up on a sandy beach to drink a six-pack and barbecue a couple of *ulua* fillets. Alone on the ravaged isle, they had wandered up an old footpath to the island's highest point—after the Navy had obliterated its former summit with its practice bombs. There, past ruins of shrines and next to an ancient bell stone, they gazed down at Kealaikahiki Channel, "the pathway to Kahiki," mythic land of their ancestors, and pondered the history of their people.

Despite Cookie's warning, Calvin had struck the stone, and the uncanny echo scared him. Something mysterious was afoot on that island, something ancient yet alive that spoke to his blood. Now, as Haku Kane and Lankowski talked of gambling and money and power, Calvin felt the same anguish he had known that day on Kahoʻolawe.

"Calvin?" Lankowski said.

"Lots of compromises," he mumbled, his gaze shifting to the thick red drapes hung from golden rods above his desk.

"What's that?" Kane barked, but the governor's eyes were still distant. Kane shrugged and lit another cigarette. "Anyway," he said, addressing Lankowski, "with all this crap about Hualalai, the Maui group is threatening to back out."

"Gee, that *is* a problem," Lankowski said with a hint of sarcasm, privately intrigued—even entertained—by the turn of events.

"A problem we all share." Kane's eye twitched faster. "And that includes you, Calvin."

The governor's eyes snapped back into focus.

"I thought you politicians were the masters of handling these press idiots."

"This is turning into a nasty one, isn't it," Lankowski admitted, struggling to keep a wry smile from creeping over his ashen lips.

"You don't know what nasty is!" Kane struck the desktop, and Calvin watched his official gold pen bounce onto the carpet.

"Don't worry, Haku. There will be a response," Lankowski said, still slouched in the leather couch.

"Oh yeah? From who?"

"USGS. Not exactly a retraction, but, well—"

"And how do you know this?"

"I've already contacted the congressman. He understands the need to put a very different spin on this immediately. By now he will have talked to the Interior secretary, who will have talked to USGS."

With that, Calvin experienced his first bit of relief since Kane barged in. It was for just this kind of situation that he depended on Lankowski.

"When?" Kane asked, glancing at his watch.

"I doubt tomorrow, but maybe this weekend," Lankowski said.

"It'd damn well better be." Kane got up from the governor's chair and turned to Calvin, who automatically stood up too. "So you'll be there Saturday?"

"Yes . . . of course." Calvin's stomach churned as he forced out the words.

"Good." Kane slowly moved to the door. "As you know, I have friends in the movement. I'll see what I can do to derail the protest."

Calvin, hurrying to the comfort of his own chair, didn't respond.

As Kane grasped the door handle, Lankowski leaned forward. "Oh, one more thing, Haku," he said. "Nothing big, just something to think about."

Kane slid his eyes to the side.

"I've checked the veracity of the HVO report with some people who ought to know. The conclusions are actually *under*stated—due to pressures brought by our friend on the Hill."

"So?"

"So that volcano might actually be getting ready to blow."

"Don't be ridiculous," the governor said, his confidence returning now that he was sitting in his own chair again, holding court from his own desk.

Kane tightened his grip on the door handle, knuckles whitening. "I don't give a shit, as long as it happens after the project is complete and the contracts are paid."

"Really?" Lankowski said in mock astonishment. "What about the casino?"

"Life's a roll of dice," Kane replied, stepping through the door.

46 ∫ The Clandestine Gathering

LATE THAT NIGHT HIGH UP IN THE MOUNTAINS . . .

Their meeting spot was secret, a place long recognized for its mana. People had trekked up the mountain to pray at its stone shrine for more than a thousand years. Four volcanoes were visible from the altar upon which these kahuna placed their offerings, and a fifth, below Mauna Loa's shoulder, showed its presence with a volcanic glow on the clouds above it. The identity of the ten people coming to the ceremony had also been a secret until that very night. Even then, while the blue light of the waning moon revealed their faces, few knew the others' names, for most had been in hiding on their various islands. These were the men and women whose blood carried memories of the earliest Polynesians, the ones who remembered how to communicate with the gods.

For some, the call to gather had come in vivid night dreams. For others, it came from voices in the forest where generations had hunted birds, harvested herbs, and picked maile for their leis. Four had heard the message in their own voices, echoing from a place deep within their naʻau. A few, in reverie or contemplation, had seen this gathering projected like a movie on the inside of their eyelids. And one, Aunty Keala Huelani, had actually conversed with two of the gods on the same night that the great whale shark came to greet her near the foot of the Moʻokini temple.

By whatever means the message had come, its portent was clear to all ten kahuna: Gather on that night at this place to exercise your kuleana—your right and responsibility—to protect the destiny of the people. Three others who had heard the call failed to act upon it, one because she would not believe it and two because they were afraid.

"It is time to go beyond the foolish ghost stories told in tourist brochures," declared a bony old man whose arthritic body had required two younger ones to help him cross the half mile of lava between the old road and the shrines. He was the most wizened of those gathered under mahina—the moon form of the great goddess Hina—but his black eyes sparkled in the light of the *kukui* nut torch held by his middle-aged daughter, an enormous woman draped with a lei of white kukui nuts. "They will never again portray our religious beliefs as 'superstition,'" the old man declared, trembling under the blanket his daughter had wrapped over his shoulders.

"No more fables of elf-like *Menehune* dutifully building fishponds and temples for ali'i overlords," muttered another middle-aged woman in a big blue sweater, her sweet moon face flushed with cold and emotion.

"No," agreed an old cowboy, his muscled hands stuffed in the pockets of a jean jacket buttoned tight against the wind. "This time is for real."

They all nodded, but none more vigorously than the young man with the soft round eyes who had lied to his foreman—claiming illness in the family—in order to get free of his construction job on Maui. Too many times he had remembered his grandfather's deathbed charge. "Follow the will of the ancient ones, Bobby, not the demands of the haole or the confusions of Christianized Hawaiians. Listen to the ancestors," he had whispered into the young boy's ears as he slipped away into another realm.

Each of those standing before the old stones had, in their own way, come to the same conclusion—it was now time to take 4,000 years of Polynesian wisdom out of the closet, call on the ancestors, and urge the gods to save the innocents and Hawai'i. To do so meant overcoming generations of hesitation to transcend the constraints imposed by the white man's faith and once again touch the source that had defined Pacific Island cultures for centuries. These were the deities that had guided their sailing canoes back and forth across the great sea and, in time, led them to the erupting island of Hawai'i.

All eight islands were represented by the kahuna huddling in the torchlight, even uninhabited Kahoʻolawe (by a very old Maui woman who had lived on the McPhee-Baldwin ranch before the military seized the island). Few outside their families knew of their sensitivities and power, although some of their friends probably suspected. Just as their ancestors had gone underground after the arrival of Paʻao and the Tahitian aliʻi and stayed there during the missionary era, so these modern Hawaiians had guarded their bloodline secrets with the care of dissidents protecting their ideas under a tyrannical regime. It was rebellious enough to support Hawaiian sovereignty in an American state, let alone to admit the practice of a pantheistic faith that exalts the power and mystery of nature over the supremacy of man.

But the wounds of repression did not translate into anger that cold windy night. Instead, they expressed deep aloha for one another, the ʻaina, their ancestors, and the gods—and compassion for those whose disregard or confusion had led them to go along with the haole vision for Hawaiʻi. They shed rivers of tears for sacred things despoiled, for gods ignored and ancestor spirits neglected, and for their many Hawaiian brethren adrift on drugs, violence, suicide, and crime.

Each kahuna had brought one sacred object from their island, and together these became the instruments of the ceremony. They prayed vigorously that night, and the ancestors made their presence known in ways appropriate to the sensitivities of each kahuna. The gods, they hoped, would acknowledge their bloodlines and devotion, and listen to their pleas.

The same pleas had been made in other times of peril, but not for many years. The kahuna asked the gods to help the foreigners recognize their *hewa*—their grave offense—and change their ways before more innocents died. They pleaded for the gods to guide the people back to their forgotten Polynesian wisdom gathered by 150 generations of sea voyagers migrating island by island from far western shores. Finally, they asked the gods to rebuke Hawaiians who had succumbed to fear and now wished to teach the Westerners a lesson by turning nature's supreme creative powers into a curse. They hoped kahuna elsewhere were doing the same. They knew the destiny of Hawaiʻi and its blessed aloha now depended on the strength of their prayers.

47 Tremors

SHORTLY AFTER MIDNIGHT ON JUNE 16 . . .

Joe Murdock was none too happy about driving back up to the Hawaiian Volcano Observatory on a cold, wet night, especially to meet Gus Parker about new earthquake tremors beneath Hualalai.

"I don't suppose this can wait till morning?" the scientist in charge had asked, having just consumed his second beer and a bag of pretzels watching a late-night broadcast of the 1947 volcano classic *Stromboli.*

"No, Joe," Gus said. "We've got a resumption of the earthquake swarms we saw Wednesday morning, but now at higher magnitude."

"How many?"

"Already more than a hundred, some in the magnitude two range."

Murdock could have set up a meeting for the next morning, but if the swarms continued, he knew he would regret that decision. He was already concerned about his job after the starchy e-mail he'd received that afternoon from his USGS boss in Menlo Park; pressure from Washington was apparently already building after the day's press coverage.

As Murdock raced up the forested slopes of Kilauea in his USGS Blazer, he worked out the sequence for notifying the public if the new tremors indicated an eruption. The first step would be to phone Mike Takahashi, the island's Civil Defense director. After nineteen years with that agency, Mike was used to calls in the middle of the night—from HVO, the National Weather Service, or the Pacific Tsunami Warning Center. The Big Island was a perfect place for a man like Takahashi, where multiple crises tested three important traits handed down by his Nisei father—efficiency, cool-headedness, and compassion.

Joe Murdock, on the other hand, had long since shed his enthusiasm for crises. After two decades with HVO (two years as scientist in charge), Murdock's attention was focused on his retirement, just three years away. Murdock disliked controversy, and another public announcement on Hualalai would be controversial, whether the mountain erupted or not.

As Murdock unlocked the heavy metal door of the observatory, Gus sat upstairs in the Crisis Center, his feet propped on the big table map of volcanoes, thinking about how to explain to Murdock that two minutes after their phone conversation, the needle on the seismic drum had gone flat. "She's teasing us," Gus muttered to himself, aware of footsteps echoing in the darkened stairwell leading to the Crisis Center.

Murdock paused on the top step to refill his lungs. "Evening, Joe," Gus said, pointing to the center of the table where the latest seismic record waited for Murdock's inspection. "There it is."

Murdock snatched it off the table and plopped into a chair across from Gus. He carefully examined the jagged portions of the line.

"How long did it rumble?"

"Maybe forty minutes. It stopped right after I called you. One hundred seventy-three distinct tremors above one point oh magnitude. Maybe fifty of those were two point oh or higher. The biggest quake was about a three."

"So someone in Kona may have felt it." Murdock stroked his fat cheeks.

"It's a tough call," Gus said.

"Not really," Murdock replied, lifting himself out of the chair. He walked to the window, cupped his hands against the glass, and tried to discern Halema'uma'u crater through the foggy dark. "We've had evidence of deformation for two years. Now we've got seismicity. That means magma's moving—albeit slowly and erratically. And no doubt, with all those subdivisions above Kailua, somebody felt it. We'd better contact Mike Takahashi before one of them does."

Gus smiled, knowing that as soon as that phone call was made, a whole new ball game would begin, in which local scientists rather than Menlo Park called most of the shots.

Murdock looked back from the window. "Agree?"

"Agree."

Murdock walked to the stairway just as Lelehua Chin arrived. Behind her were the interns, Debbie and Richard, whom she had picked up on her way to the observatory. All looked sleepy.

"I called Lelehua," Gus said, "just in case we needed another opinion."

Murdock shrugged his shoulders, then acknowledged the three latecomers with a nod. He disappeared down the darkened staircase, to make the call to Civil Defense.

"Well?" Lelehua said softly, picking up the seismic record. "What's the verdict?"

"He's calling Civil Defense right now."

"Wow!" Richard exclaimed, at last tying the loose laces of his tennis shoes.

Debbie thought for a moment, letting the implications organize themselves in her mind. "You really think this activity justifies warning the public?" she asked.

Gus scoffed and got up from his chair. "I'll bet you want to work at Menlo Park someday."

"Oh yes," she replied.

"You'll do well there, I'm sure." He walked over to the Hualalai drum. The needle continued to scratch a flat line across the paper. "By the way, what did you three find at Royal Gardens?"

"Lots of big cracks," Richard exclaimed.

"It was a flank shift," Lelehua stated, "a substantial one." She ran her finger across the table map as if sketching the new fissures.

Gus joined the three at the table and leaned on the glass, staring at the volcano's southern flank. "Maybe, on top of everything else, Kilauea's going to start separating—big time."

Lelehua let out a nervous laugh. In the late 1980s, scientists had discovered underwater avalanche debris off every Hawaiian island, evidence that verified something long suspected—huge chunks of the volcanoes had collapsed into the sea. The last time part of Mauna Loa collapsed—scarcely 110,000 years ago—a monstrous tsunami was generated that embedded shards of coral reef a thousand feet up into the sea cliffs of Lana‘i.

Fortunately no such collapses had occurred since humans arrived on the islands, but devastating flank shifts had. In 1868, Kilauea's southern flank shifted seaward thirty feet, producing earthquakes that shook the island for days, including a 7.8 magnitude temblor, and generating a devastating tsunami. In 1975, the same flank lurched outward again, another thirty feet, causing the Kalapana coastline to slip underwater and generating a 7.2 quake and another killer tsunami. Those were minor events—mere precursors—to what scientists now believed was possible. Gus and Lelehua knew that a cataclysmic landslide today would shake the islands as never before experienced by anyone on earth and generate tsunamis that would wash away two-thirds of the archipelago's cities and towns. They also knew such collapses were inevitable, especially on the still-forming Big Island, where three areas were most likely to give way—Kilauea's active rift zone, the southwest rift of Mauna Loa, and the Kona side of Hualalai.

"I need to verify the numbers," Lelehua replied, pointing her finger at the coastline below Royal Gardens, "but I think the flank may have moved outward as much as five feet in some areas."

Richard hopped in between Gus and Lelehua. "Do you really think a cataclysmic landslide is possible?"

"It's going to happen," Gus replied.

"But of course, we don't know how many thousands of years from now," Lelehua quickly added. She placed her hands over Kilauea's southern half. "But each time this shifts outward—every year by at least a few inches—we move closer to the eventual collapse of that side of the island."

"Jeez," Richard replied, "what would Civil Defense do in a case like that?"

Gus shook his head. "At that point, it won't matter."

48 ∫ The Curse of Knowledge

SHORTLY AFTER DAWN THAT SAME FRIDAY MORNING . . .

A young Hawaiian broke the surface of Kiholo Bay, his dive mask flashing in the morning light. He held a spear and trailed a stringer of fish behind him. As he rose out of the breaking surf, sparkling water beads streamed off his modeled body. His wet ponytail swung side to side as he strode through the waves. Reaching the shallows, he hoisted his catch—two large *nenue*, several *palani*, a parrotfish, and at the very end of the line, a small octopus dangling above the water.

Just inland, on a surf-flooded ledge of lava, his aged grandfather stalked the reef, a net draped over his bony shoulder. Silver hair sprouted from his head, chest, and arms. Half-crouched, frozen in concentration, he tracked the yellow and silver flashes beneath him, waiting for the school from which these vagabonds had strayed.

Off the point a half-dozen boys floated on surfboards, rising and falling with the swells. Each waited for that certain wave that held within its rolling blue the power of flight—if he knew how to catch it. These boys did, a scene repeated countless times during the past two millennia.

Robert Conway drank in the view, already relaxing. He had driven to the far side of Kiholo Bay, to a small black sand beach created by the 1801 eruption, an undeveloped bit of shore he had donated to the county for public access. He sought relief from the tumult of the resort—buzzing with last-minute preparations for tomorrow's grand opening—and hoped to forget the bizarre spectacle he and Mali'o had witnessed two days earlier. He had since concluded that fatigue, wine, and darkness must have distorted what they'd seen. The shark, he convinced himself, was an aberrant baby whale that had strayed too close to shore, and the kahuna a silly old woman mumbling gibberish. His logical mind could not abide such foolish mysticism—and yet, despite his rationalizations, he was still haunted by it.

So he had come down to the bay to center himself, leave all the complications behind, and try to renew his dream's luster. He would swim in Kiholo Bay, as he had after the groundbreaking three years earlier. It would be a kind of ritual, his own way of thanking God, if there was one, for giving him the gift of imagination and the will to realize it.

He slipped off his shirt and sneakers and walked into the bay.

"Aloha," said the spearfisher as they passed each other.

"Hi, there." Conway smiled, his delight at being there obvious. The youthful Hawaiian picked up on it immediately.

"Enjoy the water, brah," he said.

Conway nodded.

All the way there—down the gravel road and footpath—Conway had avoided looking at the resort. He would wait until after his swim to gaze upon his masterpiece as if for the first time. He kept his eyes to sea as he swam laps parallel to shore, his tension draining out into the cool wake. When at last he returned to the beach, he did so underwater, delaying his emergence until his lungs were out of air, and he burst through the waves to stand waist deep.

The King and Queen's Towers gleamed above a tropical jungle that two years earlier had been a lava desert. Gone were the thorny kiawe trees and scrawny ironwoods, replaced with green jungle accented with splashes of color—of orange and purple bougainvillea and yellow and white ginger, the red and gold of *heliconia*, and assorted hues of plumeria. The thatched huts of the Hawaiian Village Suites and Conway's replica of the *Resolution* further transformed the bay into something out of a South Seas dream.

More than satisfied, Conway stepped from the water and strode up onto the beach. The young Hawaiian sat under a coconut tree, gently pulling each fish off the stringer and placing it in a large white bucket. He glanced up, catching Conway's eye.

"How was it, brah?" he asked.

"Very nice," Conway replied absently, transfixed by the resort.

The fisherman looked over his shoulder to see what had caught the stranger's attention. "Too much, eh?"

"Yes," Conway replied, taking the remark as a compliment.

The Hawaiian shook his head. "I'll nevah understand how some people believe they can improve on God's work."

Conway's jaw tightened. "I don't know," he replied. "It looks pretty good to me."

The Hawaiian continued to unstring his fish.

"You don't like it?" Conway asked.

"Whoever built that thing obviously never spent any time at Kiholo. Otherwise they wouldn't have ruined the place."

Conway bristled. "There wasn't much of anything here, was there?"

The young man looked up. "You never saw Kiholo before they built the hotel?"

"I swam here three years ago."

"Then you remember how quiet it was. How the reef was full of fish. How there was freshwater here, ponds now buried under those fake Hawaiian huts." Again, the young man shook his head. "I guess some people are satisfied with things that aren't real."

"Very true," Conway replied. Surely romanticizing the shrub and rock that was this desert before Conway applied his magic hand was living in a fantasy of the past. Conway began to wonder if this articulate young Hawaiian was one of the activists.

"So people around here are pretty upset about the resort?" Conway asked, taking advantage of his anonymity to probe for information about the rumored protest.

The fisherman shrugged his shoulders. "Hard telling. People getting a little numb—you know what I mean? They don't get upset—they just feel sad." The affable young man opened a small cooler at the base of the tree and pulled out two cans of guava juice. He handed one to Conway.

"Thank you," Conway said, sitting down on the black sand.

"I'm a fisherman. I worry what all this development will do to the reef."

"What do you mean?"

"Ciguatera."

Conway had heard about the problem. Every now and again someone got sick from eating Kona reef fish tainted with ciguatera. Fish got it from ingesting algae that environmentalists alleged thrived on reefs polluted with fertilizer runoff from golf courses and lawns. It had first shown up on O'ahu, then Maui and Kaua'i, and was now on the Big Island—shadowing the resort industry like a plague. State experts questioned the environmentalists' charge, citing "causal uncertainties," an ambiguity that gave Conway and other developers an excuse to ignore the issue.

"We could always get clean fish at Kiholo," the young man continued, "because the resorts were far away. Now, I don't know."

Conway changed the subject. "How long have you been coming here?"

"Since I was a little boy. That's my grandfather over there." He pointed to the old fisherman on the ledge. "He's been fishing that reef more than seventy-five years. His father and his grandfather before that. *He's* the one can tell you stories about this place.

"Our family used to camp here. Big luaus too, all the aunties and uncles and cousins. And when the old folks got going—oh, *mean*, brah, the stories." He raised his muscled arm and pointed through the trees to a small clearing behind the beach. "Over there was a Hawaiian village, right up till the 1940s. There's ruins all over the place—houses, canoe sheds, petroglyphs, old temples, even a refuge cave."

Conway remembered hearing about all that, but he hadn't bothered to *really* read the archaeological reports.

"We been camping here right up until the resort bought the beach a few years ago. We still sneak in sometimes, but there's no way once that place opens." He pulled a small cellophane bag out of the cooler and held it toward Conway. "Smoked marlin? My cousin caught it right off this coast. 'Ono, brah." Delicious.

Conway took a piece. The fisherman broke off a large chunk and wolfed it down.

"So they don't let you camp here anymore?" Conway asked. "Even on the land given to the county?"

"Naw, they don't want a bunch of Hawaiians messing up their beach. Bad image for the tourists."

"Huh." Conway knew nothing about the county camping ban and wanted to say so, but he didn't dare jeopardize his anonymity.

"Happens every time. My family used to go to Waipuna Beach too, but no more. They built a resort on it, put up all these Do Not signs. Now it's mostly just tourists."

"That's too bad. But then whoever owns the land has the right—"

"Ya know, that's another thing. According to our genealogy, my ancestors come from Kiholo. But the title's unclear and there's papers missing. When it came up in court, we got screwed." His face flushed a little.

"You're pretty upset about all this. You going to the protest tomorrow?"

"No. I'm a fisherman, not an activist."

At that moment, the old Hawaiian on the ledge heaved his net into the sea. Its green mesh fanned out, then sank beneath the waves. He followed the net into the surf, quickly gathering up its ends until he corralled the trapped fish inside. A moment later, he climbed out of the froth, his bulging net of twitching fish slung over his shoulder.

"Hey, hey!" his grandson called out in congratulations, holding high his can of juice. The elder said nothing. He was quietly thanking the fishing god Ku'ula for his bounty, painfully aware that it might be one of his last from the Kiholo reef.

The young Hawaiian grinned, obviously admiring his grandfather. "He's a good fisherman—wise too. He's taught me many things." He inhaled deeply, and let the air out slowly. "He says, hey, all the kanaka are talking about sovereignty. What's sovereignty? It's freedom, he says, and the only kind of freedom that really matters is *personal* sovereignty, brah, the freedom to be yourself. That's my bag. So I learn all I can from my grandfather—how to throw net, spearfish, dive down eighty feet without busting your ears. He showed me how to plant taro and harvest breadfruit. I do all this, and for cash, I teach guitar—slack key. I'm not getting rich, money-wise, but when

"What's sovereignty? Personal *sovereignty, brah, the freedom to be yourself."*

it comes to freedom, I got lots. More than when I drove hotel vans."

"So you never got political?"

"Naw, I don't do politics, brah. Waste o' time. I do religion instead."

"Religion?"

"Yeah. Give my mahalo to the akua—our gods. We leave hoʻokupu—offerings—and we pray. You'd be surprised, brah, how much difference prayer can make."

Conway didn't know how to respond.

"Like my grandfather says, our gods went away—not after the missionaries came—after our people abandoned them. In the Hawaiian way of thinking, if you neglect the gods, you break their hearts and they have no choice but to go. Then you're left to wander through the mess alone." He finished putting away his fish and prepared to leave.

Conway realized he wasn't going to learn anything about the protest from this Hawaiian. "Well, I should be going too."

"Work today?"

"Yeah."

"Oh, too bad. Where you work?"

"To be honest . . . I work at the new resort."

The young fisherman shrugged. "Well, you know how it is, brah. Everybody's gotta make a living. At least you got work out of the deal. Some of my friends applied—to be bartenders and stuff? No way. Nothing against you, but they want haoles for the real visible jobs, mainlanders especially. To keep an image for the tourists, you know what I mean?"

Conway thought of his receptionist, Brook, the Indiana blonde with the studied smile. "I don't think that's true," he said, suddenly realizing how little he'd paid attention to his manager's hiring practices.

"I've got a friend who's gonna play Hawaiian music in one of the bars. He told me the Paradise Bay has a rule—any worker, including musicians, can only be on the premises one-half hour before and after their shift."

Conway shook his head sympathetically, but he didn't really want to hear all the details.

"And us locals are not supposed to socialize with the customers. I mean, what is that? Since when does a musician *not* socialize with the customers? That's part of the job."

Conway shrugged. "I don't know. It doesn't affect my job."

"What do you do over there, anyway?" the young man asked innocently.

Conway was stuck. He was proud to have built the resort, but he did not want to talk about the acquisition of the land, the destruction of Hawaiian ruins, or the bulldozing of the ponds. He didn't know much about poisoned reefs or employee rules. Those were someone else's responsibility. *He was the visionary.*

"Maintenance." It was the first thing that came into his mind. "I'm in maintenance." Immediately he felt foolish about his deceit, and his cheeks flushed.

The Hawaiian eyed him suspiciously. Conway, with his smooth, tanned skin, his neatly trimmed nails, and his mainland-style manner, didn't look like the kind of guy who worked with lawn mowers or wrenches. A bartender or waiter maybe, but a maintenance worker?

"Got the bucket, Puna?" the old Hawaiian asked, walking up to the two men on the beach.

"Hi, Grandpa, this is—" He threw his hand out toward Conway.

"—Bob," Conway said.

"Aloha." The old man shook his hand, haole-style. He dropped his net of wriggling fish on the sand and sat down.

"We were just talking about the resort. Bob, here, works over there."

The old man's dark eyes flashed. "You work for those bastards?"

Conway wanted to leave, but he had to defend himself and his dream—somehow. "If the resort was going to cause so many problems, why do you think they went ahead and built the place?" he asked. "Just for the money?"

The old man cocked his head in astonishment. "Why else?"

"Jobs?"

"For who? Not my people."

"But it's magnificent. You have to admit, they created a paradise out of—"

"It's ugly." The old man began pulling fish out of his net.

"Ugly? What about the flowers, the palms, the ferns, the pools?"

The old Hawaiian looked up from his net, a fish squirming in his hand. His ancient eyes glowed like polished kukui nuts. "They ruined our ancestral homeland. They destroyed the 'aina that is my flesh and blood. And for what? The cheap entertainment of tourists who don't even appreciate Hawai'i anymore. Look!" he said, pointing his muscled finger at the *Resolution*. "They even had the nerve to put Cook's boat out in the bay, to salt our wounds with their symbol of foreign invasion—from when they came to 'discover' us!"

Now Conway was hot under the collar, his blue eyes flashing. "So you think they're evil, these builders of the resorts?"

"No, brah," the young man interjected thoughtfully. "Just ignorant."

"How can you say that?"

"If whoever built that had just taken a little time to get to know the place, talk to us Hawaiians, maybe camp down here—but they made their plans in a boardroom in Honolulu or the mainland."

"You people *are* going to protest, aren't you?"

"No," the young man replied.

The old Hawaiian pursed his lips and looked out to sea. "We will keep praying until our old ways come back."

Conway was shocked to hear such nonsense in this day and age. "Human progress is inevitable," he said.

"I don't think so," the young man replied. "I used to read a lot of history when I was at the university, and it taught me a few things I still remember. Think back to the Dark Ages, and the Depression, and Germany in the 1930s. These were all steps backward, and I think we're in a time like that again." He held his hands out before him, as if urging his listener's understanding. "I also learned that the world can change when you least expect it . . . and sometimes, given the chance, people do noble things."

"There is an ancient Hawaiian prophecy"—the old fisherman gazed at the waves breaking on the sand—"from a time long ago: *E iho ano o luna. E pi'i ana o lalo. E hui ana na moku. E ku ana ka paia.* In English it means, 'That which is above shall be brought down. That which is below shall be lifted up. The islands will be united. The walls shall stand upright.'"

Conway didn't know what to say.

"I was stationed in France during the war," the old man continued. "I don't accept that it's over for my people, any more than the Jews in Europe thought it was over for them."

"See all these lava flows," the young man said, pointing to the enormous heaps of jagged stone stretching from the coast to the upper reaches of Hualalai. "My great-, great-, great-grandfather was a young man when these flows poured down the volcano, destroying villages and fishponds all along the coast. Everyone was shocked. Now they say she's getting ready to blow again. And you know what? I'm glad. Maybe she will come down the mountain and take that ugly resort away."

The elder Hawaiian scowled with disapproval. "Puna, do not ask the gods to take on your anger."

Conway was aghast. How could anyone hope for the destruction of such an accomplishment? Of his realized dream? The entrepreneur got up from the sand and stood before the two men. "I built it," he said defiantly.

"I know," said the old man. "You're Conway. I saw your picture in the paper."

His grandson's mouth dropped. "What?"

The old fisherman rose from the sand and stepped close to Conway. He was shorter than the strapping entrepreneur, but his mana—his spiritual strength—made him seem bigger.

"I don't know why you sat here all this time talking to my grandson, but I'm glad. When you go back to your fantasyland you will not be able to forget us or what we have said. You are now cursed with knowledge." He stepped back and sat down next to his kin.

Robert Conway peered into each man's face, his exasperation rising, and stomped off across the sand.

49 ∫ Known Suspects

LATER THAT MORNING IN HILO . . .

They all looked uneasy, but no one more than Kimo, the only person not seated in the small briefing room at the Hilo Police Station. His blue uniform had been neatly pressed for the meeting and his hat brushed clean. He knew he would be reprimanded for venturing out that night with Aka, maybe even have wages docked. He was still standing because he didn't know where to sit—with Uncle Aka and the others across the table, or in one of the three chairs reserved for officers. Instead of deciding, Kimo slouched against the green blackboard and fidgeted with his police department keys, his swollen split lip still blue-black from the previous day's encounter with Jake Bluestone's fists.

Jimmy sat next to Aka, restless as always. The room smelled identical to the one where officers had accused him of stealing Mr. Yokoyama's lawn mower—of Lysol attempts to wash away the sad odor of human frailty. It was not a place Jimmy thought he belonged.

Captain Jack sat away from the table, on a chair propped against the wall. He *knew* he didn't belong there, although he was familiar with the station, having once been hauled in for refusing a Breathalyzer test. He couldn't recall which cop had stopped him that night in front of the Queen Kapiolani Bar, but he examined every officer's face as they passed the room's window.

Maile sat with Aka, unconsciously thumbing the red folder inside which she had tucked her detailed notes about the incident. Next to her was the empty chair she hoped Gavin would sit in if he had received her message about the eleven o'clock meeting. She touched Aka's hand and he smiled, but the usual sparkle in his eyes was gone. His shoulders sagged forward. Even his beard seemed grayer.

"Something wrong, Uncle?"

His eyes moistened. "Hawai'i isn't a peaceful place anymore. I'm glad I won't live much longer. I don't want to see what it becomes."

Maile's gut twisted. Uncle Aka had never seemed despairing, always heartened by the things that remained pure—the sea, the mountains, his family, the gods, and his guardian ancestors. "The momentum has to break, Uncle. Things can't get much worse."

The old Hawaiian nodded halfheartedly.

The door opened and Lieutenant Vincent Machado strode in, police hat tucked under his arm and a large manila envelope in his hand. "Everyone here?" he asked, his voice as crisp as the pleats in his blue uniform.

"Everyone but Dr. Gavin McCall," Kimo replied. "He's on the mountain, and we're not sure he got the message."

Machado set his hat and the envelope on the table and sat down. "Let's begin. Thank you all for coming." His dark eyes paused on each face. "I've taken statements from most of you this morning, but I have a few follow-up questions."

He turned to Jimmy. "Mr. Anderson, are you absolutely certain you've told us everything you know about the murder?"

Jimmy's face pinkened. "Yes."

"Our investigators have been out on the lava this morning." Machado reached into the envelope and pulled out an empty film canister. "Yours?"

"I don't remember losing one."

"What about this?" He held up the blue cellophane bag he and Kimo had discovered on their first search. The green maile leaf was now gray. Memories of that awful night instantly flowed back into Jimmy's mind. His ears reddened, and behind his wire rims, his eyes watered.

"That's the sack that held the lei they threw onto the dead man."

"This isn't a bag from the store where you bought your film?"

"No, I—"

Captain Jack leaned forward in his chair. "Wait a minute, Machado. What're you gettin' at?"

"I'm saying we have little solid evidence to back up his story that a murder took place out on the lava flows."

Everyone gasped, and Kimo's head jerked back in surprise.

"Where's the victim? No one's reported a missing person and we've found no body out there."

Jack shook his head. "Ya gotta be kiddin'!"

Aka leaned over the table. "This young man is telling the truth, officer."

"He may well be, but I've got to have something more than his word alone to pursue this."

"This is nuts!" Jack growled. "Jimmy had to go into hiding for almost two weeks!"

"How do we know he wasn't just harvesting marijuana with Bluestone?"

Jack's face almost turned purple.

"What about the leaf in the blue bag, Lieutenant?" Kimo interjected quickly—before all hell broke loose.

"Ah yes, the leaf." Machado plucked it out of the bag. "That may be our only supporting evidence. I'll have verification of the plant species later today. On the other hand, all this stuff—bag, leaf, and canister—may just be trash from lava-hunting tourists."

Maile finally jumped in. "Lieutenant Machado, I corroborated Jimmy's story this morning. I saw the murderers too."

"We examined the area where you claim to have seen the two men—"

"Claim?"

"We found the skylight, but no physical evidence of a procession of men or even of your presence."

A young officer appeared in the window and knocked. The lieutenant opened the door and the officer whispered into his ear. "Send him down," Machado replied.

Maile straightened in her chair. "So, you doubt my word?"

"Let's put it this way, Dr. Chow. I can't find anything to prove your statement or disprove it. We'll find out what Dr. McCall has to say about that night in a moment."

Maile's face brightened, just in time to shine through the window for Gavin. Kimo let him in.

"Glad you could make it, Dr. McCall," Machado said, glancing at his watch. "Please sit down." The astronomer took the chair Maile had saved for him, and she reached under the table for his hand.

"Sorry I'm late," Gavin said. "I got your message last night, but I had a bit of trouble getting back down this morning, what with the storm and all." He turned to Officer Machado. "Spun out on Saddle Road, and it took forever to get her back out of the ditch."

"Is there snow on the mountain?" Jimmy asked.

"Bloody blizzard, lad. I reckon the summit looks a bit like your Minnesota."

Captain Jack pointed his pipe at Machado. "I'll tell you one thing that wouldn't happen back there in Minnesota—a whitewash like this!" He stood up. "We're wasting our time."

"I agree," said Machado, rising to step between Jack and the door, "unless we get some hard evidence, Jimmy. Did you take pictures that night?"

"Of the lava, yes."

"Of the murder?"

"I was too scared to take pictures."

Machado's eyes narrowed.

"Hell," Jack scoffed, "that kid's pure as North Woods snow—unfortunately! If he says he didn't take any pictures, he didn't."

It was, in fact, the first time Jimmy had ever lied to a police officer, and Jack was proud of him for doing it.

"Mr. Anderson," Machado said, "have you had any contact with Jake Bluestone since the earthquake?"

"No, thank God. He's gone crazy."

Machado got up and paced in front of the window.

"We've put together a composite drawing of Bluestone based on descriptions by Mr. Anderson, Kimo, and his uncle here, Mr. Kaikala. We're searching for him all over the island. The warrant reads kidnapping, assault, and propagation of a controlled substance. Kimo—"

"Yes, sir?"

"During your captivity, did Bluestone say anything about the alleged murder? Specifically whether he had seen it?"

"Naw."

"Mr. Kaikala?"

Aka shook his head.

The police lieutenant stopped his pacing in front of Jimmy. "How about you, Mr. Anderson? You were with Bluestone for more than a week. Did he tell you that he had also witnessed the murder?"

"I sure didn't see him there."

"That's not what I asked."

Captain Jack, still standing by the door behind Machado, shook his head.

Jimmy followed suit. "I don't recall him saying anything about it, sir."

"So we're back down to that leaf," Machado said, glancing over his shoulder at Jack.

Just then a police sergeant stuck his head into the room. "Talk to you a minute?" he asked the lieutenant. The two conferred outside the window, and when Machado returned, he dismissed the group.

"Thank you for your cooperation." Then a more emphatic statement: "Make sure to notify this department if you have any additional information—or you plan to leave the island."

As the group followed Machado down the hall, they passed the sergeant's desk. Seated with him was a striking young Filipina in a chiffon blouse, black miniskirt, and heels. Tears streaked her beautiful face and profound grief stood in her eyes. Maile overheard the policeman introduce her to Machado.

"This is Mali'o Rivera, the woman from Honoka'a. She's here about her missing cousin."

50 ∫ The Soldier's Retreat

NOON ON KILAUEA . . .

Jake Bluestone, panting with pain and exhaustion, slumped against the cave wall. Blood was ballooning into the bandage on his thigh, where the shard of broken window had stabbed him when his cabin collapsed in the quake. Maybe up here, in one of the volcano's dead lava tubes, he could at last find sanctuary and live like the animal they'd made him. They would never suspect he would flee up onto the active rift—away from the subdivision and the roads.

Bluestone had bolted from the ruins of his place after spotting several police vehicles drive up to Royal Gardens. At first he assumed they were after him for kidnapping, but when a police helicopter zoomed over the treetops above him, a new idea planted itself firmly in his mind—he needed to be silenced. He had, after all, seen the murder of the young Hawaiian, even spotted Jimmy behind the rock taking pictures. He had recognized two of the men at the execution—native vice cops who worked Pahoa town—and it didn't take him long to conclude it was a Hui thing. Through his binoculars he had spied on other Hui body dumps, usually in skylights, but that was the first time he'd seen a *live* man thrown into the molten streams. One of Bluestone's war wounds was a tendency to paranoia, but this time he knew he was right to worry—Jimmy had blown his cover. Now the Hui knew someone still lived in the cabin on the hill overlooking their wicked dumping ground.

He scanned the tunnel-like cave, surveying its sanctuary possibilities, when the roar of another helicopter reverberated through the stone above him. "Too easy to ambush—keep moving!"

Limping up the cavern, he contemplated a dash across the open lava. He knew that at least one police chopper was out there, and that tour helicopters flew to the erupting cone about every twenty minutes. If Bluestone could just make it to the forest on the other side, the geologists' trail there would lead him to Highway 11, where he could hitchhike into Hilo. But then what? By that time, his mug would be pasted on every airline clerk's computer screen, and escape by sea would mean chumming up with harbor union sleaze that might still be tied to the underworld. Maybe he could get to the FBI office in Hilo, but they had their own closet skeletons—from paranoid operations against Hawaiian activists. Still, the feds were like pit bulls when it came to underworld crime. Bluestone felt sure the G-men would listen to his story and keep him alive long enough to tell it to some federal judge.

Fortunately he had stuffed a few things into a rucksack—canteen, flashlights, binoculars, a government-issued .45, and three pounds of canned food. He grabbed a flashlight and picked his way up the tube. He knew enough about the volcano to know that it led more or less straight to the erupting cone—and halfway to his forest escape route. Unlike other tubes he'd been in, this one was still hot, having recently carried lava to the sea. His feet grew warm inside his jungle boots and he wished he'd brought gloves to protect his hands against the hot rock. As he made his way up the cavern, seams of glowing red occasionally appeared in its walls, indicating active conduits nearby.

"I'm finally going to hell," he would observe. "I'll meet the rest of you bastards there!"

Twice during the journey, skylights let in the cool mountain air and gave Bluestone's lungs a break. Both times he stopped, but only briefly, certain the enemy was closing in. "Discipline is survival," he would holler into the cave, listening to it echo back like a taunting sergeant. Following his wagging beam up into the bowels of the volcano, he commanded himself to "step lightly and stay alert!"

Meanwhile, four police officers searched his cabin ruins and the lean-to he had made from its debris. A half-dozen others threaded their way through the forest, guns drawn, searching for what the department had told them was a wild man.

Among the group were two officers familiar with the terrain, having been there the night of the murder. They were prepared to ignore the department's admonition about using firearms only if necessary, determined to bring the suspect in dead rather than alive. Both knew Bluestone would carry a weapon and that the open terrain presented opportunities for manipulating ballistic evidence. It wasn't long before all four officers broke free of the forest and started plodding across the lava. They might have turned back at the tree line, but one rookie thought he'd heard the words "stay alert" drift over the rocky terrain. A mile and a half beyond them towered Pu'u 'O'o, belching a poisonous plume that looked like the exhaust of a hundred steamships combined. As usual, afternoon clouds hunkered down over the 600-foot-high cone and it began to drizzle. Everything grew dark. The rainwater evaporated instantly on the hot flows near the cone, creating a massive whiteout that migrated downslope toward the officers.

The shroud of steam was fortunate for Bluestone, since his journey through the tube was about to end. Rubble below the third skylight blocked the rest of the cave. He climbed the stony heap and stepped out onto the decimated landscape. Now a half mile from the cone, he would have to dash across a bizarre terrain of pumice, rock, and cinder, maintaining cover with the only thing available—murky waves of steam advancing over the land like legions of ghosts. Sulfur fumes permeated the mist, stinging his eyes and the laceration on his leg. His ponytail funneled raindrops down his back, and his teeth chattered inside goosebump-riddled cheeks.

Bluestone screamed obscenities at the spirits he saw in the mists, demanding, "Get the hell off my back!" and "Go hassle the enemy!" His chilled flesh grew pallid, as if he, too, had become a ghost. But inside, his heart and lungs remained warm, fired by the will to survive, even as he lost his bearings and marched straight to the erupting cone.

Coughing on volcanic fumes, Bluestone struggled up its steep incline, loose cinder giving way each step. While resting high up on the cone, he noticed, between waves of mist, blue figures scrambling over the lava. No doubt they had spotted him. The last tour helicopter to chance the fog startled the Vietnam veteran when it momentarily passed through a hole in the clouds, camcorders pressed against its windows.

The air turned warm as he climbed, and he soon found out why. One flank of the cone had collapsed and what remained was riddled with deep crevices pouring forth scalding steam. With visibility only a few feet, Bluestone moved cautiously toward the fissures, seeking respite from the deathly chill that had settled into his bones. A strange chomping sound made him stop, as if some giant beast lunched on the rock—*kayawachawa—kayawachawa—kayawachawa.*

He moved ahead slowly, the noise louder with each step. The heat intensified, and a glowing red mist enveloped Bluestone at the cone's rim. He all but forgot his pursuers as he stared down into the lake of lava, a steamy skin of undulating rock ruptured in places by upsurges of magma. Each tear was fluorescent orange, a jagged window into the molten stew just beneath its dark membrane. Here and there, the ruptures bubbled over with bright red lava, splashing iridescence onto the lake's surface and against the cauldron walls, and geysers of lava fountained as high as eighty feet. At one point, the undulating skin folded over itself as the restless currents of the lake pulled it down into the bright red stew. Bluestone's pupils narrowed against the volcano's blinding light, and heat blasted his face, tossing his damp hair straight up. He remembered a close call with a napalm drop on a village in the Mekong Delta, but that fiery scene paled compared to this.

"I've died and gone to hell!" he hollered, oblivious to the two policemen approaching the rim. He dropped to his knees and stared into the cauldron.

"No, you're not in hell," said the panting officer stepping into the glow. He pointed his gun at the back of Bluestone's head. "But it won't be long."

Bluestone swung around as the second officer reached the rim. These were the Hawaiian vice cops he'd seen at the murder.

"Anybody with you?" the one with the drawn gun said to the other.

The cop shook his head. "McCarthy 'bout a quarter mile back, and Correo went to da uddah side of da cone. I t'ink Machado's copter headed back down—no more visibility."

“Then it’s just the two of us and hippie here.” He placed the gun barrel against Bluestone’s brow.

At that moment the volcano roared like a B-52 on takeoff, and a hot wind blasted out of the chasm with such force that both policemen fell backward down the pitch of cinder, their hats caught up in the gale. A swirl of pumice and ash flew out of the crater and raced headlong down the cone, knocking over Officer McCarthy. The little tornado—with police hats in tow—spun across the lava all the way down to the jungle. Red glow overwhelmed the entire landscape, and the chomping growls of the roiling lake grew so loud it seemed the beast would consume the whole cone inside out. The two Hawaiians crept back up the cinder, hunkering low to avoid the heat blasting out of the crater.

Bluestone was gone.

“No more haole,” shouted one of the cops. “I t’ink he wen fall in.”

They crept to the rim and peeked over the edge. A twisted char lay on the surface of the lava lake, engulfed in yellow flame.

“Mean!”

Another blast rose from the chasm, singeing the hair and eyebrows of the two startled Hawaiians. As they turned away from the heat, one of them thought he caught a glimpse of a woman dancing on the lake.

51 ∫ Na'au

THAT AFTERNOON IN KEAUKAHA . . .

The soft cooing of doves under the eaves of Maile's bungalow added to the dreamlike quality of the afternoon. Making love to Maile had left Gavin pleasantly disoriented and certain this passion was deeper than any he'd felt before. Despite their different worlds, fire had passed between them, fusing a connection that stirred his spirit in mysterious ways.

For the past two days Gavin had tried to do science in the base camp library, but his mind was fixated on Maile. He often found himself staring through the rain-streaked window, watching thunderheads boil above distant Mauna Loa, its snowline lower each time the clouds receded. Kept from Mauna Kea's summit by a blizzard now in its second day, Gavin had resumed his normal sleep schedule, and for two nights he had experienced the same fantastic dream:

He and Maile stood arm and arm inside a tiny dome, stargazing with the college telescope he'd used when he first grasped the physics of what had excited him all his life. The couple peered at hot young stars shrouded in wisps of cosmic afterbirth and at old red giants consuming the last of their fuel. They marveled at galaxies—vast spirals of suns spinning in a dynamic dance set to the rhythms of the big bang.

At one point, Maile tugged Gavin away from the eyepiece, urging him outside, where they stood atop a lone high peak. The twinkling town lights were so tiny that at first Gavin thought they must be peering down from somewhere *above* Earth.

"Look," Maile said, pointing to the night sky.

One by one, stars swooped down next to the mountaintop and began communicating with the astronomer through a series of excited color shifts and flashes. Although Gavin knew everything science had taught him about the stars, he was unable to comprehend their language. But Maile understood, so she translated for him, and in the phantasm common in dreams, did it all without words, as had the stars. The wonders Gavin learned were even greater than the marvels science had revealed.

On each of the two mornings following the dream, Gavin lay in his little base camp bed trying to retrieve those meanings, but alas, they eluded his conscious grasp.

Although the weather had thwarted almost all of his team's observation work, Gavin could only feign disappointment. The storm had gotten him off the hook, and when Maile's message about the meeting at the police station arrived, it was almost easy to abandon his work. He needed to see Maile—to touch her, talk with her, just be in her presence.

In the quiet of the cottage, he lay against her body, exhausted by the explosive power of their lovemaking. Her caramel skin seemed somehow more natural than his own pallid flesh. Moist heat radiated from her, penetrating his own body. He recalled Maile's startled eyes and the swell of her enormous black pupils as he entered her body; her open mouth and quiet moans as he struck deep inside; her jumbled hair trembling as she shuddered into climax. Maile's final cries echoed in his head amid the island melodies playing softly over the radio.

Maile heard the music too—sentimental vocals accompanied by guitars. She drifted with the tunes, relaxed but alert, her skin still tingling. The balmy breeze caressed her breasts as Gavin breathed into her hair. She was surprised at the familiarity of his breath—sweet, tangy, alive. She could have identified it in the dark.

The tumble into each other's arms had been precipitous, although not unusual for lovers so recently fallen into desire's abyss. Gavin had agreed to meet Maile at her seaside home, presumably to discuss the police investigation. Once inside the cozy bungalow, with soft afternoon light filtering through its cotton curtains, only minutes had passed before they were sprawled naked on the carpet. The rest happened quickly, with the desperate fervor of new lovers separated for more than two days. Aware that neighbors might overhear their moaning, Maile had switched on a Hawaiian radio station.

Now, as Maile and Gavin recuperated, a stark silence interrupted the broadcast, and a moment later a voice came over the air: "This is a Civil Defense message for Friday, June 16, issued shortly after one o'clock. I repeat, this is a Civil Defense message—"

"Hey, where's the music?" Gavin said dreamily.

"Listen!" Maile replied, rising up on her elbows. Keenly aware that she lived on a coast twice devastated by tsunamis since World War II, Maile had learned to pay strict attention to the voice of Mike Takahashi. For years he had warned Big Islanders about hurricanes, eruptions, flash floods, earthquakes, and other disasters.

"This is eruption information bulletin number one, affecting all residents on the west side of the island of Hawai'i . . ."

"Eruption?" Maile queried. "On the west side?"

"Early this morning, seismographs at the Hawaiian Volcano Observatory detected a swarm of low-magnitude earthquakes emanating from Hualalai volcano above Kailua-Kona."

Maile sat up on her knees.

Gavin tried to refocus, but it was difficult with his naked lover kneeling beside him. "Bloody hell!" he said, grinning. "We've started an eruption, Maile."

"Shhhh!"

"The swarm lasted eight minutes and included almost two hundred individual quakes. The highest was a magnitude three-point-one temblor occurring at 12:07 a.m., felt by a number of people in Kailua. Scientists believe this earthquake swarm, the third to occur during the past several days, may indicate movement of magma inside Hualalai."

"Oh my God," Maile muttered.

"All residents on the Kona side of the island—from Keauhou to coastal Waikoloa—should be on the alert for the possibility of volcanic activity. While there is no evidence yet of actual lava being erupted—I repeat, there is no known eruption at this time—residents should be prepared to evacuate at a moment's notice. Scientists are concerned that activity might resume at the site of the last Hualalai flows, in 1801. If so, the areas most susceptible to catastrophic damage include coastal and upslope sections of North Kona between the airport and Kiholo Bay."

"Where the resorts are," Maile said, getting up from the floor.

"Good heavens," Gavin muttered, finally grasping the magnitude of the news.

"Scientists are closely watching Hualalai for additional signs of activity, but little has occurred during the past twelve hours. As a precaution, Civil Defense personnel are now in the area, making preparations in the event that evacuations are necessary. Please stay tuned for additional updates . . ."

Maile picked her shirt and panties up off the carpet, slipped them on, and started pacing the room. Her mind raced. Who did she know in Kona that might not have heard the announcement?

Gavin started searching for his trousers.

Most of Maile's family lived on the Hilo side or in the Ka'u district. She ran the faces of family members and friends through her mind.

"Ah hah," Gavin blurted, spotting his pants bunched up under the dining room table.

"Aunty Keala!" Maile declared, suddenly remembering that she lived on the slopes of Hualalai, near the village of Holualoa. Odd that *she* should come to mind; Maile hadn't seen the renowned elder in three years, not since she'd interviewed her for the Kiholo archaeological surveys. Yet Keala Huelani's face was the only one that popped into her mind. "Do I even have your phone number?" she wondered aloud as she stepped next door to her study.

"What number?" Gavin asked, pulling on his pants.

"Aunty Keala's," she replied absently, scanning the addresses in her iPhone with an urgent feeling that somehow it was *her* responsibility to notify the woman. She checked under H, then K, and in desperation, dove into the A's just in case she had misfiled it under "Aunty."

"Auwe! I don't have it," she declared.

"Who are you trying to reach?" Gavin asked, puzzled by Maile's agitation.

"Aunty Keala! An elder I worked with a few years ago," she replied impatiently. Maile flung open the phone book and pored over the names listed under H. "Huebner, Huehue, Huemiller, Huey. She's not here!"

"Maile, it's just the first bulletin. Calm down."

"I can't," she shouted. Maile yanked open a drawer of the desk and pulled out a shoebox containing old address books and numerous slips of paper on which she'd scrawled contact information over the years. Surely she still had her number.

Gavin got up from the sofa and stepped toward her. "What *is* going on?"

She thrust her hands up between them. "No!" she said in a tone that meant, no more questions allowed.

Gavin ignored this. "Why is it so bloody important to reach this woman?"

Maile looked up from the scraps of paper strewn across the desk. Grave lines etched her face and big viscous tears stood in her eyes. "I don't know! But I'm getting a clear message—GET HOLD OF KEALA HUELANI *NOW!*"

Both paused to think. Then Gavin said, "How can I help you, Maile?"

She shoveled the papers back into the box, grabbed it, and stepped into the living room. "Help me look through these old addresses and phone numbers." She dumped the contents on the carpet, and the two began sorting through the mess. Ten minutes later Gavin found the entry in an old address book.

"'Fraid she's unlisted, luv," Gavin said, handing her the address book.

Maile sighed. "Now what?"

"What choice have we?"

"Right," she replied, "Let's go."

"Have we time to shower?" Gavin asked.

Maile glanced at her half-naked partner. "No, but I think we'd better."

"Here we go again," Gavin said, getting up from the floor. "More adventure."

She shooed him toward the bathroom with a pat on the backside. Maile reread the entry and noticed some notes scribbled under Aunty Keala's name:

> Local knowledge of North Kona, including Kiholo
> Friendly but reticent to reveal too much
> (Local rumor: is this kahuna . . . a kaula—seer??)

"Kahuna," Maile said softly, "are you calling me?"

As she waited to shower, Maile gathered a few things for the trip—a change of clothes, some water and snacks, and her notebook. Almost as an afterthought, she added the camera and her field notes on the petroglyph cave. Then her na'au kicked in with a curious message: *You'll need protection.*

Maile obeyed it. She placed her lizard talisman around her neck.

At that moment she remembered something else about her last encounter with Aunty Keala. The elder, sensing Maile's good Hawaiian heart, had invited her to come visit anytime. Maile recognized that this was the teacher offering to help a student. Preoccupied with her work, perhaps apprehensive of what might be required, Maile had never followed up.

Maile's Jeep climbed the steep winding road leading to the saddle between the two giant volcanoes. A second Civil Defense bulletin came over the radio shortly after three o'clock. It contained the same information as the first but now included the locations of three evacuation centers—two in Kailua and one in Waimea.

"Establishing these centers is only a precaution," said Mike Takahashi. "Hualalai is a steep mountain and lava flows are expected to move rapidly. In 1801 lava reached the sea in less than an hour. Residents must know exactly where to go since there may be no time to think about it once the emergency is under way."

The weather seemed fine until they crested the saddle, where dark thunderheads towered over both summits. About that time, the coastal radio station petered out.

"That's where the blizzards are," Gavin commented.

Something struck the windshield.

"What the—!" Maile slowed the vehicle.

Another hit the window, then the hood, and soon the whole Jeep was pelted. Inside the metal cab, a popcorn popper.

Gavin rolled down his window and stuck out his arm.

"Ouch!" he hollered, yanking it back inside. He unfolded his fingers to reveal a half-inch chunk of ice.

"Look, Gavin!" The ditches of lava were turning white.

By the time they passed under the hailstorm, a mile beyond the observatory turnoff, the wipers were jammed with ice. And yet only ten miles farther, as the saddle dipped toward Kona, patches of blue sky were visible again, peeking through streaks of cirrus clouds moving in from the west. Eventually they turned off the Saddle Road onto the upcountry highway leading toward Hualalai and the town of Kailua. Once again they were able to pick up a radio station. KING FM ran a statement from Mike Takahashi on the top-of-the-hour news. It also broadcast a two-minute interview with Dr. Lelehua Chin identifying various pathways the lava could take. She kept her message calm and academic, until the frustrated reporter finally drew her out:

"Look, Dr. Chin, you've included three-fourths of the Kona coast in your possible inundation areas, but you haven't told us what that really means in terms of possible impact. What's the worst-case scenario?"

"Worst case?" Lelehua replied. "OK, picture scores of people killed, hundreds of homes and businesses destroyed, and billions of dollars lost. "

"Good God," Gavin said, looking through the windshield at Hualalai, a small volcano compared to Mauna Kea. "Could it really be *that* dangerous?"

"I'll show you just how dangerous in a few minutes," Maile told Gavin. Ten miles later, she pulled over where the road crossed an 1801 lava flow that still covered the volcano's flank all the way to Kiholo Bay. "Oral histories document this event as a battle of wills between Pele and Kamehameha, the most powerful king ever to rule Hawai'i. The goddess humbled the man, but not before destroying villages along this coast— " She stopped midsentence, flashing on something Lelehua Chin had just said over the radio: *The entire area below the Buena Vista subdivision could be inundated . . .* "I've got to go back to that petroglyph cave," she said. "I haven't even started the *most important* part of the inventory."

"'Fraid you're not going to get a chance, luv—not if this volcano erupts."

"The eruption is exactly why I have to go. Gavin, that is not just any lava tube."

Gavin recalled the formidable stone guarding the rest of the cavern, and a chill ran through him.

"There's more to the cave than I let you know. It may contain the bones of King Kamehameha."

52 Rendezvous with the Kahuna

THAT EVENING ON HUALALAI . . .

Maile could not remember the exact location of Aunty Keala's driveway, so she drove the narrow Holualoa road slowly, watching for a cue—a familiar patch of taro, a distinctive mailbox, or a unique stone guarding the drive.

"I'll bet she lives right around that bend," she said, suddenly easing back from the wheel.

"You recognize the turn in the road?" said Gavin.

"No, I just have a feeling."

As the Jeep rounded the bend, a large Hawaiian woman came into view. She stood, back to the road, waist deep in a patch of ti plants, gathering leaves. Weighty clouds obscured Hualalai's summit, but the descending evening sun bathed the elder in golden light. She stopped cutting and spun around, her eyes shining with anticipation.

"Stay here," Maile said to Gavin as she got out of the vehicle. Aunty Keala's face was open and alert, watching Maile in the same way a cat observes the approach of a friendly stranger. "Do I know you?" Aunty Keala asked, noticing the bone lizard peeking out from inside Maile's shirt.

"I'm Maile Chow. We met three years ago."

"Oh yes . . . the anthropologist. Your family is from Ka'u. You're the daughter of Alana Keamoku Chow."

"Yes." Maile was encouraged.

"So why are you here?"

"I think I came to warn you about the eruption."

"The eruption of Hualalai? Yes, I am well aware of it."

Maile, suddenly confused, stared at the old woman's face. "That's not why you called me?"

"I called you?"

Maile paused to check her feelings. "Yes, Aunty. I think you called me."

The elder's eyes sparkled. "Come inside."

Aunty Keala noticed Maile glance toward Gavin, still back in the Jeep.

"Bring him too," she said.

After brief introductions, the elder escorted the couple to the lanai of her old coffee shack, directing them to two chairs across from her big koa rocker. "I was just steeping some tea," she said. "Would you like a cup?"

"Please," Maile replied. "May I help?"

Aunty Keala shook her head. "I'll be just a few minutes." Time to prepare, not just tea, but her na'au for the encounter.

As she stepped through the doorway, Gavin noticed the altar of lei-draped stones inside. "Are you sure I should be here?"

She squeezed his hand. "Yes, I'm certain."

"What about the elder?"

"She's trusting my judgment. Besides, she's probably already sensed your good character."

Gavin rolled his eyes. "What's going to happen here, anyway?"

"Something *huna*—hidden—and you must respect that."

"OK," his voice tentative.

"Aunty Keala is a revered cultural expert in the Hawaiian community, active in educational and civic affairs. What most people *don't* realize is that she is also a kaula—a seer."

Gavin drummed his fingers on the arm of the chair.

"Nervous?"

He shrugged. "We've been through more nerve-racking things than this, eh? But I could use a bit of background."

"Well, some kahuna can detect illness in people. Others experience visions or see omens in the sky. Some are known to communicate with plants and animals. A few can even contact the spirit world and the gods, or do other, more fantastic, things." She chose not to mention the dark sorcery of ʻanaʻana. "Obviously such knowledge is protected, and those kinds of kahuna went underground long ago."

"When the missionaries came?"

"Even before that. Most societies willingly embrace religious priesthoods, with their pomp, ritual, and rules. But in every culture there are also shamans, and they have a different function. They discover truth, wisdom, and prophecy—messages sometimes coming straight from the gods—and that can threaten the powers that be, including the priesthood."

"Ahhh."

"I imagine the Hawaiian royalty didn't always appreciate the advice of these kahuna, some of whom came from bloodlines predating the Tahitian invasion, an early bloodline that persists today."

"Fascinating. And these people know this about themselves?"

"Yes. You see, there was one island not overthrown by Paʻao and his Tahitian warriors—Molokaʻi—and islanders there have never forgotten that."

"And Aunty Keala is one of those descendants?"

"Yes." She leaned close to Gavin. "Even today—*especially* today—these powerful kahuna keep a low profile, and not only because of the haoles."

Gavin's eyes burned with curiosity.

"Most of my people now embrace a Christian outlook, and many of them are uncomfortable with kaula, even while acknowledging their power. High craftspeople—canoe builders, toolmakers, and herbalists—are considered kahuna if they embody the spiritual as well as functional mana of their crafts. They enjoy the respect of Hawaiians, but these other kahuna are not always so fortunate."

Gavin nodded, aware that he was learning things rarely accessible to Westerners, let alone scientists.

"I appreciate your confidence, Maile. I'm trying to stay open."

She smiled. "I know. It feels right to share this with you."

"Here we are," said Aunty Keala, lumbering across the lanai with a tray of three steaming mugs. "I hope you like *koʻokoʻolau* tea."

Aunty Keala set the tray on the table and sat down in the big rocker.

"I'm glad you came over, Maile. I did not know exactly who I was calling for help, or whether hearing the call, they would heed it."

"But you did know why?"

"In part, but not completely. I have to wait for more information."

For another vision, Maile thought.

Aunty Keala leaned forward, her intensity palpable. "Are you going to the grand opening of the Royal Paradise Bay Resort tomorrow?"

Maile, stunned by the question, pulled back.

"I thought perhaps you'd been invited," the elder continued. "After all, you did do the archaeological surveys."

Maile's eyes welled up with tears, and Gavin took her hand. "Oh, Aunty. I feel so ashamed."

"Don't. Your surveys saved some important things—a third of the petroglyphs, some of the ponds, and the refuge cave. Besides, all that is past, and I need you *now*. Your having done those surveys may help us."

Maile wiped away the tears. "What can I do?"

"Have you learned to listen to your na'au?"

"Yes . . . I'm trying."

"Well, you will need to listen to it tomorrow. For reasons I cannot completely disclose right now—please trust me—I need you to attend the grand opening. I have been called away on important business and cannot attend myself. But something is going to happen there, something I need to see through your eyes."

"I have heard there might be a protest. Is that why you want me there?"

"No. I need a Hawaiian who will be perceived and treated as a special guest, who can freely socialize with the dignitaries."

Certainly Conway and his staff would have expected the contract archaeologist to join their lavish party, but when Maile received their slick, nauseating brochure, she resolved not to even answer the invitation. "What am I looking for?" she asked.

"I don't know precisely. But whatever it is will be of sufficient surprise—it may even shock you—that you will immediately recognize that this is what Aunty Keala was waiting to see."

"How should I contact you when whatever happens, happens?"

The kahuna smiled. "The old way. Get out of the fray, call my name, and send the message. Don't worry, I'll get it."

The strange instructions stirred almost forgotten memories of conversations overheard at her mother's knee with one of the old Hawaiians in Ka'u. Maile paused to absorb it all. "I think Gavin should come with me."

"Then take him," the elder replied. She grasped both their hands. "Stay close to each other, observe with both sets of eyes, and consult. Together you will know what to do."

"Can't you give us anything more to go on?" Gavin asked, leaning forward.

"That's all I know at this point. Shall we find out what Pele is doing on Hualalai? Maile, would you go into my study, around the corner past the living room, and turn on the radio. We can listen through the window." Maile went inside, and Aunty Keala took Gavin's arm and pulled him close.

"Protect her, Gavin. Tomorrow you must be Maile's second na'au. Can you do that?"

Gavin nodded, although he was not at all sure that he could—or what new terrain he had entered.

The radio came on, playing a contemporary Hawaiian song. When Maile returned, her face seemed strained. "Aunty Keala, there's something else I need to do in Kona . . . You know Nupa 'Io, the cave with the petroglyph chamber?"

"Yes?"

"I've been studying it on and off for the past year—on my own time. I think one of the branches of the tube may contain some very important historical evidence. If Hualalai erupts, it could be sealed forever."

Aunty Keala's expression turned severe. "Just as well."

"No, Aunty, you don't understand—"

"Let it be, Maile."

"But I think that cave contains the bones—"

"Let him rest in peace."

"If Hualalai erupts, those bones will be buried and with them the secret of Kamehameha and his relationship to Hualalai, to Pele. It is—"

"—best left unsolved by Westerners!"

"But I'm Hawaiian!"

Aunty Keala peered into her face. "Not yet," she said. "Not yet."

Maile's almond eyes misted over, and through her shirt, she clutched the bone talisman.

The elder shook her head. "Go to the resort. Forget the cave."

Maile pointed at her stomach, her na'au. "But down here, I know, I must return."

"That's only your head talking." Aunty Keala stood up. "That place is dangerous. It has protection. The spirits there could attach themselves to you like maggots on a carcass. You cannot go without a kahuna by your side."

"Then maybe *you* will go with me." As soon as the words tumbled out of her mouth, Maile knew it was a mistake. Aunty Keala turned away toward the ocean and replied with a riddle.

"Today's sun will soon set on our beloved island. When darkness emerges and familiar light fades into the sea, it becomes difficult to distinguish earth from sky. For Hawaiians, and for Westerners, the new day always begins amid the darkness."

Gavin and Maile rose from their chairs as the sun—blood red through the volcanic haze blown over from Kilauea—touched the water.

Gavin put his hand out to the elder, and she pulled him forward to offer her cheek. "Take care of her," she whispered in his ear. "And keep her away from that cave."

"I'll try."

The two women embraced in a lengthy hug, and then Gavin reached for Maile's hand. "I'll meet you at the Jeep."

"I'm sorry, Aunty," Maile said, once Gavin had left.

"Shhh. Don't worry about it."

"May I ask you one more thing—about Gavin."

The elder nodded.

"Why has this haole come into my life?"

Aunty Keala smiled. "Do you not know?"

"It *feels* very right, but that's what confuses me."

"Because of his race? Surely you know it is his heart, not his skin color, that matters."

Maile nodded, a little embarrassed.

"I have only met the man today, but I can tell you this, Maile. Through the mirror of a mate, love helps us see ourselves as we truly are. Perhaps that is why Gavin has come into your life. The work this island and your culture ask of you is crucial, and it can only be accomplished once you fully accept who you are—who your ancestors left here to carry on. What little I have seen of Gavin I like. He listens. He is a thinker, yet he does not seem to fear his emotions."

"Aunty, he's been seeing Pele in his dreams."

The oracle smiled. "Of course. She is very active just now. Perhaps she is preparing to meet him . . . and you."

53 ∫ A Matter of Trust

EARLY EVENING NEAR KALAPANA . . .

Four men and a dozen empty beer bottles crowded the old cable spool that served as Captain Jack's lanai table. Jack, Aka, Kimo, and Jimmy had already polished off most of the celebratory dried squid and smoked pork. Dusky cirrus clouds streaked the sky and crickets chirped in the waning light.

"I had no idea what I was getting into when I stepped off that plane," Jimmy said, shaking his head.

Jack leaned into Jimmy and laughed. "The understatement o' the night."

"And I'm not even talking about the murder or crazy Jake Bluestone. I'm talking about this island. Rocks that glow, owls that guide, old men who harbor strangers in need. I'm blown away by it all."

Aka smiled, his teeth white inside his beard. "Miracles happen on these magical islands."

Jimmy smiled back. "Even to a dumb tourist like me."

"Yeah," Jack said, lighting up his pipe. "I'd say you've had a bonafidee adventure—even got a few scars to take back—and it ain't over yet."

"Let's hope it is," said Jimmy, raising his bottle of beer. "By this time tomorrow I'll be jetting home, as long as the cops don't find out I'm skipping town." Everyone joined him in a speechless clink of glass.

Home. Jack pondered the word. More than forty years had passed since he'd left Minnesota, more than a decade since his last visit. For the first time in years, he felt a melancholy tug on his roots. Gazing into the jungle, he recalled the smell of the North Woods, sunlight filtering through misty stands of white pine, spruce, and fir. He imagined soulful loon songs echoing across Lake Superior and romance with the Scandinavian beauties inhabiting the woods around Grand Marais. Jack puffed gently on his pipe's vanilla smoke. After all the intrigue and corruption, the sad reminders of Alana Chow, and a Kalapana eruption that had forced half his adopted community to move away, Jack was almost ready to go back to the mythic land of milk and honey—Minnesota. And there was something else. When the old adventurer finally decided to lend a hand to Jimmy, a dormant place in Jack's male heart had stirred. Now the young man who had shaken loose those emotions was getting ready to leave—like so many other people in Jack's lonesome sailor's life.

Aka noticed moisture in the old man's eyes. "Where are you?"

Jack removed the pipe from his mouth and pointed the stem at Jimmy. "For a minute, there, I was going back with the boy."

"I know that's your 'aina, but isn't it mighty cold up there?"

"Cold? Sweet Jesus, is it cold! Why, it's so cold . . ."

Aka missed the colorful description, his attention diverted by an owl landing in a nearby tree.

"Just don't forget to mail that envelope," Jimmy said to Aka.

"It's already in the glove box of my truck, ready to drop off on Monday."

"This afternoon I called my buddy whose dad is the judge. He says they've already notified the Minneapolis FBI that the roll of film is on its way."

"Can you trust judges back in Minnesota?"

"More'n you can most places," Jack interjected with home state pride. "Why I'd say—"

"What's he doing here?" a startled Kimo interrupted, seeing Lieutenant Machado's black Chevy Tahoe pull into the drive. Everybody sat up in his chair.

"Remember, no mention of my leaving," Jimmy warned, "or the film."

Machado, dressed in black jeans and an aloha shirt—tucked in—got out of the SUV. Jack noticed his clean white sneakers. "Doesn't that guy ever get shit on his shoes?" he said under his breath.

"That kind never do," Aka whispered back.

"Well, he's about to get a heap o' bullshit from us."

"Evening, guys," Machado said, stepping up onto the lanai.

Jack stuffed some stronger shag into his pipe. "Well, Officer Machado, what brings you all the way down to my dump?"

"Sorry to barge in on your party, but some information came my way that I wanted to share with you folks. I tried to call, but apparently you don't have a phone out here." Despite his plank-straight back and tidy appearance, Machado seemed less formidable out of uniform, and Aka noticed a new weariness on his face. "May I join you for a few minutes?"

Jack motioned to the one empty chair. "Pull up a seat." Aka grabbed a beer out of the ice chest and offered it to Machado, who surprised everyone by taking it.

"Officially, I'm not here." He glanced at Kimo. "OK?"

His fellow officer shrugged. "Sure."

"Let me go straight to the point. I'm under a lot of pressure to close the books on this murder allegation. That's why I handled you guys a little rough this morning at the station. Then a lady came in saying her cousin's missing, a guy I think I can link to the Hui."

The four remained silent, no one willing to respond independently of the others.

Machado turned to Jimmy. "My hunch is he's the young man you saw murdered. There's something else too. That Vietnam veteran, Bluestone? Well, he's dead too. Apparently he fell into the volcano."

The startled faces of the four spoke volumes. Still, no one commented.

"Look, guys. I need your help. I'm worried there's some men in my own department who may be involved—vice guys that I've long suspected cut some kind of deal with the Hui."

Jack leaned forward. "How do we know yer bein' straight with us?"

Machado laughed. "Up until a few hours ago, that's exactly what I asked myself about you. But too much of what you've told me fits with the story from the lady. Not only that, but suddenly everybody's jumpy in the department. I've seen that before and it usually means something slimy's about to surface, maybe involving bad-apple cops."

"So what's new?" Jack taunted, watching for Machado to flinch.

A stain crossed the police officer's eyes, leaving them a darker hue. "What you say is true—too true for my tastes. I got no time for crooked cops. My father was one." His face reddened. "Besides, I've got a weird feeling about all this, that it's much bigger than even the murder. Don't ask me why. It's a gut thing."

He turned to Jimmy. "Anyway, I want to take you into custody to make sure you stay alive—and get some help from the FBI. With Bluestone dead, you're our only witness."

Jimmy's cheeks flushed and sweat started beading on his brow.

"I also need to know the truth about whether you took pictures that night. A set of negatives could break this case wide open."

"Is that what you *really* want?" Jimmy asked.

Machado turned to the two old men. "Listen, now that Jimmy's been down to the station—twice—he's marked. The bad guys will assume he's going to try to get off the island—and take his pictures with him. If they decide to go for Jimmy, trust me, they'll get him."

"You're talking about the Hui," Jack said.

Machado lowered his voice. "A number of people can be connected to the missing man, and some of those connections lead to prominent people. You guys following me?"

They all nodded.

"If I'm right, this was no ordinary execution. That guy was made an example to scare the hell out of people inside *and outside* the Hui. If I have this figured right, even *I* oughta be nervous. You guys too."

"Then you know what it's all about?" Jack said.

"Not yet—and that's the truth. I have some ideas, but they won't be of any use unless we get Jimmy some protection."

They all looked at one another, each assessing his own feeling about the cop. Aka was the first to speak up, guided by his well-honed instincts—and because an owl had landed on a tree just before Machado showed up.

"I think you should let this man help you, Jimmy. I think you need FBI protection *now*, before you try to leave the islands."

Jack was still not sure. "How do we know we can even trust the FBI? There's plenty o' folks round here would say they're not clean either. Why, just last year—"

"I have a cousin," Kimo interrupted, "works as an agent in Honolulu." He turned to Aka. "Aunty Momi's son, Neil. I'm sure he's clean."

Aka nodded, and Jack laughed.

"You kanakas and your cousins. You've got one for every occasion."

"What's his name?" Machado asked.

"Neil Kaiko," Kimo said. "But let me talk to him first."

Machado nodded. "I'll arrange a private jet to transport Jimmy to Honolulu—and Kimo, you can be his protection on the way there."

"What do you say, Jimmy?" Captain Jack asked.

"I guess I'd rather trust Kimo and Officer Machado with my life than hope the Hui won't catch up with me."

Machado got up from his chair. "Good. I'll make all the arrangements from the Pahoa station and be back in an hour to personally protect our witness. Kimo, I'd like you to stay the night too."

Kimo nodded.

"That leaves only more question, Jimmy. What about the pictures?"

Jack squeezed Jimmy's arm. "M'boy, I guess you oughta level with 'im."

Jimmy got up, walked to Aka's old pickup, and returned with the roll of film. He handed it to Machado.

The officer shook his head. "Haven't seen one of these in a while. Captain Jack said you were old-fashioned when it comes to photography."

"I don't know how much I caught that night—I was too scared to remember and I'd never taken pictures by the light of molten lava—but here's whatever I got." The officer tore a page out of his notebook and scribbled a detailed receipt, then signed it. He also had Kimo and Jack sign as witnesses.

"Keep this in a safe place," he said, handing the receipt to Jimmy, "just in case something happens to me."

They all got chicken skin with that comment—including Machado.

54 ∫ The Force of Will

AN HOUR BEFORE MIDNIGHT AT THE RESORT . . .

Cyrus Bond, Conway's young resort manager, sat down across from Robert Conway on the vast unpeopled lanai of the Golden Coconut Saloon. "We're almost ready for tomorrow," he said, loosening his tie.

It's a miracle, Conway thought, considering everything that had happened that day. First, he'd had to shake off the two fishermen and their sour allegations. He'd quizzed his staff to put to rest the Hawaiians' various claims about the resort's employee policies and land use, but all were corroborated. Bond defended the resort's hiring practices and the rules limiting local workers' contact with customers. The public relations manager explained how "some of the archaeology and brackish ponds had to be removed" to make way for golf courses, the Hawaiian Village Suites, and an overflow parking lot. And the lawyer verified that there *were* title problems with some Kiholo parcels due to recent claims made by "local natives," but he assured Conway that "with our judicial connections," those titles should be "cleaned up in no time."

Agitated, Conway had retreated to his suite to compose his grand opening speech—and try to repolish the resort's image in his own mind. Yellow legal pad in hand, he settled into a lanai chair overlooking the pools, but his words on paper were flat and redundant.

At 1:05 p.m., Cyrus Bond had phoned to tell Conway about the Civil Defense alert that an imminent Hualalai eruption was possible. That news caused a deep quaking inside his body. "Call the Civil Defense director and find out whether he thinks this will affect our grand opening plans," he had insisted, his hand shaking as he held the phone. Mike Takahashi was in the field and couldn't be reached for two hours, but an assistant advised that in the meantime evacuation plans should be readied "just in case." Within half an hour of the eruption bulletin, phone calls came in from two Big Island investors. Conway assured them he was in touch with Civil Defense and that the information given him so far did not merit alarm. Conway knew that when the eruption scare reached the mainland and Japan, shaky investors there would be harder to calm.

By two o'clock Conway had broken a personal rule he'd followed since his poverty-stricken days on the North Shore—never drink before four in the afternoon. It was only a beer, but it represented yet another way in which his personal control seemed to be slipping away.

He thought back to earlier times when events had overwhelmed his plans—getting dismasted in a hurricane off the Mexican coast, and being wiped out financially by his ill-timed geothermal venture. In both cases, he'd survived by force of will. Conway made a vow—to ride out the waves of trouble now pummeling his resort and to do it with strength and dignity. His pride demanded it. His dream depended on it.

Later that afternoon, as the last decorations were hung and all but the final food preparations were complete, Conway had begun feeling the potent effect of his vow as he gazed down on his magnificent lobby from the balcony of the Java Jazz Espresso Bar. He'd beaten the odds before and he would do it again.

No sooner had his commitment solidified than Lankowski called. Conway decided to use the encounter as an opportunity to further steel himself, and by the time he'd reached the lobby office phone he was more than ready, convinced that in adversity he could outmatch *anyone*.

"What's on your mind, Andy?" he had said cheerily.

Lankowski was taken aback. "Haven't you heard the news about Hualalai?"

"Oh yes, the one o'clock bulletin. Not entirely a surprise, given what the scientists have been saying. Could provide a spectacular show for the grand opening."

"But—"

"Of course, we're taking every precaution in case the lava flows reach this far."

"Bob, the governor's office has already received several calls from investors—"

"Me too," Conway interrupted. "I told them not to panic until we had some solid reason to do so. You agree, don't you?"

"But an eruption—"

"Don't tell me the governor's losing his cool over this," Conway said. "After all, you guys warned us this might happen."

Conway could hear Lankowski fumbling for a cigarette. "Bob, have you talked to—"

"Civil Defense? Yes. In fact, Mike Takahashi and I will confer within the hour." A slight exaggeration.

"Yeah?"

"Anything else, Andy? As you can imagine, I'm very busy right now."

"Uh, only that Calvin's decided to attend the grand opening, to make the speech."

"I'd have hated him to miss it. It's such a great opportunity for a politician."

"Yeah. Yeah. That's right."

"Thanks for calling, Andy," he said, hanging up before Lankowski could say another word.

Conway laughed quietly to himself. "I bet the weasel was so thrown off he didn't even light his cigarette."

Conway's final walk through the resort with Cyrus Bond had further buoyed his spirit. Now, gazing across the lanai of the Golden Coconut Saloon, Conway finally began to relax. He raised his gin and tonic. "You've done a great job, Cyrus, you and your whole staff. The place looks fabulous!"

Bond raised his glass of Dewar's. "Thank you, sir. It's been a pleasure—mostly." They both laughed, keenly aware that they were still far from out of the woods.

A sliver of moon struggled to shine through the swelling bank of clouds rushing in from the southwest. The energy in the air reminded Conway of the open sea.

"Storm coming," he commented, sipping the last of his drink.

"Maybe it'll clear by tomorrow," Bond said.

Conway watched the clouds swallow up the moon.

"Unlikely, but that's OK. We'll get a chance to show off those fancy canopies we had sewn for just this kind of weather." Bond marveled at the man's ability to look on the bright side, even in the midst of such deep trouble.

"Well, I'm heading upstairs," Conway said, stretching his arms outward with a yawn. "Big day tomorrow."

Bond drank the last of his cocktail and prepared to stand. "Morning meeting?"

"Yes. Have everyone gather at eight for a final briefing. Two hours later the fun begins." Conway rose from his chair and inhaled deeply. "Tomorrow will be a famous day," he said, smiling out to sea.

As Conway strolled across the lanai, waves of fatigue rushed over him, finally overwhelming the barriers guarding his public façade. Rising up out of those waves was a reef of anxiety, steaming with red lava that could well sink his ship. He shook his head and pushed past the carved Polynesian woman on the door of the Golden Coconut Saloon.

As he entered his suite, Conway thought of Mali'o, expecting that later she would join him in a private celebration on the eve of the big event. He set out two champagne glasses, then switched on the radio, a jazz program from Honolulu. A brief newscast at the top of the hour included the latest word on the eruption threat:

"Scientists breathed a cautious sigh of relief this evening when, for a second day since tremors were detected under Hualalai, the volcano remained quiet. But they urged the public not to get complacent, noting that little is understood about this Kona volcano. 'It wouldn't be the first false alarm in Hawai'i,' said a visiting geologist from Menlo Park, California."

Now in survival mode, Conway took everything moment to moment, and from that perspective the news could not have been better. Considering it a reward for maintaining his composure, he stepped out on the lanai to have another drink. He sat down at the glass table and tried to relax, but watching the sky thicken with clouds was tough duty. A rustle inside the suite broke Conway's meditation.

"It's just me," Mali'o hollered as she shut the front door.

Already? Conway glanced at his watch, startled it was after 1 a.m. He went inside. The possibility of companionship—probably even some lovemaking—immediately began dissolving his funk. Mali'o stood in the foyer, still in her stage clothes—tight silk blouse, black miniskirt, and four-inch heels. Her silver bracelets rattled softly as she slipped out of her dark stockings and draped them over a chair. She was such a welcome sight that Conway failed to notice the strain in her face.

"God, you're a stunning creature," he declared, moving toward her.

"I don't feel all that stunning tonight," she said, removing her earrings.

"Well, tomorrow's the big day!"

"Yeah," she said absently, walking past him. "The lobby looks real nice." She stopped at the hallway mirror and took off her pearl barrettes. Her beautiful hair tumbled down around her shoulders.

"I think we're finally ready," he said. "Now we're just waiting on the volcano."

"I don't believe that will happen," she scoffed. "I mean, if there was any real danger, wouldn't they have discouraged people from building over here?"

Conway shrugged, finally seeing her fatigue reflected in the mirror. "Tough gig?"

"The audience seemed satisfied enough." She unfastened her necklace. "But I was preoccupied."

He stepped close to her, aware of her scent, a mix of perfume and perspiration. "I'll bet you sang your heart out."

She shrugged.

Conway grasped her slender waist and kissed the base of her neck. "I like the way you sing for me."

"I'm not in the mood right now." Mali'o tried to pull away, but Conway, his passions rising, began unbuttoning her blouse.

"Bob, please . . ."

He eased the silk off her shoulders. "Yes, baby?"

"Bob, I really can't do this."

"But this is the eve of the grand opening," he urged, reaching to unhook her brassiere. "I wanted to celebrate."

"No!" she cried, pulling free of his arms. She yanked the blouse back up over her shoulders.

"But why?"

"I just want to know what happened to Kalama."

"Who's Kalama?"

"My cousin," Mali'o replied, "Kalama Ho'eha'eha." She dropped into the snow-white couch and started to cry.

Conway sat down beside her, wondering why the name seemed vaguely familiar. "Do I know him?"

"No, you two never met." Another gush of tears.

"What's happened?"

Mali'o tried to focus on Conway, but he was just a blur through her damp grief. She dabbed her eyes with the cuffs of her blouse. "Kalama's missing, for two weeks now. The family was told he was working on O'ahu. But my aunty finally got suspicious, and they asked me, 'the sophisticated one,' to talk to the police. I did, this morning. They think he's dead."

"Good God, how?"

Her eyes suddenly cleared, gleaming back at him like polished gems. "He crossed the Hui," lips trembling on the words.

A chill ran up Conway's spine, followed by a wave of recognition. Fragments of a memory filtered into his mind like grains of sand slowly filling a gap between stones. He remembered a high-rise apartment in Waikiki about two weeks back, crowded with stylish people, some of the old Nisei crowd and businessmen from Tokyo and the mainland, everybody with a checkbook open and an accountant on the phone. They had youngish wives or girlfriends in tow, with jeweled chains around their throats, and chauffeurs on the street guarding Jaguars, BMWs, and Cadillac SUVs. Lankowski, he was there too, saying something about a guy named Kalama Ho'eha'eha, the difficult pronunciation clucking awkwardly off Lankowski's tongue. What was Mali'o's cousin doing in this picture? Conway searched his memory without success.

"Unusual name," he muttered.

"It means 'heartbroken,'" Mali'o replied, struggling against another wave of tears.

Conway got up and walked to his immense window overlooking Kiholo Bay, but all he could see in the now rain-speckled glass was the blurred reflection of his dark beauty weeping on the couch.

"What else did the police say?"

"That Kalama may have been murdered to keep him quiet."

A knot of anxiety twisted Conway's gut as more images from the party trickled into his mind. Lankowski's rodent face loomed large in Conway's memory, his pallid skin flushed with alcohol and sweat from an active evening of hustling the crowd for his boss. He had looked beat, having just helped Governor Kamali'i dodge yet another kickback scandal, this time about some Convention Center contracts. He was many cigarettes into the evening and enjoying the open bar a little more than usual. Gripping Conway's shoulder, he had cocked his head toward a Hui man planted in the corner.

"Haku Kane never misses a beat," he'd muttered, knowing how much Conway loathed his own unwanted connection to the underworld. "Eyes and ears everywhere." Lankowski sighed. "They're especially jumpy right now, I guess 'cause someone on the inside's been spilling beans—a Big Island guy named Ho'eha'eha. Could affect your resort, Bob," Lankowski said with subtle glee. "Haku thinks he can control the activists in his ranks, but he's wrong, not unless he shows some real force *soon*. You watch. It won't be long before he makes an example of someone . . ."

Conway turned from the glass and walked back to sit with his lover. "Why do the police think the Hui murdered your cousin?"

"Because he was trying to get out, like any number of Hawaiians snared when they were young. Officer Machado thinks they made an example out of him, to keep the rest of the clan in line."

Almost the exact words as Lankowski's. Conway began to sweat.

"Why would they choose *him*?"

Mali'o peered into Conway's stormy face, searching for the right words, an explanation Conway could absorb.

"Kalama was sick of all the changes in the islands and tired of feeling exploited by the Hui, so he got involved with Kapu Hawai'i."

Mali'o frowned. "He was an idealist about everything—probably this sovereignty stuff too. Full of dreams he could never achieve." Fat tears fell onto her blouse, staining the white silk with blue-black drops of mascara.

"Of course, I had to brag to him about your damn resort, your big-shot friends, and, stupid me, your plans for the casino." Mali'o held her hand to her mouth, trying to avert the convulsion that came anyway. "I . . . I . . ." She struggled to regain her voice. "I didn't realize he was collecting information to use against the Hui, that he would try to report all that to Kapu Hawai'i."

"Good God!" Conway grabbed her arms and pulled her forward. "Where did you hear this!"

"Officer Machado and I figured it out," she said, trying to tug free.

Raw anxiety shot through Conway's body, and his fingers tightened their grip.

"You're hurting me!" Mali'o screamed, leaning away from him.

Understanding surged into Conway's mind, washing away a wall of denial he'd so long maintained. His grip slackened, and Mali'o pulled away. They sat on the sofa, mute, absorbing the revelation that Mali'o's cousin had probably been murdered to protect Conway's resort.

"Mali'o, you must believe me, I didn't know anything about this."

She nodded. "I know, Bob. I know." She reached over to touch his face and noticed tears forming in his eyes. "In some ways, you are as naive as Kalama."

Conway got up and shuffled to the bar at the back of the suite. He tossed some ice cubes into a glass and drenched them with bourbon. Cocktail in hand, he opened the glass door leading outside. A cold damp wind poured in. Conway placed one foot on the lanai, then turned to face Mali'o.

"Why would anyone risk death to oppose the building of another hotel?"

Mali'o shook her head. "You're not building just another hotel, Bob. You're planning to transform this island into another Las Vegas. Kalama must have believed exposing that was worth the risk."

Conway shook his head, amazed at how little he understood the islanders.

"Bob, you of all people should know that a determined person will chance even danger if he thinks the goal is worthwhile."

Conway, jaw clenching, nodded.

55 The Dead, Reckoning

SATURDAY, JUNE 17, AT 1:30 A.M. ON KOHALA . . .

Haku Kane, wide awake beside his sleeping wife, peered into the darkness. The bedroom was sweltering, the sheets soaked with sweat, even though the rest of the mansion was cold. Rain pounded the metal roof and thunder rumbled over Waipio Valley. Images from his dream rushed back into his mind, and his left eye twitched so agitatedly that he had to shut the eye to still it. Kane had heard of dreams like that but had never experienced one. So terrifying was the spectacle that at first he wondered if some kahuna ʻanaʻana had conveyed the pictures into his mind to drive him mad. If so, he could do something about that—identify the evil sorcerer and put an end to it. But he was powerless against those who had just entered his dreams—his own ancestors, come to reproach him.

They had sailed into his subconscious in five Polynesian canoes. Guiding the flotilla was a gigantic mano, Kamohoaliʻi, Pele's brother in his shark form. Kane immediately recognized many of the boats' occupants, because his mother had recited his genealogy to him, admonishing that one day he would need that information. That day had come. There were his parents and grandparents, his uncles and aunts, even his great-grandfather. He deduced the identity of the others from the positions they held on the boats, ancient progenitors of his Kohala clan of fishermen and cowboys. His great-grandfather, an imposing man with an immense white beard and shark tooth tattoos on both arms, stood in the bow of the lead canoe, pointing an accusatory finger at the Hui chief.

"Your ancestors are upset, Haku."

"Why?" the descendant replied. "I have prayed to you."

"Yes, you called upon us every time you were in trouble but ignored our counsel when it conflicted with your desires. Or perhaps your head is so full of yourself that you can no longer hear."

Kane bristled. "What is your complaint?"

"You began as a warrior, in your own way fighting for the dignity of Hawaiians, but now you are nothing but a common criminal, who—with the haole—has betrayed the 'aina and harmed its people. You shame your ancestors."

Some of the women began to *ue*—sob uncontrollably—a lament for the family's disgrace. One was Kane's mother. And at that moment, the line between watching the dream and being inside it dissolved, and the safety of his slumber disappeared. Kane would later tell his wife that he was wide awake for the worst of their assault. The canoes vanished, and suddenly his ancestors crowded the bed, wagging their fingers or throwing up their hands, so upset that one long-dead uncle threatened to pummel him with his fists if he did not "open his ears." His mother's face popped into view right in front of his own, her cheeks moist with tears.

"Auwe! Auwe! The gods work in mysterious ways. Your father and I were taken from the physical world when you were a young man still in need of guidance. Oh, when did you take the wrong turn?"

"Mama—"

Tears welled up in her enormous eyes. "You put on the airs of a god, yet your life is filled with acts of evil. What happened to the aloha for which our family was known?"

"It thrives inside MY family," Kane replied forcefully.

"What about OUR family?" said one of the women, pushing her face so close that he could taste her sour breath. He tried to turn away, but her withered face followed. "What of the children of Hawai'i? *All* the children?"

"All? I care only for those of our own blood, not the foreigners who have taken almost everything—"

"—your allies," said his great-grandfather, his whiskered face now looming above.

"—your friends," added his mother from somewhere behind the older man.

"This is a mockery," Kane declared. "I hate the haole and his Asian subordinates! What I do, I do for Hawaiians!" He thumped his fist against his chest.

The kind face of his favorite grandmother appeared to his left. Seeing her again seemed to lighten the spiritual darkness around him. "Do you not know, child," she said, "that eons ago, our people came from that stock too, that our veins run rich with the blood of the yellow and the white? That we are all related?"

Kane had always refused to accept the genetic evidence of the early Caucasoid and Oriental linkages to the Polynesians, insisting that whatever relations he held with them derived from money, not blood. But, overwhelmed by the appearance of his ancestors, he said nothing.

"Good," said his great-grandfather, "just listen and consider these truths."

Then came the odor of sulfur, followed by an orange glow that flooded the room. Out of this radiance emerged a hot red flame bearing the distinct features of the volcano goddess. Sweat streamed from Kane's whole body, and his slumbering wife stirred beside him. Pele looked old, her face worn from countless battles and years of perpetual vigilance, yet her iridescence was irresistible, and Kane sat up in the bed.

"You murdered our brother, Kalama Hoʻehaʻeha," she accused. "You have made me a party to an unjust deed—violated my kuleana. The volcano is my domain and responsibility. Her voice sharpened, and new waves of heat blistered the paint on the walls. "You, Haku Kane, have maligned both of us and brought evil upon our beloved people. You shall pay for this!"

The crime boss cowered, covering his face against the blinding heat.

"I have accepted Kalama into my family of fire," Pele pronounced, "and he resides, at *my* behest, on the slopes of Hualalai!"

Like a flame extinguished by a sudden wind, Pele dissolved into darkness, and all of his ancestors vanished, leaving Kane alone in the sullen darkness. A chill passed across his bed that made him think of the damp crypt where lay his mother's bones. He retreated under the sweaty sheets, shivering. For many minutes Kane stared into the darkness, as if expecting them to return. Eventually he fell asleep, exhausted by the encounter. But there was little peace in his retreat. Another shocking dream—even more terrifying than the first—reeled across his subconscious:

He moves through the mansion's spacious rooms, gathering up his two daughters and three sons. Then, as his puzzled wife looks on, he leads them onto the huge lanai overlooking the back of Waipio Valley. Waterfalls flank the view, tumbling over the mossy cliffs to the stream a thousand feet below. One by one, Kane leads his children to a freshly sawed opening in the railing. Unsuspecting of their father and spellbound by the view, they fail to resist his powerful grasp. In rapid succession he pushes each one over the cliff and watches their bodies disappear into the misty canyon. When the last child, his little five-year-old girl, is gone from view, Kane turns to his astonished wife, who has just stepped onto the lanai, her face frozen in disbelief. All that remains of her children are footprints in the fresh sawdust.

Out of sheer force of will, Kane shook himself into consciousness, only to be confronted again with the troubled face of his wife.

"Haku, you shoved me off the bed and started shouting."

Kane rubbed his face, relieved that the ordeal was finally over but hesitant to relive it by telling his wife. Yet he had always relied on Leilani for advice, and so recounted some of what he had seen. Leilani knew exactly what to do—call in her husband's personal kahuna.

56 ∫ Help from the Evil Sorcerer

Keawe Kanuha arrived at Haku Kane's mansion at six o'clock Saturday morning, after driving forty miles through the storm from Kona. The guards waved the small dark-skinned man through. They weren't sure what role Kanuha played in their boss's world, but they knew it must be important. He had unlimited access to Haku Kane, and no one else was allowed to display such gruff audacity with the underworld chief. His age was also a mystery, in part because of the two-toned coloration of his hair—snow white on top with a jet-black beard containing a single jag of silver at the corner of his mouth. His boyish face was smooth and shiny, yet heavy purple bags sagged beneath his eyes. As usual, he wore a knit golfing shirt, inside which hung a talisman of human bone, an image of Ku, the war god.

Kanuha slammed the door of his Buick Park Avenue, cussing the rain and the early hour, and stood for a moment on the mansion's sprawling lanai. Wood smoke scented the wet jungle, but it was not the only odor the kahuna noticed among the lush ferns and 'ohi'a. The stench of evil spirits could not elude the discerning nose of Keawe Kanuha. He flashed a challenging smile and bounded up the steps. One of Kane's bodyguards greeted the kahuna with the customary half bow of the head (as instructed by Kane), then escorted him into the hallway.

Kane's wife waited in the crime chief's den. She was small and muscular, that morning in designer jeans and a sweater. Although younger than her husband—in her late forties—her face carried the stress lines of an older woman. She smoked anxiously, the room hazy with nicotine fume.

"Good morning, Leilani," Kanuha said, striding in. She wrapped her arms around his compact shoulders and kissed him on the cheek.

"Aloha, Keawe. Haku is really upset. In all our years together, I've never seen him this way. I knew we would need a religious man." She motioned toward the sofa in front of the crackling fireplace. Kanuha plopped into one corner of the leather couch and Leilani sat in the other.

"Tell me everything," he said,

"Haku is convinced he was visited last night by his ancestors, including Pele."

Kanuha was suddenly wary. He'd occasionally been called upon to conduct dark sorcery against Haku Kane's adversaries, most recently the activist Wailani Henderson and the old Ka'u rancher, Uncle Sonny Kiakahi. He'd even responded to visitations from spirits. But he had never dealt directly with Pele.

Keawe Kanuha had first become a part of the Hui's innermost circle when, after one of his dreams, he alerted Kane to an FBI sting that came the closest ever to snaring him. Before that, Kanuha was known for killing a man in cold blood and going to Halawa Prison for it. Kane realized that a man with both abilities could be very useful to him.

"He saw Pele?" Kanuha asked skeptically.

Leilani drew heavily on her cigarette. "Haku says she spoke to him."

"Hmmm," he frowned. "Many people mistake—"

Leilani grasped his arm. "She was here, Keawe. The paint on our bedroom wall is peeled from her heat."

"Show me."

Leilani marched him into the bedroom and pointed at the paint blisters near the bed. They looked similar to damage done when tropical moisture penetrates walls, but the trace of sulfur in the air was unmistakable. Kanuha stared into Leilani's face and gently fingered the silver vein of his beard. For the first time in many years, he wondered whether he might be in over his head.

She escorted him to their private breakfast room, a nook at the end of a glass hallway surrounded by jungle. Heavy rain pummeled the roof, and thunder rumbled through the dark forest, occasionally rattling the floor-to-ceiling windows. Haku Kane was hunched over his breakfast at the head of the table, staring into the forest. One hand held a biscuit, and the other a knife, from which a small lump of butter had slid off onto the mauve tablecloth.

"Haku," Leilani said. "Keawe is here."

Her husband's trance remained unbroken, his face peering into the trees.

"Haku," Kanuha said, walking over to his patron. The kahuna placed his hand on Kane's shoulder. "Haku!"

The Hui chief slowly turned his head and gazed up at the bearded man. Kane's face, typically beaming with energy, was pale, and his mouth was pulled inward as though holding something too bitter to swallow. He uttered no words and made no sign that he recognized the two people who had just entered the room. His only response was to resume the task he had begun ten minutes earlier—buttering his biscuit. And even that he did absently, without realizing that the lump of butter had long since fallen off the tip of his knife. Kanuha released his grip and glanced over at Leilani, who shook her head.

The cook arrived with their plates of food and they sat down on either side of Kane. He consumed his breakfast mechanically, his mind still digesting the dream. As they ate, Leilani grew more agitated and, between bites, puffed a cigarette she kept lit in the ashtray near her plate.

Kanuha poured himself a cup of coffee, then freshened the one in front of his boss. "Tell me what happened," he said gently.

Kane, his expression indifferent, shook his head.

"Please, Haku. I cannot help if you—"

"I don't need your help," he replied.

Shocked, the kahuna said sternly, "Listen to me, Haku! You must tell me what happened this morning!"

Kane shook his head again, firmly, at last showing his usual obstinacy.

"Keawe has driven all the way up here from Kona," Leilani protested. "You agreed that I should call him. Well, here he is."

"I've changed my mind," he growled, still gazing into the jungle.

Kanuha motioned for her to join him a short distance down the glass hallway. There, the two spoke, watching Kane finish his breakfast.

"He's mad!" Leilani declared. "Could he be under some kind of spell?"

"It's possible, but I cannot say until I know in detail what occurred last night."

She recited everything her husband had told her, but it was only a portion of what had actually happened. Kane had not recounted the dream in which he sacrificed their own children to the valley. He'd also failed to mention that Pele had accepted Kalama Ho'eha'eha into her family, that Kalama was now poised to avenge his own murder with volcanic power. Even so, when Kanuha heard about Pele's reprimand, his face grew as ashen as the bolt of silver in his beard.

"Leilani, I believe your husband was in fact visited by his ancestors, including Pele, and that they're angry."

Leilani had feared as much, but hearing the kahuna confirm it awakened her suppressed ambivalence about such things. Ostensibly Christian and urbane, Leilani found it difficult to accept the idea that sentient spirits had come into her bedroom to denounce her husband.

"It means we must pray," Kanuha declared.

"Pray?"

"We cannot change their minds, but we can say we're sorry."

That idea was even more difficult for her. Leilani had long ago rationalized the victims of her husband's business—thousands of girls and young women enslaved through prostitution and pornography; countless souls hooked on heroin, cocaine, and ice; Hui members terrorized for disloyalty; and innocents murdered to maintain secrecy—journalists, politicians, and police who disappeared without a trace. Those rationalizations may have taken a toll on her lungs and her once-youthful face, but Haku Kane had provided Leilani with wealth and social prominence, and a semblance of respectability among the haole and Asian American leaders of Hawai'i. Leilani was *recognized*. She was the wife of one of the most powerful Hawaiians of our time. Apologize? Ridiculous!

As Kanuha guided her back to the breakfast room, lightning split a giant ʻohiʻa tree next to the mansion—and startled a yelp out of Leilani. The crack of thunder shook the whole building, and ʻohiʻa splinters pelted the glass hallway. The jungle lit up with eerie illumination, and Kanuha glimpsed five shadowy figures among the giant ferns, the same evil spirits he had smelled earlier. Goose bumps erupted on his arms.

Kane rose from the table when Kanuha and Leilani walked back into the room.

"Haku," Kanuha said, placing himself between the Hui chief and the door, "I think I know what's going on."

"So do I."

"Sit down and let's talk about this."

"I don't have time."

"Why?" said the unnerved Leilani. "Where are you going?"

"To the stable, to saddle up."

"What! It's pouring out there." Just then a gust of wind pitched a limb against the glass, cracking it. "It's a goddamn thunderstorm!"

But Kane's eyes were wide open now, the one susceptible to twitching calm for the first time in hours. Kanuha saw in Kane's face the same resolve he had observed whenever Kane was called upon to act. Kane had regained some vision of what was required of him, and the kahuna knew it was now out of his hands.

"I'm going to ride down into Waipio," Kane declared, walking away.

"Are you crazy?" Leilani hollered after him. "What about the storm? What about the grand opening? What about the casino? What about—?"

"It doesn't matter," he said, his voice disappearing down the rain-pummeled hall.

Leilani dropped into one of the chairs and lit another cigarette. She glared at the kahuna. "He's gone overboard, and I want to know what you're going to do about it!"

"There's nothing I can do. He's gone to be with his ancestors."

57 ∫ *Message from the Snow Goddess*

THAT SAME SATURDAY MORNING AT 3:33 A.M. . . .

The chill came suddenly, a spirit wind seeping through the cracked planking of Aunty Keala's coffee shack. It was definitely a mountain zephyr—and not from Hualalai. The wise old kahuna stirred in her bed, emerging from a dream that had taken her up the slopes of Mauna Kea. She opened her eyes and probed the room's darkness, but there was nothing unusual in the shadows. The chill settled into her back like a brace of ice, but she felt aloha in the cold, an urgent call from the snow goddess Poli'ahu.

Somehow Aunty Keala knew this would not be one of their regular encounters, and she set about meditating on why, with all that was happening, this luminous deity so close to the heavens on Mauna Kea beckoned her now. She knew that when clouds shrouded the mountaintops, the gods were concealing themselves from the islanders below.

"What are they up to?" she muttered, uneasy.

58 ∫ The Mysterious Blur

THAT SAME MORNING AT 5 A.M. IN HILO . . .

"You owe me, Machado—big time," the slender Chinese American said, unlocking the darkroom as he glanced back down the narrow hallway, his round spectacles catching the light of a security lamp. "If the newspaper finds out, I'm in deep *kim chee*."

"Relax, Ray," the police officer replied. "Nobody gets here Saturday morning before eight."

"How would you know that?"

"Cops know everyone's routine in a city the size of Hilo—when the first batch of doughnuts comes out of Lanky's pot, who arrives late every day at the County Building, and what time Mrs. Suzuki's male friend visits after her husband goes to work."

Ray Ho's oval eyes flashed mischievously. "Which Mrs. Suzuki? Up on Haili Street?"

"C'mon, let's get that film developed so we can get out of here."

"We should have done this last night," Ho said, stepping into the darkroom.

"I know, but I was busy." Machado had spent all night guarding Jimmy at Captain Jack's, and only a half hour earlier he'd put the young man and Kimo on a charter plane to Honolulu to meet Kimo's FBI cousin. "Handle this carefully, Ray," Machado said, handing him the film canister. "We can't afford to lose the evidence I think it contains."

"And when will I find out the significance of my work?"

"Soon enough, but if these negatives show what I hope they do, you won't want anyone to know you're the one who turned them into pictures."

The little man held the roll of high-speed Fujicolor next to his face and flashed a crooked grin. "Mrs. Suzuki?"

Ray Ho had thirty years of developing experience, twenty in this stinky little darkroom next to the loading dock of the *Hilo Times*, where he worked as the paper's photographer. Machado chose Ho to do the covert job because even though he'd long been shooting digital pictures processed on the *Times'* computers, Ho would likely still have access to its old darkroom, maybe even used it now and then. Machado also knew that outside the newspaper, the bachelor photographer lived a solitary life, and that Ho would never reveal a clandestine favor done for the only Hilo High athlete who hadn't pushed his skinny face into the ball field dust or in some other way humiliated the nerdy kid when they were together in school.

Ho turned off the lights to load the film into a steel developing tank while Machado rocked on his heels next to the sink. A minute later Ho switched on the fluorescents. "I haven't used these chemicals in a year," he said, "for some exposed rolls I found in Mom's attic, but hopefully they'll still do the job." Machado grimaced. Ho then began the elaborate developing process, pouring chemicals into the tank while monitoring his timer. A few minutes later, he opened the tank and dropped its spool into a bath of running water.

"Have we got something?" Machado pressed.

"Doesn't seem to be much here," Ho replied, squinting at the last negatives on the reel, "but we'll look at them closely after they're washed." Machado paced the cramped darkroom until Ho finished the wash and held the damp negatives up to the light.

"What are these?" Ho asked, peeking over his fogged glasses.

"Lava at night."

"I guess that's why there's nothing much on them."

Machado commandeered the film. "Let me see!" The amber negatives were mostly clear—capturing the black of night—with only small highlights of boiling steam, lava, and fire.

"This is just tourist stuff!" Machado declared, slumping against the door.

Ho reclaimed the roll and continued his own perusal.

"Wait! Who are all these people standing around this fire?" Ho asked, squinting at the last few frames. "Looks like a luau or something."

"What!" Machado straightened up. "You can see that?"

Ho grabbed a magnifier from the enlargement table. "Kinda hard to look at these wet negs, but yeah, there's some people here. Hey, one guy's got a gun in his pants—"

"Let me see!" Machado leaned close to Ho and both men peered at the negative. Just then steps echoed outside the door, footfalls of at least two people.

"Uh-oh!" Ho whispered, killing the fluorescents. He flung open his drying cabinet and clipped the strip inside, then locked the darkroom door. The two sat silent in the dark.

Bang! Bang! Bang! Three fists against the door. "Machado! You in there takin' a crap or what?"

Hand on his gun, the policeman eased open the door.

"Me an' Aka's been waitin' out front for twenty minutes!" Captain Jack said. We seen yer big SUV in back, so we came in through the loading dock."

"Who are these guys!" Ray Ho asked, irked at having his old private domain violated.

"The men who gave me the film."

Ho eyed them suspiciously. "How did you find my darkroom?"

"Easy," Jack replied, pointing at the bumper sticker on the door:

Photographers do it in the dark—and they love multiple exposures.

"Time to move, guys," Ho said, eager to get the crowd of strangers out of his darkroom. "You'll have to wait in the staff lounge while I dry the film and make prints."

Machado pulled Ho aside. "Ray, please print anything that has people on it, even if they're dark or blurry."

"Sure." Ho dropped his voice. "Vince, what are these negatives, anyway?"

"If we're lucky, they're pictures of a murder."

Ho raised his eyebrows. "If there's anything on the negs, I'll pull it out of 'em. Meanwhile, leave me alone so we can get out of here before someone else—like my boss—shows up. "

Machado escorted the two men to the lounge, where they waited almost an hour.

"What's taking him so long?" Jack said, drumming his fingers on the Formica table. "Can't be that difficult to turn them negatives into pictures."

"You're right. Something must be wrong." Machado marched down the hallway and rapped on the darkroom door. "Ray!" he hollered. "Are you OK?"

The door opened slowly, revealing the photographer draped in a heavily stained lab coat, cradling a plastic tray of almost-dry color prints. "You're as antsy as my editor!" he complained, striding past the policeman to the lounge, where he placed the tray on the table. "These are good pictures," he announced. "Whoever shot these knew what he was doing."

The three men huddled over the table, amazed at the first print Ho pulled from the tray—six Hawaiians and a Filipino gathered in front of a glowing hole, their faces red in the light.

"Look how steady he held that old camera," Ho said, pointing at the crisp resolution on the towering Hawaiian in front. "Must have been at least a one-second exposure, but you can even see detail in the gun."

"That guy looks familiar," Machado said.

Aka nodded.

"You have a closer shot, Ray?"

Ho held up a portrait of the Hawaiian's mustached face. "He must have had a zoom."

"I think we just caught ourselves a very big fish," Machado announced. "That's Makaha Nuiloa, a prominent Hui operative, key man in their music operation."

"Mean bugga," Aka said, unconsciously stepping back.

"You know him?" Jack said.

"Everybody's heard of Makaha."

"Yep," Machado affirmed. "Originally from Maui. He's the one Haku Kane sends to fund-raisers, hearings, rallies, and the like—wherever a visible Hui presence is necessary to show influence or stir up fear. The feds tried to finger him once, but no one would testify."

With that, Ray Ho pulled out a third picture, a wider shot showing

Kalama Hoʻehaʻeha being shoved into the lava, embraced by a swirl of red fume. His falling body was blurred but the expression on his face was sharp—astonished eyes wide open, yet with no trace of terror, more like awe. The others were frozen in shock, except Makaha, whose face seethed with anger.

"No wonder Jimmy was half-crazed when he came to my place," said Jack. "Think o' the nerve it took to shoot them pictures."

"What was it all about, anyway?" Aka asked.

"To make an example of the victim," Machado answered.

"Who'd they want to impress?"

"That's a good question. Ray, let me see that first photo again." Machado examined each man's face with the magnifier. "Well, there's the victim," he said, pointing the glass at the man slumped between two others. "And those two guys holding him are my crooked cops, Mau and Lalama." He shook his head. "I'm not surprised."

"This Filipino with the machete, he's Makaha's sidekick. But who are these two?" Machado tapped the magnifier against the remaining figures—a young ponytailed Hawaiian with heavily tattooed arms and chest, and a white-haired man whose face was obliterated by his movement during the shot. The lieutenant studied the other photos. In each case only that man's face was blurred.

"Could he have known there was a photographer?" Ray Ho said.

"How could he?"

Aka stared at the blur. "Maybe he just sensed it."

"What's that around his neck?" Ho asked.

Machado again peered through the magnifier. "Looks like some sort of talisman."

59 ∫ Hawaiians Prepare for Battle

EIGHT O'CLOCK THE SAME MORNING . . .

Wailani Henderson gathered ti leaves for the day's protest from a roadside patch in front of the Holualoa Church. The heavy showers had paused for the moment, but the dark clouds rafting into Hualalai continued to build.

Her angry rival, ʻIolani Carvalho, didn't notice Wailani as he stepped out of a silver Buick into the crowd gathering on the damp lawn. She did not recognize the car's white-haired driver with the silver jag in his beard, the kahuna, Keawe Kanuha. But her gut twinged as if a centipede had bit her insides. She noticed his bone tiki of the war god Ku and was surprised to see such a portentous talisman worn outside his clothing, in full view of anyone.

The driver glanced over at Wailani, startled that she had seen him. He covered the tiki with his hand, slipped it inside his shirt, and drove away. She took a deep breath, recalling Aunty Keala's words at the hospital: "The spirit of evil cannot overwhelm one who knows she cannot be conquered. Aloha is your protection. Believe this." Wailani glanced back at the empty roadway, certain that ʻIolani and the man with the talisman had just returned from some dark ceremony.

"Makaʻala!" she warned herself. Eyes open! Evil forces had already claimed Uncle Sonny's life, the old cowboy having died that morning from stroke complications. But Wailani was all the more committed to carrying out Uncle Sonny's plan—to expose the real purpose of the Royal Paradise Bay and the corrupt cadre behind it.

She felt bolstered by her defeat of the evil spell placed upon her, but she was still physically drained from the gall bladder surgery two days earlier. During the recovery she had moved her bed onto her lanai so she could watch the sea and ready herself for the protest. She drank medicinal teas and ate taro, sweet potato, and reef fish caught by friends. Each morning she took a *hi'uwai*—a spiritual cleansing bath—in the sea to release any residual fear or anger that could damage her aloha or confuse her na'au.

That very morning at sunrise, Aunty Keala had led Wailani and a dozen other protest leaders in prayer, asking the gods and ancestors for guidance. They gathered in the rain at Mahai'ula Beach, the same strand of white sand where in 1801 King Kamehameha had disembarked to take his sacrifice of hair to Hualalai's craters. Naked to the elements, the group entered the pounding surf where each Hawaiian released whatever hostility had lodged in their soul from past fights and disappointments. Aunty Keala had instructed them to stay in the water until all anger had dissipated. For some, the hi'uwai took only minutes, for others it required a chilly half hour or more.

During the cleansing, a pod of spinner dolphins had entered the bay, twirling in the rising swells. Beyond the view of the bathers, but clearly visible to Aunty Keala above the beach, was a speck of dorsal fin on the horizon, the giant whale shark guarding the bay against wayward tiger sharks that might harm the praying Hawaiians. By the end of their water ritual, the love and power of the wise sea god Kanaloa had restored them, and the happy group milled about the beach—chatting, laughing, and munching breakfast until it was time to depart for the larger gathering at the church.

Watching 'Iolani Carvalho and his cohorts gather on the church steps made Wailani wish she had urged *all* the protesters—not just the leaders—to attend the early morning ceremonies. Although the crowd was generally upbeat, Wailani sensed a hostile undercurrent, emanating mostly from 'Iolani's supporters. She did not want to add to that negativity, but she knew that somehow she had to break the news that the "old boys" intended to make the Royal Paradise Bay Hawai'i's first gambling casino.

Dressed in a bright pareu, she strode into the church and up to the pulpit with a vigor that heartened those who had heard about her recent gallstone attack. Seeing her at all surprised ʻIolani, and a flash of confusion crossed his face.

"*Aloha kakou!*" she announced in greeting.

"Aloha!" replied the audience.

People packed into every pew and stood cheek to jowl against the walls, while others spilled out into the vestibule. Sprinkled among the generally youthful crowd were a number of elders—the women dressed smartly in long *muʻumuʻu* and the men in colorful aloha shirts, some elders wearing hats brimmed with leis. The children remained outside, playing on the wet lawn or putting final touches on placards they'd helped their parents prepare for the protest.

"Today we will carry a message to the governor about the disputed lands of Lapalapa Ranch on Hualalai," Wailani declared. "They have arrested our brothers and sisters, and they think we are defeated. But they are wrong! We are stronger and more encouraged than ever!"

"*Pono!*" someone cried out in support. Righteous!

"The developers and politicians do not want us camping on the ʻaina of our ancestors, so we will take our message to their latest, most profane outrage, the Royal Paradise Bay Resort, playground for the rich—

"Rich haoles!" shouted one of ʻIolani's lieutenants.

"—anchor for shopping centers and condominiums!" Wailani continued, unruffled.

"White men's retirement homes!" shouted another man standing next to ʻIolani.

"And," Wailani added, "—the future home of Hawaiʻi's first gambling casino."

The shocked crowd stirred in reaction.

"Not!"

"Doesn't surprise me."

"What next?"

"No wonder Hualalai is shaking!"

"Yes," Wailani resumed. "This next atrocity will lead Hawaiʻi into the world of blackjack, keno, and slot machines—run by the corrupt clan who already plays too big a role on our islands."

Many people clapped, but the indirect attack on the Hui made some listeners nervous, especially since some of its known operatives were in the crowd.

"And who do you suppose is behind this one?" she asked rhetorically, glancing over the faces riveted to the pulpit. "Robert Conway, of course. But there are others."

"Governor Calvin Kamali'i!" several people shouted.

Wailani smiled, her dark eyes gleaming. "How did you guess?"

"Our esteemed Big Island Congressman Yamashita?" somebody asked mockingly.

A man close to 'Iolani cupped his hands round his mouth and shouted: "You eat da coconut and da banana together, you git one bad case indigestion!" The crowd laughed uproariously.

"Yes, the governor and the congressman, but who else?" Wailani asked, leaning way out over the pulpit. "Who else is *always* there, the evil shadow lurking at the edges of the political machine, forcing even them to cower like the rest of us?"

A wave of recognition passed through the room, but no one dared say the name.

"Haku Kane!" she declared, her eyes blazing.

The crowd murmured with a hundred sideways glances.

"And are we surprised?" Wailani continued. "Haku Kane is so enamored with his power that he no longer walks among his Hawaiian brothers and sisters as he did years ago, before he bedded down with the business and political establishment. Now he sequesters himself in his grand fortress above Waipio Valley, counting American greenbacks he makes off the abused bodies of young women, the ravaged souls of addicts, and the questionable loyalties of the thugs, developers, and politicians he coerces to do his bidding!"

An almost inaudible but simultaneous inhalation swept the room.

"The fact that Haku Kane is a force behind the Royal Paradise Bay reveals just how much he has lost touch with the reality of our people, of whom he claims to be so proud. It is time to gather our courage and face *all* our adversaries in this struggle for the 'aina, be they white, yellow—*or brown!*"

At first, the audience remained silent. Everyone knew that to attack the Hui directly—especially its chief—was to put oneself and one's family at risk. Wailani knew this too, but she had come to the point idealistic leaders sometimes reach, where their hearts can no longer abide the self-censorship required to remain effective *and* safe.

"Pono!" shouted a very old woman in a woven *lauhala* hat with an heirloom feather band. Several people clapped, but most just glanced about the room for some Hui reaction. ʻIolani and his people got up from their seats and headed for the door.

"ʻIolani Carvalho," Wailani shouted after him, "don't leave before we honor one of our elders who planned to be here today—had he lived."

ʻIolani clenched his jaw and turned to face Wailani.

"Help us, ʻIolani, honor the man who planned to reveal the real reason that the lords of power want this resort. I ask everyone to stand in a moment of silence for Uncle Sonny Kiakahi."

ʻIolani's comrades watched him for a cue. Everyone else rose from their seats, their attention shifting back to Wailani. ʻIolani had no choice, but he knew his showdown with Wailani would come later that day. He raised his fist and declared: "To Uncle Sonny." His clique of confused supporters looked at the floor. Wailani smiled like a warrior astride a fallen adversary with spear set to his throat. She felt the presence of her ancestors, in fact was certain that the idea of calling after the departing ʻIolani had come from one of them.

"Uncle Sonny," she said quietly, bowing her head. The room went silent. During the last moments of the tribute, a fresh breeze blew in through the open windows, ruffling the hair of the people in the crowd, then issued out the door with such a distinct presence that the men in the vestibule turned to watch its departure toward the road.

Wailani looked up from the pulpit, her eyes shining with confidence and aloha. "Uncle Sonny loved Hawaiʻi, and in his own quiet way fought to defend the ʻaina—our homeland. He had no time for mean-spirited people, especially if they came from our own Hawaiian community." She glanced piercingly at ʻIolani. "No matter how dismayed he became, Uncle Sonny maintained his aloha, knowing that to yield to anger was to forfeit something basic in our Polynesian character. The last time

I spoke with him was right here, in this church, and he gave me this advice: 'Aloha is the strongest weapon against greed. Our adversaries have money and power, but they do not have aloha, the one thing that makes our people unique in the world.' "

"Maika'i no!" shouted one of the elders. Most fine!

"Maika'i!" shouted many others.

"This is a waste of time," 'Iolani muttered to his allies. "C'mon!" A dozen Hawaiians followed the young radical as he left the church. Several elders shook their heads, and one older man trailed the group outside to lecture them as they descended the stairs. Wailani ignored all this.

"So today we begin a battle for much more than the lands of our sacred island. We fight for the preservation of ourselves as Hawaiians. The international reporters and photographers coming to Kiholo today expect an extravagant party for the world's largest resort. But what they will actually witness is a celebration, not of Western opulence, but of Hawaiian sovereignty and determination. This is the opportunity to take our righteous struggle to a world court. Let's make the most of it!"

The crowd leaped up from the pews and cheered, and the church surged with a potent energy as if all the ancestors of the congregation had joined them. At that instant the earth shifted, knocking people back into the pews with a jolt that rocked the church and shattered three stained glass windows. With a wood-splitting moan, the old roof rose at three corners, and the pews creaked against their bolts on the floor. The quake hurled Wailani against the altar, while candles, cups, and other ceremonial items slid onto the ground.

A second jolt struck, and the enormous wooden crucifix broke free of the wall, crashing onto the pulpit. Those who had regained their feet flew headlong into the pews, and Wailani fell to the floor. Despite continuous ground vibrations, the children outside rushed up the steps to join their parents inside as a third jolt incited a mass exodus from the church.

Wailani dragged herself up onto the splintered pulpit and leaned forward over the fallen crucifix. "Everyone please calm down!" she shouted, but her words couldn't penetrate the panic, and the throng crammed against the exit.

Suddenly, the vibration ceased and people stopped in their tracks, waiting. Nothing came, and a nervous chatter rose from the crowd as they made their way down the steps to the lawn.

"Is everybody OK?" Wailani called out from the vestibule.

"Aunty Mildred's pretty shaken up. Keanu's taking her back home."

"Anybody else hurt?"

"Mostly cuts and bruises, Wailani," reported a man wiping blood from his wife's forehead.

"It felt so close," someone said.

"Hualalai," said another. Many nodded.

"The island churns," said an older man as lightning flashed inside the dark clouds gathering over the slope.

"Listen up!" shouted a hefty bearded man inside his red pickup parked on the lawn. "The radio's got a report!" He swung open both truck doors and turned up the volume. The crowd hushed, waiting for word from Mike Takahashi.

"This is your Hawai'i County Civil Defense. At 8:26 a.m., a major earthquake shook Kona, apparently . . . excuse me. Please stand by." The half minute of dead air could not mask the muffled argument audible in the background. When Takahashi returned, his usual calm voice was tense. "I repeat, a *significant* quake has struck Kona, *apparently* centered above the town of Kailua on Hualalai. We do not yet have an official confirmation from the Hawaiian Volcano Observatory, but eyewitness accounts in Kona indicate a maj—significant quake, perhaps between six point oh and six point five in magnitude."

The crowd on the lawn surged toward the truck.

"At least two major shocks have been reported, and shaking continued for at least one minute."

"Three quakes!" someone shouted.

"Seemed like five minutes to me!" said another.

"Some minor damage has been reported in Kailua, Waimea, and along the North Kona coast. There are scattered electrical outages in West Hawai'i, but so far they appear highly localized, due to fallen trees and power poles. Residents should remain vigilant because this seismic activity may be related to three smaller earthquake swarms on Hualalai earlier this week. Scientists at HVO said yesterday that an eruption of Hualalai is possible, and they are monitoring the situation closely."

A murmur passed through the crowd.

"Because Hualalai's last eruption occurred before we had scientific observation, the volcano's behavior is unpredictable. Scientists believe it is very possible—"

Strident background voices again pulled Takahashi from the mic.

"I know that!" he was heard to whisper. The Hawaiian inside the truck cranked up the volume, and although someone's hand had obviously covered Takahashi's mic, his disagreement with whoever was there could be heard over the air. "The public has a right—"

"They got trouble down there, yeah?" the Hawaiian said, lifting his eyebrows. The crowd nodded.

"Give me some basis—" Takahashi could be heard saying, but barely. The truck's owner leaned close to the door speaker and began relaying the argument. "Mike says that's shibai." Bull. "And he won't repeat it."

Everyone laughed, and half of them applauded.

"Now Mike says he doesn't give a damn whose office called, even if it was Yamashita!"

The Hawaiians cheered.

A loud thud came over the air, blasting the Hawaiian away from the speaker, then the creak of the microphone being adjusted. "I apologize for the interruption of this Civil Defense broadcast," said Takahashi, with an edge immediately recognized as anger. Muffled talk behind him showed that the argument was still under way. "We now have an HVO confirmation on the quake and a preliminary estimate of six-point-one magnitude. They think this may be a precursor to a volcanic eruption, that magma may have shot up into a subterranean dike, or storage area, inside the volcano, waiting for sufficient pressure to erupt. For this reason, I'm reissuing the volcano watch for the entire Kona coast, from Kailua town to coastal Waikoloa. Residents and visitors to this part of the island must begin preparing for the possibility of an evacuation . . ."

Everyone crowded even closer to the truck. Directly above the throng, noticed only by Wailani, sat an owl on the tallest ʻohiʻa limb in the yard.

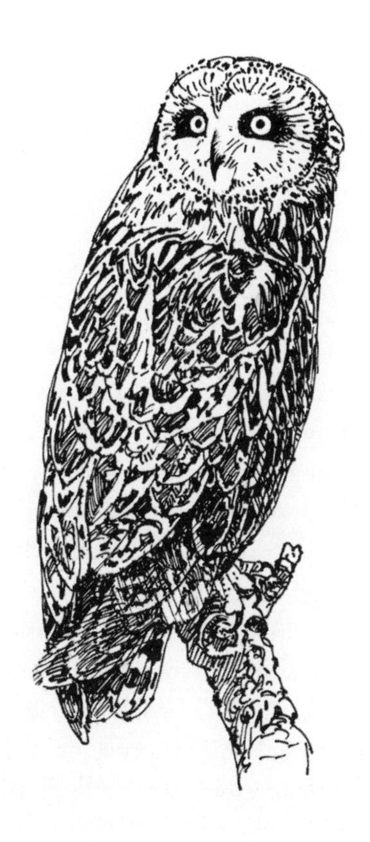

Directly above the throng, noticed only by Wailani,
sat an owl on the tallest ʻohiʻa limb in the yard.

60 ∫ "He Knows Everything . . ."

JUST AFTER 9 A.M. HIGH UP MAUNA KEA . . .

Dense clouds covered the entire island, with the astronomers' base camp right in the middle of them. The dining room was dark, its view of Mauna Loa obscured by fog and rain blowing against the windows. Thunder rattled the glass, and four feet of snow already blanketed Mauna Kea's summit.

Frustrated astronomers in sweaters chatted over coffee, several eyeing the beautiful Hawaiian woman eating breakfast with their colleague. Gavin, aware he had broken the rules by bringing a guest to the base camp after their visit to Aunty Keala, resisted the impulse to tell the other guys to "bugger off!" Instead, he pressed his leg against Maile's and recalled snuggling in his twin bed after their exhilarating high-altitude lovemaking. They were still sound asleep when Hualalai shook and did not realize what had awakened them until later, when they overheard the cooks at the serving line speculating that the quakes might be signs of a possible eruption. That also helped explain the jokey addition the road crew had made to their snow-closure message in the lobby:

8:45 a.m. Temperature on Mauna Kea: –2 degrees F.
Temperature on Hualalai—hot and getting hotter!

"We haven't had a storm like this in decades," Maile said as she and Gavin walked through the lobby to the front door. "It brings to mind the elders' stories of the icy tempest that struck the mountain in 1967, when they were carving up the summit for NASA's first big telescope."

"I may have no data when I get home, luv, but I'll have tales to tell—blizzards, earthquakes, murder, maybe even a new eruption!"

"And that's the least of it," Maile replied with a gleam in her eye.

His eyes met hers. "Yeah. That's the least of it."

If the drafty camp building was uncomfortable, going outside was downright miserable. Sheets of icy rain swept over the couple as they bolted for Maile's Jeep. The vehicle protested the cold at first but eventually fired up. They drove through three torrential downpours before turning onto the Saddle Road and heading for Kona.

Maile shivered, even after the heater began pushing warm air through the vents. Her tropical blouse and skirt for the grand opening just wasn't enough insulation. Gavin offered his sweater and Maile pulled over to make the exchange inside the vehicle. A lone pickup with two people inside sped past in the opposite direction. Maile turned to glimpse the silhouettes in the pickup's back window. "That was Aunty Keala! I'm sure of it! Watch. Aunty's going up the mountain."

Sure enough, the truck turned onto the observatory road.

"I'm surprised she didn't recognize your Jeep. Why didn't she stop?"

Maile turned to face her companion. "She doesn't want anyone to know what's she's doing."

Gavin's eyes glowed with curiosity. "Why? What's up there?"

Maile just smiled.

An hour later Gavin and Maile joined the line of cars entering the Royal Paradise Bay Resort. Kona winds rocked the huge bronze scepters flanking the drive, and the avenue of palms bent inland, their fronds rapidly shredding. Visibility was less than a quarter mile in the heavy rain, and mud from the fresh sod ran brown along the curb. Private security officers in bright yellow rain gear stood along the route, and manned police cars were parked throughout the jungle near the resort. Because of the volcano alert? the couple wondered. Or for the protest?

With the resort full of overnight guests and no evacuation orders yet from Civil Defense, Cyrus Bond had gotten Conway's swift approval to press on with the festivities. Despite the weather and the morning quakes, visitors thronged the lobby, and Gavin and Maile had to wait for a valet. A handsome young haole ran out to meet them, his sodden black slacks and purple aloha shirt stuck to his skin. "Good morning," he exclaimed with practiced cheer, oblivious to the irony. He leaped in as Gavin and Maile got out, and sped away through rivulets rushing down the pavement.

A pair of pretty island girls in bright pareus greeted the couple. "Aloha! Aloha!" the girls declared in unison, draping the couple with purple orchid leis. "Welcome to the island of Hawai'i!" Their greeting belied the general mood of the hotel staff, already weary from reassuring guests about the earthquakes and picking up numerous flower arrangements, artwork, and other things knocked over by the temblors.

The crowd was also subdued, despite the fanfare—hula dancers in the hallways, lei-draped staff greeting monorail passengers, and islanders playing 'ukulele on every sloop plying the artificial waterways. Music groups performed in lobbies and on lanais, including a big band, a jazz combo, a salsa dance troupe, two slack-key guitar ensembles, and a small orchestra playing Vivaldi, Mozart, and Brahms. Food-and-drink tables were everywhere, each adorned with ice sculptures, flowers, and servers sporting purple chef's hats and smocks.

Conway's birds, meant to add exotic sights and sounds to the celebration, were disoriented by the storm. Agitated parrots and parakeets flew back and forth among branches of the lobby's banyan. Drenched ducks, swans, and flamingoes shivered in gardens and pools while distraught peacocks incessantly called out in the rain.

Open-air hallways were shuttered against the storm, and colored rain canopies sheltered the immense lanais where the festivities took place. Muddy water puddled on the slick tile floors, and windblown blossoms and leaves littered the garden walkways. Rain poured through the lobby's atrium, overwhelming the roar of Conway's giant waterfall. A cool clamminess clung to the guests, making short work of elaborate hairdos and finely pressed suits and gowns.

A television crew videoed the crowd gathered at the falls while a skinny young reporter with too much lipstick rehearsed her lines behind a fern. A limousine of Japanese dignitaries strode into the lobby with the same self-confident air Americans had mastered decades earlier. Meanwhile, in the executive dining room off the Royal Ballroom—the King's Chamber—special guests and speakers had begun assembling for a private ten o'clock brunch. At eleven the larger ballroom party would begin with speeches by Robert Conway, Governor Calvin Kamali'i, and US Representative Harold Yamashita.

Gavin and Maile worked their way through the crowd to a vacant section of the lanai overlooking Conway's artificial pools. Kiholo Bay was blue-black under the darkening clouds, its surface churned with whitecaps. Conway's magnificent reproduction of the *Resolution* bobbed violently against moorings designed to withstand strong easterly trades, not this Kona gale from the southwest.

"This place is amazing," Gavin said, as a sleek train flew by on the monorail.

"*Disgusting* is the better word," Maile replied, appalled to see the fantasy she had viewed in drawings made real in concrete, steel, and glass.

"To think this was all just lava a couple years ago. I mean, Christ, it's like the palaces of Europe. The bastard's even got Cook's ship out on the bay! All me life I've admired the bloke who discovered Australia. I'd really like to tour that ship."

Maile was shocked at Gavin's reaction.

"You've got to admit, Maile, what Conway's done here *is* incredible. I mean, what a man can do if he's got heaps of money—"

"—and doesn't care what was here before he arrived. First Cook, then the missionaries, and now the Americans."

"Hey, Maile, don't forget about your Polynesian priest, Pa'ao. He showed up with his warriors and his kings and took over the whole bloody culture."

Maile gazed at the *Resolution* tugging its lashing. Why, she thought, are the destroyers of culture lauded as purveyors of progress and admired for their conquests? Why do the dreams of one culture seem always to destroy the destinies of others?

"Look, Maile, I agree with you a hundred percent about the losses, but—"

She looked at Gavin in disbelief. "It's just Disneyland. And there were important things here. Our heritage. Conway walked on the prayers of my people. He trampled the voices of our past, and in so doing threatens our future. Without those prayers and voices, native cultures like mine lose their way."

Gavin recognized the deep sorrow beneath Maile's anger, and he moved close to her. A huge tear collected in her eye, then collapsed onto her cheek. Gavin reached out to wipe it away, but she turned to face the raging sea.

"And I—who should have known better—contributed to this." She shook her head slowly, and her beautiful lips trembled. *"E kala mai ia'u."* I'm sorry.

Gavin cradled Maile in his arms. Her sad eyes gradually took on an expression of resolution. "This is no time for self-pity," she said softly, gently pulling out of Gavin's embrace. "Aunty Keala has given us a task. Let's finish it. And then I have something else to do before Hualalai erupts."

"The cave?"

She nodded, gazing at the waves, their hue now turned from cobalt to iron.

"Remember Aunty Keala's warning."

"She may be wrong about *this* one. Something in there is drawing me back."

"But is it good or evil?"

"I don't know yet," she replied, slowly turning to face the crowd behind them. "But I sense there's evil here, right now."

She peered into a line of people loading up plates from a food table decorated with huge bouquets of birds of paradise. Her eyes zeroed in on a Filipino man in an aloha shirt too big for his small frame. He gobbled a doughnut while loading up not one plate but two with pastries.

"See that man over there?" she said to Gavin. "Imagine him with a machete."

"Good God," he muttered, suddenly back at the skylight on Kilauea, "that was one of the . . ."

"Shhh!"

The man finished filling his plates, then strutted through the crowded lobby like a pirate loaded with treasure. He made his way to a plush purple couch in the middle of the room. Seated there were two Big Island politicians that Maile recognized—a state legislator and a county councilman—talking with someone in a tall wicker chair, its back facing Gavin and Maile. The Filipino approached with one of his plates extended, and a hand much bigger than the plate reached out to take it.

"I want to know who's sitting in that chair," Maile said, stepping forward, the feeling in her na'au acute. She moved through the crowd, searching for a better vantage point as Gavin followed. Maile positioned herself along the far wall and suddenly knew at least one reason Aunty Keala had asked her to attend the grand opening—to identify this man.

As Maile maneuvered around a knot of businessmen and their wives, a commotion developed near the front door. The crowd surged forward, and many people rose to their feet, including the man in the chair. He was tall, his head towering above the crowd. At that moment, the throng between him and the front door parted and the face of Governor Calvin Kamali'i popped into view. His bold native features stood out in the mostly white and Japanese crowd. At his side was his haole wife, Marsha. Applause broke out around the governor, and a TV cameraman flooded the mob in light. This caught everyone's attention, yet at that moment, inexplicably, the big man at the wicker chair turned to look over his shoulder. His dark eyes fixed on Maile's for reasons neither could comprehend, but the sensation Maile felt in her stomach made her nauseous.

This was the mustached man she and Gavin had spotted quarreling with the Filipino on the night of the murder. But the view in the well-lit hotel was much better than in the dim, fumy light of the eruption. She was almost sure he was the Hui figure Makaha Nuiloa. The giant Hawaiian received an effusive greeting from the governor as the politician passed through the crowd on his way to the private brunch in the King's Chamber.

A new round of applause issued from the front of the lobby, this time with the arrival of Congressman Harold Yamashita. Photographers' strobes flashed above the swarm, and a TV crew moved into position.

Yamashita ambled through the crowd at a studied pace, smiling, nodding, shaking hands, and exchanging a word or two with business and political associates along the route. He knew the drill well after all these years. Harold Yamashita had returned from combat with a generation of Nisei Japanese after World War II—the war against their parents' countrymen. A tall, muscular boy, he had lied about his age to get in on the action and was one of the few in his unit not wounded. Having proved their patriotism and being committed never again to sweat for white plantation managers, the Nisei set out to overthrow the political machine of the old plantation and shipping Goliaths of Hawai'i. With discipline and patience, they rose to power, including Hilo-born Yamashita. Before long, the young business graduate and real estate broker was a rising star in the new state's senate. The youngest but most patient of the Nisei bunch, Yamashita quietly waited for his big break, an appointment to the US House of Representatives after the death of the eldest Nisei. His charisma, razor-sharp mind, and ruthless moxie saw him rise to a position in Congress that rivaled that of any senator. Eventually, through deft patronage at home and tough politicking, he inherited the whole sprawling Hawai'i political machine, its linkages reaching into every major development project in the archipelago. Now nothing moved without his approval.

At the sight of the old congressman, Maile's feet took over, guiding her toward the throng clustered around him. Moments later, she stood so close to the current commander of the old-boys' regime that she detected the sweet scent of his cologne. It had been a decade since she had seen Yamashita in person, and she was shocked at what the years had done to his face. He looked like a man in an ancient Japanese *Noh* mask, his eyeballs recessed inside almond-shaped holes on a face whose flesh had turned to hide. Deep crevices marked the corners of his mouth, downward lines that belied all the public smiles. These were the lines found on old men after a lifetime of fretting and frowning, of carrying burdens beyond their psychological capacity. Had the eighty-five-year-old Nisei's ambition finally got the better of him? Or was this the destiny of politicians who spent most of their lives protecting the turf they'd so diligently acquired?

Yamashita, flanked by photographers, moved into the middle of the room, noticing the state legislator and the county councilman. He happily accepted their extended hands and greeted each by first name, but when his eyes landed on the big smiling face of Makaha Nuiloa, he withdrew his hand abruptly and veered away.

Makaha, surprised, glanced at his political cohorts for their reaction, but they were caught up in the fanfare of the congressman's mingle with the rich and powerful in the room. The politicians had not noticed the rebuke, but Maile did, and her naʻau processed its meaning instantly—Yamashita knows *everything.*

61 ∫ Obeying the Call

9:30 A.M. ON MAUNA KEA . . .

Had someone at the astronomers' base camp noticed Aunty Keala's old truck climbing the mountain road, they might have wondered why anyone in their right mind would drive up Mauna Kea in the middle of the tempest lashing the island. But the kahuna trusted the call she had received. She also believed that with help from her eldest son—a hunter intimate with the mountain roads—she could reach her sacred destination by noon, the most auspicious time for such spiritual encounters.

The paved road ended just above the base camp, and her son, Keone, shifted the pickup into four-wheel drive. Rain poured through the swirling fog, and blood-colored torrents saturated with ash streamed along the roadside. The second switchback was badly eroded, and water gushed against boulders that had rolled into the road. Fortunately the truck had oversize tires, and Keone bypassed the rocks by driving up the stony embankment. The next switchback was even worse, and Keone had to gun it through several deep ruts in the road. He glanced over at his mother, his face filled with concern.

"I have been called to the mountain," Aunty Keala said with confidence. "Don't worry. We'll make it."

After another mile the road all but disappeared, and the little pickup struggled through gully after gully, each overflowing with torrents pouring off nearby cinder cones. As they climbed higher, snowy slush whitened the landscape.

"What's this!" Keone peered past the sleet-encrusted wipers. An upper gate, 2,000 feet below the summit, had been pulled shut—and secured with a padlock.

Aunty Keala's heart dropped. "It can't be."

Keone leaped out into the ankle-deep slush and clumped over to the hefty lock. He yanked on it fruitlessly, then turned to flash his mother a doleful look.

"Can you cut it?" she hollered from the truck.

He shook his head. "Don't have the right tools."

Keone watched his mother push open the door against the snowy wind and slog to a steep overlook a short distance from the road. The barrage of wet snowflakes immediately soaked her shoulders, face, and hair. The kahuna gazed up at the riotous clouds, trying to decipher in them meanings beyond the logical realm. Nothing came. She turned to trudge back to the truck when a sudden change came over her. She cocked her head as if listening to a far-off sound, and the name "Makaha Nuiloa" formed in her mouth.

This message had come not from the clouds, but from Maile at the crowded grand opening. The kahuna closed her eyes and saw the gangster's mustached face peering over his broad shoulder.

"So it *was* the Hui after all," she muttered.

Another man loomed in the picture conveyed by Maile—Congressman Harold Yamashita, his mask-like face frowning.

"As I suspected." She shook her head in disgust, not only at the connivance of the politician who for years had conveniently turned a blind eye to the Hui, but also at her own complicity in accepting the many federal grants Yamashita had secured to fund her cultural programs. Others would say it was the least the congressman could have done for the Hawaiians in return for all the exploitation he and the other Nisei had funded through their pork barrel politics. But Aunty Keala had always felt uncomfortable accepting these crucial but tainted monies. She knew her own ancestors had to make similar compromises to survive the royal tyrannies of the Tahitians after *they* took over the islands. But now there would have to be an end to it, or the gods, also disgusted, would take more innocents.

"We have tried!" she called out into the sky, her tears already congealing on her cheeks. "With all our hearts—over many generations—we have tried!"

Lightning flashed inside the clouds and the thunder roared.

"You must give us more time to make things right!" she pleaded, but the sky only darkened.

Her son, standing before the locked gate, observed all this in silence. He had seen her this way before and dared not interrupt, but he worried how long she could withstand the snowy winds. Aunty Keala slowly turned toward the volcano's snowcapped summit. Dark, mottled clouds swirled about the upper cones in shapes she knew only too well, a parade of all the deities known to Hawaiians. All, that is, but one, the most powerful, whose name is so sacred it is never uttered in Polynesia.

"Now only you can help us," she said with great humility in words Keone was too far away to hear. With that, the trance broke, and the shivering kahuna trudged back to the pickup. Keone rushed to his mother's side and helped her into the truck.

"Did you get an answer?" he asked.

"Yes. We have to go higher," her face full of resolve.

"But, Mom, how—?"

"I know of a certain place on the northern slope that may be high enough. I'm told there once was a road—"

"Can you show me on the map?" he asked, pulling out a USGS topo from the glove box.

She hesitated a moment, wariness in her eyes, a look Keone never expected from his mother. She could trust her son with the sacred location, but he could never go with her to the place. Even Keone, with his indisputable strengths, would be overwhelmed.

She placed her hand on his. "This place I must go is so kapu that even I—with the training and the blood—may perish with what I have to do."

He knew better than to argue, but melancholy filled his big brown eyes.

"The northern slope?" he asked, passing his finger over several cinder cones on the map.

"Yes."

"I think I know the road, but I'm not sure the truck will make it in this weather. It's an old hunting trail that follows this gulch." He traced the route with his finger, stopping at the base of the biggest of the cones. "It's supposed to go all the way to here."

Aunty Keala glanced at the clock on the dash. 9:55 a.m. "How long?"

Keone stared at the topo, rubbing his forehead. "At least an hour and a half—*if* the truck makes it."

Aunty Keala did the arithmetic—only about thirty minutes to spare. Thirty minutes she would need to hike to the spot—and in the storm, at high altitude. The kahuna stared through the windshield at the lock, wishing she had the power to break it.

"OK, we *hele*!" Let's go!

62 ∫ Conway's Nightmare

9:45 A.M. AT THE ROYAL PARADISE BAY RESORT . . .

ALOHA SHUTTLE NUMBER 7 sped through the bustling resort, carrying Robert Conway to the Royal Ballroom—and his destiny. Alone in the monorail's end car, Conway gazed at his distorted reflection in the window's convex glass. He was too preoccupied to worry that he was running late for the dignitaries' brunch next to the ballroom.

Five hours earlier—at 4:30 a.m.—he was lying sweaty in his bed, struggling to find meaning in the disturbing images of a nightmare. In the dream, Conway had wandered into the lobby in pajamas and bare feet. A desk clerk in a plastic smiley face mask pointed to a dozen Native Hawaiians huddled under the spreading limbs of the lobby's huge banyan. "There are some people to see you, sir," she said.

"Why are you here?" Conway asked the Hawaiians.

The old fisherman Conway had argued with on the beach stepped forward. "We're waiting for the funeral."

"Who died?"

Just then a Mercedes hearse pulled up to the curb and Conway ran over to peer through the window at the open casket. He saw himself laid out in the same blue suit and tie he'd worn at the Waikiki party where Lankowski mentioned Mali'o's cousin Kalama. His lifeless eyes were still open, and the embalmer had set the face with a broad cheesy grin. Aghast, Conway glanced into the gleaming fender of the hearse to compare the corpse's visage with his own, only to discover that the awful grin was there too!

He awoke, and these images were quickly crowded out by the awful memory that Mali'o, grief stricken by her cousin's murder, and now disillusioned with Conway, had decided not to be there today to share his glory. Unable to fall back to sleep, Conway had gone out to the lanai. He stood in the Kona gale, naked, staring at Captain Cook's storm-washed ship. The biting rain took him back to the *Transpac*, racing with his mentor Gieselmann straight into a squall that blew them off course. But they eventually caught up—even placed in the race—because of perseverance. Conway, soaked but trembling with fire, again declared his commitment, this time shouting into the storm, summoning its power for strength.

Despite the early hour, he'd decided to further fortify himself with a final "captain's inspection" of the Royal Ballroom's party finery, but when he got there everything seemed drab and artificial. Conway had tried to reinvigorate his commitment, but after Mali'o's news, his vision had slipped away. Just as termites gnaw away the beams and braces of island homes, so realities Conway had long denied—particularly his debt to the Hui—consumed the underpinnings of his outlook. He shook a fist at the great dome of stained glass, a vivid depiction of an erupting volcano. "I've been up against more than this, and survived!" he declared, but growling thunder and the hammer of rain battering the glass overwhelmed his words.

Things only got worse. The 8 a.m. staff briefing, meant to be an appreciative pep talk, had deteriorated into a squabble among division managers over the distribution of orchid leis for the staff. Then the Hawaiian minister scheduled to do the Christian blessing (a customary ritual for island development projects) called to cancel the prayer, not because his native brethren planned to protest the resort, but because flash floods off Kohala volcano had made his morning arrival impossible.

Conway's mood blackened further when the resort's in-house "wildlife specialist" reported the drowning of a peacock, washed into a drain pipe when the artificial rivers running through the Crocodile Jungle overflowed. A female crocodile named Bloody Mary was also unaccounted for after the deluge, thought to have perished after plummeting over a high falls near the Hawaiian Village Suites, although no one had been able to find the reptile's body.

Gazing into the train window, Conway thought that on top of everything else, he had forgotten to shave. But the shadow in his face came from *beneath* the flesh, a dismay that added ten years to his appearance. No question about it; he was losing his nerve. Spotting Lankowski waiting for him in the crowded lobby off the Royal Ballroom brought some of it back. Beneath each person's cerebral cortex lies the remnant of a reptile's brain from an earlier evolutionary epoch, a chunk of gray matter that still regulates territoriality. While reptiles had no capacity for vision, they did know how to defend themselves, an attribute Conway hoped might help him survive the day. The weasel stood smoking beneath Conway's fake royal scepters, a smattering of cigarette butts on the lava tiles at his feet. As the train slowed, Conway felt bile fill his gut. He bared his teeth, pleased with the effect on his reflection.

The train doors opened, and dozens more people poured into the already packed lobby. "Good morning, Bob," Lankowski said, spotting Conway as he stepped from the car. "Too bad about the weather," a hint of needle in the weasel's voice.

"I understand your boss has made it to the opening after all," Conway replied tersely.

"Had to. Biggest Big Island event in years."

"I just assumed the Hui ordered him to be here," Conway said, striding past him.

Lankowski, once again thrown off by Conway's abrasive manner, fell in behind the tall entrepreneur.

Conway grinned savagely. "Or maybe Calvin just wanted to witness the eruption firsthand."

"Well, I—he—"

"I'm late for the breakfast, Andy." Conway picked up his pace.

"It's the eruption I need to talk to you about," Lankowski declared, trying to keep up as Conway wove to and fro through the horde.

"Oh, really? Tell me, Andy, what good news do you bring this time?"

"We can't hold Takahashi back any longer. Civil Defense is going to bump it up from a watch to a *warning* tomorrow—and that means evacuation."

Conway stopped and faced the weasel, the poison in his gut rising to his throat. "A warning?" he boomed. "Tomorrow? So tomorrow the world will learn that Hualalai's going to vomit all over Robert Conway's casino!"

Several of the well-heeled in the milling crowd glanced over with snobbish disapproval. Lankowski puffed his cigarette mightily. "Bob, let's go somewhere private."

"No!"

"Listen, Bob! Did you hear me? Takahashi will have to order a full evacuation."

"You people!" Conway shouted. "For all your talk and intrigue, you don't accomplish a damn thing!" He stormed ahead, but Lankowski grabbed his arm and forced him to stop.

"Hey, Mr. Big Shot, we've done our best. If it weren't for our office—and Yamashita's—Civil Defense would have issued that warning yesterday!"

Conway could taste the rage in his mouth.

"Over here, Lankowski," he said, motioning to an alcove near the men's room. The weasel trailed him into the darkened recess, his cigarette sagging from his mouth. Conway spun around and grabbed the lapels of Lankowski's suit. He pulled the weasel's face right up to his own, so close he could smell the rancid breath. "Cynics like you make me want to puke!"

"Bob? What the hell are you doing?"

"You know what I'd really like to do, Andy? I'd like to put you out of your misery!"

As Lankowski tried to squirm away, Conway let go of his jacket, and the governor's aide stumbled out of the alcove into a Japanese visitor headed for the men's room.

"*Konnichiwa*," Lankowski muttered as he and the man tumbled to the floor.

Conway, his face suddenly calm, stepped over both of them and ambled toward the King's Chamber, where the dignitaries were already eating breakfast. He opened the door and peered inside. Noticeably absent—much to Conway's relief—was Haku Kane. The crowd chattered their superficial gab, kowtowing to one another, repeating the same old lines. Conway wondered if a single one of them shared his vision, or even understood it. He panned the faces of the most celebrated of the dignitaries holding court at the head table. Was there even one dreamer among them?

Maybe Yamashita, he thought. He and his mentors had pushed aside the corrupt powers of the white oligarchy and built the most vibrant political machine in the history of modern Hawai'i. But as Conway watched the old congressman glad-hand one approaching political hack after another, he realized that even Yamashita had lost track of his dream. Years of compromise and self-aggrandizement had tarnished its original idealistic gloss, leaving as the "Nisei revolution's" primary legacy the personal wealth they had all made through "public service." For the first time, Conway noticed that Yamashita's once-handsome face had lost its shape and luster, that cynicism had disfigured even him.

Conway, still red in the face from his encounter with Lankowski, walked up to the head table. He stepped to the podium, and the crowd began to quiet. What could he possibly say to these . . . these philistines? Nothing more than the typical platitudes they deserved—and counted on.

"Welcome to the Royal Paradise Bay Resort," he began. "I hope you're having a good time, despite the weather." As if in reply, thunder boomed along the coast and a murmur of nervous laughter rose from the audience. "Let me say how much I have appreciated all your help—public officials, investors, contractors, and, of course, my staff." He nodded toward Cyrus Bond, who stood near the exit. Conway wished he could switch places with him and slip out the door.

"Without all of you, it would not have been possible to turn this dream into a reality, to transform these barren lava fields"—a picture of the Kiholo Hawaiians, elder and grandson packing up their fish, popped into his mind—"to transform these barren lava fields into the largest, finest, most luxurious resort in the world. And that's not all. As you know, today marks not only the opening of this resort, but the beginning of the most ambitious development project ever undertaken in the Hawaiian Islands."

He stopped, vaguely aware of someone standing in the shadowed corner of the room. His peripheral vision revealed an elderly Hawaiian man dressed in a malo, a loincloth, with a fishing spear in hand. But when he turned to look, the phantom disappeared.

"We have . . . we have very big plans for this development, a proposal that when realized will turn the Big Island into the single most important visitor destination, not only in Hawai'i . . ." Again, out of the corner of his eye, Conway saw several shadowy figures in the back of the room. He looked straight at them, and this time their image held steady. Half a dozen Hawaiians stood there, some in loincloths and pareus. They vanished when lightning flashed outside the window. The blood in Conway's face drained away.

". . . ah, not only in Hawai'i," he stumbled, "but, ah, in the Pacific."

"What's wrong with Conway?" the governor asked his aide. Lankowski shrugged, unwilling to alarm his boss by disclosing what he actually believed—that Conway was unraveling.

"These plans will be unveiled in about thirty minutes. In the meantime, I want to thank Governor Calvin Kamali'i, whose full support of this project is greatly appreciated." The crowd applauded and Kamali'i stood, waving his big hands and mouthing the word *aloha*.

Conway gasped. The entire back wall was now lined with Hawaiians—fishermen and farmers, native women with children, hula dancers and drummers, chiefs dressed in feather robes, and warriors with spears. In front of them were Hawaiians of more recent eras, some dressed in Mother Hubbards and Victorian work clothes, some in surfer shorts and aloha shirts. He blinked and the apparitions disappeared. A cold sweat broke out under his clothes as he gazed, dumb faced, at the wall.

The room hushed, every eye on Conway. Clearly something was wrong.

"I, ah, also want to acknowledge, ah, Congressman Harold Yamashita. We appreciate your coming all the way back from Washington." The congressman did not rise, but flashed a perfunctory smile and waved from the table.

Native Hawaiians now stood along every wall, completely surrounding the gathering. Conway, ashen and sweaty, blinked several times, but the apparitions would not disappear. The storm thundered again and again, rattling the huge windowpanes, adding to the crowd's distress as they watched Conway come apart.

"Thank you all for coming," he muttered, stumbling away from the microphone. Once off the platform, he bolted for the exit, where Cyrus Bond was waiting.

"Are you all right?" the young manager asked once they were safely in the hallway.

"No," Conway replied, slumping up against the door, his breaths labored. "Something is terribly wrong."

At that moment, a commotion near the monorail station seized their attention as scores of Native Hawaiians, many carrying signs, poured out of the train, flooding the lobby in front of the ballroom.

"It certainly is," Bond replied.

63 ∫ Armed with Ancestors

10:40 A.M. . . .

More than 200 Hawaiians had infiltrated the resort, arriving in small groups not easily noticed in the crowd. Most dressed neatly in accord with the wishes of Uncle Sonny Kiakahi. Even those sporting traditional topknots, ponytails, and tattoos looked reasonably respectable. The only party questioned by a policeman was 'Iolani Carvalho's group, after drawing attention to themselves by stepping out of the crowd to approach a Hui acquaintance moonlighting as a security guard. But that association got them off the hook, when 'Iolani explained to the cop that they were there, not for the protest, but at the request of Haku Kane.

Kapu Hawai'i had smuggled their placards inside suitcases carried by three haole sympathizers assumed to be hotel guests. Once inside, half the protesters positioned themselves in the resort's various lobbies while the rest headed for the Royal Ballroom. At the appointed time, the protesters all pinned big red *ALOHA 'AINA!* buttons on their chests. Some guests assumed the Hawaiians were greeters for some local celebrity until someone explained that *'AINA* was not a name. Two people at the head of the throng unrolled a long multicolored banner urging guests to *VISIT HAWAI'I AND MEET THE PEOPLE—HAWAIIANS.* Other signs said *GIVE BACK OUR ANCESTRAL LANDS,* and *GOVERNOR KAMALI'I, WHERE'S YOUR ALOHA?*

Already excited by the celebrities and the extravagant resort, the media fell into a frenzy when the Hawaiians arrived. All but a handful were travel, restaurant, or entertainment writers, completely unaware that Hawaiians were anything but satisfied with modern island life. Some, like the New York television crew of *Playtime for the Famed and Fortunate*, were put out that Hawaiians would discard their image as friendly natives eager to please visitors. Even so, the reporters soon recognized that a confrontation was brewing, the kind that could land their story on the front page. It didn't take them long to locate Wailani Henderson.

"We are here to welcome with aloha these visitors to our island," she told the swarm of reporters gathering around her under the lobby's Gauguin. "We hope, in return, that they will listen to what has happened to our people and our land."

The reporters listened intently, searching for news hooks that would interest their editors. Most were ill informed, asking questions that struck wide of the mark, such as the one from a *Today Show* host broadcasting live from the resort. "Isn't your real concern that Native Hawaiians won't get the jobs created by this resort?" he asked with rehearsed sincerity.

"Yeah, right," Wailani smiled. "We're breaking down the doors for the chance to change sheets and clean toilets for $7 an hour." The host, stung by the rebuke, took a quick commercial break.

Wailani was shocked to discover how little even the American journalists knew about the fiftieth state. None were aware that Hawai'i had been seized in a military-backed coup d'etat or that many Hawaiians viewed the 1959 statehood vote as illegal.

A *San Francisco Chronicle* reporter muscled her way to the front. "Ms. Henderson," she said, "thousands are here celebrating the resort's grand opening. Do you really think these people—far removed from the problems of Hawaiians—will pay attention to a couple hundred protesters?"

"They will if they open their hearts to the island," Wailani replied cheerfully, her face beaming confidence. "I think our conversations will make a real difference. And by the way, we are far more than two hundred. When Hawaiians get ready for battle, we pray for assistance. This morning, hearing our call, our ancestors walked in with us."

Her comment was viewed as picturesque by most reporters, but a young Latina from the *LA Times* followed up by asking Wailani whether she thought the eruption threat from Hualalai had anything to do with the opening of the resort. Wailani peered into the reporter's brown eyes, trying to connect with her earth ancestry.

"For 2,000 years Hawaiians have lived in the shadow of volcanoes, and we have learned a great many things. One lesson is clear. When something is hewa—deeply wrong—our gods are obliged to set it right. Our job, as custodians of the island, is to stop what's hewa before there's a catastrophe that endangers innocent people."

The reporters had trouble locating Robert Conway, who, with Cyrus Bond's help, had slipped away via the underground tunnels normally reserved for workers. Loyal to the end, the young hotel manager was determined that no one from the media would see the great entrepreneur in his bewildered state. The two fashionable haoles seemed out of place in the electric cart racing toward the King's Tower and Conway's suite. Speeding on nerves, Bond swerved around other electric carts, food pantries, and huge trolleys loaded with employees, luggage, and linen supplies. He took the last corner so fast that his dazed boss nearly spun out onto the floor, then parked in front of the freight elevator for the King's Tower.

On their way up to the eighth floor, Conway kept muttering over and over again, "They got Cook too." Once there, Bond guided Conway down a short hallway to his private suite. A half-dozen reporters waited at the door, having overheard a receptionist transfer a call from Lankowski to the suite.

"Mr. Conway! Mr. Conway!" shouted a smartly dressed woman from the *New York Times* travel section. "Was this protest something you expected?" Conway gave her a baffled look, slow to comprehend that the swarm around him were reporters.

"Come in," he said mechanically. Hushed mutterings replaced their rapid-fire questions as the reporters beheld Conway's extraordinary suite. Not a single one failed to notice Mali'o's black stockings draped over the white chair just inside the door, or the four-inch heels she'd kicked off in the hall. Two reporters fingered the silk wallpaper, while another ogled the gold-plated telephone. Others found their way to the living room, where they admired the ivory Bösendorfer grand piano in front of the window.

"You play?" asked the *Times* reporter.

"No," Conway replied, still confused. "My girlfriend." Sadness swept over him like a cold wave, only adding to his distress. Who were these people and why were they asking all these questions?

"Is this real silk?" someone asked.

Cyrus Bond interceded, stepping in front of his boss. "Yes, handmade from Pakistan. Would you like to see Mr. Conway's private bath and hot tub?" Everyone nodded and the reporters followed Bond down a corridor hung with Conway's private collection of Gauguins.

Suddenly alone, Conway drifted toward the sliding glass doors in front of his lanai, where three potted ferns had tumbled over in the storm. Droplets of water seeped in along the edges of the door, and the glass rattled in the wind.

"You know what the Hawaiians did to Captain Cook after they killed him?" came a question from a shadowed corner of the suite.

Conway spun around, certain the voice belonged to yet another of the spirits that had haunted him all morning.

"I'm not interested in where you pee," the voice said. Stepping into the light was a dark young man in black jeans, sneakers, and an aloha shirt with a 1950s design—brown natives fishing with a *hukilau* net under billowed clouds.

Conway stared into his intelligent black eyes. "You're not with these other people, are you?"

The man shook his head.

"They hauled him up the pali," Conway said, turning back to the window and the raging storm, "to a temple. They built a fire, roasted his body, and stripped the flesh away."

The dark visitor smiled. "Then they shared the bones among the island's chiefs."

"It was an honor actually," Conway explained, staring at the gale-tossed *Resolution*. "They wanted a piece of his mana because they recognized he was special." Tears welled up in his eyes, and his chin quivered.

"Or maybe they wanted to desecrate his bones—defile the invader by carving his limbs into fishhooks. You think they're going to roast *you?*"

"Yeah," Conway nodded. "Yeah, I do."

The visitor ambled to the window and stood next to the entrepreneur. Conway shuddered with the chill creeping in around the glass.

"It's too bad, really," said Conway, nodding. "There aren't enough dreamers, let alone dreams."

"Imagination is a potent thing," the man replied, "but it's always challenged by realities."

"And they grind everything to a halt," Conway muttered. The tears in his eyes finally fell.

"Well, people have a stake in things."

"Yes . . . I know. Their *own* dreams."

The bay darkened, the sky turned purple, and the coconut fronds flailed about like the wings of frantic birds trying to escape Earth's grip. Lightning struck up the coast, and in the momentary flash, Conway again saw the spectral figures of hundreds of Hawaiians in the dark jungle surrounding the hotel. The thunder shook the suite. Paintings jiggled off their hooks and a table lamp tumbled to the floor.

"Earthquake! Earthquake!" shouted the reporters clamoring back down the hall, recognizing that the danger was more than just thunder and lightning, and the dark young man fell in with them. Suddenly alone, Conway stepped outside into the storm.

Downstairs, the already-edgy crowd bolted for exits and dashed under tables. The tremors stopped in fifteen seconds, leaving the visitors more shaken than the building.

"That's our cue," Maile said, hustling Gavin through the hotel's main lobby. "We've got to get to the cave."

"What about Aunty Keala?" he asked, pushing several tourists aside.

"I witnessed what she needed to see, and I'm certain she got the message."

Gavin followed her out the entrance and handed the valet the claim check for the Jeep. They were surprised at how dark the morning had become, the purple sky as dim as evening—and darkening. The downpour had paused, but the Kona winds blew stronger than ever. The coconut palms lining the road swayed like drunken sailors as lightning flashed inside the clouds that capped the three volcanoes visible from the resort.

Maile gazed up at Mauna Kea. "The winds must be incredible up there."

The sixty-mile-an-hour gusts that buffeted Aunty Keala's truck had such force that neither she nor Keone felt the earthquake as they four-wheeled up the back side of the mountain. A river of runoff poured down the steep grade, sloshing over branches and rocks washed out of the embankments. Lightning flashed all around them, illuminating the concentration in Keone's face as he peered through the windshield, his view all but obscured by driving rain.

KA-THUNK! The truck came down hard on its axle, its oversize tires having slipped into a chuckhole and off the side of the road. Without hesitation, Keone dropped the transmission into first and gunned the engine, all four wheels churning through mud and stone until the truck was back out onto the road.

"Maika'i!" Aunty Keala exclaimed, patting him soundly on the shoulder. Most fine!

"I don't know about this, Mom."

KA-WHOMP! The front wheels dropped into another gully, lurching the whole truck forward. Water splashed over the hood, spraying the windshield with muddy ash before the truck bounded up the other side. Aunty Keala grasped her son's shoulder and closed her eyes, falling into a trance, her lips trembling ever so slightly with the words of a prayer.

Up, up, up they climbed, past a crudely painted sign marking 11,000 feet. The engine's high-pitched whir nearly drowned out the howl of the winds. Heavy sleet replaced the rain, plastering the back window. Keone's knuckles, white from his grip on the wheel, grew cold as the truck climbed higher. He turned the heater up full blast, and using his free hand, pulled out a yellow blanket from behind the seat and eased it over his mother's shoulders. "Are you OK, Mom?" he asked, feeling the effects of the brain-numbing altitude.

"Just fine," she smiled, her eyes glassy from prayer.

"We should reach the north side in a mile or so," Keone said without taking his eyes off the road. "Perhaps then the mountain will block these Kona winds."

The kahuna did not hear. She was listening to voices from a place far beyond the noise of engine and gale. The whitened road angled up a sharp incline, past two huge cinder cones towering above the last of the shrubby *mamane* trees.

"The turnoff's got to be around here somewhere," Keone muttered to himself, glancing at the topo map on the seat between them. The gale ceased abruptly, and for the first time in an hour the windshield was clear. Aunty Keala opened her eyes, as if awakened from a deep sleep. Keone stopped the truck on a level spot in the road and got out. Snowflakes fluttered onto his shoulders as he watched a small breach form inside the black clouds. The fissure brightened, then opened a slim blue hole from which a ray of sunlight issued. The golden beam jagged across the shadowed landscape until it illuminated an old tower of stones perched on a rocky outcrop—the hunter's cairn marking Alakea Gulch—the Gulch of the White Path.

"That's it!" Keone exclaimed.

Tears welled up in Aunty Keala's eyes. "Mahalo, Poli'ahu," she said.

64 ∫ Back to the Source

11:20 A.M. . . .

The resort's opening gala went ahead without Conway, and Lankowski urged the governor to make the casino announcement in his stead. Right in the middle of Calvin Kamali'i's speech, but before the announcement, Hawai'i County police burst through the towering koa doors of the Royal Ballroom. The governor was actually relieved. He did not want to be there hawking the casino while his brethren marched against him. Like most politicians, he was toughest when bathed in praise and a weakling when confronted with criticism. For two days—since Haku Kane's threatening visit to his office—Calvin Kamali'i had tried to muster the courage to skip the grand opening and had even fantasized making a brave speech challenging the casino, but his survival instincts won out against such foolishness.

As the Kona storm intensified, the pulse of Kamali'i's Hawaiian blood had quickened. Ancestral memories encroached, telling him this was no ordinary storm—that the gods were exhibiting dismay. But it was easier to dismiss these "old superstitions" than face the disapproval of his political cohorts and the wrath of Haku Kane. Still, he wondered at the shadows he glimpsed at his vision's edge each time the lightning flashed and worried that the tingle in his back was more than just a chill from the wind.

As police rushed into the ballroom, Kamali'i watched the crowd's attention shift to the huge doors at the back. Instinctively seeking a better view, people surged toward the action, all except the Hawaiian protesters, who like a countercurrent instinctively drew back, away from the doors. During the mass distraction, Kamali'i stepped off the stage and slipped out a service door. He urged Congressman Yamashita to do the same, but the old politician was too thick-skinned to be bothered by whatever negative publicity might result from the action about to unfold.

The protesters had been scattered at tables throughout the room, their identification made easy by their big red *ALOHA 'AINA!* buttons. They were more surprised than anyone when the cops bypassed them for dearer quarry. Astonished celebrants looked on as six of the blue-uniformed men stormed Makaha Nuiloa's table, led by a tall Portuguese lieutenant. The giant Hawaiian was so shocked at the affront that Officer Machado, with Kimo's aid, handcuffed his huge wrists before he could raise his arms in protest. Two other cops tackled Makaha's Filipino companion as he bolted from his seat two tables away. The rest of the dozen police fanned out through the room looking for the other suspects in Jimmy's photograph.

The arrest might have been more discreet, but Machado had been determined to apprehend his suspects without a hitch, and surprise was essential. His two murderous cops were already behind bars, but Machado was worried that other crooked officers among the numerous policemen stationed at the resort might try to derail Makaha's arrest, so he kept the names on the warrant to himself until the last minute. The issuing magistrate, Judge Yoshihiro Yamanaka, unable to stop the warrant (Jimmy's crime-scene pictures were simply too overwhelming as evidence), had tried to notify Haku Kane, but he was told that the underworld chief was unavailable. By the time the judge overcame his hesitation about leaving the tip with underlings, it was too late for Kane's lieutenants to respond. Now Machado just had to nab the other two murderers if they were at the resort too.

'Iolani Carvalho had been sitting at a table with several Hui henchmen. Luckily for him, he left the Royal Ballroom during the governor's speech to make an anonymous phone call intended to discredit Wailani Henderson and Kapu Hawai'i—a bomb threat against "Coconut Cal" (the governor) and the "Kiholo disaster" (the casino). But the public phones outside the hall were mysteriously out of order, so 'Iolani headed for the lobby. By that time police officers were all over the place, and although ‘Iolani knew nothing of Makaha’s arrest, his gut told him something dangerous was afoot.

‘Iolani’s ponytail and vivid tattoos would have been easy to spot in the crowd had the resort not been filled with numerous other Hawaiians similarly adorned. Machado had warned his men against harassing the Hawaiians—he didn’t want anything to challenge his arrests—but his admonition got lost in the brouhaha and the cops started manhandling the protesters. Fortunately, Wailani Henderson had given Kapu Hawai‘i members instructions on how to respond to police or security abuse. So amid the tumult of agitated cops, puzzled visitors, flabbergasted reporters, riotous weather, and celebratory fanfare, Wailani’s protesters sat down on the floor and with tremulous voices, chanted a prayer asking the gods for protection. ‘Iolani was able to vanish in the chaos, never making the bomb threat call.

The other suspect—the blurred face on the photograph—was not at the resort. Hours earlier, Keawe Kanuha, the kahuna, had disappeared into a coastal cave where the somber stones of an altar and the bleached bones of old Hawaiians marked the threshold to another, darker realm.

That cave was half an island away from the one that now drew Maile and Gavin. As they sped down the coastal highway named for King Kamehameha’s powerful queen, Ka‘ahumanu, Gavin recalled the dancing figures and screaming bird etched on the cavern’s walls and the tall upright stone marking the termination of their last exploration. Four times he’d protested Maile’s decision to return, and four times she ignored his pleas, convinced that whatever lay inside that cave was something she was meant to see, although she admitted she didn’t understand the source of the compulsion.

Aunty Keala fully understood the forces driving her ever higher up Mauna Kea’s snowy slopes—she had been called by her guardian deity to plead one more time to prevent the coming calamity. Now only 2,000 feet below the cloud-draped summit, with the blizzard again in full force, the truck continued up Alakea Gulch. At these higher elevations, the "gulch" broadened into a treeless plain of cinder and stones washed there by a river of ice-melt 10,000 years earlier, when the glacier atop the mountain yielded to the warming of the earth. The tread prints of hunters' trucks that marked the "road" were impossible to discern under the drifting snow, and Keone had to watch for snow-covered cairns marking the trail. The only other landmarks were the two giant cinder cones ahead. On USGS maps they bore names made up by haole scientists, but Aunty Keala knew that the larger of the two—their destination—was Pu'u 'Ikuwa, the Hill of the Voices of the Gods.

Gusty winds spun into snowy whirlwinds that danced around the pickup as it climbed, and somewhere above 12,000 feet, with snow filling the wheel wells, the tires lost traction. Ahead lay deep snowdrifts that Keone knew he could not plow through.

"Oh, my God!" he exclaimed as a snow-white tornado spun out of the clouds and raced toward the gulch. Keone slammed on the brakes, and Aunty Keala jerked forward, the blanket tumbling off her shoulders. Her eyes opened dreamily, then shut against the physical reality of the truck. The view ahead disappeared in a blast of spinning ice crystals against the glass, and the pickup rocked violently, as if a giant hand had taken hold of it. Then, as quickly as the blast had arrived, it departed, and the snow gyrating against the windshield collapsed in a heap on the hood.

Keone watched the tornado spin up the side of Pu'u 'Ikuwa and into the swirling summit clouds. He gazed through the windshield, dumbfounded. The twister had swept away the drifts, and the old truck treads on the trail were now visible on the cinder slope. The winds eased and only a light snow fell from the sky.

Aunty Keala opened her eyes, and smiled. "How far?"

"Less than a mile to the end of the road," Keone replied, still shaken.

"Don't be so shocked, son," his mother said, patting his hand. "When the people abandoned the old beliefs, the gods retreated, but they did not leave the island. We cannot falter now. We have entered their realm. What time is it?"

Keone looked at his watch. "Eleven thirty-five."

Aunty Keala peered out the window at the huge cinder cone

towering above the side of the volcano, its southwest face plastered with snow. "Hele!" We go!

They bounced inside the truck as it raced up the gulch. Aunty Keala noticed a white bird soaring in and out of the clouds above the cone. She smiled.

"What's up there, Mom?" Keone asked.

The kahuna peered into the face of her man-child. "There is a shrine, from the oldest epoch of our people, long before the rule of the ali'i, when navigators—wedded to the heavens by the stars that guided their canoes—wisely steered the helm of our culture. A time when wisdom, not bloodline, formed the basis of society. It is said this shrine was among the first constructed in Hawai'i, and for 2,000 years its upright stones have aided the oracles in communicating with the gods."

As the son of a leader of Hawai'i's cultural revival, Keone had danced and taught the most traditional hulas and prayed to the gods and his ancestors. But he was young, not yet ready for the step his mother had been called to take—to confront the Supreme One. She wondered if even she was ready. "You will leave me at the base of the cone," she said, buttoning her jacket. "I'll hike in from there—alone."

"I'm going with you," he insisted, shocked that she would consider doing the trek without him. "Is the shrine at the top of the cone?"

His mother shrugged her shoulders. "I do not know, but I will find it."

"Mom!"

Aunty Keala shook her head. "It is I who have been called, and I who must go." They locked eyes. "Your assignment is different."

Keone drove to the base of Pu'u 'Ikuwa, a cloud-capped cone so tall it seemed like a miniature mountain. Though the blizzard had subsided, the icy temperatures continued to drop, well below freezing. Keone persuaded his mother to slip his jacket over hers, put on his work boots with double socks, and don his wool cap, scarf, and gloves. Nose to nose, they exchanged breaths of aloha—Keone transmitting his youthful vitality for her trek ahead, and Aunty Keala one more time giving her son her sacred mana.

She stepped from the truck into the frigid air and marched through calf-deep snow toward the cone's upslope side. Each step yielded a sharp crunch she had never heard before. Directly above, soaring high on convective winds, circled the bird—a snow-white hawk. Aunty Keala's breaths, strained by thin air and the exertion of the climb, echoed inside her skull: *haa-ahhh, haa-ahhhh, haaa-ahhhhhh*... A tingle settled into her fingers and toes, and a surge of warmth filled her chest. Her head began to spin, her ears rang, and the whitening light distorted her vision. She defocused her eyes, yielded to the dizzying mystery, and let the weight of the mountain pull her forward.

Keone, wrapped in the blanket, shuddered inside the truck as he watched his mother disappear around the cone's far side.

"Directly above, soaring high on convective winds, circled a snow-white hawk."

65 ∫ Sulfur?

NOON . . .

A thuddy rumble echoed down the lava tube that Gavin and Maile had just traversed to reach the petroglyphs. "What's that!" Gavin exclaimed.

"A collapse?" Maile muttered, fingering the bone lizard on her breast.

"That's all we need," Gavin groaned.

While Maile's gut had drawn her back to the cave, Gavin's had resisted, but his loyalty to Maile prevented defection. Under grim skies flashed with lightning, he had followed her through the tall grasses laid flat by the storm. Down they had gone, into the damp tunnel of rock, treading inside tiny envelopes of illumination created by their flashlights. Along the way they'd passed several branches of the labyrinth, finally reaching the chamber of ancient carvings. Maile wasted no time documenting the site with her digital camera. Gavin's light immediately fell on the carved hawk he'd seen in his second Pele dream. The open, screaming beak further unnerved him, stirring the same claustrophobia he had experienced five days earlier. He felt as if a huge stone pressed upon his chest and thought again of Aunty Keala's warning.

Suddenly his feet went wobbly. "Did you feel that!" he shouted, placing his palm against the wall.

Maile lowered the camera from her eye and panned the cave with her flashlight. As its beam passed over the tall sea-burnished stone guarding the passage beyond the petroglyphs, the lava tube shook with such force that Maile flew sideways into a wall and crumpled to the ground, the beam from her light disappearing. Gavin, also thrown down during the five-second temblor, got up to search for her amid the rocks on the cavern floor. Through suspended dust in his flashlight beam, he noticed that the guardian stone had fallen. "Maile! Are you OK!" he hollered into the darkness, finally catching her gleaming eyes in his light.

"Smell that?" she asked.

Gavin rose to his feet. "What?"

"Sulfur. I think I smell sulfur."

Five people huddled around the table in the HVO Crisis Center, pondering a map of Hualalai. Dr. Lelehua Chin leaned over the topo, studying the little red dots marking possible epicenters of the two earthquake swarms and the two large temblors that had shaken Kona during the past three days. Joe Murdock sat quietly at the far end of the table while Gus Parker paced the windows overlooking Kilauea's foggy caldera. Southwest winds blew hard against the glass, streaking the huge panes with rain. The two Stanford interns flanked Lelehua; Debbie was somber, and Richard, his face alight, chewed excitedly on a pink wad of Bazooka bubblegum.

"We don't even know for sure that these are the epicenters," Lelehua complained. "They may be just exceptionally big gusts of wind."

"It's hard for me to believe that the whole seismic detection system is of no practical use," Debbie said.

"When you've got extraordinary winds like the ones occurring on the other side of the island, the seismographs' antennas rattle and big trees sway, shaking the ground around the station," Lelehua explained. "Any of this can mask the seismic record, creating so many lines you can't tell what's what."

"Same thing happened when Mauna Loa erupted in 1984," Gus added. "We didn't know about it until a telescope operator on Mauna Kea stepped outside and spotted lava fountains across the way."

"Look, Debbie," Lelehua said, pulling aside one of several wide strips of paper at the table's far end—the latest records from seismographs on the west side of the island. "This is from Hualalai's northwest rift," the geologist said, pointing at the two largest pulses on the jagged line. "It's almost impossible to pick out even the big quakes among all that noise."

The phone rang.

"HVO. Joe Murdock," answered the scientist in charge, swiveling his chair toward the blustery window. It was Civil Defense director Mike Takahashi. "The problem is those winds, Mike," Murdock explained. "We can't be sure of anything. We have two men in the field, but they've got lots of territory to cover, and until the storm subsides we don't dare do a flyover . . ."

Across the room, Richard pointed at several large jags on the Mauna Loa record. "What are these, Dr. Chin?"

Lelehua, still eyeing the Hualalai sheet, glanced over at the seismic record in the young man's hands. "The winds atop Mauna Loa are the worst," she replied. "Those are probably just exceptionally high gusts."

Gus walked over to examine the record for himself. "We could call the NOAA weather observatory and see it they felt anything this morning," he said.

"I can't imagine Mauna Loa would also act up right now," Lelehua replied, "but it wouldn't hurt to give them a call."

No one answered the phone at the tiny monitoring station 11,000 feet up the giant mountain. Buried in snow, it had been abandoned hours earlier. "Probably just wind," Gus conceded, turning to eavesdrop on Murdock's conversation with Takahashi.

"I sympathize with you, Mike. If I had some hard data to give you, I would, but with the storm . . . uh-huh. Yeah, I agree. Hard to evacuate without something more tangible. On the other hand . . ."

Richard stepped over to Debbie and whispered loudly into her ear, "This is great! I think *we* ought to go over to Kona and check it out."

"This isn't TV, ya know!" Gus said, firing his gaze at Richard. "There are lives and property at stake."

An awkward silence hung over the group, finally broken when Murdock hung up the phone. He walked over to the Hualalai drum. "Mike says there's been another quake in Kona, at least a five point oh, judging from resident reports." He bent over the Hualalai drum and looked for a pulse standing out among the myriad lines marking the background wind shake of the instrument. “Sure enough,” he said, pointing at an especially large jag in the line. “Quake number five. Twelve o’clock noon, exactly when people said they felt it.”

The phone rang again, but this time it was one of HVO’s field geologists back from a chopper flight over the Pu‘u ‘O‘o cone. Murdock jotted down her report.

“Well, gang,” the scientist in charge said, swiveling his chair to face them, “on top of everything else, Kilauea may be taking a rest.”

They all looked back over their shoulders.

“The lake inside Pu‘u ‘O‘o is empty, and so are the tubes. Park rangers saw no plumes when they got down to the coast this morning, and the chief ranger invited Dobbs on the flyover. Sure enough, the red stuff’s gone.”

“That means it shut down sometime last night,” Gus said.

“Something we could verify if our seismic records weren’t so full of wind shake,” Lelehua added.

“Interesting timing,” Murdock muttered “what with lava probably filling up Hualalai.”

And maybe Mauna Loa, Richard thought.

“Hualalai’s so seismically active right now,” Gus said, “it’ll be a miracle if it’s *not* erupting. But those winds make it hard to pick out the big quakes, let alone harmonic tremor from moving magma.”

Murdock shook his head. “Good thing we sent Simmons and Wray over there yesterday to start the field work.”

“Yeah, right,” Gus said, “two guys wandering around blind in the storm.”

“Not quite blind,” Murdock replied, getting up to examine the Hualalai topo, a map detailing every vent and flow from previous eruptions. “They’re checking every vent anywhere near the suspected earthquake epicenters.”

“So where do *you* think it’ll unzip, Joe?”

“Who knows? Conventional wisdom has long assumed that the 1801 vents would be likely candidates. But the fact is”—Murdock swept his hand over both rifts of the volcano—“it could blow out of any of these vents, from Huehue to Waha Pele.”

Lelehua leaned across the table and ran a finger along the four red dots marking the suspected quake locations. "They seem to be clustered in two areas—near the summit and down the southeast rift in the vicinity of Waha Pele."

Gus scratched his chin. "If that's accurate, it could flow either way—toward the North Kona resorts or down into Kailua town and Keauhou Bay."

Murdock nodded.

"How about this latest quake?" Richard asked, popping his gum.

"Looks like it's also near the summit, directly above the airport."

"Too bad about the weather," Gus said, dropping into a chair. "Otherwise we could check it out with choppers."

"Damn it!" Murdoch complained. "Right now low clouds are shrouding the upper two-thirds of the mountain. We won't know what's happening, or where, until lava flows reach below that ceiling. By then there won't be enough time to get out of the way, let alone evacuate." Murdock straightened up. "We can't do an overflight. The seismic network is almost useless. Our field crew is looking for needles in a haystack. And with all those clouds, the people of Kona won't even see the glow."

"Too bad we didn't issue our report earlier, eh, Joe?" said Gus.

"Even that wouldn't have mattered," Murdock replied, deflated. "Civil Defense has never evacuated until we've confirmed lava on the ground. In this case, that requirement may prove fatal. Mike wants to start the evacuation tomorrow, but he's under pressure from the big boys who don't want to set a new precedent for evacuation."

"Do you suppose it's already started?" Lelehua asked, her dark eyes fixed on the topo.

Murdock took a deep breath and plunged his hands into his pockets. He didn't say it, but he knew that if Hualalai did erupt that weekend, he would be looking for a new job.

"Well, it's not your fault Menlo Park ordered us to revise our report," Lelehua said. "Given the delay, it seems to me you've done everything you could, Joe."

Murdock shook his head. "I'm afraid that's not how it works."

66 ∫ Aunty Keala's Plea

12:15 P.M. . . .

Twenty minutes after Aunty Keala disappeared behind the snowy cone—at noon—the winds on Mauna Kea had ceased blowing and a strange stillness settled over the mountaintop. Keone sat in the truck, watching snow steadily pile up on the hood. Now and again he ran the engine to warm the cab and run the wipers. As the minutes passed, a sense of momentous change replaced his anxiety about his mother's safety; it was as if he was in the middle of something larger than himself or his mother. Even his worry about snow stranding the truck before her return had faded. He rolled down the window and peered at the fog-capped cone with his hunting binoculars, certain he was about to witness something special.

Just then the white veil atop the cone parted and he spotted his mother on the rim a half mile away, bundled up in his jacket, cap, and gloves. Arms outstretched, she spoke into the sky, in a posture he had seen many times before—when she chanted on the rim of Kilauea's crater, atop the rocky seashore, or at the edge of the rainforest. Now and again, she dropped her arms, as if listening for reply. Each time she resumed her pleas, her gestures became more adamant. Gradually her posture changed, she ceased chanting, and her arms fell to her sides. The winds began to blow again, fog shrouded the cone, and the mountaintop grew dark.

Keone found another sweatshirt behind the seat, slipped it on, and stepped out into the now-blowing snow. But then an inner voice stopped him from making the trek. He recalled the moment an hour earlier when his mother shared with him her breath—and he suddenly realized that this aloha was meant to be final, that she had no intention of returning to the truck. Tears stung his eyes and spilled down his face.

He stepped forward into her snowy tracks, but again the inner voice stopped him. He stared up at the dark clouds draped over the cone, struck by his mother's faith and courage—and the realization that she was now gone. More tears streamed down his cheeks. Then the warmth of her presence came over him, and he remembered her saying, "Your assignment is different." A keen sense of purpose filled his heart. He must carry on, just as she had done. Her ancestral memories, all the teachings of her elders, were now his to share.

The white hawk they had seen earlier spiraled out of the summit clouds, soaring higher and higher until it was just a speck moving behind the falling snow.

Keone got back into the pickup. Despite his inner message and the outward sign, he waited two more hours until the winds again subsided and the clouds on the cone parted. Through his binoculars he saw that the snowy rim was empty, no sign of his mother, and he knew with certainty she had gone to join their ancestors. It would take him another hour to clear the wheels of snow with the small camping shovel he kept in the truck. By the time he headed back down the mountain, his face and hands were frostbitten, his body chilled to the bone, and his heart heavy with grief and a new sense of responsibility.

67 ∫ Secret of the Cave

12:15 P.M. AT THE CAVE . . .

I don't smell it," Gavin said, stepping close to Maile.

She turned full circle to sniff the stale air for sulfur. "I don't either . . . *now*. But I'd swear—"

"This place gives me the creeps," Gavin interrupted.

"I know you're uncomfortable, Gavin, but I *have* to go on. I'll walk you out and come back on my own."

"I'm staying with you. That's all there is to it, luv."

Maile smiled.

"OK, girl-o, let's take care of this damned obsession of yours—and get the hell out of here," Gavin said, leading the way past the fallen stone. The couple moved swiftly down the tube whenever its floor was reasonably smooth, and gingerly through areas with a low ceiling or collapsed debris. Sometimes they had to scramble on all fours over heaps of fallen rock. Twice Gavin noticed other branches of the cave and stopped to consult with Maile. Having never been beyond the petroglyphs, she could rely only on her na'au. Finding it too difficult to "feel" her way through the labyrinth without being in front, Maile soon reasserted her role as leader.

About a mile beyond the fallen stone, Maile stopped at a bend in the tube where the ceiling dropped low. "We need a short break," she said, taking off her little yellow backpack. She pulled out a liter of water and handed it to Gavin. "How are you feeling?"

"OK," he replied, taking a long drink, then handing it to Maile. "I still have that sense of foreboding, but I'm trusting that you know what you're doing. So I feel like I'm supposed to be here—at least here with you."

She smiled. "What's happened with you and me is no accident—all these things we've done together. I don't know about you, but I feel changed by it all."

"For me too, Maile."

"If you and I hadn't met, I wonder if I would have ever reconnected with Aunty Keala." She took another sip from the bottle. "Maybe I would have continued to deny my Hawaiian kuleana—my responsibility. Ancestral memory tells us what our kuleana is, a destiny revealed through the naʻau. You may not realize this, Gavin, but you have helped me act upon the responsibilities I now understand are mine."

She glanced at her watch. 2:30 p.m. They'd been inside the volcano for more than two hours.

"Let's keep moving," she said, stowing the water bottle in her pack. "For all we know, Hualalai could be erupting right now."

"Yeah, picture that," he said with a nervous chuckle, "stepping out of the cave into the middle of a lava flow."

The ceiling became lower, perhaps, Maile thought, because they were now under the broad plain between the base of the pali and the coast. They had to watch out not to bump their heads.

Maile stopped abruptly. Standing in their path was another upright stone, its strange features lit up in the beam of Maile's light. Four feet tall and a foot thick, the trapezoid-shaped rock was steel gray and smoothed by centuries of a previous life in the sea. A half-dozen deep pockmarks covered its face, like Picasso eyes peering out from the wrong places. It leaned forward with a foreboding stance—anticipating intruders, warding them away.

"This guardian stone is old," she muttered, chicken skin all over her arms.

"Gives me the heebie-jeebies, like it's watching us."

Maile crept closer. "I'd swear I've seen pictures of this stone—but where?"

"Notice that *this* one didn't tumble in the quake," Gavin commented.

Maile slid her backpack off her shoulders and unzipped the pocket containing her camera, then thought better of the idea.

"There is a god in this stone," she announced, pondering its many eyes.

Beyond the monolith, in the distant illumination of the flashlights, other stones stood in a line against the cavern wall, and visible beyond them were flecks of red and gold.

Maile inhaled, her pulse rising, and yet her tone and manner became more professional, almost academic. "Scholars have long speculated that the bones of the legendary King Kamehameha are tucked into a cave adjacent to one of his royal fish ponds, but nobody's known for sure. No archaeologist has proved otherwise—until now."

She stared at the stone. Its half-dozen eyes gazed back. "Gavin, behind that stone may lie the answer to one of the great mysteries of Hawaiian archaeology—and we stand just a few paces from discovering it."

She took a step forward, but Gavin grasped her arm. He caught the face of the monolith in his beam of light. "What does that stone tell you? Your gut feeling—as a Hawaiian?"

Maile took a moment to answer, then sighed. "Kapu." Off limits. "Absolutely kapu."

"OK, there's your answer."

Maile was suddenly filled with deep apprehension, realizing it was not her Hawaiian na'au that had brought her back to the cave, but the professional drive she'd inherited from her Chinese American father. "Let's get out of here," she said, abruptly turning from the stone. Gavin fell in behind her, and they hustled back up the tube.

"We scientists can't help being a bit too nosy," he said. "It's in our nature."

"Yeah, well, that kind of thing can get you into serious trouble," she said, quickening her pace. "I should have been paying better attention to my na'au."

And Aunty Keala, Gavin thought. "I wish I trusted my instincts better. I might have done a better job keeping you away from this bloody cave."

"Don't worry, Gavin, you'll come to trust your na'au too—if you stay. I can already see it happening."

He stopped in his tracks. "If I stay?"

She didn't need to reply. The hope in her voice had said it all.

At that moment, a blast of warm air passed over them.

"Where did *that* come from?" Maile said, slowing to a stop.

"Sulfur again," Gavin said, feeling it tickle his throat. "This time it's not your imagination."

They looked at each other, their minds racing.

"I've heard of it," Maile said. "Lava entering old tubes. It's definitely getting warmer down here."

"And the smell's changing, too—like—like—burnt bittersweet chocolate."

"That's the smell of molten lava, Gavin." She held up her palms to feel the rising heat. "And it's getting closer."

"Which way should we go?" He flashed his light in both directions, its beam dimmer now from an afternoon of use.

"We can't continue back upslope. That's toward the lava flow."

"All right then," he agreed. They jogged back down the tube, but soon stood again before the stone monolith, its many eyes quivering in their flashlights' glow.

"We've got no choice," she said, licking the sulfur brine off her lips.

"What about taking a side vent?"

"The last one was at least a quarter mile back."

The Australian ransacked his mind for another alternative. Beaming his light beyond the guardian stone, he saw vague outlines of whatever lay waiting in the shadows. "Any advice?"

"First, don't touch anything. If it is a burial, it's important nothing be disturbed."

"Right."

"Keep moving. Get past it as quickly as possible."

"OK."

"And pray."

"Pray?"

"Burials are full of spirits, wandering souls searching for their ancestors. They can cling to you as you pass by. Some are just curious, but others are desperate, eager to feed on the mana of the living."

"Good heavens!"

She took his hand and squeezed it hard. "Listen to me, Gavin. I love you. I don't want anything to harm you. Pray!"

"Christ, I haven't prayed since grade school. I don't even remember the words."

"Think of it another way. Call on your source, whatever it is that makes you feel whole and strong. Whatever helps you do that, do it now!"

"But the lava flow—"

"You cannot walk through this burial without protection!"

"All right, all right. Just a moment." He turned away from the huge stone and pondered his "source" while Maile readied herself.

"Can I pray to the wonder of the universe?"

"If that's what strengthens your spirit."

Gavin closed his eyes and tried to envision a vaulted universe of stars and planets.

"Oh blast!" he cursed. "I'm stumped, Maile."

"You've got to let your source know you're here. If that means asking for help, then ask. If it means giving thanks, then do it. If it means praising the source for its wonder, then tell it so!"

Closing his eyes made the heat and odor seem even more suffocating. Rather than succumb to an encroaching fear, Gavin used these heightened sensations to propel his mind into the heart of creation—and put himself right into the middle of it. He danced through clouds of nebulae where stars are born, and soared along the edges of the great whirlpools of stars that men call galaxies. Connected to all these dynamics, Gavin felt a strength—and a newfound serenity—that surprised him.

"Righto," he announced. Maile nodded, and they advanced.

Stepping around the monolith was like entering another realm. A charge passed over them, giving them goose bumps, and Maile heard a cacophony of ancient Hawaiian voices spoken all at once. She could make no sense of the words, except that the spirits were agitated. She continued to pray to the gods and her ancestors to guide their safe passage.

Much of the burial was masked in the moving shadows formed by their lights, but as they began passing it, Maile couldn't help noticing a sailing canoe tucked into a side chamber of the cave, its mast, rudder, and sail laid flat over the outrigger. Stacked along the chamber wall lay several bundles of bones, each wrapped in white tapa cloth, and nearby stood two spears and two royal feather scepters. Amid all this, on a rock ledge above the other corpses, stood a small sennit casket intricately woven into a god figure with eyes of shell and a cape of golden plumes—a treatment reserved for the bones of kings. Opposite the burial, on a fine rock altar, lay the collapsed remnant of an offering. Time and decay had broken the dried fibers of the ti leaf bundle, spilling its contents out onto the stone—desiccated remains of breadfruit and fish, and ample locks of gray-black hair.

"He's waiting for her," Maile said, her mind whirling back to 1801, when the king was compelled to apologize to Pele with a sacrifice of his own mana-filled hair—the same eruption that had formed this cave. What untold part of the tale remained hidden in its mute rock walls to explain these gifts? Left for Pele when next she would return? Was this the secret protocol given to Kamehameha by the prophet of Pele?

Reminding herself to keep moving, Maile slipped between the altar and the bones, into the dark passage ahead. But her muttered prayers were broken by a commotion behind her. She spun around, expecting to see Gavin in her tracks, but he was not there.

A low moan rose from the ground. Maile's flashlight located him facedown between the altar and a ghastly wooden tiki standing near the bones. Maile had been so stunned at seeing the offerings that she had failed to notice the carved god image, its crude mouth pursed in revolting affront, arms and legs astride in defiance. Its presence confirmed Maile's burial conclusion, for King Kamehameha was known to possess ancient Moloka'i images carved of *kalaipahoa* wood. These spoils of war he kept—and used—as a follower of the evil sorcery of 'ana'ana. So lethal was this sorcery, said the lore, that just touching one of these consecrated images could kill.

68 ʃ Pele Arrives!

2:45 P.M. . . .

Jimmy Anderson peered out the airliner as it approached the Kona airport from Honolulu, another load of tourists brought in before Civil Defense decided to close the airport. Squeezed next to FBI Special Agent Neil Kaiko, the young photographer was a little self-conscious taking pictures out the window, but he did it anyway after several local passengers claimed they'd "never seen anything like it." A single monstrous cloud—pulsing with lightning—capped the island, while the rest of the archipelago was clear.

Jimmy was returning to the Big Island to identify the suspects Lieutenant Machado had arrested that morning. The FBI agent, Kimo's cousin from Honolulu, was there to protect him—and to make sure the Hawai'i County Police handled the prisoners properly.

"God, what's that?" asked an elderly Nebraska woman, pointing a bent arthritic finger out the window.

"Looks like a forest fire," said a brawny vacationer from Oregon.

A cocktail waitress from LA dropped her makeup kit into her purse and pushed her doll face up against the glass. "Where might that be?"

"Over there, just under the clouds," replied the Oregonian.

"Above that little road?"

"Yep."

They watched as tree after tree burst into flames above the old highway near Holualoa, smoke billowing into the clouds.

"Must be pretty darn hot to burn 'em like that in the pouring rain," boomed a Texan a few rows up. "Wonder how it started?"

"Lava, that's how," Jimmy yelled, steadying his zoom lens. "I can see the flow!"

A couple across the aisle leaped up from their seats to get a better view, and before long everyone was craning to see out the left-side windows, a number standing in the aisle. Some tourists displayed the glee of voyeurs witnessing another tragic incident, like those featured nightly on television. Other visitors were confused, unable to imagine the dangers of a volcano erupting above Kona. But the island residents on board knew that their homes, businesses, schools, churches, and loved ones were in jeopardy. They fell silent amid the uproar of tourists straining for views and reaching for cameras.

"Please remain seated until the plane has landed," a flight attendant urged over the loudspeaker.

Although lava had erupted from the Hualalai's Waha Pele vent two hours earlier, it had remained hidden in the giant cloud until moments before Jimmy spotted it, shortly after three o'clock. Civil Defense sirens started blasting ten minutes later, about the same time Jimmy and the passengers deplaned onto the tarmac, but most people at the airport had no idea why. Five more minutes passed before an announcement finally came over the public address system, one obviously not recited from an emergency manual:

"Listen up, everybody. This is airport security. We just got a call from Civil Defense. Believe it or not, Hualalai volcano is erupting. Lava flows have been sighted above the Mamalahoa Highway two miles west of Holualoa. These flows are heading toward Keauhou Bay—and they say they're moving real fast. Civil Defense has ordered the immediate evacuation of Kailua-Kona, and they're asking you to stay here until further notice. Basically, they don't want you guys getting in the way of the evacuation. Residents living north of Kailua, you can go home. Kailua residents, wait at the baggage carousels for instructions . . ."

Agent Kaiko escorted Jimmy to the late-model station wagon serving as the Kona Isle Taxi Service. The huge Hawaiian behind the wheel pushed open both doors from the inside. At 300 pounds (in shorts, aloha shirt, and flip-flops), that was easier than struggling in and out of the car.

"Welcome to Big Island, cuz," he said to Agent Kaiko. "Thanks for the call."

"No problem, Bobo. To the police station."

"Are we safe there?" Jimmy asked.

"The station's on the outskirts of Kailua, in the opposite direction from the lava flow," Agent Kaiko replied.

A dark cap of cloud shadowed the whole Kona coast as they drove the five-minute route to the police station, but the earlier heavy rains had turned to drizzle.

"Heckuva day fo' come Kona," the driver said, his moon face absent its usual smile. He turned down the radio a notch, but a repeating Civil Defense message still played.

"Pele prob'ly goin' take half da town," he said, pulling onto the Queen Ka'ahumanu Highway.

"You think so?" Agent Kaiko replied, unwilling to speak pidgin in front of his haole charge.

"Dey say da flow jammin'—nine, ten miles an hour."

Agent Kaiko spotted the distant smoke out the window. "Pretty hard to outrun that."

After witnessing a murder, dodging the Hui, getting kidnapped by a disturbed veteran, and being guarded by the FBI, Jimmy had no trouble believing he might experience another calamity. The highway was not busy yet, and there were few visible signs of the emergency—an orange fire department helicopter hovered over the slope and two police cars, sirens blazing, sped past on their way to Kailua.

"Bad timing for an arrest," Agent Kaiko commented ruefully, "what with Kona about to get slammed by Pele." That comment put the driver's big eyes into the rearview mirror.

"This is Hualalai eruption update number three," said Mike Takahashi on the radio. He spoke in a calm, even voice, but his message was alarming. "At about three o'clock this afternoon Kona residents and local police spotted a massive lava flow crossing the Mamalahoa Highway, heading southwest toward Keauhou Bay. Scientists estimate it will reach the sea before sunset. The flow is expected to enter the Kona Mauka Home Lots subdivision within fifteen minutes. Residents of that area should evacuate immediately. There is no time to gather up belongings. I repeat, there is no time to evacuate your belongings. Access roads to the subdivision will soon be closed off by lava, certainly within the half hour. Civil Defense personnel and helicopters are on their way to assist. Please follow their instructions . . ."

"Mean, huh?" the driver said, connecting with Agent Kaiko through the mirror. The agent flashed his eyebrows.

"Wildfires ignited by the flow are burning pasture and forest within the Kaukohoku Ranch. Thirty-five-mile-an-hour winds are fanning the flames, spreading rapidly to the northeast. Several houses and farm buildings have already caught fire . . ."

Agent Kaiko shook his head, his eyes glistening. He leaned forward to squeeze the driver's shoulder. "Bobo, do you need to get somewhere?"

"Good t'ing I no more live Kailua. I stay up Kona Paradise subdivision, above da airport."

"What about family?"

"All Hilo side."

"You're lucky."

"Pele wen' leave us alone many, many years, but no mohr. She take 'em now."

Jimmy leaned forward. "Why now?"

"She no like all kind development action, you know. She no like 'take dis, take dat,' no mohr respect li'dat."

Agent Kaiko nodded his agreement as they sped past two new shopping centers. Like the police station, these buildings stood almost alone in the middle of vacant land miles from downtown—on old Hualalai lava flows county planners had designated for more urban sprawl.

When the taxi turned into the station parking lot, only two cars with blue police lights remained in front of the tiny building, the rest having been called to the eruption. Agent Kaiko noticed the bumper sticker on one of them, the slogan of the island's biggest construction firm, Tamaguchi Brothers Limited: "Building the Islands Forever." He shook his head, thinking, Stay on your toes, Kaiko. You can't always trust these Big Island cops.

69 ∫ Lava Closes In

3:13 P.M. . . .

"Gavin!" Maile shouted, rushing to her lover sprawled on the cavern floor near the formidable tiki.

"I tripped on something," he said, raising his head, his fingers bleeding from the fall. Maile took his arm and guided him away from the burial. He wrapped the bloodiest cuts with his handkerchief. "What was that tiki, anyway?"

The clamorous voices Maile had heard earlier echoed in her head. "Something from the dark past." She wiped the sweat off her face. "Pele's getting closer."

Gavin unbuttoned his shirt as they hustled down the tube. "Keep your eye peeled for side vents. We've got to find an exit."

"This is a burial cave, Gavin. There may not be another way out."

A distant boom echoed through the darkness.

"Now what!" she said, slowing her pace.

"Keep moving!" Gavin shouted, tugging her arm.

Another boom, this time closer.

Maile stopped abruptly and shone her light back up the tube. She began trembling. "Oh, Gavin . . ."

He rushed back and pulled her into his arms. "We can't panic, luv, or we won't make it."

She blinked a tear onto her cheek. "I'm scared."

"So am I," he admitted, "but together we can get out of here."

"I love you, Gavin."

"I love you too, Maile, and I swear, you and I are going to swim in that lovely Hawaiian sea again—soon."

Again, the lava tube resounded with a boom, the closest yet.

"That's rock exploding," Gavin said, urging her forward. "From heat expansion?" he wondered aloud. If so, the lava wasn't far behind.

Side by side they hustled down the tube, but they were slowed by great heaps of debris from two old ceiling collapses. They cut their hands climbing over the sharp-edged rocks. After almost three hours underground, their flashlights had grown dim, and Gavin's light had to be shaken back to life every few minutes. Temperatures rose steadily, and the thunderous booms of swelling rock continued, each time startling the fleeing pair into greater effort. Air pressure inside the tube increased, pushing the lava's fumes well ahead of the flow. Breathing got difficult, and a new smell mixed with the odors of lava and sulfur—the sweet scent of burning wood, bone, and leaves.

"There goes your burial site, Maile."

Sealed in a sarcophagus of stone, its secret was now buried forever, save perhaps for the inborn memory of some offspring whose ancestors had been entrusted to conceal the bones. Maile decided right then and there she would never reveal Kamehameha's secret—*if* she survived to exercise that choice—and she added that pledge to her prayers.

"How far back was it?" he asked.

"No more than ten minutes. Lava moves fast inside tubes, so it must be hung up on those debris piles."

"Then maybe we've still got a little time."

Gavin's light flickered off again, but no amount of shaking could bring it back to life. "Damn! The torch is gone!"

"Here," Maile said, shining her light for both of them as they sped toward another bend in the cave. The turn also dropped ten feet, and they had to climb down carefully. Maile stumbled, nearly tumbling to the floor. At the base of the chute, Gavin suggested they stop for "a quick breather," and they slumped wearily against the opposite wall. It was warm, and they saw no sign of an opening in the tube ahead of them.

Poisonous fumes seared their lungs. Perspiration streamed off their faces and arms, and their clothes were soaked. They finished what little water was left in Maile's bottle.

"Let's save our batteries," Maile said, switching off the one good light. Sounds became all the more evident in the dark—the boom of cracking rock, the hiss and pop of lava, and their own agonized breathing. As the flow moved down the tube, they could hear its hardened edges scraping the walls, like claws tearing at the stone. But they were too exhausted to move, even if there had been a way forward.

"You were right, Gavin," Maile said, unconsciously fingering her lizard talisman through the damp fabric of her shirt. "I should have listened to Aunty Keala."

A dim ruby glow began to replace the darkness, illuminating the grave faces of the couple huddled against the wall. Tears seeped out from Maile's shuttered eyes, and her lips trembled as she muttered a Hawaiian prayer. The tube soon glowed with rosy light, and the steamy air shimmered. The flow, still beyond the bend, projected a dancing shadow on the far wall, the figure of a woman, her long skirts and flaming hair bouncing wildly side to side.

"Pele," Gavin muttered, his mouth agape. Finally free of his logical mind's resistance, Gavin prepared to meet the goddess. For days now—ever since their dreamy encounter on Maile's lanai—Gavin's gut had told him that the meeting was possible. But he had not imagined it would happen at the moment of his death.

Maile opened her eyes as the lava appeared around the bend, and the dancing shadow vanished in a flood of orange light. The glowing river, two feet thick and wall to wall, moved swiftly, carrying with it boulders and other rocks snatched up along the way. For the first time in hours, the entire cavern was brightly illuminated. The flow pushed up along the bend and spilled down the chute.

"I'm so sorry, Gavin," Maile said.

He turned to face her, searching for his last words. "Maile, you have shown me a deeper world than the one I knew. I'm only sorry we cannot explore it further—together."

Then, suddenly, in the glow that filled the cave, Maile noticed a small tube entrance five feet up the far wall. They bolted for the hole just as lava poured onto the floor at the chute's base. Maile climbed up first, with Gavin pushing from behind, and then pulled Gavin up after her. Lava oozed against the wall below the upper tube, blasting Gavin with scalding heat as they scrambled along the tiny cavern on hands and knees, feeling their way in shadows cast by the lava light behind them. Maile switched on the one serviceable flashlight, revealing at least ten more feet of tube.

"Let's hope that wall ahead is just a corner," Gavin gasped, tortured by the heat blasting from behind.

"I can't breathe!" Maile sputtered.

He unwrapped his bloodied handkerchief from his fingers and handed it forward. "Hold this over your mouth!"

The wall ahead *did* mark a bend, and Maile led them to a wide spot fully illuminated by a small glowing hole in the floor. She crept carefully along the hole's edge, glancing down as she passed. The lava flow had become a surging river, splashing halfway up the walls of the lower tube. Blue gas jets burned atop the flow as it swept down the stone conduit. The temperature of the upper cave—already nearly unbearable—rose further, and the rock over which she scrambled became almost too hot to touch. Once past the hole, they entered a chamber large enough that the couple could again take to their feet. Ceiling cracks allowed tiny breaths of fresh air into the cave, and drops of runoff from the storm dribbled onto their faces, giving them hope that they would soon find a skylight through which to escape.

But their optimism was short-lived. Within minutes, rising heat moved through the tube, followed by more gassy air. They both recognized that this meant lava had filled the lower tube and was now pushing up into their escape route.

Two lava flows now poured down Hualalai above Kona. The first flow to emerge from the clouds—the one Jimmy had spotted from the plane—was the smaller of the two and the one farther south. By late afternoon, it had already left a 300-foot-wide swath of destruction and was headed straight for the Sheraton Keauhou Bay Resort. The other flow, much wider and somewhat slower, emerged from the clouds thirty minutes after the first flow was sighted, moving parallel downslope and closer to Kailua town. It had crossed the highway three miles from Holualoa, burning and then burying four houses, including the home of Aunty Keala's neighbor, and was now expected to cross Ali'i Drive and enter the sea an hour or two after sunset. Several condominium complexes and the twelve-story Outrigger Keauhou Beach Resort seemed to be its target.

At 3:55 p.m. Mike Takahashi came over the airwaves to announce that Governor Calvin Kamali'i had finally declared a "state of emergency" for the whole Kona coast. It had taken almost an hour to locate the governor. After ducking out of the Royal Ballroom, he'd eluded even Lankowski by slipping into one of the hotel's many bars to contemplate his response to the arrest of Makaha Nuiloa, a man with whom the governor had had his picture taken many times. At a secluded table overlooking storm-whipped Kiholo Bay, his mind drifted on swells of old memory, recollections from his youthful days before he'd become a pawn of the political machine. Kamali'i was so caught up in his reverie that even the bolt of lightning outside the window failed to stir him from the past. It had taken the grasp of a husky bartender bearing a message from the Civil Defense director to shake him back into his predicament.

Meanwhile, a Civil Defense field command post was established at the Kona police station—a day later than Mike Takahashi would have begun preparations had he not been deluged with complaints from politicians, real estate agents, and developers following his Friday radio bulletins. Never had he experienced such political pressure. But Takahashi was among the youngest of the *Sansei*—offspring of Hawai'i's first-born Japanese Americans—and he disapproved of the political shenanigans that many in his father's generation had profited by. While his Sansei connections had helped him land the Civil Defense post, he held a more altruistic view of public service, one inherited from his principled Shinto father.

Takahashi's own friends, startled by his radio announcements, had urged him to "ease up on all this disaster talk," explaining that "summer is the critical time for Kona retailers and hotels." But those with profits at stake were not alone in their denial. Scores of citizens called the mayor's office and Civil Defense to complain that Takahashi was "unnecessarily scaring the hell out of people." Despite a convincing presentation by HVO's Joe Murdock, the mayor had refused to declare a state of emergency, leaving Takahashi no choice but to get the governor to do it.

Pressure also came from the Hawai'i congressional delegation. One senator faxed a message accusing the director of having "lost his mind," and a congressman sent an e-mail urging "Mike" to "move cautiously" in light of the "sometimes overstated worries of USGS scientists." The other congressman, Harold Yamashita, had exerted his influence through a brief "courtesy visit" to Civil Defense headquarters in Hilo early Saturday morning before flying over to the resort's grand opening. Takahashi, already weary from the mayor's pestering, had struggled through his postquake broadcast while Congressman Yamashita scowled on the other side of the radio booth with menacing eyes.

That morning's broadcast had been the last Mike Takahashi made from the Hilo headquarters. The director was then whisked over the mountains by helicopter to personally direct the evacuation of West Hawai'i. Also on their way to the field command post were numerous county, state, and federal department chiefs. By late afternoon, the police station parking lot was crammed with Civil Defense Jeeps, county fire engines, National Guard Humvees, and the drab Blazers of HVO, Army leftovers from America's three Middle East wars. Joining these were vehicles from the National Park Service, US Coast Guard, Hawai'i County Public Works, the mayor's office, the State Harbors Division, the Civil Air Patrol, and the gas, electric, and telephone companies, as well as the American Red Cross, the County Medical Association, the Salvation Army, and the Humane Society.

Meanwhile, growing activity at the Kona police station had overwhelmed Special Agent Kaiko and his charge, Jimmy Anderson. Machado was expected to arrive any minute with Makaha Nuiloa and his henchman, but there was little hope of a thorough police consultation now. Heavy rains had resumed, and steam boiling off the flows filled the forests with fog, obscuring their locations. Hot lava ignited pockets of methane from rotted vegetation under old flows. The booming explosions were so frequent—dozens a minute—that homeowners scampering to collect their possessions might well have wondered if the crisis was precipitated by the approach of warring artillery.

Shortly after 4:30 p.m. several HVO scientists, including Lelehua Chin and Gus Parker, helicoptered into the field command post. Murdock remained with the seismic instruments above Kilauea, and an assistant took his post at the Civil Defense headquarters in Hilo. The two field geologists who had reached Hualalai's summit cones were instructed to head down the southeast rift to pinpoint the exact location of the vent or vents feeding the flows. They were, however, at least three hours away, depending on weather and terrain. News of the eruption reenergized the drenched pair, both men addicts for volcanic adventure. A break in the weather might give them a chance to witness the glow from the first Hualalai eruption in over 200 years.

70 ∫ The Weasel Finally Gets His Due

5:30 P.M. . . .

"I think we're blocked," Gavin declared, after picking his way through a jumble of rocks left from another old ceiling collapse. Breathing hard through a shred of shirtsleeve tied to cover his mouth, he plopped down on a rock next to Maile. Exhausted as well, she nestled against his chest. Maile switched off the flashlight.

They held each other, waiting for the inevitable red glow to arrive. They'd managed to outrun the lava for yet another hour by breaking off into other branches of the tube, evasions that bought brief respites to catch their breath, sip rainwater from ceiling cracks, and wrap their wounded fingers with strips torn from Gavin's shirt. But the eruption continued to follow them, filling each escape route with molten stone. After nearly four hours underground, Maile concluded that they must have either doubled back or were now moving parallel to the coast. Several times they noticed the sweet odor of burning organic matter, other old bones smoldering into oblivion. At one point they heard the cry of birds echo through the tube and tried to follow them into a side vent, but the calls faded into the rock. Gavin was so tired and nauseous from fumes that he felt he might actually welcome the lava's deliverance. Maile, ashamed of her violation of the burial and weary from fear, accepted the inevitable—a final meeting with the goddess.

And yet, the glow did not appear. Had the lava bypassed them again?

"I'm going to give it one last go," Gavin said wearily, taking the dim light from Maile. She smiled at him, her eyes filled with tears. Gavin gently touched her bloodstained hands. "You stay here, luv, and rest. I'll see if I can find a route through that mess." He worked his way over the pile of rubble, probing with the light for an exit. Maile watched the dull beam flash about the rocks and cave walls until she sat completely alone in the dark. She used the moment to *pule*, to pray not just for her and Gavin, but for her beleaguered people and the 'aina.

Minutes later, a blast of heat poured down the tube. She stood up, not sure what to do. How ironic, she thought. After all they'd been through together, they would now face their deaths alone.

"Maile," said a distant muffled voice. "Maile, I think I've found a way out!"

She stumbled up the rocks in the dark, watching for Gavin's light. The heat rose and the screech of lava scraping the walls grew louder.

"Hurry!" she shouted. "She's found us again!" A moment later, Gavin's dim light popped into view.

One more time she mustered the energy to move forward as heat and glow pursued her, and Gavin saw Maile's silhouette emerge above the rocks, her glistening hair surrounded by a halo of orange.

"I smelled the sea," he said, reaching for her hand. "The exit *can't* be far."

The rich odor of Kiholo Bay, stirred by huge swells, hung in the artificial jungle fronting the lanai of the Golden Coconut Saloon. Robert Conway inhaled the briny evening air, relieved that at least this time Hualalai would take someone else's hotel. The rain had subsided and a light drizzle bled from the clouds, dampening the stone tiles just inside the purple canopies of the outdoor bar. The winds, too, had eased, but the churning clouds above the mountains suggested that the storm wasn't over. A few guests, bundled up in sweaters, huddled under the cabana watching live coverage of the eruption on the giant TV in the corner of the saloon.

The emergency had so overshadowed the grand opening that the party ended early. Half the crowd headed for Kailua town, most to find vantage points along the coast to watch lava pouring down the mountain, and some to help evacuate friends or pick up their cherished belongings. The politicians followed them into town to play "Johnny on the spot" for the media. By then the losses included twenty-five homes, two businesses, thirty-five head of cattle, and the lives of two ranch hands trapped while trying to save them. An elderly couple had also been killed. They had been napping with their television on, unaware Hualalai had erupted, and were unable to escape when their home burst into flames.

The investors gathered in the weatherproof Captain Cook Lounge to watch the news and drink cocktails, some to celebrate their "good fortune" that the volcano had erupted onto other people's developments, and others, those bound to lose money in Kailua, to self-medicate. The rest of the dignitaries drove to Hilo, where it was still possible to fly home. Wailani's protesters had long since departed, confident that Pele's response would have far greater impact than anything they might do, except for two older men still sitting on a lobby sofa holding their placards: *HAWAIIAN LANDS ARE SACRED—ASK FIRST!*

Conway eyed his replica of Cook's *Resolution*, noticing that one of its moorings had pulled loose during the storm, but he was too weary to do anything about it. That's when Lankowski swaggered up to Conway's table, a Vantage smoldering in his mouth.

"Your lucky day," the weasel said, taking a chair. His thin lips carved a smile in his sallow face.

"Shove it, Lankowski," he replied.

"Gee, Bob, I mean it. Those lava flows could have been heading here."

Conway grimaced. "People are already dying in Kailua," he said, "and thousands have been forced to leave their homes. Have you no sympathy?"

"You weren't here for Kalapana or Royal Gardens, were you?"

"Nobody *died* in those disasters."

"True, very true." Lankowski stretched out his legs and signaled the waitress.

The young haole woman came to the table. Like everyone else, she was distracted by the news droning out of the television. Still, she managed to get Lankowski's order and take it to the bartender.

"You have to admit," Lankowski continued, "there's a risk building on a volcano."

Conway recognized the sneer in the comment. He didn't want to talk to anyone, least of all Lankowski. During the past twenty-four hours, realities had poured over his dreams like lava down the pali, burning away his vision. He had come to his least crowded bar to brood alone.

"That cigarette stinks," Conway snapped.

Lankowski glanced at the burning fag with genuine surprise. "Huh?"

"Why don't you disappear like your boss did?"

Lankowski's eyes narrowed. "Seems to me you *both* disappeared."

Conway smiled sardonically. "Where is Calvin?"

"In Kailua. They're going to fly him over the lava flows before sunset."

"Our public servant at work."

Lankowski accepted a beer from the waitress. "We all lucked out, you know."

"Oh, yeah?"

"Well, every television and radio station is fixed on the eruption of Hualalai—instead of the arrest of Makaha Nuiloa at the Royal Paradise Bay. And on the day of the casino announcement—and for murdering a Hawaiian activist, no less."

"Hawai'i's seen enough of those crooks."

Lankowski stared straight into Conway's eyes. "*Your* partners."

"Against my will!"

"Ahhhh." Lankowski leaned back in his chair, insolence in every line of his body. "Old debts come due, don't they?"

Conway glared at him, but Lankowski was still smirking. "I often *give out* debts, Bob, but I never owe them. You dreamers are all alike, always gambling your future on an idea. I never count on anything beyond what's right in front of my nose. Any ambition beyond survival can be dangerous."

Conway felt his heart pound, his blood surge.

Lankowski never felt the blow. He didn't even feel the pain of his broken nose until Conway grabbed him off the floor and shook him back to consciousness.

"Where is that bastard?" Conway said, shaking him by the lapels of his rumpled suit, now splattered with blood.

"Who?" Lankowski replied, barely aware that it was Conway looming over him. A sharp pain radiated from the center of his face.

"Haku Kane! He knew not to come to this debacle! Where is he!"

Lankowski shook his head, his nose flaccid. "I don't know," he mumbled, unable to focus.

Conway shook him again. "Don't give me that, you weasel! You talk to criminals all the time." The bartender came over to break up the fight, but recognizing Robert Conway, stood back, uncertain what to do.

"Weasel?" That epithet opened the lid on Lankowski's mind, and his adversary finally came into focus.

Conway's bloody fingers, gripped tight to Lankowski's lapels, were only inches from his broken nose. Conway's face was bright red, his teeth clenched.

"Listen up, weasel!" he shouted. "You tell me where Haku Kane is or I'll blacken your eyes too!"

"OK, OK," Lankowski replied, fumbling in his jacket for cigarettes. "He's probably at his mountain spread, in Kohala."

Conway lifted him off the floor and plopped him into a chair, blood dribbling out his nose onto the glass tabletop.

"Draw me a map!" Conway demanded, handing him a napkin and a pen.

"You hurt me," Lankowski whined, still trying to fully grasp what had happened as the pain in his face intensified. He made a crude sketch of the route, hurriedly, the need to vomit rising within him.

Conway grabbed the napkin and stuffed it into his shirt pocket while Lankowski dashed to the ferns at the edge of the lanai.

"You ought to quit smoking, weasel!" Conway declared as he strode out of the bar.

71 ∫ Looking for Jimmy at the Eruption

5:45 P.M. . . .

The old Dodge Dart, leaking rain in the downpour, zipped along the Saddle Road toward Kona. It was a good thing Captain Jack's car heater worked, or he and Aka would have frozen up there between the two storm-shrouded mountains. The car radio, however, did not work, so they had no idea Hualalai was already erupting. It was just dumb luck they had chosen the mountain route, rather than around the island's south end, because that road was now blocked by two lava flows fast approaching the sea.

Jack and Aka were headed for the Kona police station, where Jimmy would be waiting with the FBI. The young man had left a phone message at Aka's house Friday, and when Jack learned that Jimmy was still safe, the old sailor cursed with joy and bawled like a baby.

The Dart encountered a roadblock at the Queen Ka'ahumanu Highway, and Jack—initially unaware of the gravity of the crisis—protested noisily, jabbing his pipe at the young National Guardsman. The soldier had only two options—let the irate island resident pass to get him out of his hair, or arrest him. The latter required hassle and paperwork. Besides, what trouble could a couple of old guys driving a beater like that cause?

They were also stopped at the police station parking lot, now crowded with vehicles and the helipad established for the Civil Defense director's chopper. But the CD officer on duty—normally a maintenance man for the county parks department in Hilo—recognized Aka and, in keeping with "local style" protocol, waved them through. The real problem was inside the police station. No one seemed to know anything about the FBI or Jimmy, and with all the eruption hubbub, the two old men were relegated to some butt-crimping plastic chairs until someone found time to help them. While they waited, a new worry seeped into their minds—was Jimmy endangered by the eruption? Twenty minutes passed before a police sergeant walked up with a sealed envelope, official stationery from the FBI's Honolulu office.

Jack ripped opened the envelope. Inside was a note and a Civil Defense pass.

> Captain Jack Hemmingson—
>
> We are accompanying Jimmy Anderson to the FBI secure house in Kailua. He is very eager to see you and Mr. Kaikala. Directions to the house—35 Ali'i Drive—are written below. Meet us there when you arrive in Kona. Use this pass to get through the roadblocks.
>
> *—Special Agent Neil Kaiko, FBI*

They left the station at 6:15 p.m. and made the seven-mile journey—through four roadblocks—in something over thirty minutes. The best and worst of human nature played out at each checkpoint. Tearful residents waited patiently in line so they could retrieve more of their belongings, while tourists and other sightseers pressured the guardsmen to get closer to view the disaster. Civil Defense personnel consoled distraught residents while television crews and photographers shoved their way past barricades, flashing media credentials for which verification was impossible.

The sun hung low over the sea as the Dodge Dart crept along Ali'i Drive behind a line of vehicles. Storm waves pounded the rugged shoreline, and the old car passed through a mist of suspended salt spray. Through intermittent rain of the now-fading storm, Jack and Aka spotted distant red streaks moving down the dark face of Hualalai.

The flows were too far away for them to fully appreciate their destructive power. Towering mounds of 'a'a lava clinkers fronted each molten flow. These jumbles of glowing embers grew higher as they migrated downhill, some reaching forty feet, then collapsing with a cacophony of shatter, like a thousand bottles breaking. Heat radiating from each rocky flow ignited grasses and scorched trees. Houses in the lava's path burst into flames, the storm's dousing irrelevant. Then the towering ridges of 'a'a bulldozed the fiery skeletons, leaving only the memory of homes.

Upslope communities, including Holualoa, were the first evacuated, followed by places closer to the coast—Keauhou Estates, Keauhou Bay Lots, Kahalu'u Bay Villas, and the tourist sprawl of Keauhou itself. Civil Defense personnel, along with guardsmen and park rangers, went door to door, calling out to residents that the time for packing was over.

As lava buried roads, police and Civil Defense officers closed sections of communities, some residents agreeing to leave only under threat of arrest. One homeowner who refused to go was Masayuki Kawamoto, a retired coffee farmer who believed Pele would never take his split-level rambler. He resisted all urgings until Mike Takahashi himself showed up by helicopter to counsel the distraught resident. Moments after lava entered his street, Mr. Kawamoto emerged from his house with the Civil Defense director, the old man clutching the only thing he could think to save in his grief-stricken bewilderment—a pot of steaming rice.

While these evacuations took place, helicopters flew over the next threatened streets, blasting an unrelenting—and still inconceivable—message: "Lava flows are fast approaching and will soon enter the subdivision. This whole area must be evacuated within ten minutes. I repeat, you have ten minutes to leave. All access into and out of this subdivision will cease at 6:45 p.m. . . ."

Downtown Kailua was on alert, but not yet evacuating. Flows did not yet directly threaten it, and only piecemeal evacuation was practical until Army and Marine reinforcements arrived the next day. Even so, Civil Defense messages over the radio and from patrol car loudspeakers urged coastal residents and tourists to "pack up and be ready to go."

"There it is," Aka said, spotting 35 Ali'i Drive, a tiny bungalow clinging to the narrow strip of rock and palms on the ocean side of the street. Jack swerved into the drive with such exuberance that the squeal of the old tires caused Special Agent Kaiko to leap up from the sofa and draw his .45. Jack blustered up the walk and flung open the door without bothering to knock. Peering fiercely at the white-shirted man pointing a gun at his face, he declared, "On this island only city hall crooks wear ties. You must be a fed."

Jimmy popped out from behind the agent and a round of handshakes and hugs ensued. Jack got so emotional that at one point he tried to lighten the mood—and avoid embarrassment—by teasing the rambunctious young man. "I've got an old donkey tether in the car, just in case you decide to get stubborn again," he told Jimmy, a tear crowding his eye.

"Sounds like we need one of those for each of you," the FBI man replied.

They all laughed, and Agent Kaiko offered them Hinano beers from the fridge. Jimmy and the two old men drifted out onto the lanai overlooking the Kona coast, where, under the agent's watchful eye, Jimmy detailed his FBI custody in Honolulu and the identification of Makaha Nuiloa and the Filipino at the chaotic Kona police station. Jack lauded Jimmy for making the arrests possible "on account of them daring snapshots" he'd taken of the murder.

The clouds above the coast finally thinned, but the upper slopes of Hualalai remained cloaked in storm. The sun, half-hidden in golden bands of cirrus clouds, touched the sea. Aka lit a tiki torch on the lanai and Jack used it to light a match for his pipe.

"And the damnedest thing, Jimmy," the old sailor said, "Kilauea went dark last night—no flows, no glow from Pu'u 'O'o, nothin'!"

"Wow. You know the cops say Jake Bluestone jumped in."

"Or was tossed in," Jack replied, puffing on his old briar. "Aka, you don't s'pose it's just a coincidence?"

"Pele has her own way of doing things," the Hawaiian replied with a shrug. "Thirty years ago she visited my grandfather. She told him that if developers went ahead with Royal Gardens and all their other big plans, she would bury the whole coast, including Kalapana—and that's just what she did." He glanced up at the red flows streaming down Hualalai, his watery eyes shimmering in the tiki torch glow. "Now she's come to Kona."

"But she didn't take *our* places, Aka."

The old Hawaiian nodded, but what actually came to mind was a picture of that stone ruin in the forests above Kalapana, an ancient temple that had now survived yet another Kilauea eruption. Aka's family had a relationship with that temple dating back a thousand years, to a time long before the arrival of the Tahitians. The koa tree marking its place had its own multigenerational tradition. It was the second towering tree to be planted there by Aka's ancestors, the first having been felled by lightning when the Tahitian canoes made landfall.

Captain Jack threw his muscled arm over the young man's shoulder. "So you can come back and visit us anytime, Jimmy."

"Without all the *pilikia*," Aka added. Without the trouble.

"I thought I heard you say something about going back to Minnesota, Captain Jack."

The old sailor pushed his ruddy face up to Jimmy's. "What would *I* do back there? Sit around the library in my long johns, dreamin' o' the South Seas? Not a chance," he replied with a grin, although Jimmy detected a crack in his voice when he said it.

The conversation came to a halt when Agent Kaiko approached the screen door with the latest news from the TV: "A hotel is being taken right now."

All four gathered on the far side of the lanai. "There's smoke over there!" Jimmy shouted, pointing toward a stub of shoreline a few miles away.

"That's the hotel going up," Agent Kaiko said, handing his binoculars to Aka.

"The Sheraton Keauhou," Aka announced, sharpening the focus. His eyes narrowed at what he saw next, an owl soaring above the smoke plume.

"I smell it too," Maile said as they rounded another bend in the tube. "The sea can't be far away."

The thought of cool water might have brought them psychic relief, but the screech of boulders dragging across the cavern floor meant that the river of molten rock had plowed into the heap of debris they'd just climbed over. The flashlight, having flickered on and off for half an hour, finally died, and darkness enveloped their path. Gavin shook the light in vain. "It's gone," he said.

Maile slipped her hand inside the crook of his elbow. "We'll have to feel our way," she said. Step by step, Maile guided them down the twisting tube solely on instinct, one hand outstretched for protection. Each imagined the cave's exit in their own way—for Gavin, the blue of sky, and for Maile, the blue of the sea.

The scrape of rock grew deafening and the oppressive heat rose. Maile's concentration finally broke and she screamed. The couple cowered, hands pressed over their ears, so they did not hear the suck and draw of water surging into the tube, or realize their shoes were wet. An inkling of ruby glow rose behind them, issuing from just beyond the last bend. Maile, exhausted, dropped to her knees. She felt small waves against her arms and legs, but believed the sea had come only in her imagination. Gavin, fumbling in the dark to find his partner, also discovered the water.

"It's here!" he shouted, dashing in up to his thighs. "The sea! We're at the sea!"

Disbelief turned to glee as a red glimmer on the wave tops confirmed their discovery. Maile cupped her hands into the surge and poured cool water over her fevered face.

"Mahalo, mahalo, mahalo," she said over and over.

Gavin ran further into the waves, immersing himself.

"Is it night, then?" he yelled, looking up for stars. But the reddening cavern walls held the answer. To their horror, the brightening glow revealed that the cave continued underwater. Maile gazed at the rise and fall of the surge at the end of the tube, still struggling to grasp their predicament when the cave lit up with vivid orange light. Both looked back when the lava angled around the bend, boulders and other debris now embedded in its flow. They shielded their faces against the heat.

Gavin pulled Maile up from the water and kissed her mouth so desperately that her lips tingled after his release. "I love you," he said, peering into her shadowed face. "More, I think, than I've ever loved another."

Tears welled up in her eyes.

"C'mon, luv, it's not over!" he said, guiding her into the onrush of waves until they lapped against their chests. "Here's our way out."

A finger of lava kissed the sea inside the tube, sending up steam that sprayed the cavern wall.

"You're the swimmer, Maile. Take a big enough breath for both of us."

He let go of her hand, and they inhaled, glancing one last time into each other's eyes. Gavin paused an instant to watch Maile disappear beneath the waves, then followed her into the inky black surge.

72 ∫ A Big Enough Breath for Two

6:59 P.M. . . .

The swell, aided by the mightiest strokes Maile could muster, pulled her well down the tube. *But where's the light at cave's end?* she fretted. Molten rock exploded as it entered the water, sending shock waves and a deafening thunder down the tube. *Where's Gavin?* Maile glanced back through the watery darkness. *Why don't I feel his presence?* She kicked madly against the backwash of tidal swell as streams of heat surged into the cool water around her. *How long can I last down here?* The surge reversed, pushing her outward again, but the opaque water, the pressure of depth, and the rising heat ignited panic inside her chest. *Keep going!* Again the swell shifted. Her lungs ached, and bubbles spilled out her nose. *Go! Go!* She kicked off her shoes and flailed out of her jeans. On animal adrenaline, she fought the reversing surge. *Holding ground! Making it!* A black patch drifted across her brain, and her head began spinning.

What's that light over there? The glimmer grew in size and brightness, but it was not the white of sunlight. *It's red! Red!* Her mouth emptied, bubbles into her jumble of hair. *Out of air!* She kicked all the way up through rocking waves and gulped down mouthfuls of air—air saturated with warm steam that made her cough. She opened her eyes and found herself in fog. She tongued her lips. *Sulfur?* Moist clouds skimmed the water, and through their passing veil she saw the red sun touch the horizon. Bobbing about on huge chaotic swells, she felt nausea seep into her gut.

A glowing rock scorched her elbow, hissing with steam as it spun atop the wave. She thrashed backward, but more lava chunks—still buoyant on gas—surrounded her, blistering her skin, singeing her floating hair. Temperatures rose in the waves. Treading water, her bare legs passed through clouds of hot lava sand, a thousand pinpricks. The sea roared.

She swam toward the vanishing sun, where the air freshened and the clouds in her mind began to part. *Gavin, where are you?* She spun around, searching for his head among the swells and glittering lava. Through an auburn fog, she spotted the shore, steep cliffs awash in froth.

"Gavin!" she screamed from atop a giant swell. "Gavin, are you here?" All alone, another panic pierced her chest. She bit off a chunk of air and dove deep beneath the wave, propelled on adrenaline aroused by a new source—her heart. Back through the hot sand and into the heat.

Great pillows of fuming rock tumbled out of the underwater cave, and in their glow Maile noticed a ruddy shadow moving slowly away from the entrance. Riding the inward pull, she drifted close enough to spot an arm, then legs, the limbs dangling as if lifeless in the surge. *Gavin!* She swam to him, grabbed his tattered shirt, and dragged him to the surface. Out of a muffled world into noisy chaos. Waves thundered against nearby cliffs, steam raced over rolling swells, and gyrating lumps of glowing lava hissed atop the waves. Clouds of black sand surged beneath them, prickling Maile's exposed limbs. But she was oblivious, her attention on the man cradled in her arms. Purple twilight shrouded the scene as the couple rode up and down the billowed swells, wave tops shattered by the gale.

Then she realized he wasn't breathing. *Don't panic now!* She opened his mouth to clear the tongue, rolled him over on the wave, and treading water to get above him, thumped hard on his back. No response. "C'mon, Gavin!" she screamed, her lips trembling. She struck again, this time so hard a red mark rose on his skin. He gasped, then coughed, and finally vomited seawater. The convulsion over, he gulped breath after breath. Maile's eyes burned as she watched him revive, finally opening his green eyes. He looked about, dazed, like a child thrust from the womb.

"Maile?" he said. Up and down they rode the blue-black waves while volcanic steam spun in little tornadoes about them. Combers smashed against the cliff, a muffled roar through Gavin's water-plugged ears. A lump of steaming lava floated by his nose. "Did we make it?" he asked tentatively.

Maile nodded. Tears, gated during the crisis, flowed freely down her cheeks.

Suddenly the sea exploded with a rocketing blast of steam that triggered an offshore wave and obliterated the view, and the entire river of lava, finally free of its subterranean passage, disgorged into the Pacific. A thousand floating embers lit up the water—instantly scalding hot! No words of alert were needed, and once more Gavin and Maile strained lung and limb to escape.

Neither stopped to rest until they were a thousand feet offshore. From there they could see the towering plume of steam, which almost obscured the runway beacons and observation tower of the Kona airport. Subdivision lights sparkled on the slope above the airport, but farther down the coast—where most people lived—the volcano was oddly dark, save for two glowing red streaks heading toward the sea. A shroud of blue-gray storm still hid Hualalai's upper slopes, but out over the water, stars were becoming visible in small gaps in the clouds. And one bright planet shone as a beacon—Jupiter.

A dark object moved into the periphery of Maile's view—a huge dorsal fin slicing a swell near the now-reddish steam plume where molten rock poured into the sea.

73 ∫ In the Hands of the Gods

7:04 P.M. . . .

No one was more surprised than Mike Takahashi when the ocean fronting the airport exploded with volcanic steam. The Civil Defense director was buckling himself into a chopper when it happened—on a tarmac only 300 yards from where lava poured out the underground tube into the ocean. The crisis was only four hours old, and he was already fed up with surprises. Never before in his twenty-five-year career had he lost a life during an eruption, but by the time Hualalai's lava had reached the sea, the death toll was already fifteen. Most were old or infirm, unable to escape before lava engulfed their homes. Four were dead before the first Civil Defense siren had even blown, including two sleeping children on a coffee farm near Judd Road.

Takahashi could not bear the deaths of the children. Their mother had left the three- and four-year-old unattended during their afternoon nap so she could make the ten-minute trip to Holualoa for milk. The first lava flow stranded her when it crossed the old highway, something she learned when she arrived at the store. She called several neighbors for help—having switched off her home phone's ringer to let the kids nap—but by then they'd all abandoned their homes. She raced up and down every farm road she knew to gain access to the other side of the flow, but lava had severed them all. Insane with panic, she abandoned her car and tried to cross the hardened skin of the fresh flow in her flip-flops. Exhausted, her feet blistered from heat, she finally reached the farm, only to discover the house burned and all but buried beneath a swath of steaming black pahoehoe.

The destruction of the Sheraton Keauhou Bay Resort was also a point of regret for Takahashi. A miscommunication between his field crew and the hotel's bewildered management had delayed the evacuation. Although every guest and employee got out before lava poured into the lobby, gas lines to the kitchen had been inadvertently left on during the shutdown of utilities, causing explosions that undermined the structural integrity of the first floor and eliminated any possibility of salvaging the building. The blasts also damaged a dozen vehicles parked out front and injured three diligent employees loading up one last van of hotel valuables.

By the time that flow had reached the Sheraton, seventy-five structures, including homes and condominiums, had also been destroyed. Meanwhile, the second flow, a quarter mile north, had turned into a river of fast-moving pahoehoe, which would likely reach the Outrigger Keauhou Beach Resort before moonrise.

Takahashi had boarded the helicopter for a predusk air reconnaissance when the underground river of lava passed beneath the airport runway and into the sea. Strong southwest winds bent its plume landward, and within minutes the terminal was engulfed in a haze of acid rain, steam, and glass particles—including golden strands of Pele's hair. Emergency personnel, stationed at the airport following its evacuation, dashed behind ticket counters and the half walls of the open air terminal. Those with dust masks or particulate inhalers put them on, and the rest shielded their mouths with handkerchiefs or bandannas.

"Keep the ship running," Takahashi shouted to the pilot over the chopper's roar. "I'll be right back."

"If these fumes keep up, I'm gonna have to move her," the pilot hollered back. "They'll trash my engine in no time."

Takahashi held up five fingers. "Five minutes. That's all I need."

Takahashi used the first minute to reach the terminal, and the second to bark out orders to Civil Defense underlings for keeping an airstrip available for emergency traffic. He used the third and fourth minutes for a brief but superheated phone conversation with Joe Murdock at HVO.

"Good God, I've got a lava flow a hundred yards off airport property, and you guys don't know a damn thing about it! I need better information than that, Joe!"

"I know, Mike. I know," said Murdock, "but until those mountain winds subside, we can't trust what our seismographs are saying."

"I don't care if I get *inaccurate* information. I want to know about anything—*anything!*—that even hints of activity on Hualalai."

"Problem is, we're getting ground shake at all four Hualalai seismic stations—say nothing about what's showing up on the Mauna Loa record."

"Mauna Loa?"

"We're getting impulses from virtually every Mauna Loa station, but one in particular—on the volcano's northern flank—shows a persistence that has us a little concerned."

"Northern flank? But there's no rift zone over there."

"Radial vents."

Takahashi thought for a moment. As Earth's largest volcano, Mauna Loa was so huge and powerful that its eruptions could tear open a vent almost anywhere on its flanks. Just as Takahashi's mind formed the words, Murdock said them: "The 1859 vents."

"Oh, Joe," Takahashi said, rubbing his forehead. "The last time a Mauna Loa flow reached North Kona it came from those vents. Eight days later, it poured into Kiholo Bay."

"It's probably just wind," Murdock said, trying to reassure his trusted colleague. "Especially given that side of the mountain's exposure to the storm."

"Keep me posted on that—and on anything you have about Hualalai. What's the word from your men in the field?"

"They've been feeling all kinds of earthquakes but they couldn't reach the vents before nightfall. So unless they see glow tonight, we won't know any more until tomorrow."

"Are you going to send someone to Hualalai's northwest rift too?"

"As soon as possible, now that we know there's lava at the airport.

Hard to believe she's erupting on *both* rifts, Mike."

Takahashi glanced at his watch, about to enter his fifth minute. "Joe, should I clear the airport?" Just uttering the words brought beads of sweat to his brow. That would mean evacuating two airliners, numerous small planes and helicopters, scores of emergency vehicles, and more than a hundred personnel.

"My scientists—Chin and Parker—are just down the road at our Kona field command post. I'll call them, but they're probably already on their way. In the meantime, I'd get ready to move."

"Tell me what's possible—the worst-case scenario."

"OK, Mike. One, a surge of lava breaks out of the tube aboveground that threatens the airport. Two, a littoral cone forms at the coast, throwing spatter onto the runway and anything that's parked there. Three, a wholly new eruption vent opens up. Since we don't really know how Hualalai behaves, you'd better be ready for *anything*."

"You're talking about more than the airport then?"

"Hell, yes. There's a lot of houses built on that part of the mountain. Fact is, Mike, you might want to consider an evacuation of everything, Kailua included."

Takahashi was already having trouble getting people out of the upland subdivisions currently threatened. He could hardly fathom a total evacuation, especially with military reinforcements not due to arrive until the next morning.

"Joe, didn't you guys have any idea this might happen? What have you been doing up there?"

"Fighting with the USGS bureaucrats on the mainland!" Murdock blurted. "We've been trying to get this information out for more than two years. Why don't you ask Congressman Harold Yamashita and his Chamber of Commerce buddies those questions!"

Takahashi winced as if a boot had struck his gut. He gazed out at the fiery steam plume, its height growing.

"Sorry, Joe," his voice in defeat. "You can tell me all about it later, over beers or something. In the meantime, keep me posted."

"We'll do our best, Mike, but we need that wind to stop shielding our data. The Weather Service is baffled. They say the storm is only on the Big Island now, a low-pressure system convecting right above the mountains."

Takahashi looked up at the sky and noticed a star or two out to sea. "The rain stopped here half an hour ago, and the winds have dropped a notch. Maybe tomorrow we'll be able to see what we're dealing with," he said, wondering what kind of body count he'd have by morning.

Strong ocean currents, fueled by days of storm, carried Gavin and Maile up the coast and away from Kailua. In fading twilight they watched for a safe place to exit, but huge combers pounded the whole shoreline, the task made all the more difficult by the giant swells on which they rode, some fifteen feet from trough to cap. Maile asked Gavin to keep Jupiter in sight, supposedly to maintain a fix on their position, but her assignment was actually meant to keep his mind off what would soon be a chill in his bones.

Maile watched the passing shore, knowing that even if they missed the sandy bays at Mahai'ula and Makalawena, there was always Kiholo, which should be easy to spot with all the lights of the Royal Paradise Bay Resort. Slowly the couple drifted out to sea, and the airport lights and glowing red plume grew distant. A fog passed over them, cutting visibility to less than a hundred feet. Eventually even the crash of waves against the shore faded. Only the intermittent glow of Jupiter in the passing clouds of fog assured them that currents were still moving them up the coast.

Gavin was the first to shiver from hypothermia, but Maile was also affected, and she knew that fatigue and cold would soon sap whatever rational judgment remained after their ordeal. As a precaution, Maile linked herself to Gavin with the straps of her little backpack. Tired and barely kicking, they were flotsam rising and falling on the swells.

Now and again, little whirlwinds spun out of the fog, pausing next to the couple, then swirling away. Over time, the wind's maddening drone transformed into a soft harmonic murmur. Maile heard the voices first, a sweet low chorus singing in some lost Hawaiian dialect.

She had heard the melody once before, as a child swimming at night in a cove on the Kaʻu coast. Its source had been a mystery, but she accepted its reality, and assumed the song was sung for her.

She looked over to check Gavin's reaction, but he was lost in his own thoughts, staring at Jupiter's diffuse glow. She heard the soft swish of water as if a hull was slicing through the waves farther out to sea. She turned away from Gavin and faced the sound, and a small Polynesian outrigger with a lone paddler emerged from the fog. Tattoos adorned his strong young body, and Maile recognized the elaborate bold designs of the Marquesan Islanders, Hawaiʻi's original settlers. He sang with the rhythm of his paddle stroke, accompanied by voices in canoes beyond the foggy veil. He passed to her left, smiling softly as he floated by. She heard the splash of the other canoes and listened to their chorus fade into the waves.

"I'm losing it," Gavin muttered, his head bobbing, eyes half-closed. "I'm sorry."

"Did you see them?" Maile asked, the bone talisman floating close to her face.

"Only Jupiter."

Maile tightened the straps of her pack to raise Gavin's head well above the water. "Sleep a little, if you can," she said, brushing her fingers over his brow. "We may have to wait until morning to make a landfall."

"I love you," he said, shutting his eyes.

Maile began to shiver in the foggy night air. She realized they were probably lost, and that by morning Kanaloa's currents might even take them beyond sight of land. A prayer chanted by fishermen on journeys far out to sea came to mind. Her mother loved that pule and had recited it to her daughter on stormy nights when Kona winds rattled the louvers of their Pahala home. The words came easily, and Maile muttered them to the rhythm of the waves, keenly aware of the carved lizard tugging gently at her neck. She closed her eyes and would have dozed had she not felt the wake of a nearby sea creature.

Even when its huge blue back broke the surface one swell away, she was not afraid. Water poured off its flanks, revealing its stunning coat of white spots. The giant whale shark moved easily through the water,

The Marquesan sang with the rhythm of his paddle stroke, accompanied by voices in canoes beyond the foggy veil. He passed Maile, smiling softly as he floated by.

first circling the pair, then falling in next to Maile, where it gently brushed its tail fin against her body.

"Kamohoali'i," she whispered, reaching out to his fin. She held fast, and with Gavin strapped to her back, sailed through the water under the shark's strong, steady tow. Feeling an onrush of love that warmed her whole body, she closed her eyes and vanquished all thought, and for the first time since her youngest days, Maile was aware only of her na'au. There was no memory and no future; all before and after was opaque. The moment was so alive and vivid that it was easy to trust the shark and know she was now in the hands of the gods.

74 ∫ The Fateful Meeting

9:55 P.M. . . .

The rain had ceased by the time Robert Conway reached the turnoff to Haku Kane's estate. For the first time in more than a week, a few stars shone over Kohala, and the slivered moon had just risen off the island's eastern coast. Even the clouds on Mauna Kea had begun to recede, exposing fresh snow all the way down to 7,000 feet. Remnant wisps of ground fog bounced off Conway's Range Rover as he sped up the narrow drive leading to the mansion. In the moon's first light, Conway thought he saw a wild boar along the road, a persistent phantom until he reached the security gate. An immense Hawaiian bundled up in a wool jacket strolled over from the guard shack where two pit bulls paced their cage.

"What do you want?" the guard asked in a tone as cold as the mountain's night air.

"Haku Kane." Conway let out just enough rage to sound dead serious and handed the man his driver's license. "I'm Robert Conway, builder of the Royal Paradise Bay Resort. Lankowski sent me."

The guard stared back, miffed.

"Nobody told *us* you were coming." The big man peered at Conway's face with cold discernment.

Conway stared right back. "Nobody knew Hualalai would erupt."

"Got any weapons?"

"Yeah, but you'll have to get Haku Kane's approval before you search *me*." It was an impulsive bluff, but it worked.

"Hold on a minute, Mr. Conway." The guard lumbered back to the shack to make the phone call. Inside a small television buzzed with the ten o'clock news.

"The Outrigger Keauhou Beach Resort is the second hotel overrun by lava tonight," said the reporter, "and a new flow threatens the Four Seasons Hualalai Resort just north of the airport. The loss of a Hawai'i Power lineman brings the eruption death toll to nineteen, and no one's even attempting to estimate property damage . . ."

The guard returned after several minutes. "Mr. Kane's not here, but Congressman Yamashita is. He says you should come in."

Yamashita? Was this a ruse?

"When do you expect Haku to return?"

The guard shook his head. Conway's mind reeled, but at that point he was following a course set moment by moment.

"OK, let me in."

The guard ambled back to the shack and switched on the electric gate, which whirred open just long enough to let the Range Rover through, then sealed shut behind him. Conway took a deep breath and watched the huge mansion, lit up with spotlights, appear through the trees. He'd only heard about Haku Kane's estate above Waipio Valley—the armed guards, the vicious dogs, the expensive furnishings befitting the mighty crime chief.

Conway was a young man when he last spoke with Haku Kane. It was a brief encounter at the Sheraton Waikiki, back when Kane was still a minor figure in the underworld—though already a fearsome presence. Conway had been drinking there with several Korean businessmen one week after making his final payment to Buzzy Kamaka, the Honolulu loan shark from whom he'd borrowed half a million dollars following his geothermal fiasco for financing some leverage capital to persuade his Asian contacts to invest in Hawai'i's imminent '80s boom. Only later he found out that Kamaka worked for one of Haku Kane's mentors as the bagman who delivered exorbitant payoffs to city officials. Kane, at the Sheraton to hear a Hawaiian band, had strolled up to Conway's table, patted him on the back, and said, "Glad to see you're back in circulation, Robert." He then withdrew two Macanudu cigars from his sports jacket, placed one next to Conway's highball, and unwrapped his own. "Buzzy tells me you're the man to watch in the future," Kane said, igniting his cigar with a large gold lighter. "And I fully intend to do that." He ambled back to his table, the smoldering Macanudu protruding from his mouth.

Now, driving up to Haku Kane's mansion, Conway remembered the sinking feeling of impotence that had seized him that evening, and he was determined to purge it tonight.

Two guards waited on the lanai, where Conway was unceremoniously frisked.

"Where's the piece?" asked one of the brutes.

"I keep it locked in the trunk," Conway replied. Fortunately, the men didn't ask for his keys. While being escorted to the door, Conway noticed storm damage to the house—windows cracked, pieces of roofing gone, and deep ruts from runoff along its stone foundation. The guards took him inside and down a long hallway to Haku Kane's den. Yamashita sat inside, tucked into the leather couch in front of the crackling fireplace, smoking an impressive cigar. He did not rise to greet his visitor, but in a lord-like way offered his hand. Conway didn't take it, instead moving toward the overstuffed chair across from Yamashita. The congressman observed him with dark eyes that gleamed amid the hardened features of his face.

"Cigar?" he said, pointing at a box on the fireplace mantle. "I'm sure Haku wouldn't mind." There was unmistakable sarcasm in his voice.

Conway, brazen with resolve, smiled. "Good ones?" he asked, opening the box.

"He has surprisingly good taste," replied the old Nisei with a smug smile.

Conway plucked out two Havanas, pocketed one, and sat down in the chair with the other. "Where is the man?" Conway asked, biting off the cigar tip. He eyed the congressman, half-convinced that Kane was hidden in the shadows or listening by intercom.

Yamashita shrugged his shoulders and laughed. "Nobody knows."

Conway replied with a puzzled look.

"He was last seen riding his finest thoroughbred down into Waipio Valley."

Conway located a desk lighter from the coffee table and lit the cigar. "When?"

"Early this morning."

"During the storm?"

"I'm told he was not, ah, himself." Yamashita leaned forward on the couch and looked hard at Conway. "Can you shed some light on this?"

"I don't track his personal habits."

"His wife tells a fantastic story, of visions and ghosts." Yamashita raised his eyebrows. "I have not been able to determine which of them has lost their mind."

Conway puffed the cigar. "Easy to lose one's bearings after years of deceit."

The congressman frowned.

"I have no idea why Haku Kane would choose to disappear at this particular time," Conway continued, "but I'm damned disappointed. There are a few things I want to tell that bastard."

Yamashita's face showed no particular interest, but the gleam in his eyes intensified.

"There is another man who's gone missing," Conway said, "a young Hawaiian, Kalama Ho'eha'eha. I have a feeling, Congressman, that you know what happened to him."

Yamashita's eyes narrowed, the gleam gone.

Conway leaned forward. "As you know, they've arrested Makaha Nuiloa for his murder."

Yamashita's hand, resting on the chair's arm, clenched. "Your business is with Haku Kane, not me."

Conway rose from his chair, the long cigar protruding in his mouth. He walked over to the couch and looked down at the old politician.

"You were once a great man, a dreamer. Fighting against enormous odds, you and your comrades pushed out the old guard and brought a breath of fresh air to Hawai'i. That took real courage. But being in Washington all these years has changed you, vanquished your rebel spirit. Now you're just a power-drunk old man—like Haku Kane."

Yamashita's eyes flew open at such disrespect. No one—save a few noisy activists—dared criticize one so well positioned. Here was the great entrepreneur—one of them!—breaking the unspoken rule by which all with power abide: never attack a fellow broker, least of all with damaging personal truths. "Don't associate me with him," he said. “I don’t approve of his methods any more than you do.”

“Then why are we both here?”

A commotion in the hallway stopped the conversation, rapid-fire words outside the den’s wooden door. A woman screamed.

Yamashita lifted himself from the couch, holding his body stiff.

Conway strode to the door and opened it. The hallway was crowded with people, standing stunned above the body of Haku Kane sprawled across the floor. Leilani, terror in her eyes, dropped to her knees and threw her arms around him, as their five stricken children looked on in shock. Mud caked his riding pants and rain slicker, and muck oozed from his boot tops onto the carpet. His big hands—in rigor mortis—still grasped the reins his men had severed in order to pull him off his drowned horse in the swollen stream. His stiffened body still held his riding position, legs bowed from the saddle and arms stretched forward as they had been around the neck of the submerged beast. In deference to Leilani, one of his men had already closed Kane’s horror-filled eyes, but his bloodless face was ghastly—mouth agape and neck strained from his final attempt to draw air above the water’s wake.

Conway and Yamashita stood in the doorway with their smoldering cigars.

“Hawai‘i just changed,” Yamashita muttered.

“It’s about time,” Conway replied, stepping back as the family and guards huddled closer to the body. He slipped out unnoticed. Once on the lanai, he tossed his cigar and drew in a breath of fresh mountain air. The moonlight caught the tops of the trees and the sky was filled with stars. Conway walked across the lawn to his Range Rover, and as he opened the door, heard a rustle in the brush. A huge black boar darted through the trees, grunting loudly, and then the mountain shook with a force that threw Conway to the ground.

Shocked, he watched as trees swayed, limbs snapped, and the land around the mansion seemed to drop a foot. The sounds of glass shattering and wood splitting filled the forest as the mansion pulled up from its footings. Muffled screams issued from inside. Two of Kane’s children, a son and a daughter, appeared in a window, their little hands pressed against the fracturing glass, mouths open in terror. The big front door flew open—all the panicked shrieks within let out!—and

Yamashita dragged himself onto the lanai. But the twisted house had already tilted back toward Waipio, and he faced an uphill climb. Slowly, with inexorable force, the mansion slid toward the valley as the cliff beneath it tore away from the bluff, leaving an enormous gap in the woods.

Struggling upward from the shaking ground, Conway got to his feet as the crash echoed out of the valley. The earthquake stopped and the forest fell silent, except for the grunt of the boar foraging in the dark. Heart pounding, Conway dashed to the new cliff edge. The valley's sheer walls glowed in the moonlight, its many waterfalls tumbling into the abyss like rivulets of diamonds. The swollen Wailoa River meandered over the dark valley floor to the sea, where milky combers pummeled the shore. For an instant Conway thought he heard a voice call out in pidgin from the shadowed forest below, but the words failed to come again, and he concluded it was only his imagination.

Haku Kane's wife—bloody from having broken a window to escape—and five of the compound's surviving guards converged along the ridge, yelling out to anyone who might still be alive. Conway, unnoticed, sprinted back to the Range Rover and tore down the drive. Luckily the gate had collapsed during the calamity, and the spooked dogs were nowhere in sight. Ten minutes later, when Conway reached the highway, a strange calm settled over his soul.

He parked his SUV on the edge of the road and got out. The storm had finally dissipated, and the island gleamed under the moon's glow. Mauna Kea, now draped in the heaviest snowfall in decades, lorded over the scene. Hualalai loomed as a shadow above the Kona coast, its summit also crowned with snow, as orange lava flows flickered on her slopes and two red plumes boiled up from her shore. Much closer, the lights of the Royal Paradise Bay twinkled in the darkness.

For the first time in weeks, Conway felt relief, having finally said his piece to those who had contaminated his dream. He inhaled deeply, then climbed back into the Range Rover to make the long drive to Kona. His body vibrated with a vague sense of insight, and his head resounded with voices, mostly from his past. The most distinct words washing up into his mind had been spoken by his mentor, Helmut Gieselmann, during one of their private moonlit sails on San

Francisco Bay, the city's lights shimmering on the dirty water through which Conway, at the wheel, cut a clean, even wake. His mentor sat in the cockpit, several bourbons into the night, reminiscing about early business exploits and the grand times he'd had in North Beach, at the St. Francis Yacht Club, and at his other San Francisco haunts.

"The city doesn't have the same hold on me as it once did," Gieselmann had commented wistfully. "We've plenty of change in our pockets, but now we have to live with the change." Tipsy, he had laughed at the turn of his own phrase, but a tear crept out the corner of his eye, caught for an instant in moonlight. "Ah," he said, shaking his head, "the magic's been chased away."

Above the ruin of King Kamehameha's colossal war temple, Pu'u Kohola, Conway was moved to pull over and get out, to look again at the moonlit sea. The temple's stone walls formed a stark silhouette against the shimmering swells, and the waves thundered like the approach of a far-off storm. A huge black frigate bird—an *'iwa*—flew up from the sea, soaring so low over Conway that he felt the rush of wind beneath its eight-foot wingspan. A chill ran through him as he watched the bird disappear toward Mauna Kea. Beyond that mammoth peak, on the glistening white slopes of Mauna Loa, he noticed a pulsing red lava flow that was aimed in the direction of North Kona.

75 ∫ The Ghost of Makalawena

EARLY SUNDAY MORNING, JUNE 18 . . .

Maile awoke slowly on a remote beach called Makalawena, a strand of powdery white dunes built up by the waves of tumultuous Kona storms. The huge swells of the night had subsided, but waves breaking against the dunes still carried a trace of their former energy. The sun had not yet risen over the shadowed hulk of Hualalai, and a cool breeze coaxed open Maile's eyes. The splash and draw of combers lulled Maile back from the dreamy images of the Marquesan paddler and the whale shark, giving way to the sudden recollection of Gavin foundering in the fog.

She sat upright with a jolt and scanned the shoreline. The dunes surrounding the aqua cove were empty, save for the sodden yellow backpack at her side. She gasped on a stark emotion she had felt only once before, when her Aunty Pualani announced that Maile's mother had gone to join the ancestors. Maile's eyes searched the watery horizon as spasms of grief overwhelmed her. She had only just begun to know Gavin—the man with the dazzling eyes, the inquiring mind, and a thirst for all wondrous things, a man to whom she had at last opened her heart fully.

Slowly, feeling as if her briny body weighed a thousand pounds, she pushed herself up off the sand and stood on the beach. Her legs wavered, forcing her to sit back down and fight the sea-spin vertigo left from her ten-hour ride on storm swells. Her stomach flip-flopped and a dull ache rose inside her skull, throbbing with the rhythm of the waves. She fell back on the sand, hoping the whirling would pass, and watched the storm's remaining cirrus clouds grow pink in the day's first light. Several minutes later her equilibrium returned, and she managed to prop herself on an elbow. As the cobwebs spun away, thoughts of Gavin filled the void and again she ached with grief.

She stood up, still wobbly but cognizant enough to recognize the possibility that Gavin had emerged somewhere else along the coast. Maile resolved to search, but she first needed to wash away the fog muddling her brain. She might have restored herself in the blue cove, but she just couldn't face any more salt water. Instead, she wandered over the dunes to locate one of Makalawena's freshwater ponds where she could also get a drink. Far off, under a grove of hala trees, an ivory figure, its back to Maile, rose above one of the pools. It moved so slowly and seemed so out of place that Maile assumed she had returned to the mystical world of the shark. She moved slowly toward the ghost.

Gavin stepped out of the pond, his lean body glistening. With a shout, he started across the sand, his smile undiminished by their fifteen-hour ordeal. And in his eyes, love.

Maile, suddenly aware, cried back. She bolted toward him, arms outstretched, and they fell into each other's embrace, both lovers sobbing.

"I thought you were gone," she said, choking back tears.

"I'm sorry I frightened you," he replied, caressing her cheek. "I tried to shake you awake but you didn't budge. You were breathing normally, but your body was so cold, I decided to gather wood for a fire. When I discovered the pond, I just had to wash the sea salt out of me soul."

"I am so happy to see you alive," she said, peering into his green eyes, luminescent with tears.

Gavin and Maile bathed together in the little pond as the sky lightened and the sun warmed the sea wind blowing over the dunes. They washed each other gingerly, appreciating each caress as though it were their first. A school of tiny shrimp, ʻopaeʻula, flitted about the pool as if celebrating the reunion. Above it all, in an ironwood tree planted long ago by ranchers, a hawk watched in silence, unnoticed by the pair.

"Do you know how we got to the beach?" Maile asked, gently probing to see if Gavin had experienced what she had the night before.

"Yeah. After we found the cove, I hauled us up on the sand."

"So you stayed awake then."

"Naw," he said shaking his head, "only long enough for us to land. Before that I was well out of it."

"Then you didn't see the shark?"

Gavin's eyes darkened and his smile receded. "Oh yes, I did."

She waited for more, but none was forthcoming.

"He was a big mano," Maile said.

"Indeed, he was."

Gavin leaned back in the pool and examined the fatigue lines etched in Maile's face, yet she seemed more beautiful than ever.

"I saw the Polynesian as well," he continued, "and heard the spirits sing."

Surprise passed over Maile's face.

"I'll be honest with you, luv. I haven't a place in my brain to put these experiences, but I know I can't deny them. And, frankly, after all that's happened to us, I have no desire to do that. But I'll need a guide."

Maile's lips curled into a smile, and a sparkle rose in her eyes. She grasped his hands and pledged, "You've got one."

They both looked up when the hawk spread its wings and flew back to the mountains.

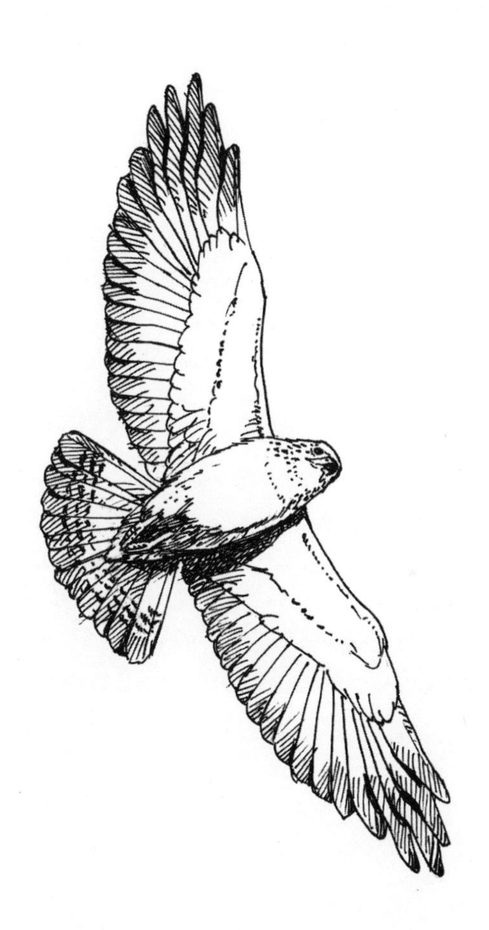

Epilogue

The Mauna Loa lava flow Robert Conway spotted creeping down its snowy slopes that night after leaving Haku Kane's mansion stirred new worries, but its slow progress and remote location behind Hualalai kept Kona residents focused on the destruction wrought by the volcano right behind them. Hualalai continued to erupt for six more days, disgorging from three separate vents enough molten rock to fill up Robert Conway's resort twenty times over—had that been its target. Instead it inundated 2,000 acres of land a dozen miles south of the Royal Paradise Bay Resort and added several miles of new coastline.

Scientists eventually determined that the eruption had begun on Hualalai's southern flank at a centuries-old vent named Waha Pele—"Pele's Mouth"—sending down lava torrents that wiped out two resorts, countless homes, a small boat harbor, and a beach park, and left a wide swath of steaming pahoehoe in front of homes along the coast. A few hours later, an 1801 spatter cone high above the airport also erupted, reactivating an old lava tube near the coast, but no one—save for Maile and Gavin—knew about that until the subterranean flows reached the sea that evening (and no one else ever learned the secret of the cave). Subsequent surface flows from the same cone inundated the airport and the shoreline fronting the Hualalai and Kona Village resorts, both closed indefinitely due to smoke damage from lava-sparked wildfires. During that time, Hawaiians and other islanders, singly and in small groups, brought offerings to the flows, most asking Pele to stop the destruction and all to revere her beauty and power.

The last vent to erupt, an old cone near the summit, was the most spectacular. In the middle of the night, it burst forth in lava fountains 2,000 feet high that startled even the tourists on Waikiki Beach 200 miles away. It continued on and off for two days, and people lined the Kona side of the Saddle Road to watch the distant spectacle, including Captain Jack, Aka, and Jimmy, who had ridden over with Gavin and Maile. Awed by the fountains, Jimmy decided that night to accept a photography job at the Hilo newspaper (arranged by Lieutenant Machado through his friend Ray Ho), and Jack offered Jimmy "a berth" in his cabin until he could find "less dumpy digs" closer to town. As Hualalai spewed cinders into the starry sky, Gavin and Maile uncorked a bottle of champagne to announce their engagement, at which point Aka broke out a fresh batch of ʻopihi he'd gathered near Jack's place that morning.

"I've already arranged to do archaeological surveys for some Hawaiian groups that work closely with traditional elders," Maile had said, her face bright in the distant fountain's glow. "And Gavin's going to seek an observatory position."

"Yeah, I think the mysteries I've experienced these past few weeks will enhance my science," he had added, winking at Maile, "though it may puzzle me colleagues at first."

But their celebrations ended the next day when flows from that same cone plowed straight through downtown Kailua, filling in part of Kailua Bay. Among the losses were the first Christian church in the archipelago and the royal summer palace, Hulihe'e, where the nineteenth-century ali'i had vacationed in European aristocratic style. Miraculously, Kamehameha's temple, Ahu'ena, remained untouched—but surrounded by lava—and the nearby Hawaiian Homelands settlement, finally built after decades of public outrage, was missed entirely.

Sixty-four people died during Hualalai's eruptions, twenty-three having lost their lives in the 7.2 quake that had thrown Haku Kane's mansion into Waipio Valley and damaged other buildings throughout the island. Even before it finished, Hualalai's eruptions were already being called Hawai'i's worst natural disaster, its toll including lost homes, cars, trucks, boats, roads, golf courses, public buildings, and utilities, as well as the casualties. At one time or another Civil Defense closed every portion of the Kona coast between Keauhou Bay and the airport. Kona tourism came to a halt, but sightseers booked every hotel room in Hilo and Waimea, and the helicopter tour companies (now moved to East Hawai'i) experienced a heyday. Not only could they hover near Hualalai's flows and fountains, but they also thrilled their passengers with the massive Mauna Loa flow moving slowly toward the North Kona coast.

The most peculiar aspect of the Hualalai eruptions was the number of people, native and nonnative, who reported having strange experiences of one sort or another during the crisis—long-dead relatives coming back to visit, ghostly processions along the coast, voices in the forests, and odd sightings of spectral craft by fishermen at sea. Dr. Lelehua Chin and her Stanford interns, while working near the Waha Pele vent, were startled when a young barefoot Hawaiian, draped in a maile lei with a guitar slung over his shoulder, approached so stealthily that none heard his footfalls on the fresh cinder and ash. He had said little in response to their questions, except that he was "the guardian of the mountain" and that his name was Kalama. The most bizarre and widely seen apparition was a white-wigged sailor in an eighteenth-century British captain's uniform wandering around in the kiawe trees atop the cliffs above Kealakekua Bay. Seen by more than a dozen residents, some described the phantom as agitated, constantly peering offshore for something beyond his view. News commentators attributed the various sightings to the rattled nerves of residents still reeling from the eruption and its quakes, but local elders knew otherwise.

On the evening of June 24, one week after the eruption had begun, Hualalai's fountains and flows stopped, and people's attention turned to the still-distant Mauna Loa flow. Even so, Kona residents breathed a sigh of relief, thinking the worst was over and that any comparable calamity must be generations away. HVO geologists acknowledged such statements with hopeful nods, but Gus Parker, still fuming, got up at the post-eruption press briefing—where Joe Murdock had also announced his early retirement—to remind the audience that Mauna Loa's flow might still reach the coast and that Hualalai was not the only sleeping volcano that could surprise residents. "Mauna Kea and Maui's Haleakala may look peaceful today," he said, "but you can bet they'll erupt someday too!"

That same morning, Kapu Hawai'i, led by Wailani Henderson, held a prayer vigil up on Hualalai—near the spot where King Kamehameha had once offered his apologies and his hair to Pele—to mourn the innocent victims of the disaster and plead with Pele and the other gods for reconciliation.

Superstitious speculations about the reasons for the destruction spread like lava-ignited wildfires. Island-born businessmen privately discussed who among them was responsible for provoking Pele's wrath, and the consensus was that haole "newcomers" like Robert Conway had gone too far too fast. Conway was a logical target for reproach because, until June 26, his resort had remained unthreatened.

Mauna Loa's eruption may actually have begun before Hualalai's, but storm winds lashing the mountain's upper slopes had initially hidden it from scientists, and when the clouds finally cleared, lava flowing from a radial vent on Mauna Loa's northwest slope had already traveled eight miles. As Hualalai spouted lava fountains from its summit (two days before it shut down), Mauna Loa's monstrous flow—a quarter-mile-wide swath of pahoehoe—swept around the north side of Hualalai and moved steadily toward Kiholo. Within days it crossed the highway and stood on the threshold of the Royal Paradise Bay.

The approaching flow grew even wider on the coastal flats, slowing to an unnerving crawl as it filled in low spots and stalled while its hard crust cooled. Constantly replenished by new lava from Mauna Loa, the black crust would crack open at its different flow fronts, spilling forth more molten stone that crept ever closer to various parts of Conway's vast resort. During that time fleets of trucks finished hauling away Conway's collections of art and artifacts, his Bösendorfer pianos, and whatever furnishings and equipment could readily be salvaged. Conway's young manager Cyrus Bond, who was supervising the evacuation, had urged his boss to abandon his elegant suite, but Conway insisted on staying at the resort, and at night was its lone occupant.

Conway, pacing his lanai, had not believed his eyes when the flows buried Dusty Smythe's signature golf course. The next day, from the decks of the *Resolution*, he watched lava ooze into the landscaped jungle fronting his resort. Then the pools and canals overflowed with steaming pahoehoe, and a boat shed housing all his little sloops went up in flames. That night on his lanai, raging in the glow of the incineration, Conway saw the thatched bungalows of the Hawaiian Village Suites blaze in a fire that cast eerie shadows on the two hotel towers and filled the great banyan lobby with smoke. He wept the following morning when a note arrived at his suite reporting that scores of birds and other animals were dead or missing after the first two days of flows, despite the staff's valiant efforts to save them.

Bloody Mary, the crocodile that had gone missing early in the storm, eventually did show up, unfortunately right when a TV crew was filming the governor "inspecting" the resort during one of his tours of the continuing Kona destruction. Andy Lankowski had come along to help Kamali'i nuance his media statements, and just as the aide bent over to snuff out a cigarette on the doorstep of a charred bungalow, the croc, hidden inside, lunged forward and snapped off his hand.

That evening, with lava stalled outside the resort's main building, the entrepreneur sat alone on the darkened stage of his vacant ballroom at what had been the grand opening's head table. Exhausted and dismayed, Conway had decided to spend his last moments at the resort in what was to have been Hawai'i's first gambling casino. With his Italian loafers propped up on the purple tablecloth, he sipped a bourbon and wistfully recalled Mali'o's enthusiasm about the glittering stage shows, the fancy balls, and the frenzy of people winning and losing money. A cigar smoker only on special occasions, Conway had lit one on his final walk through the doomed resort, the Havana he'd plucked from Haku Kane's stash, discovered while boxing up his own belongings. Musing about the loss of his girlfriend, who'd moved to Honolulu for a gig in Waikiki, Conway had let the cigar go out in his bronze ashtray.

Conway was alone with his thoughts when he spotted a man slip in through one of the huge koa doors, its soft *whoosh* drawing his attention. The dark figure crossed the parquet dance floor, the muffled slap of his rubber slippers echoing through the cavernous hall. In the dim illumination of the stained glass skylight, Conway observed the figure's slow steps as he looked around at the chandeliered room, his face hidden in shadow.

Why a looter now? Conway wondered. The last of the valuable stuff had been hauled out that afternoon. "What are you looking for?" he asked the intruder, startled by the boom of his own voice in the empty hall.

"I came to see what all the fuss was about," the man replied, stepping into the light. It was the old Kiholo fisherman Conway had met on the beach the day before the grand opening. Conway pulled the cigar out of the ashtray and relit it.

The old man, seeing Conway's face flicker in the match light, laughed. "Oh, it's you. Captain going down with the ship?"

Conway shook his head. "I imagine you're quite pleased by all this destruction."

The old fisherman stopped beneath one of Conway's darkened chandeliers. "No, I'm not pleased at all, but I have no more say about it than you do."

Conway croaked softly, his head spinning a little on the potent nicotine of his twice-lit cigar.

"Some of my ancestors made the same mistake," said the fisherman. "Like you, they got big ideas in their heads. Power makes a man crazy. Read history, and you will know your place. The books are filled with stories of empire builders like King Kamehameha—the so-called Napoleon of the Pacific—and you too! We read them over and over, but always take the wrong lesson. Even Kamehameha eventually understood and stepped away from the war god who'd helped him build his empire. Me? I walk lightly, take things as they come, and pay attention to the echo of other people's prayers. Then I act accordingly. It is a beautiful world, Robert Conway. The gods have given us all we need to live and thrive."

Conway stared at the cigar smoldering in his hand. "Fisherman, you've been to sea?"

"Many times, on diesel boats and outrigger canoes."

"Me, too, on sailing yachts. Then you know that after the thousandth wave, dreams begin to invade your mind."

The old man acknowledged the comment with a hearty laugh.

"Well," Conway said, "I *act out* my dreams."

"Ahhh," the fisherman replied.

Conway looked up at the dim skylight. "What was it Thoreau said?

'The mass of men lead lives of quiet desperation.' I wanted more than that. I've always known I was destined to—"

"Conway," the old man said, shaking his head sadly. "Your culture is filled with those desperate men—people who do not know their place in the world, lost souls. I have thought about this for many years, trying to understand my haole friends and even some Hawaiians who now buy into your kind of dreams. People from your culture are desperate not because they do not dream. I think it's because they cannot feel. They do not touch the sacred that is all around us. Their dreams interfere. Only a people who are blind and deaf and numb could do to these beautiful islands what has been done."

Conway sat up in his chair and snubbed his cigar into the ashtray with such force that it rocked on the table, but his eyes were filled with tears. "My mind is alive with ideas! Images of a better future! How can I just leave these in my head?"

"I think you misunderstand the meaning of dreams. For my people they carry messages, not from you or me, but from the ancestors and the gods. But you do not listen to those voices. You make up your own. My elders trained me to listen and observe, and to respect prayers."

Conway got up from his chair. "We live in different worlds, you and I."

"No," the Hawaiian replied. "We share the same world, and that is why you're going to lose your resort. My people tried to prevent all of this, even prayed to stop it, but the disrespect and harm were too much, and we were too late."

The next morning Conway's ballroom was gone, collapsed when the massive flow outside bulldozed its foundation. But the Royal Paradise Bay Resort was not *completely* destroyed. The King and Queen's Towers, though damaged by smoke, survived. Lava surrounded them, just as it had surrounded Kamehameha's temple in Kailua, and the ivory towers stood as monuments amid the vast steaming destruction of the Kona coast. The bay itself was also filled in, leaving Conway's replica of the *Resolution* stranded in a sea of black pahoehoe.

It remained there for many years. On moonlit nights, the lava gleamed, and the ship, collapsed slightly to one side, looked like the great explorer's vessel on a run through heaving seas, searching the

Pacific for those fabled lands conjured up in the minds of white men. None of the places Captain Cook "found" were like the ones Europeans envisioned. The Northwest Passage and Antarctica were solid ice, and Australia, harsher than hoped, became a dumping ground for convicts. The white colonists sought no advice from the people who lived there—even though they had walked the earth as long as any—and their Australian descendants are still puzzled when the "Aborigines" dance beside midnight fires, blow their didgeridoos, and spin their bullroarers to call the gods from the dreamtime.

As the years passed, the simultaneous eruptions of Hualalai and Mauna Loa during the great summer storm became a central story in the lore of the Hawaiian Islands, reminding people of Kamehameha's sacrifice to the dismayed goddess Pele. The new legend became one of those narratives of momentous transition, like the fall of the Roman Empire, when events present an opportunity to put aside archaic ways for a renewed future. Even non-Hawaiians, although quick to create their own heroes and scapegoats for the crisis, ultimately accepted the deeper, more potent interpretations offered by the island's native people. The gods had spoken, and this time some people listened.

The memory of Aunty Keala and her brave snowy trek grew, and many came to believe she now worked as a spirit maiden with Mauna Kea's snow goddess Poli'ahu. Meanwhile, Mike Takahashi's heroic efforts during the disaster—and his starkly honest report of the political machinations that had led to its delayed announcement—became legendary. Pressed by a public demanding real change, he ran for mayor on a program of reform, providing young islanders with a new, uncorrupted symbol after whom to model themselves. Robert Conway, after his last meetings with investors, insurance representatives, and salvagers, bought a sturdy blue catamaran and launched a solo journey to the South Seas to consider what to do with the rest of his life.

As stories of the calamity's amazing occurrences spread from tongue to tongue, each telling amplifying their symbolic meaning, a spiritual renaissance began to emerge, this time involving men and women from *all* the myriad cultures who called this volcanic isle home. Visitors who returned eventually saw a different Hawai'i, one with fewer resorts and golf courses, more native forests and open shorelines, and a more authentic, less materialistic island culture built upon the Polynesian tradition of aloha for all and for the sacred land that sustains them. Maile and Gavin's children were among those who would become leaders of the change.

Native Hawaiians, rather than disappearing from the face of the earth—as the missionaries and purveyors of plantations and hotels had expected—saw their influence grow, as people from around the world began to ponder their ancient stories and contemplate the significance of their mysterious volcanic island situated midway between the Orient, the West, and the Pacific Islands from which those first called to Hawai'i had come.

And all of that would bring about a very different kind of story.

Ho'opau!

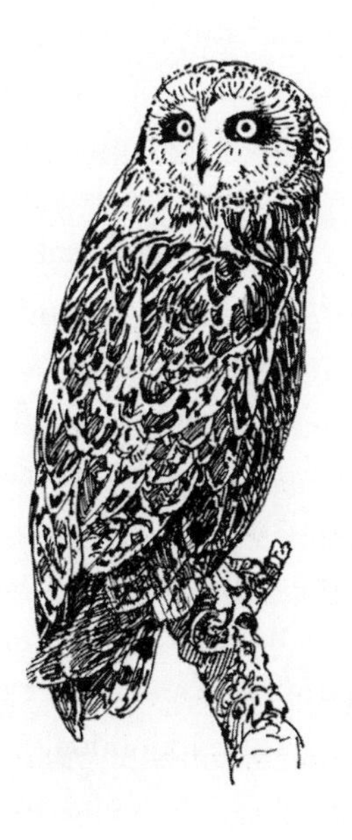

Afterword

Hawai'i, with its remote volcanic islands, extraordinary blend of cultures, and turbulent history, is a place that well illustrates the cliché that truth is often stranger or more fantastic than fiction. This presents a Hawai'i novelist with a challenge. Does he tap his imagination to push the story beyond the real wonders and eccentricities of his subject? Or should he fictionalize reality, trusting that Hawai'i's intrinsic qualities will fascinate and move the reader and perhaps even illuminate important truths? In *Daughters of Fire*, I chose mostly the latter approach.

While the characters and events of the narrative are fictional, its historic, cultural, and scientific backdrops parallel Hawai'i realities. For example, the story's geological scenarios are indeed possible. These types of events have occurred at one time or another, including the simultaneous eruptions of Hualalai and Mauna Loa, as well as eruptions where lava flowed from multiple vents. The kinds of extreme weather portrayed near the end of the novel have also occurred, including fierce Kona storms, summertime mountain blizzards, and low-pressure systems centered over a single island. Similarly, the novel's magical realism fits closely with traditional Hawaiian perspectives, practices, and events found in the historical and cultural literature and enunciated by contemporary cultural practitioners. The novel's political and economic landscape, while fictionalized, draws upon genuine aspects of Hawai'i's milieu at various times since statehood.

Daughters of Fire's many characters are fictional renderings or fanciful composites of the sorts of people one encounters in Hawai'i—Native Hawaiians, local and haole islanders, scientists, politicians, developers, underworld operatives, and resort employees—but they certainly do not represent specific individuals now or in the past. A few real people are mentioned in the story, such as Hawaiian musician and activist George Helm and fisherman and park ranger Kimo Mitchell, who disappeared in waters off Kaho'olawe while returning to Maui from one of their protest landings on the then US-Navy-controlled island.

I have taken literary license with some particulars to forward the novel's themes, keep the reader engaged, and simplify technical details that might clutter or confuse what is already a complex story. For example, "Waipuna Beach" is a fictional composite of the many Hawai'i beaches developed for tourism following statehood and now built up with hotels and resorts. For simplicity I refer to Hualalai's last eruption as having occurred in 1801, although it may have begun in 1800. Dates for its various episodes vary widely in the oral histories, some suggesting the eruption occurred even earlier. Several brief and varied versions of King Kamehameha's sacrifice to Pele exist in the literature, all of which inspired and informed my fictionalized portrayal. For general background I relied most on the renditions in S. M. Kamakau's *Ruling Chiefs of Hawai'i* and William D. Westervelt's *Hawaiian Legends of Volcanoes*. Where King Kamehameha I is buried remains a mystery, and my portrayal of its location and nature is pure fiction.

Islanders may notice that I took slight liberties with some pidgin and Hawaiian dialogue to ensure that non-island readers could understand them. I was also selective in my use of Hawaiian words (and in some cases simplified their glossary definitions) so as not to overwhelm or frustrate readers not yet familiar with that wonderfully vivid language. I chose to include glottal stops (*'okina*) in the text but, for readers' ease, left out the macrons (*kahakō*). For those readers interested in learning the proper Hawaiian pronunciations, both diacritical marks are included in the pronunciation guide and glossary that follows, presented in accord with Pukui and Elbert's *Hawaiian Dictionary.*

I sincerely hope that you, the reader, have enjoyed *Daughters of Fire*, and that through the story and its characters you have felt the enduring enchantment of this volcanic island and the Native Hawaiians who love and defend it.

Mahalo.

Tom Peek
Volcano, island of Hawai'i
March 2012

Further Reading

If your interest in Hawai'i has been stirred by *Daughters of Fire*, you may wish to read more. Dozens of excellent books and articles exist. Here are a few to get started.

FICTION

Shark Dialogues, Kiana Davenport (Plume, 1994)

The Last Aloha, Gaellen Quinn (Lost Coast Press, 2009)

Bird of Another Heaven, James D. Houston (Alfred A. Knopf, 2007)

The Last Paradise, James D. Houston (University of Oklahoma Press, 1998)

The Descendants, Kaui Hart Hemmings (Random House, 2007)

Moloka'i, Alan Brennert (St. Martin's, 2003)

Hawaii, James Michener (Random House, 1959, 2002)

The Shimmering (Ka 'Olili), Keola Beamer ('Ohe Books, 2002)

Under Maui Skies and Other Stories, Wayne Moniz (Koa Books, 2009)

NONFICTION

Voices of Wisdom: Hawaiian Elders Speak, M. J. Harden (Aka Press, 1999)

Na Mamo: Hawaiian People Today, Jay Hartwell ('Ai Pōhaku Press, 1996)

Pele, Goddess of Hawai'i's Volcanoes, Herb Kawainui Kane (Kawainui Press, revised edition, 1996)

Ancient Hawai'i, Herb Kawainui Kane (Kawainui Press, 1998)

Voyagers, Herb Kawainui Kane (Kawainui Press, 2005)

Hawaiian Legends of Volcanoes, William D. Westervelt (Charles E. Tuttle Company, 1916; Nabu Press, 2011)

The Epic Tale of Hi'iakaikapoliopele, Ho'oulumahiehie, translated by Puakea Nogelmeier (Aiwaiaulu Press, 2008)

Tales from the Night Rainbow, Koko Willis and Pali Jae Lee (Night Rainbow Publishing Company, 2005)

Beyond Paradise: Encounters in Hawai'i Where the Tour Bus Never Runs, Peter S. Adler (Ox Bow Press, 1993)

Nation Within: The History of the American Occupation of Hawai'i, Tom Coffman (Koa Books, 2009)

Ku Kanaka (Stand Tall): A Search for Hawaiian Values, George Hu'eu Sanford Kanahele (University of Hawai'i Press, 1993)

Unfamiliar Fishes, Sarah Vowell (Riverhead Books, 2011)

A Call for Hawaiian Sovereignty, Michael Kioni Dudley and Keoni K. Agard (Nā Kāne O Ka Malo Press, 1990)

Dismembering Lahui: A History of the Hawaiian Nation to 1887, Dr. Jonathan Kay Kamakawiwo'ole Osorio (University of Hawai'i Press, 2002)

Land and Power in Hawai'i: The Democratic Years, George Cooper and Gavan Daws (Benchmark Books, 1985; University of Hawai'i Press 1990)

Ho'i Ho'i Hou, A Tribute to George Helm and Kimo Mitchell, Rodney Morales, editor (Bamboo Ridge, 1984)

Hawai'i's Plants and Animals: Biological Sketches for Hawaii Volcanoes National Park, Charles P. Stone and Linda W. Pratt (Hawai'i Natural History Association, revised edition, 2002)

Ruling Chiefs of Hawai'i, Samuel M. Kamakau (Kamehameha Schools Press, 1961; revised edition 1992)

Ka Po'e Kahiko, The People of Old, Samuel M. Kamakau (Bishop Museum Press, 1964; revised edition 1991)

Hawaiian Mythology, Martha Beckwith (Yale University Press, 1940; University of Hawai'i Press, 1970)

"The Deification of Captain Cook," Herb Kawainui Kane in *Ka'u Landing*, November 1994

The Apotheosis of Captain Cook: European Mythmaking in the Pacific, Gananath Obeyesekere (Princeton University Press, 1992)

Exalted Sits the Chief: The Ancient History of Hawai'i Island, Ross Cordy (Mutual Publishing, 2000)

He Mo'olelo no Kapa'ahu (Story of Kapa'ahu), Emma Kapunohu'ulaokalani Kauhi (Pili Productions, University of Hawai'i at Hilo, 1996)

The Polynesian Family System in Ka'u, Hawai'i, E. S. Craighill Handy and Mary Kawena Pukui (Charles E. Tuttle Company, 1958; Mutual Publishing, 1999)

Hawaiian Dictionary, Mary Kawena Pukui and Samuel H. Elbert (University of Hawai'i Press, 1957; revised edition 1986).

Acknowledgments

Like other explorers, writers of books have many people to thank along the way. At the journey's outset my parents, Mary and Roland Peek, launched me with the curiosity, skills, and confidence I needed to explore. Fine writers both, they encouraged my pen and reviewed my earliest writings and the first drafts of this manuscript. Without their belief in the endeavor and their honest counsel along the way, I might never have started or finished any of my writing projects, including this novel.

Also on my journey—during good days and bad—has been my sweetheart, exploration comrade, and wife, Catherine Robbins. For her unflinching belief in this more-than-decade-long project and her sound and creative advice during each of the umpteen drafts, she deserves a medal of valor!

My *kupuna* Aunty Leinaʻala Apiki McCord reviewed the first complete draft, encouraged me to continue, and nurtured deeper insights that ultimately influenced the outcome. But her greatest gift was all those years patiently sharing her Polynesian world with her *hanai* son from the Upper Mississippi who was trying to connect his home island and Viking ancestry in Minnesota with what he'd come to know and love about Hawaiʻi. After Aunty joined her ancestors, Uncle Ed Nalu Stevens and other elders and cultural practitioners continued with equal patience to guide me on my journey. Kealoha Pisciotta, whom I met when we both worked on Mauna Kea, has long been a source of insight and inspiration, and a guide on how to keep faith with aloha in the face of adversity. Thank you all for trusting my heart and for encouraging me to explore things not entirely conceivable to my Western mind.

I also owe a debt of gratitude to other Hawaiian friends who invited me into their rich culture in ways that made my Hawaiʻi life as formative as my Mississippi River days. Two of these people, Keola Awong and Toni Case, whom I first met on the lava flows of Kilauea, read a later manuscript. Their frank and moving reactions gave me heart to recommit to the project just when my energy and optimism had flagged. Mahalo.

Other islanders' comments and background information kept the story's geological, astronomical, political, and societal elements authentic. They include Dr. Bill Carse, a longtime Kalapana resident and former dean at the University of Hawai'i at Hilo; Dr. John Dvorak, a former USGS planetary physicist; Nelson Ho, a Sierra Club leader and Big Island activist; and Harry Kim, former Hawai'i Island Civil Defense director and later Big Island mayor. Mahalo also to former Hawaiian Volcano Observatory staff members Dr. Carl Johnson and Tom English, and HVO librarian Taeko Jane Takahashi, who provided important background information when the project was just a compelling idea in my mind.

Family members and friends tested the manuscript for readability and offered valuable suggestions and encouragement, including Anne Peek, Tom Ehlinger, Peggy Trezona, Jerry and Michelle Taube, Mary Ann Robbins, Page Robbins, David Seidenwurm, Teddy Bell, Scott Sandager, Mary Ann Mathieu, Jennifer Ho, Robert and Caki Kennedy, Barbara George, anthropologist Dr. Michael Osmera, and novelist Arthur Rosenfeld. Mahalo also to Koa Books interns Kalani Ruidas and Nicole Ka'auamo for their encouraging and helpful comments on the story, and to author David Kawika Eyre for his valuable comments and suggestions on the historical prologue.

Author and editor Cynthia Orange applied her seasoned skills to a middle draft, urging me to trim the manuscript and make its cultural aspects and Hawaiian words more accessible to non-island readers. Novelist Clemence McLaren did a detailed, near-final editorial review to further prune the work, improve the readability of its multilayered story, and deepen its interpretation of Hawai'i's contemporary milieu. Copy editor and proof reader Karen Seriguchi applied her knowledge, skill, and sharp eye to the manuscript, contributing greatly to its final polish. Koa Books publisher and editor Arnie Kotler, in addition to recognizing the need for this book, guided the final revision with his astute comments, deft editorial and artistic suggestions, and deep commitment to quality publishing. These four people are proof that a tough editor is a writer's best friend!

I'm grateful that an artist of John Dawson's skill, imagination, and stature agreed to illustrate the book with his wonderful map and drawings. Collaborating with John and his wife and colleague, Kathleen Oshiro Dawson, was a creative delight! A deep mahalo to Mrs. Herb Kane for allowing her husband's stunning portraits of Pele to grace the cover and dedication page. And great thanks to Lisa Carta for the book's beautiful page and cover design.

Hilo computer wizard Roger Lidia constantly jury-rigged my PCs with used parts, keeping the machines and novel alive when I was flat broke. During my grimmest "starving artist" days, my car mechanic Bob Bertini lent me the money to replace one junker with another when no amount of jury-rigging could keep me on the road. He also kept my faith running with enthusiastic comments after test-driving an early version of the novel. Thanks to Bob Evans, who early on recognized a struggling novelist and gave me enough ESL teaching work to stay solvent while I wrote about the island life we both love. Whenever my budget got really tight, my wise friend and spiritual comrade Greg Herbst put me on the national park schedule for firefighting work on Kilauea.

Many others supported the dream along the way, including Dr. Keith Huston, C. J. Peek, Jody McCormick, Jerry Wells, Danielle Uharriet, James D. Houston, Dr. Brad Smith, Diane McGregor, Gene Ervine, Dr. Edwin Bernbaum, Pat and Janet Durkin, Tomomasa Hyakuna, and Keomailani Von Gogh, as well as my many writing students and my friends on Mauna Kea and Kilauea. A sincere mahalo to the many other friends and colleagues whose aid and encouragement helped bring this novel to fruition.

I've been inspired by the lives and words of many writers, particularly Natalie Goldberg, James Norman Hall, Herman Melville, Joseph Conrad, and Mark Twain. And of course, I am forever indebted to Mauna Kea, Kilauea, and the island of Hawai'i for keeping me in touch with life's deepest realities after I returned from hitchhiking by boat across the South Seas.

Mahalo a nui to all!

Were it not for the aforementioned, this book would not be in your hands. Yet I alone am responsible for the story, including any mistakes or misinterpretations—and I humbly ask forgiveness if I have offended anyone with my tale. *E kala mai ia'u.*

Pronouncing Hawaiian Words

The Hawaiian alphabet has twelve letters. Hawaiian vowels (*a, e, i, o, u*) are pronounced similarly to the way they are in Latin, Spanish, Italian, and Japanese:

a is *ah* (as in *father*)

o is *oh* (as in *note*)

e is *eh* (as in *bet*)

u is *oo* (as in *blue*)

i is *ee* (as in *niece*)

Hawaiian consonants (*h, k, l, m, n, p, w*) are similar to those in English, except that the *w* is sometimes pronounced as a soft *v* when it follows *a*, *e*, or *i*, as in the traditional pronunciation of *Hawai'i ("Hah-vah~ee-ee").*

When a word has a glottal stop (*'okina*) between vowels, as in *Pu'u 'O'o*, both vowels are enunciated distinctly with a slight pause between them ("*Poo-oo Oh-oh*"). When a word in the glossary has a macron (*kahakō*) over a vowel, as in *kāne*, hold that vowel's sound a bit longer ("*kaah-neh*").

Generally, when two vowels are side by side (with or without a glottal stop or macron), both are distinctly enunciated *akua* is ("*ah-koo-ah*") and *pahoa* is ("*pah-hoh-ah*"). Some vowel pairs (certain diphthongs) are pronounced by gently sliding into the second sound from the first:

ae is *ah~eh*	(*'ōpae'ula*)	ei is *eh~ee*	(*lei*)
ai is *ah~ee*	(*lānai*)	eu is *eh~oo*	(*pareu*)
ao is *ah~oh*	(*haole*)	oi is *oh~ee*	(*poi*)
au is *ah~oo*	(*'aumakua*)	ou is *oh~oo*	(*Keauhou*)

Glossary of Hawaiian, Pidgin, and Other Words

(Pidgin English in *italics*; major gods in CAPS)

ʻaʻa (ah-ah): rough broken lava flowing in heaps of ember-like clinkers; literally "to burn, blaze, or glow"

a hui hou (ah hoo-ee hoh~oo): "until we meet again"; said instead of *good-bye*

ʻāina (ah~ee-nah): homeland, the land

akua (ah-koo-ah): god or gods, sometimes used to refer to the Christian god

akua lele (ah-koo-ah leh-leh): a fireball or flying god sent to destroy or cause mischief

Alakea (ah-lah-keh-ah): the name of a star, probably used in navigation; literally "the white road"

aliʻi (ah-lee-ee): royalty descended from thirteenth-century Tahitian colonizers; their strict, stratified social system eventually evolved into a peaceful constitutional monarchy that nineteenth-century aliʻi tried to protect after a subsequent colonization by Americans, whose descendants overthrew the monarchy and persuaded Congress to annex the islands to the United States

aloha (ah-loh-hah): love, affection, compassion, kindness; to share the divine "breath of life"; often used as a greeting

aloha kākou (ah-loh-hah kah-koh~oo): "love, affection to us all"; a greeting at gatherings

ʻanāʻanā (ah-nah-ah-nah): evil sorcery

ʻaʻole (ah-oh-leh): "no," "not," or "never"

ʻaumakua (ah~oo-mah-koo-ah): family or ancestral spirits often embodied in animals, rocks, clouds, or plants

auwē! (ah~oo-weh): "alas!" or "oh no!"

bento (Japanese): a small box lunch of rice, along with chicken, fish, and/or pork

chicken skin: goose bumps

choke: much or many

da kine (*dah k-eye-n*): fill-in word with contextual meanings, similar to *whatchamacallit*

E kala mai iaʻu (eh kah-lah mah~ee ee-ah-oo): "I'm sorry"

futless: frustrated, antsy

grind: eat

hā (hah): breath

hala (hah-lah): the pandanus tree, a coastal plant symbolic of traditional Polynesian culture; the leaves (*lauhala*) are used for hats, baskets, bowls, and other woven crafts

halaʻole (hah-lah-oh-leh): innocent

hālau (hah-lah~oo): troupe or school, as in *hula hālau*, named for the long house used for teaching the dance

Halema'uma'u (hah-leh-ma-oo-ma-oo): the name of the pit crater inside the Kilauea caldera, one of Pele's homes, "house of the *ama'uma'u* fern"; also, in some traditions, Halemaumau, "house of eternal fire"

hānai (hah-nah~ee): adopt, adopted

haole (hah~oh-leh): foreigner, Caucasian

hāpu'u (hah-poo-oo): a native giant tree fern

Hawai'i (hah-vah~ee-ee): the name of the island (the Big Island) and the archipelago; elsewhere in Polynesia the name of the underworld or ancestral home; in Hawai'i the name is said to have no meaning

heiau (heh~ee-ah~oo): temple

hele (heh-leh): to go; "let's go"

hewa (heh-vah): wrong or sinful, gravely offensive

hibiscus (English): the official state flower of Hawai'i

Hilo (hee-loh): second-largest city in the Hawaiian Islands; perhaps named for the new moon or a Polynesian navigator

HINA (hee-nah): a goddess known throughout Polynesia, associated with the moon (*mahina*) and the male god Kū

hi'uwai (hee-oo-vah~ee): spiritual cleansing in water, healing bath

honu (hoh-noo): sea turtle

ho'okupu (hoh-oh-koo-poo): ceremonial offering, especially to a chief or deity

ho'olaule'a (hoh-oh-lah~oo-leh-ah): celebration

ho'opau (hoh-oh-pah~oo): to end; finished (also *pau*)

hui (hoo-ee): association or society

hukilau (hoo-kee-lah~oo): to fish with a seine

hula (hoo-lah): traditional Hawaiian dances, many quite ancient

huli (hoo-lee): to turn over or change

hūnā (hoo-nah): confidential, covert; something to be hidden

'ikuwā (ee-koo-vah): voices of the gods in the elements; clamorous

'iniki (ee-nee-kee): to pinch or nip; a piercing wind

'ino 'ino (ee-noh ee-noh): wicked

'io (ee-oh): Hawaiian hawk whose appearance is highly auspicious

'iwa (ee-vah): frigate bird or thief (because it steals food by forcing other birds to disgorge); a sign of *'uhane* nearby

Kahiki (kah-hee-kee): the mythic land from which Hawaiians came, in some traditions Tahiti

kāhili (kah-hee-lee): feather standard that is symbolic of royalty

kahuna (kah-hoo-nah): general term for priest, sorcerer, or expert in any profession or craft

kahuna 'anā'anā (kah-hoo-nah ah-nah-ah-nah): a *kahuna* of evil sorcery, said to have the power to pray a person to death

kahuna nui (kah-hoo-nah noo-ee): high priest

kahuna pale (kah-hoo-nah pah-leh): a *kahuna* capable of warding off evil sorcery

Kailua (kah~ee-loo-ah): Kona coast's largest city, the former residence of King Kamehameha and other royalty; the name means "two seas," probably referring to currents (also the name of a city on the island of O'ahu)

Kālaipāhoa (kah-lah~ee-pah-hoh-ah): a poisonous wood associated with evil sorcery (*'anā'anā*); believed to be the tree form of two gods and a goddess

Kalapana (kah-lah-pah-nah): East Hawai'i village nearly covered by lava flows from recent Pu'u 'O'o eruptions, named for a *kahuna* of Pele turned into a stone still located there

kālua (kah-loo-ah): baked in an *imu*, or underground oven (as in "kalua pig," a Hawaiian pork dish relished by islanders)

kama'aina (kah-mah-ah~ee-nah): native born; literally "land child"

kamani (kah-mah-nee): a native coastal tree whose nuts are used for leis

KAMOHOALI'I (kah-moh-hoh-ah-lee-ee): Pele's elder brother, who guided her to Hawai'i; a guardian shark god, keeper of the water of life

kanaka loko 'ino (kah-nah-kah lo-koh ee-noh): evil men

kanaka maoli (kah-nah-kah ma~oh-lee): Native Hawaiian or Hawaiians (short form *kanaka*)

KANALOA (kah-nah-loh-ah): god of the sea and sea winds

KĀNE (kah-neh): the procreator, provider of sunlight and fresh water

kāne (kah-neh): man, men

kapu (kah-poo): sacred or off-limits, forbidden, taboo

Ka'ū (kah-oo): the southern district on the island of Hawai'i, an ancient name whose cognates are found also in Samoa and the Mortlock Islands of the Pacific; some Hawaiians in the district spell it "Kau" without the diacritical marks

kau kau (*kow-kow*): food (from the Chinese)

kāula (kah~oo-lah): a type of *kahuna*—prophet, seer, oracle

kava (kah-vah): a mildly narcotic drink used in Hawaiian and Polynesian ceremonies (also *'awa*)

Kealakekua (ke-ah-lah-keh-koo-ah): "the pathway of the god"; the bay where Hawaiians killed Captain James Cook in 1779 after he kidnapped the island's king; it's said that here a god slid down the cliff and left an imprint, and that other gods also slid here to cross the bay quickly

Keauhou (keh-ah~oo-hoh~oo): Kona settlement near Keauhou Bay; literally "the new era" or "the new current"

Keaukaha (keh-ah~oo-kah-hah): settlement and Hawaiian Homelands area down the coast from Hilo; literally "the passing current"

keiki (keh~ee-kee): child, children

kiawe (kee-ah-veh): Algaroba tree, a thorny Peruvian mesquite introduced to Hawai'i in 1828, now common in the islands

KIHA (kee-hah): Kihanuilūlūmoku, an important lizard goddess

Kīholo (kee-hoh-loh): bay and village site in North Kona; literally "fishhook"

kim chee (Korean): extremely spicy cabbage salad; the expression "getting into deep kim chee" means being in big trouble

kīpuka (kee-poo-kah): an island of vegetation surrounded by lava flows

koa (koh-ah): a famous Hawaiian hardwood tree of the acacia family; brave, bold, valiant

koi (Japanese): carp, a symbol of strength and fortitude

koko (koh-koh): blood, as in "of Hawaiian blood"

kolohe (koh-loh-heh): mischievous, referring to a rascal or prankster

Kona (koh-nah): an island's west (or lee) side or a wind coming from that direction; a name for the west coast of Hawai'i Island

konnichiwa (Japanese): a greeting, usually meaning "Good afternoon"

ko'oko'olau (koh-oh-koh-oh-lah~oo): a native plant used medicinally as a tonic in tea

KŪ (koo): the war god (Kūka'ilimoku) brought to Hawai'i by thirteenth-century invaders, or the god of male-generating power who resided in Hawai'i long before that time

kukui (koo-koo-ee): candlenut burned for light, its tree a symbol of enlightenment

kuleana (koo-leh-ah-nah): responsibility, province, jurisdiction, or concern

kumakaia (koo-mah-kah~ee-ah): traitor

kupuna (koo-poo-nah): revered elder, ancestor

KŪ'ULA (koo-oo-lah): important god revered by fishermen

lānai (lah-nah~ee): verandah, porch

lauhala (lah~oo-hah-lah): leaves of the *hala* (pandanus tree), used for weaving hats, baskets, bowls, and other woven crafts

lehua (leh-hoo-ah): the red blossom of the *'ōhi'a* tree, symbol of Pele

lei (leh~ee): a garland of flowers, nuts, plants, feathers, or shells

lōlō (loh-loh): crazy

lomilomi (loh-mee-loh-mee): crushed or massaged, as done with the fish used for the marinated salmon salad of the same name

LONO (loh-noh): god of peace, agriculture, and fertility; in European myth, the god for which Captain James Cook was mistaken by the natives at Kealakekua Bay

lūau (loo-ah~oo): a Hawaiian feast, named for the taro leaves always served at one; the more traditional name is *pā'ina*

mahalo (mah-hah-loh): "thank you"

mahalo nui loa (mah-hah-loh noo-ee loh-ah): "a very big thank you"

mahina (mah-hee-nah): the moon, in reference to the goddess Hina

maika'i (mah~ee-kah-ee): good, very fine, or righteous

maile (mah~ee-leh): a fragrant woodland vine used for special leis

maka (mah-kah): eye, eyes

maka'ala! (mah-kah-ah-lah): "Eyes open! Be alert!"

malihini (mah-lee-hee-nee): stranger or guest

malo (mah-loh): man's loincloth

Māmalahoe (mah-mah-lah-hoh-eh): Kamehameha's law of the "splintered paddle," guaranteeing safety to all those traveling a royal highway; the name of a Hawai'i Island highway, misspelled as *Mamalahoa*

mana (mah-nah): spiritual or divine power

manō (mah-noh): shark, a type of *'aumakua*, or ancestral spirit

marae (mah-rah~ee): a sacred or communal ceremonial place, often containing terraces, stone borders, or upright stones called *ahu*; a Polynesian term used primarily in the South Pacific islands; *marae* built by early settlers to Hawai'i are still found in the archipelago

mean: radical, too much, over the top

Menehune (men-eh-hoo-neh): the mythic "little people" of Hawai'i, a derogatory ali'i reference to the original Polynesian settlers

mōhai (moh-hah~ee): sacrifice

mo'o (moh-oh): lizard, dragon, gecko, a type of *'aumakua*, or ancestral spirit

mu'umu'u (moo-oo-moo-oo): a woman's loose gown, usually full length with short sleeves; designed like missionary women's nightgowns, *mu'umu'u* were intended to cover up the nakedness of female islanders

na'au (nah-ah~oo): gut instinct or intuitive knowledge

naupaka (nah~oo-pah-kah): mountain and coastal shrub with small white half flowers; a plant associated with a legend of two lovers separated because one is ali'i, the other a commoner

nenue (neh-noo-eh): rudderfish found on Hawai'i reefs

Nisei (Japanese): first-generation Americans born of Japanese immigrants; literally "second generation"

Noh (Japanese): a dance using stylized masks from Japan's feudal period

nui (noo-ee): big, great, grand, important, much

nupa (noo-pah): deep cave or chasm

'ohana (oh-hah-nah): family or clan

'ohelo (oh-heh-loh): a berry-producing plant associated with Pele, sometimes presented as an offering

'ōhi'a (oh-hee-ah): a prominent native tree whose red *lehua* blossoms are associated with Pele; first tree to sprout on new lava

'ono (oh-noh): tasty

'ō 'ō (oh-oh): a striking black honey eater with tufts of yellow feathers under its wings, made extinct by hunting with rifles and loss of habitat

'ōpae'ula (oh-pah~eh-oo-lah): native freshwater shrimp

'opihi (oh-pee-hee): a small shellfish (limpet) relished by islanders

'ōpu (oh-poo): belly or abdomen

Pa'ao (pah-ah~oh): thirteenth-century *kahuna* who conveyed a colony from Tahiti to Hawai'i

pāhoa (pah-hoh-ah): dagger

pāhoehoe (pah-ho~eh-ho~eh): smooth or ropy lava

paka lōlō (pah-kah loh-loh): "crazy weed" or numbing tobacco; marijuana

Pākē (pah-keh): Chinese or of Chinese ancestry (from Chinese)

palani (pah-lah-nee): surgeonfish

palapala (pah-lah-pah-lah): a document of any kind, writing

pali (pah-lee): cliff, bluff, or steep hillside

Paliuli (pah-lee-oo-lee): a legendary land of plenty and joy on Hawai'i Island, where the children of chiefs were raised; literally "green cliff"

paniolo (pah-nee-oh-loh): Hawaiian cowboy (from *español*, or "Spanish")

pareu (pah-reh-oo): a brightly colored cloth wrap (Tahitian); Hawaiians call it a *kīkepa*

pau (pah~oo): done or ended

PELE (peh-leh): volcano goddess currently residing on the island of Hawai'i; Hawaiians view Pelehonuamea ("Pele of the Sacred Earth") primarily as a creative force

pepehi kanaka (peh-peh-hee kah-nah-kah): murderer

piko (pee-koh): navel, umbilical cord

pilau (pee-lah~oo): rot, stench, rottenness; to stink

pilikia (pee-lee-kee-ah): trouble, difficulties, distress

pohā (poh-hah): a sweet berry used for jams, jellies, and sauces; a type of gooseberry

pōhaku (poh-hah-koo): rock or stone; stones have special significance to Hawaiians, some are said to be inhabited by spirits, and others, through the spirits in them, to act as guardians

poi (poh~ee): traditional Polynesian mash made from taro root

poke (poh-keh): Hawaiian-style marinated raw fish; literally "to slice or cut crosswise into pieces"

POLI'AHU (poh-lee-ah-hoo): luminescent snow goddess of Mauna Kea

pono (poh-noh): righteous, moral

pueo (poo-eh-oh): Hawaiian owl, a type of *'aumakua*, or ancestral spirit

Puhia Pele (poo-hee-ah peh-leh): "blown out of Pele," an 1801 spatter cone on Hualalai

pule (poo-leh): to pray; prayer

pupule (poo-poo-leh): crazy

pu'u (poo-oo): hill, cinder cone

ramen (Japanese): a traditional noodle soup, available in instant form

Sansei (Japanese): offspring of the first Japanese Americans, the generation born during or after World War II; literally "third generation"

sashimi (Japanese): raw fish slices

shaka (*shah-kah*): island hand gesture, with thumb and pinky extended

shibai (*shee-bye*): a lie (from the Japanese)

Shinto (Japanese): the aboriginal religion of Japan, which venerates nature spirits and ancestors

stink eye: a hostile or disgusted look

talk stink: talk ill of someone, especially behind their back

talk story: converse informally, chat

tapa (tah-pah): cloth made from bark (*kapa*)

taro (tah-roh): a potato-like root, the basic starch of Polynesia (*kalo*)

ti (tee): plant whose leaves are used to wrap offerings, wrap food for cooking, and make skirts, leis, and other items; viewed as auspicious or protective, it is planted near dwellings and other structures (*ki*)

tiki (tee-kee): god image or statue (*ki'i*)

tsunami (Japanese): seismic sea wave

uē (oo-eh): sob, weep, lament (*uwē*)

'uhane (oo-hah-neh): spirit, ghost, soul

'ukulele (oo-koo-leh-leh): a small guitar brought to Hawai'i by Portuguese immigrants from the Azore Islands; literally "leaping flea," the nickname of the man who popularized the instrument

ulua (oo-loo-ah): certain species of crevalle, jack, or pompano fish

Waha Pele (wah-hah peh-leh): "the mouth of Pele," a centuries-old eruption vent on Hualalai

wahine (wah-hee-neh): woman, women

Waipuna (wah~ee-poo-nah): fictional Hawai'i Island beach, a composite of the many Hawai'i beaches developed for tourism following statehood and now built up with hotels and resorts; *waipuna* means "spring water" or "sweetheart"

wikiwiki! (wee-kee-wee-kee): hurry!

MAJOR CHARACTERS' NAMES

Aka (ah-kah): shadow

Gavin (Scottish): hawk of battle

Haku (hah-koo): lord, overseer, master

'Iolani (ee-oh-lah-nee): royal hawk

Kamali'i (kah-mah-lee-ee): small child

Kamehameha (kah-meh-hah-meh-hah): "the lonely one"; he was also known as Paiea, "the hard-shell crab"

Kanuha (kah-noo-hah): the sulky one

Keala (keh-ah-lah): the pathway

Lelehua (leh-leh-hoo-ah): good thinker

Maile (mah~ee-leh): a native twining shrub with shiny fragrant leaves, the body form of female forest deities associated with Laka, goddess of the hula

Takahashi (Japanese): high bridge

Wailani (wa~ee-lah-nee): rainwater, especially when used for purification

Yamashita (Japanese): one who lives below the mountain.

ABOUT THE AUTHOR

Tom Peek lived his early life on the Upper Mississippi on a backwaters island of Minnesota river folk, beaver, and ancient burial mounds. After hitchhiking by boat through the South Seas, he settled on the island of Hawai'i, where he's lived for two decades. There, he has been a mountain and astronomy guide on Mauna Kea and an eruption ranger, firefighter, and exhibit writer on Kilauea, working closely with Hawaiian elders and cultural practitioners on both volcanoes. He lives with his wife, artist Catherine Robbins, in a rainforest cottage near Kilauea's erupting summit.

ABOUT THE ILLUSTRATOR

John D. Dawson was raised in San Diego and now lives on the Big Island of Hawai'i. From the age of three, he knew that art was his calling. He graduated from the Art Center School, Los Angeles, now the Art Center College of Art and Design. Over the last twelve years, John has illustrated US Postal Service stamps for its Nature in America series. He's also done commissions for the National Park Service, United Nations, National Wildlife Federation, National Geographic Society, and Audubon Society.

ABOUT THE COVER ARTIST

Herb Kawainui Kane, celebrated Hawaiian artist, historian, and author, cofounded the Polynesian Voyaging Society and designed the *Hokulea* voyaging canoe, contributing profoundly to the Hawaiian Renaissance movement. A graduate of the Art Institute of Chicago, Kane depicted Hawaiian historical scenes realistically, but when painting spiritual or mythological aspects of the culture—as in *Pele, Goddess of Volcanoes,* the cover image of this book—his art was expressionistic, with bold brushwork and vivid colors.

FOSTERING A DEEPER UNDERSTANDING
OF PERSONAL TRANSFORMATION, SOCIAL JUSTICE,
AND HAWAIʻI

Nation Within: The History of the American Occupation of Hawaiʻi,
by Tom Coffman

Under Maui Skies and Other Stories, by Wayne Moniz

Georgia O'Keeffe's Hawaiʻi, by Patricia Jennings and Maria Ausherman

Veterans of War, Veterans of Peace, edited by Maxine Hong Kingston

Inner Gold: Understanding Psychological Projection, by Robert A. Johnson

The Wisdom of Sustainability: Buddhist Economics for the 21st Century,
by Sulak Sivaraksa

On That Day Everybody Ate: One Woman's Story of Hope and Possibility in Haiti, by Margaret Trost

The Superferry Chronicles: Hawaii's Uprising Against Militarism, Commercialism, and the Desecration of the Earth,
by Koohan Paik and Jerry Mander

Dissent: Voices of Conscience,
by Colonel (Ret.) Ann Wright and Susan Dixon

Not One More Mother's Child, by Cindy Sheehan

Words of Wisdom, by Lama Surya Das

Koa Books
PO Box 988
Hana, Hawaiʻi 96713
www.koabooks.com